The
LAND
of
LOST
THINGS

THE CHARLIE PARKER STORIES

Every Dead Thing

Dark Hollow

The Killing Kind

The White Road

The Reflecting Eye
(Novella in the *Nocturnes* Collection)

The Black Angel

The Unquiet

The Reapers

The Lovers

The Gates

The Whisperers

The Burning Soul

The Wrath of Angels

The Wolf in Winter

A Song of Shadows

A Time of Torment

A Game of Ghosts

The Woman in the Woods

A Book of Bones

The Dirty South

The Nameless Ones

The Furies

The
LAND
of
LOST
THINGS

❖

John Connolly

EMILY BESTLER BOOKS

ATRIA

New York   London   Toronto   Sydney   New Delhi

EMILY
BESTLER
BOOKS

ATRIA

An Imprint of Simon & Schuster, Inc.
1230 Avenue of the Americas
New York, NY 10020

First Emily Bestler Books/Atria Books hardcover edition September 2023

EMILY BESTLER BOOKS/ATRIA BOOKS and colophon are
trademarks of Simon & Schuster, Inc.

For information about special discounts for bulk purchases,
please contact Simon & Schuster Special Sales at 1-866-506-1949
or business@simonandschuster.com.

The Simon & Schuster Speakers Bureau can bring authors to
your live event. For more information or to book an event, contact the
Simon & Schuster Speakers Bureau at 1-866-248-3049 or visit our website
at www.simonspeakers.com.

Manufactured in the United States of America

1 3 5 7 9 10 8 6 4 2

Library of Congress Control Number: 2023934369

ISBN 978-1-6680-2228-3
ISBN 978-1-6680-2230-6 (ebook)

To Cameron and Megan, Alistair and Alannah,
and Jennie—all old enough to read fairy tales again

Books are not absolutely dead things, but do contain a potency of life in them to be as active as that soul was whose progeny they are.

—JOHN MILTON, *AREOPAGITICA*

And now we rise, and we are everywhere.

—NICK DRAKE, "FROM THE MORNING"

I

Uhtceare

(OLD ENGLISH)

To Lie Awake Before Dawn, Too Worried to Sleep

wice upon a time—for that is how some stories should continue—there was a mother whose daughter was stolen from her. Oh, she could still see the girl. She could touch her skin and brush her hair. She could watch the slow rise and fall of her chest, and if she placed her hand upon the child's breast, she could feel the beating of her heart. But the child was silent, and her eyes remained closed. Tubes helped her to breathe, and tubes kept her fed, but for the mother it was as though the essence of the one she loved was elsewhere, and the figure in the bed was a shell, a mannequin, waiting for a disembodied soul to return and animate it.

In the beginning, the mother believed that her daughter was still present, sleeping, and that by the sound of a beloved voice telling stories and sharing news she might be induced to wake. But as the days became weeks, and the weeks became months, it grew harder and harder for the mother to keep faith in the immanence of her daughter, and so she grew to fear that everything that was her child, all that gave her meaning—her conversation, her laughter, even her crying—might never come back, and she would be left entirely bereft.

The mother's name was Ceres, and her daughter was called Phoebe.

There was also a man once—but not a father, because Ceres refused to dignify him with the word, he having left them to fend for themselves before the girl was even born. As far as Ceres was aware, he was living somewhere in Australia, and had never shown any desire to be part of his daughter's life. To be honest, Ceres was happy with this situation. She had not felt any lasting love for the man, and his disengagement suited her. She retained some small gratitude toward him for helping to create Phoebe, and on occasion she saw a little of him in her daughter's eyes and smile, but it was a fleeting thing, like a half-remembered figure glimpsed on the platform of a station as the train rolls by; sighted, then soon forgotten. Phoebe, too, had demonstrated only minimal curiosity about him, but with no accompanying wish to make contact, even though Ceres had always assured her that she could, if she wanted to. He was not on any social media, regarding it as the devil's work, but a few of his acquaintances used Facebook, and Ceres knew that they would get a message to him, if required.

But that necessity had never arisen, not until the accident. Ceres wanted him to know what had happened, if only because the trauma was too much for her to bear alone, even as all attempts to share it failed to diminish it. Ultimately she received only a curt acknowledgment via one of his associates: a single line, informing her that he was sorry to hear about the "mishap," and he hoped Phoebe would get better soon, as though the child that was a part of him were struggling with flu or measles, and not the aftermath of a catastrophic collision between a car and the delicate body of an eight-year-old girl.

For the first time, Ceres hated Phoebe's father, hated him almost as much as the idiot who'd been texting while driving—and sending a message, not to his wife but to his girlfriend, which made him both an idiot and a deceiver. He'd visited the hospital a few days after the accident, forcing Ceres to request he be removed before he could talk to her. Since then he'd tried to contact her both directly and through his lawyers, but she wanted nothing to do with him. She hadn't even wanted to sue him, not at first, although she'd been advised that she had to, if only to pay for her daughter's care, because who knew how long Phoebe might endure this half-life: turned regularly by the nurses so that her poor skin would not develop bedsores, and surviving only with the aid of technology. Phoebe had banged her head on the ground after the impact, and so, while the rest of her injuries were healing, something in her brain remained damaged, and no one could say when, or if, it might repair itself.

A whole new vocabulary had presented itself to Ceres, an alien way of interpreting a person's continuance in the world: cerebral edema, axonal injury, and most important of all, to mother and child, the Glasgow Coma Scale, the metric by which Phoebe's consciousness—and, by extension, possibly her right to life—was now determined. Score less than five across eye, verbal, and motor responses, and the chances of death or existing in a persistent vegetative state were 80 percent. Score more than eleven, and the chances of recovery were estimated at 90 percent. Hover, like Phoebe, between those two figures and, well . . .

Phoebe wasn't brain-stem dead; that was the important thing. Her brain still flickered faintly with activity. The doctors believed that Phoebe wasn't suffering, but who could say for sure? (This, always spoken softly, and at the end, almost as an afterthought: *Who can say for sure? We just don't know, you see. The brain, it's such a complex organism. We don't* think *there's any pain, but . . .*) A conversation had taken place at the hospital, during which it was suggested that, down the line, if Phoebe showed no signs of improvement, it might be a kindness to—this with a change of tone, and a small, sad smile—let her go.

Ceres would look for hope in their faces, but find only sympathy. She did not want sympathy. She just wanted her daughter returned to her.

October 29th: that was the first visit Ceres had missed, the first day she hadn't been with Phoebe since the accident. Ceres's body simply wouldn't lift itself from the chair in which she had sat to rest. It was too exhausted, too worn down, and so she'd closed her eyes and gone to sleep again. Later, when she woke in that same chair to the dawn light, she felt such guilt that she wept. She checked her phone, certain that she'd missed a message from the hospital informing her that, in her absence— no, *because* of her absence—Phoebe had passed away, her radiance finally forever dimmed. But there was no message, and when Ceres called the hospital she was told that all was as it had been, and probably as it would continue to be: stillness, and silence.

That was the beginning. Soon she was visiting the hospital only five days out of seven, sometimes even four, and so it had remained ever since. Her sense of culpability became less immediate, although it continued to hover in the background: a gray shape, like a specter. It haunted the shadows of the living room on those mornings and afternoons when she stayed at home, and sometimes she saw it reflected in the television screen as she turned off the set at night, a smear against the dark. The specter had many faces, occasionally even her own. After all, she was a mother who had brought a child into the world and then failed to protect her, letting Phoebe skip just a few steps ahead as they crossed Balham High Road. They were only feet from the curb, and the crossing was quiet, when Phoebe slipped her grip. It was an instant of inattention, but seconds later there was a blur, and a dull thud, and then her daughter as Ceres knew her was gone. Left in her place was a changeling.

Yet the presence that inhabited the dark was not a manifestation of guilt alone, but of something older and more implacable. It was Death Itself, or more correctly Herself, because it assumed a female aspect. On the worst nights at the hospital, as Ceres drifted into uneasy sleep beside her daughter, she could feel Death hovering, seeking her chance. Death would have taken Phoebe on the High Road, if only the child had landed a little more sharply on the ground, and now she remained tantalizingly out of reach. Ceres sensed Death's impatience, and heard her voice, so close to kindness: *"When this becomes too much to bear, ask, and I will disencumber you both."*

And it was all Ceres could do not to give in.

II

Putherry
(STAFFORDSHIRE)

The Deep, Humid Stillness Before a Storm Breaks

eres arrived at the hospital a little later than usual, and damp from the rain. Under her arm she carried a book of fairy stories, one Phoebe had loved since she was very young, but had never read herself. It was a book she associated only with being read aloud to, and usually at night, so that all her affection for it, and all of its power, was tied up with the sound of her mother's voice. Even as she grew older, Phoebe still took pleasure in being read to by Ceres, but from this book alone, and only when she was sad or anxious. The collection was battered at the edges, and stained by fingerprints and spilled tea, but it was *their* book, a symbol of the bond between them.

Ceres's father had once told her that books retained traces of all those who read them, in the form of flakes of skin, hairs visible and minute, the oils from their fingertips, even blood and tears, so that just as a book became part of the reader, so, too, did a reader become part of the book. Each volume was a record of those who had opened its pages, an archive of the living and the dead. If Phoebe died, Ceres had decided that the book of fairy tales should be laid to rest with her. She could take it into the next world, and keep it close until her mother joined her, because if Phoebe perished, Ceres knew that it would not be long before she followed behind. She did not want to remain in a world in which her daughter was reduced to a memory. She thought this might also be the reason why she took no comfort from looking at videos of Phoebe on her phone, or listening to recordings of her voice. These were relics, totems from the past, like a haunting, and Ceres did not wish for a Phoebe that was gone, but a Phoebe yet to be.

A notice board beside the main entrance to the hospital reminded parents that a support group for those dealing with a sick child met every Wednesday night, with refreshments available after. Ceres had attended only once, sitting unspeaking while others shared their pain. Some of the parents were much worse off than Ceres. She still had hope for Phoebe, but surrounding her that evening had been mothers and fathers whose children would never get better, with no prospect of surviving into adulthood. The experience had left Ceres feeling even more depressed and angry than usual. As a result, she'd never gone back, and when she passed any of the parents from the group, she did her best not to catch their eyes.

She recognized, too, that Phoebe's accident had resulted in a change in her own identity. She was no longer herself, but was now "Phoebe's mother." It was how the hospital staff frequently referred to her—"Phoebe's mother is here," "Phoebe's mother would like an update"—as did the parents of the kids with whom Phoebe used to go to school. Ceres was not a person in her own right, but was defined solely in terms of her relationship to her suffering child. It seemed to accentuate Ceres's sense of dislocation and unreality, as though she could almost see herself fading away, just like her daughter.

A nurse greeted her as she entered Phoebe's room: Stephanie, who had been there on that first night, Phoebe and Ceres both covered in the same blood. Ceres knew nothing at all about Stephanie beyond her name, because she had never asked. Since the accident, Ceres's interest in the lives of those around her had largely fallen away.

Stephanie pointed at the book. "The usual, I see," she said. "They never tire of them, do they?"

Ceres felt a pricking at her eyes at this small kindness: the assumption that Phoebe, wherever she was, might be aware of these stories, of her mother's continued attendance, and they might yet be capable of revitalizing her.

"No, they never do," said Ceres. "But—" She stopped herself. "Not to worry, it's not important."

"It might be," said Stephanie. "If you change your mind, just let me know."

But she didn't go about her duties, and Ceres knew that the nurse had further business with her.

"Before you leave, Mr. Stewart would like a quick word," said Stephanie. "If you drop by the nurses' station when you have a moment, I'll take you to see him."

Mr. Stewart was the principal physician responsible for Phoebe's care. He was patient, and solicitous, but Ceres remained suspicious of him because of his relative youth. She did not believe he had lived long enough—or, more correctly, suffered enough—to be able to deal properly with the suffering of others. And there was something in the nurse's face, something in her eyes, that told Ceres this conversation was not going to bring her any easement. She felt an end approaching.

"I'll do that," said Ceres, while in her mind she pictured herself running from the hospital, her daughter gathered to her breast, the bedsheet like a shroud, only for it to be carried away by the wind, floating high into the air like a departing ghost, leaving her to discover that her arms were empty.

"If I'm not there, just ask them to page me," said Stephanie.

And there it was again, this time in the nurse's smile: a sadness, a regret.

This is a nightmare, Ceres thought, *a living one, and only death will bring it to a close.*

III

Wann

(OLD ENGLISH)

The Darkness of a Rook's Feathers

eres read to Phoebe for an hour, but had anyone asked her the substance of the stories, she would have been unable to tell them, so distracted was she. Finally she set the book aside and brushed her daughter's hair, working so gently at the tangles that Phoebe's head remained undisturbed on the pillow. Phoebe's eyes were closed; they were always closed now. Ceres saw only a suggestion of the blue of them when Mr. Stewart or one of his juniors came by to lift the lids and check Phoebe's pupillary responses, like pale clouds briefly parting to reveal a glimpse of sky. She set aside the hairbrush and rubbed moisturizer into Phoebe's hands—peach-scented, because Phoebe liked the smell of peaches—before straightening her nightgown and rubbing tiny flecks of sleep from the corners of the shuttered lenses. When these small services were complete, Ceres took Phoebe's right hand and kissed the tip of each finger.

"Return to me," she whispered, "because I miss you so."

She heard a noise at the window, and looked up to see a bird staring at her through the glass. It was missing its left eye, the injury marked by twin scars. It tilted its head, croaked once, and then was gone.

"Was that a crow?"

She turned. Stephanie was standing in the doorway. Ceres wondered how long she had been there, waiting.

"No," said Ceres, "a rook. They used to haunt battlefields."

"Why?" asked Stephanie.

"To feed on the dead."

The words were out of Ceres's mouth before she could block them. *Scavenger. Carrion seeker.*

Omen.

The nurse stared at her, uncertain how to respond.

"Well," she said at last, "it'll find no pickings here."

"No," agreed Ceres, "not here, not today."

"How do you know such things?" said Stephanie. "About rooks and the like, I mean."

"My father taught them to me, when I was younger."

"That's an odd lesson to be teaching a child."

Ceres placed Phoebe's hand on the bedspread and stood.

"Not for him. He was a university librarian, and an amateur folklorist. He could talk about giants, witches, and wyrms until your eyes glazed over."

Stephanie gestured once again at the book under Ceres's arm.

"Is that where you and Phoebe got your love of fairy stories? My own boy devours them. I think we may even have a copy of that same book, or one very like it."

Ceres almost laughed.

"This? My father would have hated to see me reading Phoebe such nonsense."

"And why would that be?"

Ceres thought of the old man, dead now these five years. Phoebe had been permitted to know him only briefly, and he her.

"Because," she said, "they just aren't dark enough."

The consultant didn't have an office of his own in the main hospital, but worked from a private room in an adjoining building. Stephanie escorted Ceres to his door, even though she knew the way. It made her feel like a prisoner being led to the gallows. The room was anonymous, apart from a bright piece of abstract art on the wall behind the desk. There were no pictures of Mr. Stewart's family, though she knew he was married with children. Ceres always found it odd that doctors, once they attained a certain level of expertise, became plain old misters once again. If she had spent years training to be a doctor, the last thing she would have wanted was to forgo the title she'd worked so hard to obtain. She'd probably have had it branded on her forehead.

She took a seat across from *Mr.* Stewart, and they made small talk: the weather, an apology for the smell of fresh paint, the decorators having just been in, but neither of them had their heart in it, and gradually it dwindled to nothing.

"Just say whatever you have to say," Ceres told him. "It's the waiting that kills us."

She spoke as mildly as she could, but it still emerged sounding harsher than she might have wished.

"We think that Phoebe requires a different level of care from now on," said Mr. Stewart. "Supportive rather than curative. Her condition hasn't altered, which is good in one way, although it may not seem so at first glance. It hasn't worsened, in other words, and we believe she's as comfortable as she's likely to be, for a while."

"But that's all you can do for her?" said Ceres. "Make her comfortable, I mean, not make her better?"

"Yes, that's all we can do for now. Which is not to say that, down the line, this won't change, either through developments in treatment or Phoebe's own capacity for recovery."

He looked strained, and Ceres thought she understood why he didn't keep pictures of his wife and kids on his desk. Who could tell how many such conversations he was forced to endure every day, with parents hearing the worst news about their children? For some, being required to look at a picture of another man's healthy family while they tried to come to terms with their own grief would only add to their burden. Not Ceres, though: She hoped only that each day when he went home, Mr. Stewart hugged his children to him and gave thanks for what he had been given. She was glad that he had his family, and she wished them only happiness. The world had enough misery to be getting along with.

"And what are the chances of that?" she said.

"There is limited brain activity," said Mr. Stewart, "but there *is* activity. We have to hope."

Ceres began to cry. She hated herself for doing it, even though it wasn't the first time she'd cried in front of this man. Yes, she continued to hope, but it was hard, and she was so weary. Mr. Stewart said nothing, but gave her time to recover herself.

"How is work?" he asked.

"Nonexistent."

Ceres did freelance copywriting, which had expanded into copyediting, but that was all past tense. She hadn't been able to concentrate since the accident, and so hadn't been able to work, which meant she wasn't bringing in any money. She had already spent most of her savings—not that she'd ever had much, not as a single mother living in London—and really didn't know how she could continue. It was one of the reasons why she'd agreed to sue the driver, but he and his lawyers were resisting the payment of even a modest interim sum for fear that it might leave them open to greater liability down the line. The whole mess would have kept her awake at night, if she wasn't so exhausted all the time.

"I don't wish to pry—" said Mr. Stewart.

"Pry away. I don't have a great deal left to hide."

"How badly are you struggling?"

"Pretty badly, in every way, including financially."

"I may be mistaken," said Mr. Stewart, "but didn't you tell me that your family owned a property in Buckinghamshire?"

"Yes," said Ceres, "a small cottage not too far from Olney. It was my childhood home. My mother still uses it during the summer, and Phoebe and I spend the occasional weekend there."

Her mother had often suggested to Ceres that she move to the cottage permanently instead of wasting money on rent in London, but Ceres hadn't wanted to return. Going back to where she began would have felt like an admission of failure on her part, and there had been Phoebe's school and circle of friends to consider as well. Now those things were no longer an issue. "Why?"

"There is a care facility, a very good one, exclusively for young people, on the outskirts of Bletchley, with a considerable degree of specialization in brain injury. It's called the Lantern House, and a space has just opened up. My parents live in Milton Keynes, so I'm back and forth quite a bit, and I have a professional relationship with the Lantern. My suggestion, if you were amenable, would be to transfer Phoebe there as soon as is practical. She'll be well looked after, I'll be kept in the loop, and its status as a registered charity means that you won't have that financial concern hanging over your head—not to the same degree, at least. Given the circumstances, the Lantern might be the best option for everyone. But we're not giving up on Phoebe. You have to understand that."

She nodded, but didn't mean it. They *were* giving up on Phoebe here, or so it seemed to Ceres. And the word *charity* stung, because she'd always paid her own way, and now it was what she and Phoebe were reduced to. She felt powerless, useless.

"Let's move her, then," she said.

And so it was done.

The evening had turned cold: November, and winter in the ascendant. Already, barely minutes after ending her conversation with Mr. Stewart, Ceres was making plans to reorder her life. She wouldn't particularly miss London, not any longer. She still consciously avoided the road on which Phoebe had been hit, and the pall cast by the accident seemed to have spread from that small stretch of tarmac to all of South London and, by extension, the rest of the city. Whatever her reservations about Buckinghamshire, moving back there would help her escape one shadow, and a change of environment might even enable her to get back to work again.

The winter king on his throne, and all change in the realm.

IV

Anhaga
(OLD ENGLISH)

One Who Dwells Alone

he move took about three weeks, all told. Preparations had to be made for Phoebe's arrival at the Lantern House, and the cottage needed to be made ready for longer-term habitation. Ceres's landlord in London was sorry to see her go—she was a good tenant, which meant she didn't kick up a fuss, or cost him a lot in repairs—but any sorrow he felt at her departure was eased by the knowledge that he could now test the market by raising the rent. Ceres's friends—of whom she had just a handful, London being a hard place to make enduring friendships, especially for someone who worked alone—held a farewell drinks party for her, but it was a low-key affair, and she knew that only a few of them would keep their promises to visit. They had done their best to be considerate toward her, but people only have so much time, attention, and care to give, and the torments and sorrows of others can be draining, even for the most generous among us.

Ceres was aware that the knowledge of her daughter's condition altered the mood of any company of which she was a part. Sometimes, she knew, dinner parties or restaurant outings to which she might previously have been invited went ahead quietly without her being made aware of them, but she felt no resentment toward those involved. After all, there had been occasions since the accident when, among close acquaintances, and fueled by a glass or two of wine, she had laughed aloud at a joke or story and felt immediately remorseful, the effect as sobering as a slap across the face. Was it permissible to laugh when one's child was suspended somewhere between living and dying? When a day might come requiring a decision that would bring an end to her span on earth because of that most nebulous of concepts, quality of life?

And what, Ceres thought, if something were to happen to herself? What if she became ill, or died? Who, then, would make decisions about Phoebe? She supposed it would have to be a professional; she could not ask this of one of her friends, and even her mother might be reluctant to accept sole responsibility, especially as she was now in her early seventies. Ceres had been advised by the medical staff to set out her wishes in a will, but so far had resisted. No parent should be forced to make plans for the possibility of their child's death by the withdrawal of medical care. It seemed impossible to think of such a thing and remain sane. How could she place such a burden on someone close to her?

Then there were the lawyers: interviewing witnesses, corroborating Ceres's version of events, collecting photographs, maps, diagrams. Every week brought another letter, more questions, progress toward a hearing, a settlement. Her life had become inseparable from her daughter's, so she was not even sure that she knew herself anymore. The passage of time had lost its meaning, and whole days would go by without any sense of purpose or achievement. She existed, but, like Phoebe, she did not truly live.

On the day that Phoebe was transferred to the Lantern House, Ceres tagged after the ambulance in her car, the last of their possessions on the seats. She could have traveled with her daughter, who was hooked up to a portable ventilator for the journey, but she chose not to. She could not have said why except that, where possible, she now preferred to be alone rather than be forced to make conversation, especially in a vehicle containing her comatose child. Strangers who knew nothing of her predicament were easier to deal with—easier, even, than some friends. As she drove, she saw that the grass had still not fully recovered from the summer drought, when the land had been rendered a parched, dull yellow instead of the lusher green of her childhood. It seemed to get worse each year, but then so did many things.

The Lantern House was very modern, set on well-tended grounds surrounded by woodland that concealed it from the road. Every room, she was told, was situated so that it looked out on grass, trees, and blooms, summer-flowering plants having been replaced for the season with snowdrops, Christmas roses, mahonia, daphne, winter jasmine, and clematis. Phoebe's accommodation, once she was settled in, smelled faintly of honeysuckle, and through the window Ceres could see the cream-white flowers amid branches that were otherwise close to bare. A pair of winter-active bumblebees was flitting from blossom to blossom, and the sight of them brought reassurance. Phoebe loved bumblebees, the speed and grace of creatures both small yet also, in their way, near-impossibly large.

"But how do they fly?" Phoebe would ask. "Their wings are so little, and their bodies so big."

"I don't know, but they do."

"When I grow up, I want to be a bumblebee."

"Really?"

"Only for a day, just to see what it's like."

"I'll add it to the list."

Which included, variously, kingfishers, worms, whales, dolphins, giraffes, elephants (African and Indian), assorted breeds of small dog, butterflies (but not moths), blackbirds, meerkats, and, just to be gross, dung beetles. It was an actual list, too, kept in an envelope pinned to the kitchen corkboard: plans for a life, halted indefinitely.

A voice spoke Ceres's name.

"I'm sorry," she said, "I was elsewhere."

The staff member was big and tall, with a soft, indefinable accent. His name, he had informed Ceres upon arrival, was Olivier. Like most of the staff at the Lantern House, and the hospital in London, he came from somewhere distant from England, in his case Mozambique. All these people, Ceres reflected, far from home, cleaning, tending, consoling the children of others, often doing jobs that no one born here wanted to do.

Olivier had been speaking to Phoebe since she was taken from the ambulance, explaining to her where she was, where she was going, and what was happening as they moved her from the stretcher to the bed. He did not treat her as anything but a sentient child who heard and understood everything she was being told, and his gentleness was striking for such a big man, because Olivier stood at least a foot taller than Ceres, and she was five foot seven.

"I was just saying that we've made Phoebe comfortable," said Olivier, "and you can stay as long as you like with her. You can also visit when you please, or near enough to it. That sofa folds out to a bed if you want to spend the night beside her, although we also keep a couple of suites ready for parents. We ask only that you don't arrive after nine in the evening, unless it's an emergency, just to avoid disturbing any of the other children who may be settling down to sleep."

"I understand—and thank you, for being so good to Phoebe."

Olivier looked genuinely puzzled, as though it would never have occurred to him to behave other than as he did, and Ceres knew that her daughter had found her way to the right place.

"Well," said Olivier, "I'll leave you two alone. I'll drop by later, Phoebe, to make sure you're okay." He patted her hand before leaving.

"You're being guarded by a giant," Ceres informed Phoebe. "No one will dare harm you while he's around." But she looked to the shadows as she spoke.

The sun was setting, and soon it would be dark. Although she was wearied by the day, Ceres took the book of fairy stories from her bag and began reading to her unresponsive child.

THE TALE OF THE TWO DANCERS

*O*nce upon a time, near the town of Aachen in what is now modern Germany, there lived a young woman named Agathe. As this name was common in the region, she was known as Agathe des Sonnenlichts or Agathe of the Sunlight because her hair was as golden as the rays of the sun, and like the sun, Agathe was bright and beautiful, with a pure heart. She took good care of her widowed mother and her two younger siblings, and worked their little patch of land with the aid of her brother and sister. So mindful was she *of her family that she refused to marry, since she did not trust any husband to be as loving and tender toward them as she was—and, truth be told, since the family was not very wealthy, and could provide no dowry for her, Agathe did not have as many suitors as other women less pretty and kind than she.*

But she was also a good judge of character, having learned well at the feet of her mother, who had learned from her mother, who had learned from hers, and so Agathe was the inheritor of generations of female knowledge— which, as any wise person will tell you, is very useful knowledge to possess. Agathe could look into a man's eyes and pierce straight through to his heart, although she spoke of what she saw only with her mother, for she did not care to arouse hostility, or risk being branded a witch for what was, after all, mostly common sense and perspicacity.

If Agathe had one love, her family apart, it was dancing. When alone, she would find her feet following the patterns of a pavane or quadrille, tracing the movements on a dirt floor or a grassy field as she went, and leaving the evidence behind in the form of her footprints. On feast days she would be the first to rise when the music began to play, and the last to sit when it ended. So graceful was she, so lithe, so attuned to the rhythms of the players, that she could elevate even the clumsiest of partners, as though her gifts were so abundant that they overflowed her to spill into others. This was the cause of occasional envy among some of the less accomplished girls in the village, and even some of the more accomplished ones, too, but Agathe's disposition was so gentle, and she was so generous in spirit, that few could remain resentful for long.

Few, though, is not all. On the other side of the hill from Agathe's family lived a girl named Osanna, who was almost as beautiful as Agathe, almost as clever, almost as graceful, and for whom these shortfalls were like dagger thrusts to the heart. Sometimes she would watch from the woods as Agathe danced, willing her to stumble, wishing her to fall, the misstep to be punctuated by a cry of pain and the crack of a bone breaking. But Agathe was too sure-footed, and only in Osanna's dreams did her rival falter. Yet so fierce was Osanna's jealousy, so poisonous her rancor, that it began to transform her very being until all her thoughts, both sleeping and waking, were of Agathe.

But we must be careful of our fancies and wary of our dreams, lest the worst of them should be heard or witnessed, and something should choose to act upon them.

*I*t was the custom in that place to hold a special dance on Karnevalsdienstag, or Shrove Tuesday, a final opportunity for feasting and merriment before the commencement of the Lenten fast. As the time of the festival approached, Agathe danced away the days, and lost herself in music only she could hear. On the morning before Karnevalsdienstag, she was so distracted as she danced through fresh fields that she failed to notice another set of footprints materializing alongside her own, as though her movements were being shadowed by some unseen other, an invisible dancer as skilled as she, one who had no difficulty in matching her steps; and when she hummed a tune, as she did from time to time, a second voice echoed hers, but so low as to be mistaken for the buzzing of insects, or so high as to disturb only the birds in the trees, who fled from the sound of it.

That night, as Agathe slept, a shape watched her from the window, and it eclipsed the very darkness.

*S*o Karnevalsdienstag came, and as usual Agathe was the first to her feet when the musicians began to play, dancing with all who asked, young or old, awkward or expert. Even had she not been so adept, it would not have been in her to refuse anyone for fear she might hurt their feelings, or expose them to ridicule from their peers. She did not stumble, did not tire. The torches were lit, and the celebrations became louder and more raucous, and still Agathe danced, until no man in the town who was capable of it had not moved in step with her.

Finally, as a cloud passed across the moon—although the night was clear—and the torches flickered briefly—although no wind blew—a stranger moved through the crowd, the celebrants making way for him even before they became aware of his presence, because an old, fearful part of them, one deeper than sight or hearing, had sensed his coming and sought to protect them from it; and he did not touch them, and none touched him.

He was tall and handsome, his hair dark, his teeth white and even, his

*skin unmarked, his eyes merciless. His clothing was black and without dec-
oration, but finely made, and his leather boots shone as though worn for the
first time. And while no one could recall ever having seen him in that place
before, he appeared to them almost recognizable—and to Osanna more
than the rest. She knew him, because she had glimpsed him in her dreams.*

At last the stranger stood before Agathe, and extended a hand to her.

"Dance with me," he said.

*Agathe looked deep into his eyes, and perceived him for what he was.
What was tall without was short within, what was beautiful was blighted,
what was sweet was sour, and what was straight was crooked—so very,
very crooked.*

"I will not dance with you," she said.

"You have danced with me before."

*Only then did Agathe register the imprints of footsteps in the grass, the
buzzing of insects where none flew, the fleeing of birds where no threat was
to be found, and saw how careless she had been.*

"If I did," she said, "it was not by my own will, and that is no dance at all."

*"I wanted to be certain that you were a worthy partner. Was that so
wrong?"*

"I find it so," said Agathe.

His wintry eyes, cold gray, grew chillier still.

"I will ask you again," said the stranger. "Dance with me."

*"And for the second time," said Agathe, "I tell you that I will not dance
with you."*

*The stranger's teeth nipped at the night air, and Agathe saw that they
were now closer to yellow, like the flesh of an apple discoloring.*

*"You have danced with all the rest," he said, "so why will you not
oblige me?"*

"Because you are not what you pretend to be."

*His outstretched arms took in the gathering, because all were quiet now,
and even the musicians had ceased to play.*

*"Is anyone?" he said. "You are prideful, and that, as your priest will tell
you, is the original and gravest of sins, though you are not alone in sinning.
This one"—a finger pointed at Uwe the baker—"soaks old bread in water
to add to his dough, and thus adulterates the mix."*

The finger shifted an inch.

"This one"—Axel the blacksmith—"cheats on his wife with a woman in the next village. This one is a thief, this one dilutes his beer, and this one"—the finger found Osanna —"summoned me here out of envy of you."

Osanna looked appalled. She was not a bad person, although there was badness in her. Now, confronted by true evil, and apprehending the part she might have played in its arrival, she was both fearful and contrite—but too late, her response rendered less sincere by coming only as a consequence of being found out.

"Stop," said Agathe. "This is not kind."

"So many you have danced with," said the stranger, "and each not what they pretend to be."

"They are all flawed," said Agathe, "as am I, but our flaws are not the sum of us. That is not true of you. There is no good in you, no good at all."

The stranger's body spasmed, and everyone gathered there heard the snapping and popping of bone and cartilage. Afterward he did not stand so straight or so tall, and lesions had opened on his face. From the deepest of them a millipede crawled, only to hide itself away in his hair.

"I will ask you one last time," he said to Agathe. "Dance with me."

"And I tell you for the last time," said Agathe, "that I will not dance with you."

With that the stranger's disguise fell away entirely, revealing a crooked man.

No, *thought Agathe*, not a crooked man, but *the* Crooked Man. *It was his name and his essence, every badness made manifest. This she knew, although she could not have said how, having never set eyes on him until that night.*

"Then let the dance go on without me," said the Crooked Man, "but you will play no further part in it, and for that you may come to thank me."

His right hand made a sign in the air, and a serpentine dagger materialized in his fist. Suddenly he was no longer in front of Agathe but behind her, and with a single slash, he severed the tendons in her lower legs. Agathe collapsed instantly, but none came to her aid. None could, because each had begun to dance, all except the musicians, who commenced a tune that they had never heard before, and never learned; slowly at first, then faster and faster, and as the music quickened, so too did the steps of the dancers;

and though they tried to stop themselves, they could not, and the dancing continued for hours and hours, then days and days, and it only ceased when the dancers became so exhausted that even the Crooked Man's spell could not compel them to continue, or their limbs snapped and they dropped to the ground.

And when the spell had depleted itself, and the revels were ended, only one of the villagers could not be found: Osanna, who had brought the Crooked Man down upon them by her ill will toward Agathe. Uwe the baker thought he had seen the Crooked Man take her by the hand and drag her away toward the woods, and so a search began, led by hounds. By then a week had gone by, but the dogs managed to pick up Osanna's scent, and they traced it to the heart of the forest. There they found Osanna's body, her feet worn to stumps as she danced herself to death.

And that is The Tale of the Two Dancers.

"What an *unusual* story. I don't think I've ever heard it before."

Olivier was standing in the doorway. Ceres did not know how long he had been there. Long enough, at least, to have listened to some, if not all, of the tale.

But here was the thing: Ceres had never heard the story before, either. It was not contained in the book balanced on her knees. She had not been reading but reciting, as if from memory, yet she had no earlier remembrance of the tale, just as she could not recall having held a pen in her hand when she began. Stranger still, upon looking down at the book she discovered she had been writing the story as she told it, but set at an angle to the existing text on the page, so that by slightly adjusting the position of the book one or the other might be read. A palimpsest, or near enough to one; that was what it was called. Her father, whose work had included deciphering old manuscripts, loved encountering them, artifacts from a past when paper was too precious to be used only once.

Olivier was now by Ceres's side. He, too, had spotted her handwriting on the pages, five of which she had filled with the story.

"I didn't know you were a writer," he said.

"I'm not," said Ceres, "or not like this. Of stories, I mean. I don't know where that one even came from. I must have heard it somewhere, or read it as a child."

"Once upon a time," said Olivier. "Or 'There was and there was not,' as my grandmother used to begin them."

"Yes, I suppose so. Once upon a time."

Or "There was and there was not." There was and there was not a girl. There was and there was not her mother.

But the idea that she had somehow birthed a story was confusing to Ceres. As a young woman she had enjoyed drawing, but stopped in late adolescence when she grasped that all she was doing was trying to reproduce the world. Real artists, by contrast, rendered the world anew, which was beyond her abilities. She had knowledge, but what she lacked, she decided, was imagination. Now, perhaps, that capacity—a comfort with *not* knowing, which brought forth invention—might have been hers after all, but in a different form: words, not pictures.

Ceres stood. It was time for her to leave. She kissed Phoebe goodbye.

"She looks so small," said Ceres, not to Olivier but to some unseen other, because there was a hint of reproach to her voice. She had grown more and more used to speaking aloud her thoughts, especially when she was alone with Phoebe. It was a way to break the hush, and let her daughter know she was near. Phoebe never reacted, but that was no reason for Ceres to stop. The day she did, there would no longer be a point to anything. "Each week that goes by, she grows thinner. I can see it in her face."

This is how we sometimes lose people: not all at once, but little by little, like the wind blowing specks of pollen from a flower.

"I've seen her medical records," said Olivier. "Your daughter is a fighter. If anyone can pull through, she can."

"You're very kind," said Ceres. It was a rote response. She'd grown good at giving rote responses, but Olivier, it appeared, was not one for them.

"It doesn't mean anything if it isn't true," he said. "And I won't ever lie to you, or to Phoebe."

Ceres did not reply. Lies or truths, they made no difference now.

"I don't think I can keep doing this," she whispered. "I don't have the strength."

And somewhere a woman heard, and drew nearer.

V

Auspice
(MIDDLE FRENCH)

A Divination from the Actions of Birds

livier walked Ceres to the Lantern House's main door and remained with her as she buttoned her coat against the chill. The sky was clear, the crescent moon hanging so low over an old house to the east that one almost might have stood on its roof and touched a hand to a dead world.

"What is that place?" said Ceres. "Is it part of the center?"

"Of a sort," said Olivier. "Years ago, a writer lived there. He wrote just one book that became quite famous, published under a pseudonym. He made some money from it, but he didn't have a happy life."

"No?"

"His wife died in childbirth, along with their baby, and he never married again. He just stayed in that house, wrote his novel, and lived modestly on the proceeds. Toward the end of his life he founded a charity with earnings from the book, as well as money left to him by his father, which he'd never spent. His father was a codebreaker at Bletchley Park during the war, and afterward invented something to do with computers and coding that made him quite wealthy. That money paid for the initial purchase of the land for the Lantern House, and much of its construction. The interest from the fund still contributes to our upkeep—along with royalties, because the book continues to sell—which enables us to provide care for those without the ability to pay."

"When did he die?" asked Ceres.

She had a vague recollection of all this, a passing reference by her mother or father after she'd left home, only to be discarded as inconsequential.

"He didn't, exactly," said Olivier. "I mean, he's certainly dead now, but technically he disappeared, and may even be listed as 'missing' in some police file. Whatever happened, he was a fading, elderly man when he vanished, and that was almost twenty years ago.

"There's always talk of turning the house into another wing of the center, or giving it over to office space, but parts of it are particularly old, and subject to all kinds of restrictions on what alterations can or can't be made. At first the trustees tried to rent it out, but nobody wanted to stay there for long, and then it was briefly opened to the public as a museum, but it was just too much trouble to keep it running. After that it was used for file storage, and now it's vacant. The floorboards are rotten, and there are holes in the roof, but the charity's money can be put to better use here, and no one else wants to spend what's required to renovate it."

Even by moonlight Ceres could tell that it had once been an impressive residence, and might be so again, if someone were willing to invest in it.

"Why did nobody want to live there?" she said. She had picked up on a hesitancy in Olivier's voice.

"Old houses and all that," he said. "You know what some people are like."

"No, tell me: What are some people like?"

Olivier examined his shoes, and tried to make light of what he said next.

"They claimed it was haunted, so they didn't want to stay. Three leases were broken before everyone gave up on it."

"Haunted? You mean, by ghosts?"

"Or by memories, which may be the same thing. And not good ones, either."

"Why do you say that?"

"Because if they were good, all those people wouldn't have upped and left, would they? I'd better be getting back inside before someone starts thinking I've run away with the fairies."

"Have you been inside the house?"

"Once or twice."

"And?"

"I didn't linger." He was serious now. "It didn't feel quite empty."

As Olivier prepared to return to his duties, Ceres asked one last question.

"What was the name of the novel, the one that paid for this place?"

"It's called *The Book of Lost Things*," said Olivier. "Actually, I thought you might have read it."

"Why would you say that?"

"Because it has a Crooked Man in it, just like your story."

"No, I don't think I've ever heard of it. Or him."

"Well," said Olivier, "you have now."

Nearing her car, Ceres saw that a rough path wound east through the woods from the parking area. She wondered if it led to the house, not that she had any plans to go visiting at this hour. She might not have believed in ghosts, but she'd read enough mysteries to know that bad things could happen to a person who chose to wander the woods at night, and Milton Keynes and its environs were not immune to crime. Even a wicked witch might stand a good chance of being mugged in the wrong stretch of forest.

On the lowest branch of an oak tree that marked the entrance to the path, she spied movement: an old rook with one eye, the other lost to talons.

"No," said Ceres. "It's not possible. You can't have followed us here."

The bird croaked three times, a response uncannily like laughter. Keeping her distance, Ceres leaned down and commenced gathering stones.

"I'll show you what happens to rooks that think they've found easy prey," she said. "I'll make you wish that whatever took that eye had come back and finished the job."

But when she looked up again, the rook had departed.

VI

Eawl-leet

(LANCASHIRE)

Twilight, or Owl-Light

eres slept late the next morning and did not dream; or if she did, she had no memory of the substance. She spent the hours that followed unpacking boxes of clothing and books, among them her daughter's possessions. Phoebe had her own bedroom at the cottage, which already contained some of her things, but now Ceres added the rest, even putting up Phoebe's posters and pictures from their former London flat. She could not bear to leave the room unfinished, because to have done so would have been to admit that her faith in the possibility of her daughter's recovery might be wavering. Perhaps, too, there was an element of superstition involved, as though even by hinting at such an outcome she might bring it to pass.

The cottage was modestly sized, but with a considerable back garden, currently overgrown and distinguished by a stand of old yew trees at its northern extreme that it shared with a small cemetery fallen into disuse since the end of the nineteenth century. Ceres supposed that some might have found the nearness of a graveyard unsettling or depressing, but she never had. Growing up, she felt that it was part of the landscape—an occasionally thrilling one, as at Halloween, but otherwise an element that barely registered. Because those laid to rest in it had come from the poorest sections of the local community, it contained few headstones, and someone unacquainted with its history might have passed it by without registering its purpose. The faintest outline of a face formed from leaves, a Green Man, peered from one of the old gateposts, testament to beliefs older than Christianity.

By the northern edge of the graveyard ran a small stream, which her father used to claim concealed a water horse and a river sprite, and Ceres might be able to spot them if she stayed still long enough. But Ceres had never seen either horse or sprite, and came to suspect that her father had invented their habitancy as a means of keeping her occupied when he wanted to read, or watch football. To the east, the stream wound past a hillock, said by some to be a fairy mound, because it was once thought that fairies made their dwellings close to cemeteries, to claim the souls of those laid to rest. Her father had always been dismissive of this, if only because, in his view, it meant putting the cart before the horse: the mounds were older than human burial places, and therefore it was men, unconsciously, who chose to situate graveyards close to mounds, not vice versa. On the other hand, he was scornful of those who, out of caution, stepped around mushroom rings, ascribing their presence to the actions of fairies. As he explained to Ceres, the fungal threads, the mycelium, sprouted in a circular shape underground; this was science, and there was no mystery about it. On such esoterica were articles for folklore journals built.

But it was the trees that Ceres especially loved. They were known as "walking yews," formed when the branches of a parent trunk reached the ground, then layered and extended themselves to produce new roots—as well as interesting archways and grottos for first Ceres, then Phoebe, to explore—which regrew as sibling trees. Benignly neglected, the yews continued to thrive: evergreen, their branches sleeved in lichen, their bark, upon closer examination, not brown alone, but red, green, and purple, too. Lovely, and dangerous also: full of the poison taxine, used in the past to lace the tips of arrows, so that even a scratch might prove fatal; and, so local lore had it, once applied to the stems and thorns of a bunch of freshly cut roses, which were then sent by a baker's daughter to her rival in love, who subsequently perished in agony.

Returned to her childhood home under the worst of circumstances, Ceres discovered a new comfort in the proximity of the yews, because they endured. Damaged, scarred, blighted, they persisted. They declined to yield to death. Even the nostoc, which her mother abhorred, gave Ceres hope. Currently in residence on the garden bench, the blue-green algae, blown in as spores from the cemetery, formed clear, glutinous clumps across the lawn and furniture after rain. On one level, Ceres accepted it was undeniably disgusting, but on another, it was tenacious, resilient. Nostoc could remain in a dry, seemingly lifeless state for years or decades, only to revive again at a time of nature's choosing. Her mother, had she been present, would have sluiced it away with a hose, but Ceres chose to leave it unbothered.

When she grew weary of resettlement chores, she drove to a supermarket to stock the larder and refrigerator before, on a whim, going book shopping, something she hadn't done much of since the accident. She and Phoebe were inveterate browsers, although they preferred older, secondhand bookshops to newer ones, assuming one could still find any of the former open, charity stores having usurped them. Then again, even when used bookstores were ubiquitous, Ceres had often wondered if part of their purpose was to be closed as often as possible, just in case someone should come in and disturb their studied disorder by actually buying a book. Used booksellers' ploys were legion: BACK IN FIVE MINUTES signs that remained in place for hours, or days; a scribbled phone number to be called in order to gain entry, but destined never to be picked up, assuming it had ever been connected in the first place; and once, carefully typed on a lined card, the five words CLOSED DUE TO DEATH TEMPORARILY, which raised more questions than it answered, not least whether it was the closure or the death that was intended to be provisional.

In the Snug, nearby Olney's children's bookshop, she bought the only copy of *The Book of Lost Things* on the shelves. Since Phoebe was a beneficiary of the writer's largesse, Ceres supposed that she should know more about her benefactor's work, having learned more about his life from the internet. As Olivier had explained, it was one colored by sadness, but not defined by it. The author had found a way to turn his pain into a novel, and that novel had occasionally helped others with their pain. That was what stories did, or the ones that mattered to us: They helped us to understand others, but they could also make us feel understood in turn, and less alone in the world. Right now, Ceres thought she would be happy with that, because she'd never felt more alone.

But she remained troubled by "The Tale of the Two Dancers" that had transmitted itself, seemingly unconsciously, from mind to mouth to hand, and from there to the page. Had it not been in her own writing, she might have doubted it was her work at all. Typically, when she wrote longhand, she left a trail of crossed-out words, rethinks, and corrections. When she was contemplating the right turn of phrase, or the construction of a sentence, she had a habit of tapping the end of the pen or pencil on the paper, creating a swarm of dots. By contrast, the writing of the previous night was word-perfect, and showed no signs of hesitation or reflection.

Upon her return to the cottage, Ceres brewed a pot of tea and spent a few hours at her desk. She had forced herself to begin working again, and already had three deadlines imminent, all involving advertising copy for products she would not have wanted to buy or websites she wouldn't wish to visit, which made the task of convincing others to do so that much more difficult. Then again, if she had only consented to write about products she liked, she and Phoebe would have ended up on the streets long ago. That was one of the differences between childhood and adulthood: as a child, you often had to do things you didn't want to—including, in Phoebe's case, go to school, finish homework, and eat broccoli—because someone bigger and older told you to do them; as an adult, you still had to do things you didn't want to do, but if you were fortunate, somebody paid you to do them, which helped a bit.

Once the work was completed and the day was mellowing into evening, Ceres allowed herself a glass of wine to accompany her reading of *The Book of Lost Things*. It had been a long time since she'd opened a work of fiction for her own pleasure. Mostly she read for Phoebe, even before the accident, and she now found it hard to associate the act with anyone but her daughter. Not to be reading aloud felt odd to Ceres, so much so that it took her a moment or two to realize she could hear herself reciting the opening of the novel to the empty room, like a spell or incantation. *Once upon a time*: Who even began a book that way anymore?

And—oh!—there was that sudden sharp sting of loss again, as she caught herself using one of her daughter's favorite sentence constructions, a formulation on which Phoebe fell back when something was particularly frustrating or bewildering.

Who even *knows* that song?

When even *was* that?

What even *is* cauliflower?

God, she missed the sound of Phoebe's voice so much. It was the quiet that was so hard to bear, as though Ceres were gradually being prepared for a lasting silence to come, when she would no longer even have her daughter's breathing to console her, and remind her that she remained in the world. But how to balance this with the despair that descended on her more frequently, and most acutely in the hoary light before full dawn, although it had also come upon her as she drove home from the Lantern House the night before: the secret wish that this would all just come to an end, a resolution, for her—

Or for Phoebe.

"No!" She shouted the word to the empty room, startling herself. "I take it back. I didn't mean that."

To the dust motes caught in the lamplight.

"I will not part with her, not like this. Whatever it takes, I want her returned to me."

To the crumbs on the plate, and the spilled tea in the saucer.

"She is my child."

To the spiders in the corners, surrounded by the shriveled discards of their quarry.

"Are you listening?"

To the woman in the shadows, who heard only what she wanted to hear.

VII

Ryne
(OLD ENGLISH)

Mystery

t was dark, and the book had been set aside in favor of the nightly news, which turned out to be an error, given that it was dominated by Russian tanks bombarding villages, and scientists prophesying imminent climate catastrophe. Before the accident, the latter had particularly troubled Phoebe, who couldn't understand why politicians weren't rushing to save the planet. It had been left to Ceres to try to explain that, rather like some small children, politicians were driven by short- to medium-term gain, and rarely thought further than the next election, which only confirmed Ceres's view that politics was no proper pursuit for an adult. She gave up on the news bulletin after only ten minutes; she didn't need to be made to feel more impotent.

She stroked the cover of *The Book of Lost Things*, as she might have a sleeping cat. Although she didn't like to admit it to herself, Ceres realized she'd become distanced from fiction, so much so that she could no longer use it as a form of escape—and she had more cause than most to want to leave reality behind, if only for a while. She couldn't even blame her disengagement on the accident, because it had been ongoing since adolescence. She had fallen out of love with stories, and what had come upon Phoebe simply confirmed the pointlessness of them. What good were they? The happy ones were untrue to life, and the sad ones couldn't tell you anything you didn't already know.

Here is my story: I had a daughter once, but she was stolen from me, and left in her place was a doll in her image.

Yet . . .

The book on the table was calling to her, wanting to be read. She thought it might be because of its connection to the Lantern House, to the author's old residence rotting away on the grounds, and the mystery of his disappearance. These things gave texture to the tale. They made it more relevant, and so it was less the book than the circumstances surrounding its creation that engaged her. This is what she told herself, even as she caught the lie lurking. It was peculiar, but everything about the experience of reading this novel now made her perplexed. Earlier she had found herself becoming immersed in it without noticing, and when at last she surfaced, she was shocked to find that nearly two hours had gone by, so lost had she been in the story of a boy who loses his mother, gains an unwanted stepmother and half brother, and ventures into a land, real or imaginary (that was never clear), built from the books on his shelves, and the fairy stories that he loves. In its pages dwelt the Crooked Man, a being who, as Olivier had pointed out, bore the same name as the monster in the story she had invented for Phoebe. The only explanation Ceres could come up with was that, in the past, she must have read a review of the book, or an article about its author, and stored those details away in her mind.

She set about making supper, even though she was not particularly hungry. Her pleasure in food—like her pleasure in so many things—had been taken from her, and she ate only to sustain herself. Whatever little use she was to Phoebe at present, she would be no use to her at all if she ended up in the hospital herself due to neglect.

After supper, she read some more of the book, taking her more than halfway through. When she could read no more, Ceres called her mother, who now lived modestly in northern Spain for much of the year, and rarely went to bed before two in the morning. She'd left England not long after Ceres's father had died. She couldn't face a grim winter there without him by her side, she said, but then it turned out that she didn't want to face the English spring or autumn without him, either, although she could just about tolerate the summer for a few weeks. They had explored the countryside together, she and he, mapping old burial mounds, photographing stone circles and fairy forts, and gathering folktales, myths, even colorful old and local words to add texture to the obscure academic papers that father published, or to chapters in books destined to be read only by peculiar men and women as obsessive as he, or so Ceres had always assumed. All those yellowed pages, those withered leaves . . .

It had taken a long time for Ceres to figure out why her father's vocation had alienated her so, and *The Book of Lost Things* reminded her of the reason: She found the stories he preferred frightening. She could see the ghost of him now, sitting in his favorite chair by the empty fireplace, his cardigan smelling of earth and tobacco smoke.

"There is another England, Ceres: a hidden land, a secret commonwealth, and these tales are its echoes, its history."

But she did not care to listen to those echoes. They spoke of cruelty and viciousness. Let them fade away. Let them be lost forever. As though to spite him, she had chosen instead to read what she pointedly called her "fairy tales," a term that always made her father wince; and the prettier the princess, and the happier the ending, the better. Fairy godmothers, fairy helpers, benevolent beings with wings and wands, she adored them all.

"But those are not fairies, Ceres," he would tell her.

"They're *good* fairies."

"There's no such thing."

"Because you only believe in bad ones."

"There's no such thing as bad fairies either."

"But if they're not good, and not bad, what are they?"

"They're Other, Ceres, that's what they are: Other."

And his voice was firm and full of conviction, as of one who believed in the objective reality of such creatures, because he *did* believe. For her father, the past and present ran alongside each other, largely on parallel lines, but they touched in ancient places, where the land held memories the way graveyards stored bodies. Those memories crept into earth and stone, metal and wood, infusing inanimate materials with their essence. Around such locales, myths and legends gathered, and out of them came stories, books, histories, so that the boundary between what was real and unreal became more and more obscured, as each teller extracted layers of meaning and added new layers of their own. Actuality became shadowy, smudged, and so the world was altered.

Because, her father would tell her, once a book or story was told for the first time, reality itself shifted. The story became part of the world, and anyone who heard it, or read it, and in whom it took root, was never the same again. Stories were a benign infection, transforming their hosts—or generally benign, because some books could reshape people for the worse. Pour enough venom into a book, or warp truth sufficiently in its pages, and you could turn a weak mind hateful. But the more one read, and the wider one's reading, the stronger one's mind became. This was why, in the end, her father was content that his daughter consumed any books at all, even if they weren't always ones of which he approved. What mattered was that she appreciated the value of literature. When some idiot politician or finger-wagging do-gooder complained about the books on school reading lists because they dared to treat adolescents with respect, or acknowledge that issues of race, sexuality, and gender might be of some relevance to them as they strode the path to adulthood, he would always make the same remark: "It's not the people who read books you have to worry about, but the people who don't."

Meanwhile, the phone was still ringing in Ceres's ear. Her mother was forever darting off to some other part of her house, or wandering in the garden, day or night, leaving her phone wherever she last dropped it. Frequently she would mute it so that she wouldn't be disturbed while reading or watching TV, and forget to turn it back on again, leaving Ceres to wonder if she might not have died since their last conversation, and her body was waiting to be discovered by a worried neighbor or some unfortunate postman. Ceres had reached that age when a person spends a great deal of time worrying about both children *and* parents. Adulthood, she had long ago surmised, was very overrated.

At last her mother picked up. She had returned to England to be with Ceres in the days following Phoebe's accident, and ended up staying for some weeks, until it became clear that her granddaughter's condition was unlikely to change dramatically for the time being. By then mother and daughter had grown fractious with each other, because Ceres's flat was too small for a pair of adults to share, particularly adults who were probably too much alike in some ways for comfort, yet also too dissimilar in others. Ceres loved her mother, but she had a big personality, and big personalities didn't function well in restricted spaces. Eventually, by mutual agreement, Ceres's mother returned to Spain, but they spoke at least every other day, and Ceres knew that she would be ready to hop on a plane back to England at a moment's notice should anything happen to—

No, nothing would happen to Phoebe, or nothing worse. Ceres willed it. The new environment of the Lantern House, with its trees and flowers and birdsong, could only be beneficial. If Phoebe's spirit remained in that body, it might hear the birds and respond; and if it was elsewhere, their song could yet summon it back. Ceres just had to keep her own spirits up, and not fall prey to melancholy or despair, as she did earlier.

"How is she?" asked her mother, because that was how their conversations inevitably began.

"The same," said Ceres, "but the new place is lovely, or as lovely as it can be."

"Are you missing London?"

"I haven't had a chance to miss it, but I don't think I will. London had become too big and loud."

And empty, without Phoebe. She had filled its spaces.

"I hate to say it," Ceres continued, "but you may have been right all along about coming back here. It was always home for me. I'd forgotten how much I love it."

They had sometimes discussed selling the cottage, but it was filled with possessions and memories from decades of married life, and her mother was reluctant to part with any of them. Also, no pressing financial reason had existed for the sale, or not until Phoebe's condition threatened to alter that situation. Ceres's mother had informed her that she need only ask and the cottage would be put on the market, but living in it now appeared to be the better solution, thanks to the Lantern House.

"Well, just be careful that you don't get lonely. Do try and make some new friends, Ceres."

Ceres had never minded being alone when she was younger, because there was a difference between being lonely and alone. Books had helped back then, because a person with a good book could never be lonely. Then Phoebe had come along, and Ceres didn't have time to be alone, and was never lonely as long as her daughter was around. But with Phoebe in a state of suspension, Ceres, too, was held in stasis. She was alone *and* lonely. Something would have to be done about it. Perhaps something already was being done.

"I've started reading again," she said. "Books, I mean."

"Books aren't the same as friends."

"Aren't they? Dad would have disagreed with you."

"Your father disagreed with me on many things, which was one of the reasons we got along so well."

"Because they were unimportant things?"

"No, because secretly we both knew that I was right and he was wrong. He preferred not to admit it, and I was happy to let him have his pride."

There was some truth to this, Ceres admitted. Her father was a man who dwelt in many worlds, the real one far from being his best-loved, the presence in it of a wife and daughter notwithstanding. Had her mother not kept him anchored to the ground, he might well have floated away, a distant figure receding into the clouds, his head buried in a history of megalithic circles and underground tombs, or a paper on the differences between dryads and hamadryads.

"I worry about you, you know," said her mother. "I'm concerned about what all this is doing to you. If only you had someone by your side to share the load—"

This was another of her mother's frequent tunes. She couldn't grasp why Ceres remained single, and Ceres would have struggled to explain, even had she wanted to. She had been let down badly by Phoebe's father, which was part of it. This had made her not untrusting of men, but wary of them, especially with a young daughter to consider. She didn't want to introduce a new man into Phoebe's life just because she occasionally missed male company, or the bed was too big, and so far she hadn't met any man about whom she felt sufficiently deeply to consider allowing him in.

But it was also the case that she and Phoebe had become their own unit. They had established routines and patterns that worked, and with which both of them were content. Ceres hadn't wanted anyone else to disrupt this, not unless she was absolutely certain it was the right person; and since that was difficult, even impossible, to know, she had settled for a life without a partner. It wasn't always easy, but she was content with the decision she had made—or had been, until the accident.

"A boyfriend, you mean?"

"Just someone," said her mother.

"I might get a dog."

"A dog isn't some*one*, it's some*thing*. But now that you come to mention it, a dog might not be such a bad idea. You can talk to it, and it won't talk back."

"Like Dad, you mean?"

"Your dad didn't remotely resemble a dog. He wouldn't have dreamed of doing what he was told, even for the promise of a biscuit. It was hard enough to get him to remember what he was supposed to buy if I asked him to go to the shops. I used to wait by the phone for him to call once he'd arrived, checking on what it was I wanted him to get. I'd have blamed it on senility, except he was sharp as a tack right to the end, however much he might have pretended otherwise. And there was no point in giving him a list because he always left it behind, or somehow misplaced it in an overstuffed pocket. I did once consider writing things on his hand, but to be honest, I wouldn't have put it past him to have lost the hand somewhere between the front door and the end of the street. He was a most infuriating man, and I loved him with all my heart."

Ceres let her gaze roam over the living room of the cottage. There was so much of her father here: the books, the maps and woodcuts on the walls, his armchair, even a couple of his pipes in a rack on the mantelpiece, along with a stuffed platypus in a glass case. (He claimed not to be able to remember buying the platypus, which had shown up on the mantelpiece while Ceres's mother was in the hospital for the removal of gallstones, and refused to part with it upon her return, arguing that it added character to the room.) Nooks in the brickwork were still frosted with wax from the candles he would light, and the shelves in the hall were filled with pieces he had found in the earth during his explorations and excavations: Viking stone-carved animals, Saxon arrowheads, shards of Roman pottery, even jewelry made from semiprecious metals. He had been scrupulous about handing over valuable or uncommon items to the authorities, though he knew they would probably just end up stored in some dusty box in a museum basement.

Only one thing had he kept that he should have surrendered: a Roman dodecahedron, dating from the second or third century. It was three inches in diameter, and consisted of twelve pentagonal faces, each with a circular hole in the center, although the holes were not of the same size, and each face was surrounded by five small raised circular knobs. Her father had spotted it in disturbed soil near Hadrian's Wall, the barrier built by the Romans to fortify the south of Britain against the northern tribes, and kept it for himself. The attraction for him lay in the mystery of the object, because no one had yet been able to establish the purpose of a dodecahedron. One theory was that it might have been used for soothsaying, but the dodecahedron bore no symbols or inscriptions, so how could one divine knowledge from it? The knobs meant that it couldn't be thrown easily, so it would come to rest on the side on which it was dropped. That meant that dodecahedrons didn't work as gaming dice either. Some frustrated experts declared them to be purely decorative, but her father had never accepted this, and in the end he stopped reading other people's opinions of dodecahedrons altogether.

"It's not important to know what it's for," he would tell Ceres, as she sat in his lap, turning the dodecahedron in her hands. "It's enough to know that it *is*."

Now, the phone held to one ear, Ceres walked to the hall. The dodecahedron was still in its place, and still shining. Alone of all the collection, it never gathered dust. She clasped it in her hand. The radiator wasn't working, and she could see her breath clouding, yet the dodecahedron was warm to the touch. She set it back down. The shelf on which it stood held the books that were most important to her father, among them art monographs by Giovanni Battista Piranesi, Wenceslaus Hollar, and Pere Borrell del Caso; a copy of Robert Kirk's *The Secret Commonwealth of Elves, Fauns and Fairies*; S. R. Gardiner's *Oliver Cromwell*, from 1901, which had been awarded to his own father as a school prize, as all three men—Ceres's father, grandfather, and Cromwell—had been born in Huntingdon, Cambridgeshire; two volumes of Milton's *Paradise Lost*, which he regarded as the greatest poetical work in

English, dating from 1719; and five small volumes of Livy in Latin, bound in red and gold leather, published in Germany in the nineteenth century.

From the latter, Ceres could remember her father translating for her (behind her mother's back, of course) the story of Regulus, the third-century BC Roman general paroled by the Carthaginians in order to return to Rome and negotiate a settlement. When he got home, Regulus urged the Roman Senate to reject the Carthaginians' offer before, against the protests of his own people, returning to Carthage to fulfill the terms of his parole, under which he had promised to go back. For his troubles, the Carthaginians were reputed to have cut off Regulus's eyelids, packed him in a spiked box, and rolled him around in it until he died, not unlike the unfaithful servant in the story of the Goose Girl by the Brothers Grimm—one of the folktales of which her father very much approved, because someone perished painfully at the end.

"But why did Regulus go back?" Ceres asked him.

"Because he had given his word," her father replied, "and it was the right thing to do."

"Even though he knew he might be hurt, or die?"

"Sometimes that's the choice we have to make."

"I hope I never have to make that choice."

He kissed her head.

"I hope you never have to make it either."

Dad, oh Dad.

"I must go," Ceres told her mother. "I'm bone-tired."

"Then go to bed. I love you. If you get a dog, don't make it one of those little yappy ones, or I'll never forgive you."

They wished each other good night. Ceres turned off the lights, put a guard in front of what remained of the fire, and climbed the stairs to her bedroom. She didn't pull the curtains on the window because she liked to fall asleep by moonlight in winter, knowing that she wouldn't be woken at some ungodly hour by the rising sun. As it happened, she barely had time to register the unsheathed blade of the moon before she was asleep, and so did not hear the flapping of wings at the glass, or notice the first tendril of ivy force its way through the crumbling brickwork of the wall and curl itself quietly, almost watchfully, into a corner.

VIII

Egesung

(OLD ENGLISH)

A Fear or Dread

 lesson hard-learned as an adult is that no call in the dead of night presages any good. So it was that Ceres came awake instantly when her phone rang at 4 a.m., the display showing one word: Lantern.

"Hello?"

The voice was Olivier's. For this, if for nothing else, she was grateful.

"Ceres?" he said. "Phoebe's condition has deteriorated. I think you should come."

Phoebe's new room was different, more like the one in the hospital. There were no pictures on the walls, and no armchairs or couches. This was a high-dependency unit, designed with one purpose: to keep a child alive.

Ceres was trying to listen to what the silver-haired doctor was saying (*Beattie? Yes, Beattie, that was her name*) but the words drifted by, barely making an impression—"sudden," "unexplained," "difficulty breathing"—because her attention kept returning to her daughter. Phoebe now looked even smaller and more lost than before. Ceres so badly wanted to hold

her, to put her head to her breast and stroke her hair, to tell her that everything would be all right, that she needn't be afraid—

*But if you have to leave me, I'll understand. If there's too much pain, I want you
to let go. But if you can, I want you to stay, because I don't want to be without you.*

"Could this have been caused by the stress of the transfer from the
hospital?" she asked.

"I very much doubt that," said Dr. Beattie. "The staff responsible for
the move are so experienced that we've never had an incident, not even
a minor one. Phoebe was monitored throughout, and examined again as
soon as she arrived with us. There were no warning signs, and no issues.
What we continue to hope is that the alteration in her condition may
be related to a process of repair. Her system has been shutting down all
nonessential functions to concentrate on restoring the important ones,
and the job is ongoing."

"But if that's true," said Ceres, "how do you explain this downturn?"

"We're pretty confident that it's a temporary lapse. But I won't lie
to you: We were worried about Phoebe for a while, which was why we
thought it best to bring you in. Now we have her stabilized, and she's out
of danger, if not out of the woods."

Through the unit's sole window, Ceres could see the shapes of
branches taking form in the early-morning light, like a photograph slowly
developing in a tray. They appeared chimerical to her, intruders from an
alien environment. Here was a world of plastic, metal, glass, electron-
ics; and there one of wood, bark, grass, and sap. Somehow her daughter
straddled both, her body lying unmoving in one while her soul wandered
the other.

"Can I stay with her?" said Ceres.

"Not in the unit itself, I'm afraid, although you can take one of the
parental suites. We do our best here, but it's not the Savoy. You might
be more comfortable at home, but it's completely your choice. If there's
another change, you'll be the first to know, and you can call us at any
time to check on her. But as I said, we're cautiously optimistic that we've
arrested the decline."

Ceres could only nod. She wanted to thank her for what she'd done,
but the words wouldn't come easily, and by the time she found them,

the doctor was gone. Only Olivier remained. Together they watched a nurse check on Phoebe, her movements swift and efficient, no time or effort wasted. Only at the end, as she was leaving, did she pause to stroke Phoebe's hair, and a look of tenderness and understanding was exchanged between nurse and mother.

That should be me, thought Ceres. *I should be the one to console her.*

"I told you," said Olivier. "She's a fighter."

"No," said Ceres, "she's just a child, and a child shouldn't have to fight, not like this. It's not fair."

"None of it is fair," said Olivier, "but this is her battle, and all we can do is aid her in it. There was a moment when she slipped, when she might have lost, but we were there for her, and the fight goes on."

Ceres turned to him.

"How do you do it, Olivier?" she asked. "This job of yours, it's so hard. All these children, with all their illnesses—"

"Because it's not a job," said Olivier, "not to me, not to any of us. It's more than that, much more. And I do it because *not* doing it would be harder, if that makes any sense: *not* to be here for them, *not* to sit with them in the night when they're scared, *not* to be able to explain to them what's happening, or why. I couldn't do anything else, not now. Nothing else would have such meaning. Even at the worst moments, I've never regretted the decision to come here. Never. But I also know what I feel for each of these children, for all its depth, is infinitesimal compared to what you feel for Phoebe, and what you're going through now. All I can tell you is that I understand it, a fraction."

Ceres reached out and held his hand tightly for a moment.

"I'd like to stay here for a while," she said, "to watch over her. After that, I know you'll do the same."

"Yes," said Olivier, "I will," and he left her with her child.

IX

Urushiol

(JAPANESE)

Oily, Skin-Irritating Coating on Ivy

n the days that followed, a new routine took over Ceres's life. Despite the Lantern House's assurances that she would be notified immediately of any developments, she found that she couldn't relax at the cottage. Her nerves were constantly jangling, one ear always alert for the sound of the phone ringing. She was reminded, too, of her father's death, and how the hospital had called after midnight to say that they should come immediately, because his race was nearly run. Ceres had been staying at the cottage with her mother and Phoebe, who was then not yet three years old. Ceres had somehow managed to dress quickly, and wrap Phoebe up warmly without waking her, before joining her mother for the fifteen-minute drive to the hospital. By the time they got there, her father was dead. His hand was still warm as Ceres held it, and all she could think was: *We should have been here. We should have stayed. We knew he didn't have long. They told us it could be a day or two, but no more than that. Instead it was just a few hours, and we weren't beside him at the end. He died without us, and we didn't even get to say goodbye.*

While she willed a different ending for Phoebe, one in which her child was restored to her, she feared another. She would not allow Phoebe to be alone if that moment came. She asked the care team if she might be permitted to make use of one of the suites after all, and was told she was welcome to do so. "Suite" was too grand a word for the room, which was just about big enough to accommodate a bed, a desk and chair, a wardrobe and bedside table, and a tiny bathroom, but it was minutes away from where Phoebe was lying. The room also had a refrigerator, a kettle, and a microwave, as well as a wall-mounted television, so Ceres could make coffee, heat food, and even watch old, undemanding movies when she was too tired to do anything else. She was allowed to spend time with Phoebe as well, now that she'd been stabilized, and so Ceres resumed reading to her daughter, but this time it was *The Book of Lost Things* that she read rather than the old tales. Even though she had almost finished the novel, she returned to the start and commenced reading aloud from the first chapter, so that Phoebe, too, might know it.

In case you're listening. In case you can hear me.

But there was another reason Ceres had left the cottage, one she had not mentioned to anybody, not even her mother: the ivy. She had spotted the first of it in the corner of her bedroom on the evening after Phoebe was placed in intensive care. She'd climbed on a chair to clip it back with a pair of old shears, and the next day stopped at a garden center to buy weed killer. That afternoon, she sprayed the exterior wall, as well as the inside corner where the ivy had intruded, and plugged the hole with some filler she'd discovered in the garden shed, before returning to the Lantern House to pay her evening visit to Phoebe.

When she woke the following morning, the ivy had broken through the filler and started to spread: two tendrils instead of one, snaking south and east from the corner, the leaves no longer entirely green but mottled yellow and white, as though the poison she had sprayed had left it physically altered but otherwise unharmed. She attacked it again with the shears, but it was harder to cut than before, and she had the disturbing impression that it was actively resisting her, learning from the last assault and adding an extra layer of protection to its stem. Even after she managed to sever the branches, they fought her attempts to wrest them away, and when she finally managed to yank them free, they took a layer of paint and a chunk of plaster with them, disfiguring the wall. Also, despite wearing gloves, Ceres developed a rash on her wrists and fingers, and had to pry green, splinter-like fragments from her flesh.

But worse was to come. She went downstairs to find the ivy had entered the kitchen too, devising points of access by the windowsill and from behind the cupboards. These leaves, too, bore the new coloration. Ceres didn't even wait until after breakfast, but immediately went outside and began spraying again until the five-liter container of weed killer was empty. She could only hope that it worked; the prospect of hiring someone to remove the ivy filled her with dread. Apart from the fact that she'd always liked how it looked on the cottage, the way it had adhered so tenaciously to the walls of her bedroom suggested that wrenching it from the exterior might damage the stonework. Money was already tight without adding expensive repairs to her outgoings in order to keep the winter chill out, or prevent the cottage from crumbling around her. Lord knew what her mother would have to say about that.

Ceres went back inside, made breakfast, and did a couple of hours of work. At noon she drove to the Lantern House to read to Phoebe. She left shortly after two, bought bread, milk, and a newspaper, and was home by three. She pulled up outside the cottage, got out of the car, and took the bag of groceries from the back seat.

Only then did she notice what had happened to the ivy.

The gardener's name was Greene, which Ceres might have found amusing at another time.

"*Hedera helix*," he said, as he stood before the house. "English ivy. Strong-willed stuff. Once it gets a foothold, it's the devil to dig out."

"But why is it red in places?" asked Ceres.

The ivy on the cottage walls, green for so many years, then briefly tinged with yellow and white, now showed a claret internal structure on its leaves, as though sanguinary fluids, not water and sugar, were flowing through them.

"Could be a pest infestation," said Mr. Greene, "or too little phosphorus in the soil. Sometimes people mistake Boston ivy for English, and Boston reverts to red in autumn, but you don't see Boston ivy so much round here, and this is definitely the homegrown English variety. Know it by the leaves."

He leaned in closer, and took some of the ivy in his gloved hand.

"Never seen redness quite like this before, though," he said. "It's the midrib and veins that have turned. See?"

Ceres looked, but didn't touch. The ivy repelled her.

"It looks like blood," she said.

"Just so. Must have been happening for a while, though."

"No, it started today."

"That's not possible," said Mr. Greene. "Every leaf has changed. That would take longer than a day."

"And I'm telling you it wasn't like this when I left the house earlier. Traces of yellow here and there, yes, but not red. I sprayed it with weed killer. Could that be the cause?"

"Did you spray the lot of it?"

"Only the front part. The container ran out before I could get to the ivy at the back."

"But that's red, too," said Mr. Greene, "and the root system is different. No, it's unlikely that weed killer did this. I mean, this ivy's not even dying. If anything, it's flourishing."

"I want it gone," said Ceres. "It's breaking through the walls."

"Well, I can remove it, although it won't be this week. The next, with luck."

"Next week? But by then it may have overrun the house."

"I'm sorry, but I can't come out again any sooner. And I have to warn you, your cottage will look a sight after. You might need to consult a builder, too, because I can't promise it won't cause harm to the facade—or worse, if it's started to find its way through the stonework."

And that was where they left it, with Mr. Greene promising to do his best to tackle the problem as quickly as he could, and the cottage swathed by ivy with something like blood in its veins. This, then, was the real reason why Ceres had elected to stay at the care home for a time, while she sat by her daughter's bedside, reading, reciting.

Creating.

Channeling.

THE TALE OF THE MAN OF IVY

*O*nce *upon a time, in a land both far from this one and very near—because sometimes distant places are closer than you think, and more similar, too—lived a man named Jacob. He owned a small farm, but dreamed of owning a larger one. He was married to a pretty wife, but secretly yearned to be married to a more beautiful one. He had a scholarly, amiable son, but would have preferred a strong, forceful one.*

These desires Jacob kept to himself, because although he might have been driven by longing for all he did not have—or thought he did not have, because desire is a blinding emotion—he was not a malicious man, and had no wish to hurt his family. Only when he was alone in the woods, with no one to hear, would he permit his frustrations to show, and then he would give vent to his true feelings, speaking aloud of them to bark, branch, and blade.

One autumn day, when he had spent an hour telling nature of his longings, he heard a voice call his name. He looked around him, but the forest clearing was empty, for not even a bird hovered, nor did the tiniest of insects trouble the dirt.

"Who's there?" said Jacob. "Stop hiding and show yourself!"

"Look closer," said the voice, "and then you will see. Look to the trees."

Jacob did as the voice told him, first gazing up at the crowns, then peering behind their trunks, until finally he came to an old sessile oak, its bark overgrown with thick ivy. And there, in the heart of the greenery, he saw a face formed by the arrangement of the fronds. It had only darkness for eyes, and a hole for a mouth, yet a face it undoubtedly was, though it would have been easy for someone to miss it had they not been searching for it. As Jacob watched, the fronds at the mouth moved, and the voice spoke again; a dry whisper, a rustle, like dead leaves driven before the breeze.

"I was not hiding," said the voice. "It is one thing to hide, another not to be noticed."

"Who are you?" said Jacob. "What are you?"

"I suppose one might term me a spirit. Some might even refer to me as a god."

"But how are you called?" said Jacob.

"Oh, I have many names, some of which have never been uttered aloud by men. Today, for you, let me be called Beonot."

"Beonot it is, then," said Jacob, even as he thought that this was a curious name, for it referred to a place of bent grass, of crooked greenery. But then, this was a curious creature, whatever it might be.

"How long have you been there?" he asked.

"Long enough to have listened to your complaints," said Beonot, "and not just on this day, but all the days gone by. Long enough to feel pity for your plight."

"Pity?" said Jacob.

"You deserve better, but that is true of many people. What makes it harder for you is that you know you deserve better. A different, richer life is almost within your grasp. If it were granted you, I have no doubt you would cherish it, and value your time on earth all the more. You would no longer waste time pining for what you did not have, because all that you wished for would be yours. You would be content, would you not?"

"I would," said Jacob. "The land I farm is good land, but there could be more of it. My wife loves me, but the years, I fear, are not being kind to her. My son is liked by all, and is a tender soul, but this is not a tender world, and strength will take him further."

"So what would you have me do," said Beonot, "if it were in my power to change things for you?"

"You would give to me my neighbor's land," said Jacob, "that I might grow more crops and raise more cattle, but not so many acres as to make its stewardship a strain. You would make my wife beautiful once more, but if that were not possible, you would provide me with another who was but who loved me just as the old wife does. Nevertheless, I would not wish her to be so beautiful that other men might covet her, and would ask that you provide her with a faithful disposition, just in case. And you would take some of my son's kindliness and replace it with a robustness of body and will, but not so much as to cause him to reject me in my old age."

"Then you would be content?" said Beonot.

"Then I would be content," said Jacob.

As he spoke, Jacob believed all he said, but only because he had long *before convinced himself of the truth of it. Thus can a man become a liar while holding himself honest.*

"But what of your neighbor?" said Beonot. "Does he, too, not value his land? What should become of him if I bequeath his acres to you?"

"I leave that to you," said Jacob, "but I wish him no loss."

"And your wife? What is she to do if another takes her place?"

"I leave that to you," said Jacob, "but I wish her happiness."

"And your son? Should I make him forget his old self? What if he is content as he is?"

"I leave that to you," said Jacob, "but I wish him only to be better equipped to face the harshness of life."

By now the sun was setting, and it cast a golden glow over Beonot amid the ivy, so that he seemed to be aflame. And had Jacob not been so in thrall to his own cravings, so bedazzled by the prospect of a better future, he might have perceived that the face of Beonot was not a benign one, that Beonot's features were twisted, that Beonot's mouth was a misshapen scar, and that the concavities of Beonot's eyes were black, far blacker than any shadows alone should have caused them to appear.

"Let us be honest with each other," said Beonot. "What you desire is a life that is not the one you have, because it strikes me that you would be most happy if you could leave your old life behind, shedding it like a skin."

"Yes," said Jacob, with a confidence he had never felt before. "I wish to shed my old life, shed it like a skin."

"Then I ask that you seal our bargain with blood," said Beonot, "to show I have not misjudged the depth of your commitment. Let it drop into my mouth, for I cannot see what you are doing, and only by taste can I confirm that we are agreed."

So Jacob took his hunting knife, and with the tip he pricked a finger, so that a single droplet of blood fell into Beonot's mouth. At that instant all the leaves on the tree turned from green to pink, then red; and the ivy became flesh; and from the deadwood trunk there emerged a bent, skinless figure, even as the blood continued to drip from Jacob's finger, faster and faster, so that the drops became a stream, and the stream became a torrent, until finally nothing remained of Jacob but his skin and clothes.

The Crooked Man stretched his cramped limbs, and blood stained the dirt, hissing and smoking as it landed. He picked up Jacob's skin and fit it to his body, so that he became the image of the dead farmer. The Crooked Man, you see, was very old, and very old things may seek to make themselves look young again, for even the worst of us have our vanities. Eventually, the Crooked Man knew, his own essence would contaminate Jacob's, and he would once again resemble his former self: a gnarled, warped being, although encased in a fresh suit of skin that might last him for many years.

But while he favored the dead man, he thought he might take advantage of the fact. So the Crooked Man dressed himself in Jacob's clothing, and prepared to make the acquaintance of his new wife.

Ceres jerked upright in her chair. *The Book of Lost Things* had fallen to the floor, although how long before she could not have said. But the story she had told to her unconscious daughter was fresh in her mind, and she knew it had not come from the book she had been reading. Yet even this was not quite true, because she sensed that, while it might not have been written in its pages, the tale had come from the same world. The universe of the book, like the ivy at the cottage, was extending its reach into her consciousness, because that was what books did. She shouldn't have been surprised or frightened; it was just the way of them.

"Sleep."

a dry whisper, a rustle, like dead leaves driven before the breeze

And Ceres slept.

X

Lych Way

(DEVON)

A Corpse Road, the Way of the Dead

hen Ceres woke, she saw that someone had eased the chair into the recline position while she was sleeping and covered her with a blanket. She walked to the window. Dawn was breaking, and she could hear birds chorusing. Despite the efforts of her unknown benefactor to make her more comfortable, her body was stiff. She considered seeking the solace of her own bed, if just for a while, but the memory of the ivy convinced her that it might be less disquieting to remain where she was. She knew, though, that this was only putting off the inevitable, and eventually she'd have to return and find a way to tackle the invasive greenery.

She kept a couple of fresh T-shirts, a change of underwear, and a small toiletry bag in her rucksack. This was one of the first things she'd learned after Phoebe's accident: it might not always be possible to get home after a bedside vigil, and any stress would be made worse by having to wear the same clothes two or three days in a row, or being forced to scavenge or beg for a toothbrush.

But what do clothes and toothbrushes matter?

She stared down at Phoebe. There were fresh bruises on her daughter's arms from the insertion of new needles, and tiny frown lines—or

pain lines—on her forehead that Ceres could not remember having noticed before.

What does any of it matter?

Ceres left the room and made her way, half-dazed, to her suite, where
she undressed and climbed in the shower. Her legs felt weak, so she sat
on the base of the stall and laid her forehead against her arms.

The water coursed over her, and washed all sense of herself away.

The mind and body can take only so much—more than we might imagine or expect, but less, on occasion, than we might require. We can keep
going through force of will, without nourishment, without respite, without support, but only for so long. Ultimately we must shudder to a halt,
and our poor battered selves will seek the chance to rest.

So Ceres remained slumped in the shower stall, her eyes open but
unseeing, the water striking her for so long that it finally became afflic-
tive. She managed to reach up to turn it off before wrapping herself in a
towel, crawling from the bathroom, and lying on the bedroom floor. The
door to the suite was closed, and no one came to look in on her, assuming
that she was resting properly after a night in a chair.

Only when the water cooled, causing her to shiver, did Ceres finish
drying herself. She dressed automatically, putting on the same clothes
she had already worn for a day and a night, heedless of the fresh ones in
the bag. When she was done, she slipped on her shoes, opened the door
of the suite, and walked toward the exit of the Lantern House. Dimly
and distantly she was aware of voices from the nurses' station, of fuss
and bother, but this was not unusual and she gave it no further thought,
just as she paid no attention to her wet hair, or the aches in her back,
her shoulders, and her legs. She was both Ceres and an entity apart, a
creature dispensing with all but the most essential functions, one whose
consciousness had retreated to a place of safety deep inside. It was enough
that she could put one foot in front of the other, that she could keep moving, but what impelled her to do so, she could not have said.

Before her stretched the path leading into the woods, and from a bare
branch the one-eyed rook watched her set first one foot upon it, then

the other. Like a trained raptor following the falconer's glove, the rook glided from tree to tree, always staying marginally ahead of the woman, monitoring her progress, croaking only when she showed signs of faltering. The cry of the bird, harsh and demanding, penetrated the fog that had taken hold of Ceres, dulling the world around her. The rook tipped its beak to what was happening behind her: the forest was closing in her wake, the branches of the trees reaching out to one another, obscuring the sky, while their roots broke through the earth and formed a barrier of twisted wood from which earthworms tumbled and beetles fell.

But Ceres was not afraid. She did not want to go back, not to a world in which only the shell of her child was present. Wherever the spirit of Phoebe now dwelt, it was not there. If Ceres was to be restored to herself, if the world was to be made whole again, the part of Phoebe that had been stolen needed to be recovered; and if it could not be, Ceres did not wish to go on. It was too difficult, and she could not benefit her child only by reading stories to her in the hope that she might hear them and respond, because there was no Phoebe present to react. Ceres could as easily have recited her stories to an empty well, or howled them into the mouth of a cave, for all the good they were doing. More was required of her than that, for something had taken her daughter from her. If she could not make it surrender Phoebe, she would die in the attempt, and that would be for the best.

Ceres stood before the old house, while behind her the forest became an impenetrable thicket of trunk and branch. She followed the fence until she came to a spot where it had come loose from the pickets and posts, and she slipped through the gap. She walked along the verge of the sunken garden, the place through which David, in the book—and, who knew, in life, too, or at the end of it—had entered another realm. A sign warned against defacing the stonework, but Ceres could see graffiti scrawled and carved on it, left by readers at a time when the property had been more easily accessible.

It was the house that was summoning her. Behind the window of its uppermost room, the one that had been David's all those years before, she thought she saw a shape pass. It gave her pause, but not for long. The distant part of her that was observing herself understood that incidents from the book were blending with her own memories, and she was now seeing what David once saw, or believed he had seen: the Crooked Man creeping through these environs, seeking a child. It was not real, yet neither was it altogether unreal. The book had contaminated her, transformed her. It was part of her now, and if it was part of her, might she not also be part of it?

The rook was circling the eastern side of the house, waiting for her to catch up. The grass was crisp with frost beneath her feet, and she left a trail of footsteps behind, like an echo of the tale of Agathe and the Crooked Man, confirmation that Ceres had become both story and storyteller, dancer and dance.

Another sign by the front door cautioned against trespassing, and advised that the property was under twenty-four-hour surveillance, but she knew from Olivier that this was untrue, and the alarm system had fallen into neglect. She reached the back of the house, managed to get her fingers under the sheet of plywood covering a window, and wrenched it free. One of the panes was already cracked, so she removed a shoe and used the heel to finish the job, the glass tinkling into the kitchen sink within. When she was sure the square was entirely free of shards, she put her hand through and turned the latch, then worked the tips of her fingers between the bottom rail and the stay to force the window open. It yielded, but only with some effort on her part, and the painful cracking of a fingernail. She climbed on the ledge, balanced one foot for a moment on the old stone sink on the other side, then eased herself down to the floor. Behind her, the rook alighted on the windowsill but did not enter. It gave a single croak of what might have been approval before flying off.

The kitchen was dusty and cobwebbed, but otherwise neat. Cooking utensils remained hanging on hooks, the chairs were arranged around the table, and the empty fireplace was free of dirt and soot. Ceres discerned the scuttling of mice in the shadows, and also something larger: a rat, most likely. She wasn't frightened of rats, just wary. They were smart—not as smart as a rook, but clever nonetheless. The sound of them, and the throbbing of her broken nail, brought her back to herself. She had walked to the house in a kind of daze, but coming out of it she was aware that she was violating a private space. She wasn't worried about getting into too much trouble—she was sure the hospital would be understanding—but it would still be embarrassing. Her first instinct, therefore, was to leave the way she had entered, yet it was followed by an urge to explore, if only for a few minutes. What was it her father used to say? Might as well be hanged for a sheep as a lamb. Having gone to the effort of finding a way inside, she should take advantage of the opportunity.

But she also knew this place from the book. Being here was akin to stepping into its pages, so that she would not have been excessively surprised had some spectral David appeared before her, a volume under one arm, or the laughter of a newborn carried to her from the floor above. Ceres stepped from the kitchen into the hallway, the stairs to her left. The walls of the house were largely bare. Some of the pictures and photographs that had once graced them must have been removed for safekeeping, or even stolen, because she could see the darker patches where they had hung, though more remained in place. She was surprised by how much light there was: the plywood panels over the windows and the front door had not been positioned perfectly flush, and the orientation of the house meant that the morning sunlight shone directly on the front, sending beams through the gaps.

In the living room across from her stood the shrouded forms of furniture, her mind conjuring visions of shapes rising from armchairs and couches, their monstrousness concealed by dustcovers. She decided, on reflection, to leave that room undisturbed, and gave her attention to the stairs. There was more light at the top than at the bottom, because the windows on the upper floors had not been concealed. By the lowest step was a small glass-topped display case, perhaps from the time when the house had served as a museum. It contained various editions of David's novel, alongside a selection of items from his wartime childhood: a ration book, and ration book supplement, from the Ministry of Food; a clothing book in his name, containing unused coupons; an instruction manual titled *How to Keep Well in Wartime*; and a permit to enter nearby Bletchley Park, the property of David's father. Last of all, there was a photograph of the author with his wife. How much time had they enjoyed together before death had separated them? Ceres could remember only that it was too little.

The first step creaked loudly as she placed her full weight on it, causing her to pause momentarily. One part of her, the logical part, knew that the house was unoccupied, but another, more primitive Ceres wasn't convinced. She could blame Olivier and his talk of ghosts, but it wasn't his fault alone. After all, not everything described in the book had been invented: the author did come here as a boy, following the loss of his mother; he fought with his stepmother, who gave birth to his half brother; and incredibly, a German bomber had crashed in the huge garden, and the young David, hypnotized by the sight of the burning plane, had almost lost his life as a consequence. When the lines between what was true and untrue became blurred, so also did those between reality and unreality. For a novel to work it had to cast a spell on the reader; it didn't have to convince them to believe in the impossible, or cease to distinguish between falsehood and veracity, but it did require them to lower their defenses, to suspend themselves between realms—even, for a time, to forget one world entirely, so engrossed did they become in the other. In this house, Ceres thought, the gap between worlds was very narrow.

She reached the top of the first flight. All the doors on this level were closed, and an arched window, its panes alternately clear and stained, shed multicolored light on the old floorboards. To her right, a narrower set of stairs led to David's attic bedroom. These were completely dark, because his was the only room on the top floor, and its door, too, was shut. Ceres retraced her dreamlike walk to the house, and the shape she thought she had glimpsed by the attic window. Once again the rational and anti-rational came into conflict—

I saw something.

I saw nothing.

—before reaching a compromise that satisfied neither, which was, she supposed, the very definition of compromise:

Whatever I saw, it was not what I thought it was.

Which would have to do.

She took the attic stairs cautiously, to stand before the door. She didn't know what she would do if she found it locked. So far she'd broken only a small pane of glass, and that was already damaged. Technically, it was still breaking and entering, but the harm was fairly limited. She wasn't sure she was willing to add destroying a lock and cracking the frame of a door to the list of charges. Objectively, what she was doing made no sense. She had entered a house in which she didn't belong, abandoning for a time her catatonic daughter, all because of a book. But it was too late to undo whatever transformation the narrative had caused in her, because once read, a story couldn't be *un*read. She was a different person now, and the book had made her so.

Or had it? The tale of the two dancers and the Crooked Man had come to her *before* she opened the book. How could she have done that if she were not already acquainted with the book and its contents? Coincidence, then. Writers often had similar ideas, drawing on common human experiences—falling in love, becoming ill, losing someone dear to them—or on what was happening around them in art, politics, even war. Each writer would make a different narrative from those elements, because no two writers ever looked at the world in precisely the same way, even if what they created from their personal experiences might be understandable to many. Why should Ceres, like the creator of *The Book of Lost Things*, not have invoked visions of a crooked figure in a crooked hat, playing his crooked games with the unwary?

Because, she knew, this wasn't just a different character with a similar name: it was the same figure. Had she somehow been able to sit across from David, and prevailed upon him to draw his conception of the Crooked Man while she did likewise, they would have produced near facsimiles, of that she was convinced. *Like the devil*, she thought. If you asked two people to draw the devil, they'd come up with horns, the legs of a goat, possibly a pointed beard. Images of demons from different cultures often had those details in common, as though each of the artists had, at some point, endured the same nightmare.

Perhaps because of the trauma of what had cursed Phoebe, and all that followed from it—the anger and fear, the grief and guilt—Ceres believed that she might have found a way to access some preliterate version of herself, a form of common recall. Distinct cultures shared versions of the same stories, yet it wasn't always clear how this had come to be, because some of those tales predated contact between civilizations. It might be that some myths were so essential to our being, so crucial to our comprehension of the world and our place in it, that we produced them as a matter of course, before passing them on to succeeding generations. Ceres heard her father's voice, like an echo meant only for her ears:

"These memories teach us what to fear, so we can be aware of them from the moment of our birth, like certain smells or sounds that we know signal danger. Animals, we think, pass on this capacity, so why not humans?"

Sounds, smells. Images.

A Crooked Man.

The wind had picked up force outside, coaxing a litany of moans and groans from the old boards, dislodging rubble from the disused chimneys and sending it tumbling into the grates, and causing pale dust and flakes of paint to descend like snow on Ceres. The locked doors thudded in their frames, and the windows rattled. Down below, in the kitchen, a glass or cup, most likely encouraged by a gust through the broken pane, dropped to the floor and shattered. Now the door to the attic room was opening before her—not blown ajar, but unfastening slowly, under the control of a careful hand.

Ceres stared at what was revealed within, as two worlds started to become one.

XI

Teasgal
(GAELIC)

A Wind That Sings

he attic room was filled with ivy. It curled around the bare bedstead and over the bookshelves. It obscured the walls, hung in reddish-green clumps from the empty light fixture, and colonized the floor. And it was *moving*: a length of it appeared before Ceres's face and peered at her, the two topmost leaves at either side of the main stem turning slightly downward in puzzlement, like eyebrows furrowing. Ceres looked to her left and saw that another stem was gripping the inner knob tightly, and thus the door had been opened to her.

Amid the vegetation, multicolored insects crawled, hopped, and flew. Ceres dodged a white moth with lines of poetry inscribed on its wings, constructed from a single carefully folded page like a piece of origami come to life. A large grasshopper landed on the floor by her foot, its body formed from the green-and-gold boards of a book. Yellow-and-black-striped beetles rushed by, each with a different musical note on its back; when they brushed against one another, they chimed. In the far right-hand corner, a black paper spider, its body as big as Ceres's hand, sat at the heart of an intricate arrangement of sticky threads that extended almost to the center of the room, its lengths dotted with one-word flies.

And above the rustling, fluttering, and ringing, Ceres heard voices, as the dusty, neglected books on the shelves roused themselves to speak.

"Who is it?" asked one. "Who's there?"

It was coming from a volume on the last battles of the First World War; Ceres saw its closed pages moving like lips, and its tone was suitably clipped and military.

"I think it's a woman, or a girl," said another. "I can hear her breathing. From her tread on the stairs, I believe her to weigh approximately one hundred and seventy pounds."

"One hundred and forty!" Ceres countered, affronted, before she even registered that she was arguing with a book. Obviously, she'd taken issue with the contents of books in the past, but never with the physical object of one, although she was struggling to establish which book she was actually conversing with, so loud was the babble from the shelves, and so distracting were the bugs and ivy.

"Are you absolutely sure? You're only fooling yourself, you know."

"One forty-five," Ceres conceded. "But I'm retaining water."

"Is she supposed to be here?" asked the military volume.

"If she's here," replied the other, "then of course she's supposed to be. Why would she be here otherwise?"

"Don't take that tone with me, young fellow! I'll have you up on charges. Find out who she is. That's what you do, isn't it? You investigate. What's the point of you otherwise?"

After some muttering, which might have included a rude word or two, the second book chimed in again.

"Excuse me," it said politely, "but who are you?"

Ceres finally traced the source of the question to a copy of *Emil and the Detectives*.

"I'm going mad," she said.

"Oh, don't be like that," said *Emil and the Detectives*. "It won't help."

"Yes," said a woman's voice from a book called *The Good Master*. "You've found your way, and that's what counts. If you can hear us it's a sign that you're in the right place. There's no need to be afraid."

"Not yet."

This came from a much-read edition of *The Sword in the Stone*, its

worn covers clinging to its spine by the frailest of threads. Its contribution subdued the chattering in the room.

"We'll have to see, won't we?" said *The Good Master*. "Now, what is
your name, dear?"

"Ceres."

There was a murmuring, as the name was passed from book to book,
although some were clearly rather deaf, and Ceres heard various Ferrises,
Dorises, and Dennises being impatiently corrected.

"Are you a child?" asked *Emil and the Detectives*. "You don't sound like
a child. You sound all grown up."

"I am all grown up," said Ceres, but she didn't feel it, not anymore.

"Well, that would explain the weight business, though I still think
you ought to have your scales checked."

More mutters, and more exchanges, a number of them heated.

"I suspect there's been some terrible mistake," said Ceres. "You see, I
read a book, but it may have been the wrong book. I think it's got into my
head, and made it all confuddled."

Confuddled: one of her father's words, like "oopsident" instead of "accident" and "flutterby" for "butterfly." She hadn't used the word, hadn't
heard it spoken aloud, since his death.

"There's no such thing as a 'wrong' book," said *The Sword in the Stone*
patiently. "There is only the *right* book read at the *wrong* time."

"Don't bully her," said *The Good Master*. "Can't you tell she's mud-
dled up? Why have you come here, Ceres? What are you looking for?"

Ceres thought about the question. She might have been enduring a
breakdown, one that was causing her to see sentient ivy, evade the flight of
insects formed from living paper, and hear books speaking, but the peculiar
thing—well, the most peculiar thing, among many—was that the books were
asking sensible questions. Why *had* she come here? What *was* she looking for?

"My daughter is ill," said Ceres. "No, it's worse than that: She's gone.
Everything I cherished of her has departed, and all that's left is a body. It
breathes, but it's not Phoebe, not anymore. Someone robbed me of her, and
I want her returned. I speak to her, and I call to her, but she doesn't answer,
and it's all so hard, so hard that at times I want to give up. It's happening more
and more often now, that desire just to lie down and never rise again.

"So that's what I'm looking for: I'm looking for a way to get my daughter back, because I can't go on like this. As for what brought me here, it was the book I'm reading. It's made me sick, and caused me to see and believe things that aren't real, including all of you."

"But this *is* real," said *The Good Master* gently. "Everything you can imagine is real. You've made it so. This is the story of your life unfolding, and we are part of it, just as much as you are. And if you came here looking for your daughter, then—"

"Listen." It was *Emil and the Detectives*.

The Good Master stopped talking. All the books did, although their chattering had been ceaseless until then. They were books speaking to other books, which was what books did, because no book was ever created in isolation, and literature was a long, ongoing conversation between stories.

The wind had changed again. It was colder, viciously so, the kind of frigidity that doesn't nip but bite. The sound it made was not composed of random gusts but closer to inhalations and exhalations; and it was coming, not from outside, but from the attic room itself, from the walls, the ceiling, and the floor.

"What is it?" asked Ceres.

"Now," said *The Sword in the Stone*, "is the time to be afraid."

"You have to get out, Ceres," said *The Good Master*. "Be quick, but be very, very quiet. If you make too much noise, it will hear you. And it mustn't hear you."

Ceres backed out of the room, and the ivy closed the door soundlessly behind her. She wanted to run, but she knew that if she did, it would be noticed, and the warning of *The Good Master* had not fallen on deaf ears. So she stood on the topmost step, one hand on the banister, the other against the wall, and tried to remain as immobile as possible. Behind the door, the wind reached a crescendo before dropping entirely, only to be replaced by the shifting of leaves, as though someone, or something, were making their way through the vegetation within.

Ceres crouched until she was level with the empty keyhole. She peered through the gap and saw that the ivy was in motion, composing itself into a single mass in the center of the room. Two holes appeared in it, then a third, larger gap below, with the suggestion of a nose between.

Ceres was looking at a face, which now turned left and right: seeking, scowling. A paper moth flitted in front of it, startled into flight, and two coils of ivy shot from the green mouth and ripped the insect to shreds. The moth's remains drifted to the floor, even as the ivy extended farther, beyond Ceres's sight. When the coils became visible again, they were holding a book between them, and Ceres recognized it as *The Good Master*.

The green mouth moved, and a singsong voice came from its lips, one purposed only for mockery and malice.

"I heard you speak, book," it said. "But to whom?"

"To my brothers and sisters," said *The Good Master*, "as I always do."

Only the slightest tremble to the book's speech gave its fear away.

"No, not as you have always done," said the face of ivy. "I know the tones and patterns of each and every one of you, so long have I been listening to your prating. But another voice was heard, one that I did not recognize. Are you suggesting a new book has been added to your number? If so, show it to me. Tell me who brought it, and why."

"You are mistaken," said *The Good Master*. "There is only what you see on our shelves, just as it has been these many years."

The eyes in the greenery narrowed.

"You know better than to lie to me."

"To you?" said *The Good Master*, summoning defiance. "But we do not even know who you are. We have often felt you circling, and sometimes we have heard you pass like a breeze through the ivy, but you are not familiar to us."

"Oh, but I *am* familiar, for my spirit is in each of you. You really ought to have paid closer attention."

The Good Master did not answer immediately, but when it did, the fear was back. Ceres thought that it did recognize this apparition after all, and not newly either, though it persisted with its denials.

"Whatever you are, we have no need of you," *The Good Master* said. "Here are worlds upon worlds, so many people, places, ideas. That is enough for us. We require no more."

"Another lie," said the face of ivy. "You require a reader. What is a book if it is not read? I will tell you: nothing. It was not a voice alone that drew me. I sensed your excitement, your joy. No new book, however wonderful, could have aroused such feelings. You gave yourselves away in your desire to be read, and only the arrival of a person could have caused that. Now, I will ask you again: To whom were you speaking?"

"This is foolishness," said *The Good Master*. "Leave us be. We will not have discourse with some wraith, an itinerant phantom that has to borrow leaf and branch to give structure to itself."

"So be it," said the face. More ivy encircled *The Good Master*, gripping its pages and boards, opening it wide. "Goodbye, book."

And *The Good Master* was torn apart, just as the moth had been, the ivy reducing it to shreds of paper and scraps of cloth. Ceres heard the book cry out, but only at the start. Once its spine had been broken, it was finished, and after that the end came fast.

Now the ivy went hunting again, returning with another volume, this time *Emil and the Detectives*. Whatever the entity was, it could indeed identify the individual voice of every book. Soon it would be the turn of the military history, and *The Sword in the Stone*.

"What about you, boy?" said the face of ivy. "I fancy you'll be more sensible. If not, I will take my time with you, page by page, and I promise that you'll tell me everything you know before we're done.

"But I don't want to destroy you. You see, I like stories, so why would I take pleasure in destroying one? Let me make it easier for you. I know it was a woman who came here. I should like you to tell me her name. Will you do that, boy? Just a name. You see, I've been waiting for a woman, a very particular woman. You could say that I've been calling to her. She's important, more important than you can imagine, but I don't wish her any harm. Precisely the opposite: I want to help her."

Slowly, the ivy began to tear the title page of *Emil and the Detectives*. The book wailed with the voice of a child, and Ceres could bear it no longer.

"Stop!" she cried. "Leave them alone!"

The door was wrenched open, and the dreadful face stared out in triumph. Ivy sped across the floor, reaching for her, as from the shelves a chorus of books shouted a single word in unison.

"Run!"

And Ceres ran.

XII

Wathe

(MIDDLE ENGLISH)

The Hunting of Game

eres took the attic stairs two at a time, and only as she reached the main flight did she take a moment to check on the pursuit. Ivy was rapidly covering the walls and ceiling, and twisting around the banister rails, its lengths now studded with barbs, their points tinged with red, like blood-dipped thorns. With it came the face from the attic, reconstituting itself over and over, advancing to lead the hunt from among the foremost fronds.

The slight hesitation was enough to earn Ceres a nick on the ankle from a branch that had outpaced the rest, but it also served to spur her on. Before her was the front door, but there was no escape that way. Even if she could have opened it, a steel plate waited. No, she would have to leave as she had entered, which meant getting to the kitchen and clambering through the window, but it was now darker downstairs than she remembered. Slowly the beams of sunlight shining through the gaps in the panels were being smothered, and Ceres could hear movement on the roof. She pictured ivy pouring forth from the attic window, gradually enveloping the entire house. When it was done, she would be trapped inside, sequestered with a creature of verdure and hate, and it would do to her what it had done to *The Good Master*: it would seize her, torment her, and rip her apart.

Ceres turned sharply on the last step and skidded on the boards, almost falling before she found her balance. Another branch flicked at her right hand, cutting into the soft flesh between her thumb and index finger, but the kitchen door was ahead of her, and Ceres could still see light. It made sense: if the ivy was using the attic window to gain access to the exterior of the house, this would be one of the last places it reached. Beyond the window was open ground, and Ceres could run fast when the need arose. Once she was outside, she'd outstrip the ivy and whatever was animating it. From there she'd be in a race to the Lantern House, and safety; if the forest remained impassable, she'd have to work her way around it, but she'd deal with that problem when she came to it.

Ceres entered the kitchen, sunlight blessedly shining on her through the unobscured glass, but even as she drew nearer the ivy outside crept over the window, and the room was plunged into shadow. The only visible light was coming from under the door.

"Please," whispered Ceres. "Please."

She turned the handle as the first fingers of ivy grasped the head of the kitchen entrance. The back door was locked, and swollen in its frame, but Ceres could see that the wood was rotten, and would not withstand much pressure. She yanked hard, bracing herself against the wall with her left foot, and the door came free. Behind it was a plywood panel, not steel as at the front of the house. Ceres charged it once, then twice. The screws started to come away as the ivy invaded the kitchen in earnest. She took a step back, ignoring the pain as another barb sliced her left calf, and hurled her body full force at the plywood. It broke free, Ceres's momentum carrying her forward so that she was sent sprawling to the ground, belly-flopping painfully on the dirt as the wind was knocked from her. Her face followed through to strike the ground, and she felt her nose crunch. The shock of the impact left her stunned, but she managed to get to her feet, ready to start running again despite the pain, ready to leave the house behind forever.

But when she looked back, the house was gone.

XIII

Scocker

(EAST ANGLIA)

A Rift in an Oak Tree

eres was standing, not on an overgrown lawn, but in dense woodland, the trees so high that their crowns were lost to low cloud, and their trunks so thick that five men could not have enclosed their circumference with linked arms. The bark of the tree nearest Ceres had been mutilated by a wound that stretched from the forest floor to the level of her head, leaking viscous sap. But as Ceres stared, the hole started to close, and she grasped that this was how she had arrived. Somehow, she had run through the doorway of a house and come out by way of a tree trunk. The good news was that she was no longer being pursued by ivy, or anything else. The bad news was that she had no idea where she might be, but wherever it was, it wasn't where she was supposed to be, which was close to the Lantern House, and to Phoebe.

Ceres gripped the sides of the hole in the tree, already half its previous width, and strained hard. If she permitted the entrance to disappear, she might be marooned, and what would happen to Phoebe then? But the trunk was intent on healing itself, the bark, and the sapwood and heartwood, all reconstituting, forcing her hands ever closer and closer together until Ceres was obliged to abandon her efforts or risk sacrificing

~ 67 ~

her fingertips. She watched as the last slim fracture vanished, and then it was as though the injury to the tree had never been, and it stood identical to all its kin. Were she to wander even a short distance from it, Ceres was not convinced she would be able to find it again.

Only now did she notice the blood dripping from her injured nose. Gingerly she touched a hand to it. It didn't feel broken, but it was very tender. She flicked the blood from her fingers, only to have it flicked back at her a second later. At the base of the tree was a patch of yellow-and-white flowers, and at the heart of each was a face like a child's. The flowers were regarding her with unhappiness, not least the one nearest her, because its petals were currently dotted with blood. The flower twitched hard, dislodging more of the blood, but by now some of it was flowing toward its mouth, even as it tried blowing at it to keep it at bay.

"I'm terribly sorry," said Ceres. She found a tissue in her pocket, spat on it in the instinctive way of mothers everywhere, and leaned down to begin wiping. Before she could act, the flowers snapped shut in unison, their leaves forming a hard and sticky protective carapace.

"Well, be like that," said Ceres. "You'll be covered in it now, and it serves you right. I was only about to help."

She tried to take in her surroundings, but all she could see were trees, more trees, and clumps of the yellow-and-white flowers, which continued closing, clump by clump, the panic of one being communicated to the rest, until the forest was reduced to greens and browns alone.

Ceres contemplated pinching herself. That was what people did in stories when they thought they might be dreaming, although she'd never done it herself because being pinched rarely solved anyone's problems. Then again, the throbbing in her nose was real enough, and her breasts still hurt from the fall, but she'd also experienced pain in dreams, or thought she had. Sometimes she dreamed about the night Phoebe was born, which was about as painful an experience as she'd ever endured, and would wake up sore, the agony of childbirth pursuing her from sleep to waking.

Ceres tried to rouse herself, squeezing shut her eyes in the hope that, seconds later, she would discover herself back in one of the visitor suites at the hospital, or lying on the lawn of the old house, which would now be free of ivy because that, too, had been part of her dream—the nightmare element, admittedly, but a dream regardless. It didn't work, though, because when she opened her eyes she remained in a forest, and her nose and chest still hurt.

Is this how Phoebe now experiences her existence, she wondered, *as some kind of dream from which she can't wake, no matter how hard she tries?*

Another thought followed from this one.

If I am trapped here, might not she also be? If that's the case, I can find her. I can be with her again. Even if it is all an illusion, it will still be better than the reality of being without her, and the powerlessness of being unable to help her.

As Ceres began trying to make sense of her predicament, she reflected that she might have some idea of where she was after all. This was Elsewhere, the world of *The Book of Lost Things*. Logically, the book was in her head after her reading of it: her recollections of its structure, its incidents and characters. Her knowledge of its contents had in some way transformed her consciousness, creating a landscape for her to inhabit in her limbic state. Therefore she was unconscious, or more likely semiconscious, and concocting a version of Elsewhere in her delirium.

But logic could only take a person so far, and it began to crumble when Ceres could taste blood on her lips, and feel the tenderness of a nose that had only narrowly avoided being broken; when she could smell grass, hear the buzzing of insects, and see grains of pollen on her skin; when she could touch the bark of a tree, the leaves on a bush, and come away with fingers smeared brown and green.

Water was flowing nearby, and Ceres followed the sound. She wanted to wash the blood from her face, and she thought that applying cold water to her poor nose probably wouldn't do it any harm either. As she walked she was forced to hitch up her jeans, because they were sliding down over her hips, and she noticed that her shirt was baggier than before. She tripped, because the ends of her trousers were catching under her shoes, which had become slightly too big for her feet.

Ceres had a terrible premonition.

"No," she said. "No, no, no . . ."

She came to a stream that fed into a clear pool, and there she knelt to stare at her reflection. The face gazing back at her was smeared with blood, and the nose was badly swollen, but it was still recognizably hers, except—

Except that she looked sixteen, not thirty-two. Even her hair had changed. She had worn it short since her midtwenties, but it was much longer now, hanging to her shoulders. And while she had never been particularly tall, and had stopped growing before she left her teens, she was currently a couple of inches shorter, and more than a few pounds lighter, which explained why her clothes were not fitting her as well as before. Her breasts were smaller, and her hips narrower; of course they were, because this was no longer the body of a woman who had given birth. It was itself a child's body, or a body that was not long past childhood. It was the body of a youth, not an adult.

"Oh god," said Ceres, "not my teens, not again."

XIV

Getrymman
(OLD ENGLISH)

To Build Something Strongly, and Fortify It Against Attack

n a pallet bed, in a stone cottage with a hearth that had not known a fire for half a lifetime or more, a figure stirred. A heavy blanket was cast aside as a man got up from the thin mattress. He took in his hands, and his clothes, as though surprised by his own appearance, or even the fact that he was there at all. He was dressed in a shirt and leggings of soft green wool. His hair was short and tinged with gray. He stroked his chin and tested the stubble: a couple of days' growth, and no more, but he knew he had been asleep for longer than that. The stiffness in his body told him so.

By the bed stood a heavy axe, its blade old, but still keen and unblemished. The man laid a hand upon it, and had any been present to bear witness, they might have seen a succession of memories play across his face, a dumb show of recollected happiness, sorrow, and loss, all brought to mind by the feel of the weapon against his skin. On a rack beside it was a wooden bow, the string removed to extend its life, and a quiver of arrows. A shelf nearby held a sword in a functional scabbard, a knife in a more ornate one, and a chain mail vest that bore a light coating of grease for storage. The man recalled putting all these things away, or some version of himself doing so. It seemed such a very long time ago that he might have imagined it.

But now he was awake again. An alteration had occurred, one that required his attention; and if it required his attention, it could only mean strife. What form it might take remained to be established, which would be the task to come, but first he needed to purge the weariness from his bones. He picked up the axe, because it would be imprudent to step into an uncertain world without some protection to hand, and walked to the door, which was locked and bolted, just as the windows were secured, shuttered from the inside. He undid the catch on the viewing slit, but all beyond the cottage looked peaceful. He could see that his garden was not too disordered, and the first of the winter plants had broken through the soil, but were not yet flowering. Beyond the fence was the forest, the nearest trees thick with sleeping ivy, which was a good sign.

He opened the door and stepped outside. The cottage was made of stone, with a wooden roof sealed by mud and thatch, but the exterior was not as he remembered. Embedded in the walls, as though formed from the body of the blocks themselves, were steel spikes, each as long as a man's forearm, with more projecting from the roof. All ended in lethal points, and their lengths, he noticed, were covered in smaller extrusions, like the thorns on a branch. They were designed not alone to pierce, but also to scratch. This was not his work, nor that of any man's hand. It had been willed into being by the cottage itself, to protect its inhabitant. Warily, he examined the defenses, sniffing the metal for traces of poison, but detected none. Steel alone, it had been determined, would suffice.

Attached to the cottage was a stable, and in it stood a brown mare, peering over the half door. She nickered a greeting as he approached, and nuzzled his neck when he embraced her. Straw covered the floor, and water filled her trough. The mare's coming had been prepared for, just like his.

"You look almost as confused as I do," he said, pulling away from the horse, "but I'm glad to have you with me."

He headed to the well, where he filled a bucket, stripped himself naked, and washed. Even though he had been anticipating the cold, it was still a shock to his system, but to ensure that he banished all traces of lassitude, he emptied the remaining contents over his head before drawing a new supply. He dressed himself in fresh clothes of wool, hide, and fur, then heated some of the water over a fire, adding oats from his store—fresh, thankfully: the cottage again, although it was a pity it had not also seen fit to provide some dried meat, or a few eggs—and made a porridge for his breakfast. When he was done, he restrung the bow, tucked the knife in his belt, and picked up the axe once more. The sword he left. He was not planning to range far, not yet. He unbolted the stable door, saddled the mare, and mounted. She required only the barest touch of his heels to trot, seemingly as eager as he to be about once more.

As they reached the forest, the ivy—*his* ivy, because there were all kinds, some more benevolent than others—which had been motionless until now, stirred itself from trunk and branch, like an awakening of green serpents, and rose to welcome him. It caressed his cheek, toyed with his hair, and tugged playfully at his clothing. Around him the branches shifted, although there was no wind to stir them, and the yellow-and-white flowers regarded him without timidity as he passed. Blossoms descended, carpeting his way, and the leaves rustled their tribute.

The Woodsman had returned to the land.

XV

Gairneag
(SCOTS GAELIC)

A Noisy Little Stream

 eres had not moved from the bank, her eyes fixed on the tree. She had marked it by placing a fivepence piece in a heart-shaped indentation in the trunk, the Queen's head turned outward, the surrounding grass growing warmer as the day wore on.

She remained uncertain of what was actual and what was questionable, but she was sure of this: even if she was dreaming, or enduring some form of breakdown, the tree represented a link to all that she was. If she were to become separated from it, she feared she might forsake her sanity as well. While she sat, she attempted to bring to mind as many details of *The Book of Lost Things* as she could, but visions of Loups, sorceresses, harpies, trolls, and psychotic huntswomen did not make her feel any better about her position. Even allowing for the occasional moments of lightness in the novel, this was to be a world principally composed of threats. The only consolation was that most of the terrors she remembered had been eliminated, often violently, in the course of the narrative.

But could the story be believed? While novels might contain truths, that wasn't the same as being real. Yet here she was, stranded somewhere that shouldn't have been real but definitely felt that way. The whole affair made her head hurt.

"Good morning," said a male voice from somewhere close to the small of her back.

"Morn–"

Ceres leapt away from the bank, where a head was poking from the surface of the stream. It was the size of a small child's, but the face was wrinkled, with weeds for hair and a beard that resembled the moss found on certain old stones. The skin, on closer examination, resembled more closely the shimmering scales of a fish, while clear water flowed constantly from somewhere beneath that topping of weeds, as though the little man were at least partly water himself. Ceres couldn't figure out where the rest of his body was, because the stream was only about two feet deep at that point. Either he was very peculiarly shaped, or the head was all there was of him.

"Nice day for it," said the man, his voice bubbling, "er, whatever 'it' is," he added uncertainly, in the tone of one who has woken up and pulled his curtains to salute the new day, only to find a stranger poking around in his garden. "New here, are you?"

"I just arrived," said Ceres, "although I'm not sure where here is, exactly."

"Well, here's here," said the figure. "Stands to reason. If it wasn't here, it would be there, which isn't the same thing, not at all."

"You're right, of course," said Ceres, "although I have to say, that's not very helpful. I mean, it's not exactly handing me a map."

"No, I suppose not. Not very good with maps. Never had any call for them." A watery hand emerged from the stream—along with a very small and slightly startled snail which had attached itself to one of his fingernails—and tugged at his bottom lip in mild puzzlement. "By the way, what's a map?"

"It's— Oh, never mind," said Ceres, and then, because introductions appeared appropriate, she offered, "I'm Ceres."

"Pleased to meet you. I'm the Spirit of the Water. Just this particular body of water, mind you, not all water. Big job, that, being the spirit of *all* water. Wouldn't fancy it. Not enough hours in the day, if you ask me. I mean, what with rivers, lakes, seas, and the like, you'd never be done introducing yourself, mostly to fish, asking how they're getting along, and what they've been up to. Not big talkers, fish. Crabs neither. Come to think of it, it's been a while since I spoke to anyone who could answer back. So, to cut a long story short, I'm happy as I am: Spirit of the Water (Local Branch, Southern Section), that's me."

The Spirit of the Water gave another tug on his lip.

"Bit of a mouthful, though, isn't it?" he mulled. "Spirit of the Water (Local Branch, Southern Section). You don't want to be including subsidiary clauses and doing yourself a disservice by diminishing your own importance. Next thing you know, someone slips on a dodgy stepping-stone, and they're asking to speak to your superiors."

"What about 'Spirit of the Stream'?" suggested Ceres, as it seemed like the obvious solution.

The little man rolled the words around on his tongue.

"Spirit of the Stream," he said. "Now why didn't I think of that? I like it. It's got alliterawhatchamacallit."

"Alliteration," said Ceres.

"That's the one. Spirit of the Stream it is, then. Anyway, as I was saying, perfectly content, I am. Got my fish. Got my snails." He waved his hand gently, so as not to dislodge its occupant. "Pick up the odd tribute along the way, if you know what I mean."

The Spirit of the Stream coughed wetly but meaningfully, and tipped Ceres a wink.

"A tribute?" she said.

"Well, you did use my water to clean yourself, and I saw you take a drink, too. Don't get me wrong, I'm happy for you to do it. I keep a very clean stream, me. You could eat your dinner off the bottom of that pool, if you were a fish. But a little token of gratitude never goes amiss, does it? Nice to have one's efforts acknowledged, and all that. I mean, I appreciate you helped with the naming business, and I'm taking that into account, but a spirit still has to make a living."

Ceres searched her pockets. Her only coin was marking the tree, but she did locate a silver button that had come off her jacket earlier in the week, and which she had intended to sew back on when she was in the right mood.

"I don't have any more money," she said, "only this."

The Spirit of the Stream's eyes widened.

"Ooooh, that's lovely, that is. Very shiny, very *different*. It's worth a lot more than a quick wash of the face and a couple of mouthfuls of water. For that, you can take a bath in one of my pools anytime you like, and I'll even ask a few fish to nibble away any dead skin from your feet. If they get too enthusiastic, give them a flick. You don't want them to go chomping off a toe."

Ceres politely declined the offer. She wasn't sure that she cared to bathe in a pond that had its own resident spirit. She didn't even like using the changing rooms at her local swimming pool, never mind having some old bloke popping up to ask if she needed her back scrubbed.

"Well, the offer stands, whenever you need it," said the Spirit of the Stream, as Ceres handed over the button. "In the meantime, any trouble of an aquatic nature, just mention my name: Spirit of the Stream. Got that? Spirit. Of. The. Stream. Do you need to write it down?"

"I'm sure I'll remember," said Ceres. She didn't have the heart to point out to him that there were lots of streams, and therefore probably lots of spirits too. Nevertheless, the Spirit of the Stream's watercourse, with its cold, clear shallows, its stony pools, its fish and snails, struck her as a perfectly nice stretch to claim for one's own.

"Must be on my way," said the Spirit of the Stream, as he became one with the water again. "Things to do, rocks to clean."

"No!" said Ceres. "Wait a minute, you still haven't told me where I am. You haven't told me *anything*."

But the Spirit of the Stream was gone.

"And you cost me a button," Ceres added grumpily.

She hoisted her jeans. She'd really have to do something about them, because if she had to run for any reason, they'd be likely to end up around her ankles. But she hoped she wouldn't have to run, because if she did, it would very likely mean that she was running *from* something. She inspected the ends of her jeans and decided that the first thing was to turn them up, so she wouldn't be tripping over them, before making a belt. She considered using a length of ivy, but then thought back to her experience with the ivy in the old house, and decided she wasn't about to go hacking at any vegetation that might take it amiss. A clump of long reeds was growing close to the bank of the stream. She gave them a tentative prod, and when none objected she managed, after a struggle, to yank a piece from its moorings. It was long enough to fit around her waist, and tie in a knot without breaking. Briefly, she felt like Robinson Crusoe after he'd finished building his island hut: a triumph of man, or in this case woman, over nature.

When she glanced back at the tree trunk, the coin had vanished.

XVI

Wicches

(MIDDLE ENGLISH)

Witches, Sorceresses

or an instant, Ceres was convinced she was mistaken. She must have been looking at the wrong tree, or somehow walked farther along the bank than she thought. She retraced her steps, but not only could she no longer see the coin, she also failed to find any trunk containing a cavity shaped like a heart. They were all absolutely identical.

Wings flapped above her. On a high branch, a circle of metal shone in the beak of a black bird: a rook, and had it been closer, close enough for Ceres to make out its features, she was sure it would have possessed only one eye.

"Oh, you miserable thief!" she shouted. "You come down here right now and return that coin to where you found it."

But the rook just flitted from tree to tree, each time landing on a lower branch: taunting her, or so it seemed. Ceres, blinded by anger, went after it, heading deeper and deeper into the woods, until the stream was lost to view. Only when she was completely disoriented did the rook take flight, to vanish from sight.

"I hate you!" screamed Ceres. "I hope you choke on that fivepence!"

She could have sworn she heard a distant caw of derision, then nothing more.

Ceres paused to take in her new surroundings. The trees here were even larger and older, and the canopy they formed was so thick and dark that only thin beams of sunlight penetrated the gloom. But Ceres detected woodsmoke in the air from somewhere nearby. A fire was burning, which might mean the presence of people. Since she was now completely lost, it made no difference what direction she took, so she followed the smell until she came to a cottage in a clearing. One of the windows was open, and from inside she heard women talking. She would have been warier of a gathering of men, and might even have hesitated to approach, but she was less concerned about members of her own sex. As she drew nearer, she heard footsteps, and a young woman with dark hair, wearing a yellow cloak and a matching yellow pointy hat, came rushing toward the cottage. Over one arm she carried a basket from which poked a loaf of bread and a round of cheese. Ceres couldn't remember when last she'd eaten, only that it was far too long for her stomach and salivary glands not to react to the sight of food.

The woman paused as she spotted Ceres.

"Hullo!" she said. "You're new, aren't you? Well, hurry along. We're both late enough as it is, and if there's one thing that gets Ursula's goat, it's tardiness."

Ceres, being too tired and hungry to do anything else, did as she was told. The woman in yellow held the door open for her—"Chop, chop! We won't bite."—then closed it behind them.

The dwelling consisted of a single room, with a bed at one end, a lit fireplace at the other, and a table against the wall opposite the door. That table currently held a pie, a selection of iced buns, some sandwiches with the crusts cut off, and a number of mismatched cups and saucers beside a large teapot with steam rising from its spout. In the center of the room stood five chairs, four of which were currently occupied by women of various ages, the youngest, dressed in autumn browns and reds, barely older than Ceres—or more correctly, the age Ceres currently appeared to be—while the oldest was so elderly as to be mainly wrinkles, the rest of her, hands and all, lost beneath black robes that were too big for her, so that she resembled a balloon slowly deflating. Of the remaining women, one was silver-haired, with clothing fancier than the rest, and gave the impression that she'd have preferred to be somewhere else. The other was a cheery-looking soul with bright red hair and bright red cheeks to match, with the body of one who had never said no to another slice of cake, and the eyes of one who had never felt bad about it after. She was wearing so many necklaces, scarves, bangles, and rings that she could have passed for a human bric-a-brac stall. One of her long fingernails, painted the same shade of red as her cheeks and hair, was tapping an hourglass in a pointed manner. This, Ceres guessed, was Ursula. Seated beside her was a goat, which bleated irritably in their direction.

"We try to start at the agreed time, Rowena," said Ursula, "not ten grains after."

"Sorry, Ursula. I couldn't get my broom started, and had to come on foot."

The autumnal girl snickered, and Ursula tut-tutted.

"Now, Sage, no need to be like that. It could happen to anyone."

Sage obviously didn't agree.

"What kind of witch can't start a broom?" she jeered. "And I told you, my name's not Sage anymore. It's Belladonna."

The silver-haired woman to Ursula's left spoke up.

"Isn't Belladonna a little *obvious*?" she asked.

"She could try Onion instead," suggested the oldest participant. "That might work."

Ceres had never heard anyone actually cackle before, but the sound that followed from the old woman was undeniably cackling. Decades of practice had gone into perfecting it, making it a textbook cackle.

Sage—sorry, Belladonna—stuck out her tongue at the old woman, who responded by producing a gnarled forefinger from the sleeve of one cloak. The tip briefly fizzed with streaks of white light, like miniature flashes of lightning.

"That's quite enough, all of you," said Ursula. "It isn't helpful, and not the impression we want to give a new member. Pour yourself a cup of tea, dear, and pull up a chair. We'll get to names once you're settled."

Ceres poured some tea and did the same for Rowena.

"Would you mind if I had a bun, please?" Ceres asked.

"Buns are for after," said Ursula.

"You have to *earn* your bun," said Belladonna, giving Ceres her best who-do-you-think-you-are glare. *What a little minx*, thought Ceres, who had encountered more than her share of Belladonnas throughout her school days, girls who rarely met a compass they didn't want to jab into the nearest thigh. A therapist would have opined that Belladonna was just misunderstood, to which Ceres would have countered that there was nothing about her that couldn't be cured by a spell in reform school or the army. Casting a longing glance at the food, Ceres located a spare chair and positioned it between Rowena and the silver-haired woman.

"Right, now that we're all settled, let's begin," said Ursula. She cleared her throat. "My name is Ursula, and I'm a wicked witch. It's been five years since my last wickedness."

"Hello, Ursula," said four voices with varying degrees of enthusiasm. Ceres added hers at the end, out of time with the rest, prompting Belladonna to make an L shape from a thumb and forefinger and place them against her forehead while mouthing "Loser." Ceres wanted to thump her.

The others began introducing themselves. Rowena: two years since her last wickedness; Belladonna: eight months; Matilda, with the silver hair: five weeks, although she tried to claim it was all a misunderstanding, and she shouldn't really be there at all, at which point Ursula interrupted her to explain politely that they'd been over all this before, and a court order was a court order; and finally the old woman, Evanora: twenty years since her last wickedness, which Ceres considered very impressive. Belladonna, true to form, didn't.

"It's one thing not being wicked," she said, "and another not being *able* to be wicked because you're past it."

Evanora didn't respond, but from deep within her robes came that fizzing sound again. To Ceres, it sounded distinctly louder than before.

"And Evanora smells gross," added Belladonna. "I don't want to sit beside her next time. She's all cats and stale bread."

The fizzing ascended in pitch.

"That's very rude," said Ceres.

Belladonna cupped a hand to one ear.

"Excuse me, new girl?" she said. "*Weh weh-weh weh*. That's all I heard. Are you foreign? You can't speak foreign here. No one will understand."

"And what about you, dear?" Ursula asked Ceres hurriedly, in an effort to keep things on a civil plane. "What's your name?"

"Oh, it's Ceres, but I'm not actually a wicked witch. It's just that—"

Ursula offered Ceres her best condescending smile.

"The first step," she said, "is to admit we have a problem."

"But I don't have a problem," said Ceres. "Well, I do, only it's not being a—"

Ursula sat back in her chair triumphantly.

"See? You're already making progress. A round of applause for Ceres, everyone."

There was a scattering of claps, like a handful of pebbles falling on a tin roof. Belladonna pretended to join in, but her palms deliberately missed each other. Even had they met, they wouldn't have made much noise, since only one finger was raised on each. Some signs, Ceres realized, were universal, mostly the bad kind.

"So," said Ursula, "what good deeds have we done this week? Because . . . ?"

She waited for the required response. It took a while, but it arrived in the end.

"Because," mumbled the witches, "not doing wickedness is not the same as doing good." They sounded to Ceres like members of a hen party reluctantly admitting to a policeman that, yes, they had been the ones rolling empty wine bottles down a hill at four in the morning.

"Let's try that again," said Ursula, "with some enthusiasm."

The witches repeated the mantra, this time sounding like the same hen party addressing the judge.

"The question stands," Ursula continued. "Good deeds? Anyone? Anyone at all?"

Surprisingly, it was Belladonna who raised a hand. Even Ursula looked a bit shocked.

"Belladonna? Really?"

Belladonna composed her features into what, to someone passing at speed, might have resembled a picture of innocence.

"I left an apple pie outside the house of a sad old lady with no friends."

"Well," said Ursula, "how very kind of—"

"That's funny," said Evanora. "I found an apple pie outside my house just this morning."

There was an awkward silence while the rest of the room waited for the penny to drop.

"Oh," said Evanora. She looked momentarily dejected, before setting it aside in favor of being furious. "Why, you little—"

Ursula swiftly intervened.

"Remember, Evanora: swearing isn't caring."

"Being mean to someone isn't caring either," Ceres pointed out.

"I left a *pie*," Belladonna replied. "And who asked your opinion anyway?"

"I don't have to wait to be asked," said Ceres, "certainly not by you."

"You know, your clothes are funny," Belladonna informed Ceres.

"You know, your face is funny."

"Your mum's face is funny."

"Your mum's face isn't funny, it's just sad," said Ceres. "Because she's your mum."

Belladonna extended both hands toward Ceres, and blue lightning bolts flashed angrily at her fingertips.

"Stop it!" shouted Ursula. "We're here to help each other, not fire off spells. Remember, this is a wickedness-free space."

"She started it," said Ceres.

"No," said Belladonna, "you started it, by being born."

"Oh no." Ceres rocked in her chair as though stabbed through the heart. "That hurt *so* much, I think I might cry. *Boo-hoo*, Smellydonna said a mean thing."

"Actually," said Belladonna, missing the point of the insult completely, "it's *Bella*donna. Like, you can't even pronounce my name right."

"Like, actually," said Ceres, "it's Sage."

"I could turn you into a toad."

"Why, have you always wanted a twin?"

Belladonna's face was assuming an interesting shade of red, like a volcano on the verge of eruption.

"You take that back," she hissed.

"Sorry," said Ceres. "I take it back. *Sage*."

"It's Belladonna!"

"Or Onion," offered Evanora. "Or even 'Sage and Onion.'" She cackled again. Evanora really did have cackling down to a fine art.

"Stay out of this, grandma," said Belladonna. "This is between me and the new girl."

"Don't call me 'grandma,' " said Evanora. Her voice was very calm, the sort of calm that masked imminent chaos. "If I was related to you, I'd have disowned you long before now."

"Well said, Evanora," Ceres chipped in. "Give her a piece of your mind. You can spare it, and she needs it."

"I'll deal with you in a moment," said Belladonna.

"You're not helping," Ursula warned Ceres. "I do wish you'd—"

Belladonna put her face very close to Evanora's.

"I don't like you," she said, "and nobody else likes you either, not even your cat. It told me so. It's a cat, and even it doesn't smell as much of cat as you do. I don't know why you bother coming to these stupid meetings. I think you're just miserable and lonely. You couldn't be properly wicked if—"

White light flashed not only from both of Evanora's sleeves but also her eyes, ears, mouth, and nostrils, accompanied by the loudest fizzing yet—indeed the loudest cackling, too. The glare was so ferociously bright that spots danced in Ceres's vision, even as a cloud of noxious smoke obscured half the room. From somewhere in the midst of it, Ceres could hear Ursula and her goat coughing.

It took a while for the smoke to clear. When it did, Ceres saw that Belladonna's chair was now empty, or nearly empty. On the scorched cushion sat a shape resembling a baked potato that had been left too long in the oven. Everyone stared at it aghast, except for Evanora, who said, "My name is Evanora, and it's been"—she checked the hourglass—"two grains since my last wickedness . . ."

Ceres stood outside the cottage, Rowena beside her. Inside, efforts were ongoing to remove what was left of Belladonna from the chair, as she'd stuck to it a bit. Rowena handed Ceres a piece of cheese, a hunk of bread, and one iced cake, all wrapped in a clean handkerchief.

"I think you'd best be on your way," said Rowena. "And you ought to consider finding a different support group. Ursula's very annoyed, and we don't want to precipitate another act of wickedness, do we?"

"I don't have anywhere to go," said Ceres. "I'm lost."

"Then you can just as easily be lost somewhere far from here," said Rowena, "and you won't be any worse off."

Which put an end to the discussion. Nibbling on some cheese, Ceres returned to the forest.

XVII

Crionach

(GAELIC)

A Rotten Tree

eres walked until the cottage was safely out of sight, and she could no longer smell the smoke from the chimney, now sullied by another odor, which she guessed was charred Belladonna. She found a patch of soft, dry moss, with a tree stump to support her back, and ate most of the food, keeping back only some of the cheese, although she was hungry enough to have consumed everything, including the handkerchief.

As she was rewrapping the scraps, she caught a hint of movement against a nearby tree, and experienced the prickling sensation that sometimes comes with being observed. She didn't react, but kept the spot in view as she slipped the cheese into her pocket. Yes! There it was again, as though the tree had briefly exhaled and forgotten to inhale again, because the bark remained swollen, and buried in the resulting bulge was a pair of dark eyes. Ceres knelt, making cosmetic adjustments to the hem of her jeans with her left hand while her right grabbed a rock, the only object within reach that might usefully serve as a weapon.

There was more activity from the tree. Ceres saw that it wasn't the bark itself that was moving, but a creature perfectly camouflaged to merge with it. She could make out its thin arms and legs, and a narrow body and head.

It was about five feet long, and reminded her of a lizard without a tail. If it made a leap for her, it would be on her in an instant. Since it seemed best to preempt this, Ceres rose to confront the danger, the rock raised in warning.

"I can see you," she said. "You'd better not come any closer."

Which assumed that, whatever the creature was, it understood what she was trying to communicate. Even if it didn't speak English, it might speak rock. Everyone spoke rock, and if they didn't, they soon learned.

Now that it had been observed, the creature detached itself from the trunk. It did so slowly, but not threateningly. It was trying not to frighten her, and held up its hands in placation once it was standing on the ground. As it left the bark behind, its color changed. Its feet became a darker brown to match the dirt of the forest floor, while the rest of it gave the impression of transparency, until Ceres saw that it was reflecting the trees and bushes around it, the better to blend in with them. Only the eyes stood out.

"Don't be frightened," it said. "We won't hurt you."

Where the Spirit of the Stream's voice had burbled, this one reminded Ceres of a broom sweeping a dusty floor. But she didn't lower the rock, even though it was beginning to grow heavy. It was all well and good for something to say that it wasn't going to hurt you, but it hardly counted as a promise.

"Who are you?" said Ceres, which was becoming the question of the day.

"We are Calio," answered the creature.

"We?" said Ceres, scanning the forest nervously in case more of the creatures were hovering.

"We," said Calio, indicating themselves alone.

Before the accident, Ceres had spent enough time around Phoebe—who was very solicitous of the feelings of others—to know that if someone wanted to be referred to as he, she, we, or anything else, it was entirely their affair. If Calio was happier as "we," then it cost Ceres nothing to oblige.

"And *what* are you?"

"What are we? We are what we are."

Ceres briefly speculated whether Calio, whatever their nature, might have been spending too much time with the Spirit of the Stream. Both were doing a good job of cornering the market in unhelpful replies.

"Which would be?" Ceres persisted.

Calio considered the question.

"Dryad," said Calio, finally. They spoke clearly but uncertainly, like someone unpracticed in conversation. "We are . . . dryad."

"And what do you want?" asked Ceres.

Calio sniffed at her.

"You don't belong," said Calio. "You come from another place. These woods are dangerous, day and night. Soon all manner of beasts will begin hunting you, seeking to feast on strange flesh."

Ceres didn't like the way Calio savored the last two words, testing them on their tongue to see how they might taste.

"I can look after myself," said Ceres, and was instantly embarrassed. People only said this in films, frequently before they discovered that they couldn't.

"A child, armed only with a stone?"

Calio laughed. It wasn't a pretty laugh. Again, it reminded Ceres of girls who had bullied her in school: superior, and not a little nasty. Belladonna had probably laughed that way, until she was transformed into a burnt potato. At that moment, Ceres became convinced Calio wasn't to be trusted.

"I'm not a child," said Ceres, and the confidence with which she said it caused Calio to reappraise her. Those black eyes vanished for an instant as Calio blinked. When they reappeared, the dryad had moved closer, so close that Ceres could smell their breath, like damp, freshly turned earth.

"Aren't you now?" said Calio. "If not a child, then what?"

But Ceres didn't answer. She had already said too much, and Calio had commenced circling her, so that Ceres was forced to do likewise to keep them in sight.

"We think you should come with us," said Calio. "We can protect you."

"Come with you where?" asked Ceres, though she had no intention of going anywhere with Calio. She wanted to keep the dryad talking, because when they stopped, the trouble would start.

"To our home. It's not far. It's cool and dark. Nothing, and no one, will find you there."

Oh, I'm sure that's true, thought Ceres. *If I go with you, I have a feeling no one will ever see me again.*

"I'll stay where I am, thank you. Something will turn up. Something usually does."

Another blink, another vanishing of those dark eyes, and suddenly Calio was by Ceres's left ear.

"We can't let you stay here," said Calio. "It would be wrong."

Ceres retreated a step.

"Wrong for whom?" she asked.

But Calio had grown tired of arguing the point. They snatched at Ceres's left arm, gripping it below the elbow, and the hold was fierce and painful, like being pricked by the fingers of a thorny glove. A spur on Calio's wrist pierced Ceres's forearm, numbing it, the lack of sensation spreading rapidly toward her shoulder. Ceres knew that deadening: a decade earlier, she'd had two wisdom teeth removed under general anesthetic, and could remember the anesthetist's needle entering her arm, the sight of the syringe being depressed, and the feel of the narcotic traveling through her bloodstream to her brain, after which the world went black. Calio, like a spider attacking a fly, was rendering Ceres helpless, all the better to drag her to their lair; down, down to that cool, dark place, the one that lent its fragrance to their breath.

Except that Calio had made one crucial error: they had incapacitated the wrong arm.

With the last of her strength, Ceres swung, striking Calio hard on the side of the head. The dryad staggered back, releasing Ceres's arm, and Ceres hit them again, this time a glancing blow, because her sight was already dimming, and she was struggling to stay upright. But before oblivion claimed her, she saw Calio in their true form. The force of the blow must have damaged their camouflage mechanism, the part of their devious brain that permitted them to combine with their environment. Ceres beheld a naked form with green-brown skin; curved nails on elongated fingers and toes, the better to grip and climb; and a long, thin face with small pointed ears and two narrow slits for a nose, those mournful black eyes above, and a mouthful of small blunt teeth below. Sap, thick as honey, began pouring from a concave depression on the side of Calio's head, and Ceres thought that she might have fractured the dryad's skull.

Good, thought Ceres, as the dark came. *At least I hurt you. I hope I hurt you so badly that you—*

XVIII

Frith

(OLD ENGLISH)

Safety, Security

eres opened her eyes. Her whole body throbbed, and there was an unpleasant taste in her mouth, like sour fruit or stale wine. Her surroundings were dim, not dark, and warm, not cool; either Calio had been lying about their lair, or this was not any of their doing.

Ceres was lying on a long, narrow bed, with furs and blankets to keep her warm. To her left a fire burned, the flames adding their light to that of a trio of lamps, revealing shelves of jars, cooking utensils stacked by a stone basin, baskets of fruit and vegetables, some of the latter still with dirt clinging to them—and weapons, including a bow, a quiver of arrows, a sword, and the biggest axe Ceres had ever laid eyes on. She did not make it obvious that she was awake, but tried to take in as much as she could without moving her head. She appeared to be alone, but—

"How are you feeling?"

The inquiry came from the shadows at the far end of the room. It was not Calio's voice, which was a relief, although its owner was presumably the same person who owned the kind of axe used to cut down very large trees, and potentially cut off heads as well, regardless of size.

Ceres made out a pair of boots poking from the gloom. A chair creaked, and a man leaned into the lamplight. His hair was dark but streaked with gray, and his face bore stubble. His age was difficult to tell. He looked to be in his fifties, but his eyes, even in the dimness, were older still, as though they had been transplanted from some dead ancient into the sockets of one middle-aged. There was a familiarity to his features, although the nature of it evaded her, evanescing like overshadowed water flowing through the stippling of sunlight.

"I hurt," said Ceres.

"I'm not surprised. After all, you've been poisoned."

"Am I—?" She struggled to get the words out, either because her mouth was dry or she was afraid of hearing the answer. "Am I going to die?"

"I'm sure you are, but not today. Whatever attacked you wanted to render you immobile, no more than that. The effects would have worn off soon enough, but by then it would undoubtedly have been too late for you. No one, and nothing, wants to paralyze a young woman for the good of her health."

But Ceres had lived long enough to know that strange men who took insensible females into their cottages and put them to bed did not always do so with the noblest of intentions either. She checked under the blankets and hides, and was relieved to see that she was still wearing all her clothes.

The man got out of the chair and approached her. He was very tall, and well-built with it. Slabs of muscle shifted like tectonic plates beneath his shirt as he walked, but not the muscle that Ceres noticed on some of the young men in gyms, built purely for show. This was muscle gained from hard physical labor, raw and unsculpted. Had he felled a tree with his axe, he could have made a decent effort of dragging it home unaided. But as he stood before her, she saw that she had no cause to be frightened. His eyes—those old, old eyes—were softly, deeply kind, like her father's; this, she thought, was what had made him appear less strange to her.

"I think I'd like to get up," she said. "I'm too warm."

"Carefully, then."

He extended an arm on which she could support herself, but she noticed that he left it up to her whether to accept his aid. He would not touch her, even to help, without her permission. Ceres pushed herself up from the pillow and was immediately nauseated. Her head was spinning, but she didn't want to lie down again. She leaned against the man, and only then did he reach around with his left arm to assist her. She sat on the edge of the bed, drank an offered cup of what tasted like warm herbal tea, and waited for her head to clear. It took a while, but when it did she felt a great deal better, because some of the heaviness in her limbs vanished with it, along with a share of the discomfort.

"Better now?" asked the man.

"Yes, thank you. Not good, but better. I'm Ceres, by the way. I'm sorry, but I don't know your name."

"They call me the Woodsman," said her benefactor, "which is as good a name as any. I have questions, if you feel up to answering them, but first you need to get some nourishment inside you, including more of the infusion. It should help your body fight the poison."

A pot was heating over the fire. From it the Woodsman poured them each a bowl of thick vegetable broth, redolent with herbs and spices. They ate it with hand-carved wooden spoons, these as smoothly worked as the bowls, just like the cups from which the Woodsman drank water, and Ceres the infusion. It would have been easy to dismiss the homeware as plain, but it had the elegant simplicity that comes with fine craftsmanship.

"Did you make these?" asked Ceres.

The Woodsman looked at the cups, the bowls, the spoons, and then at the rest of the cottage, as though noticing them anew.

"Yes, a long time ago. I built this cottage, too, I think."

"You think?"

"I remember it being different, and it was, once upon a time. I've been sleeping, you see, and have only recently woken. I'm trying to get used to the world again."

"Do you mean to say," said Ceres, "that someone secretly redecorated your cottage while you were resting? It doesn't sound very likely."

"When you put it like that," said the Woodsman, "I don't suppose it does."

"And just how long were you asleep?"

The Woodsman shrugged.

"Oh, one night, I should guess, but it was a very long night and time passes differently here. Now, Ceres, where have *you* come from? Because you, I think, have traveled far for a young girl."

"Look, I'm not a young girl," said Ceres. "We need to get that straight from the start. I'm a thirty-two-year-old woman, but I'm stuck in the body of my sixteen-year-old self, and I'm not very happy about it. I didn't much like being sixteen back then, and I certainly don't want to be sixteen again when I'm really twice as old. Adolescence was bad enough first time round." And it had been: panic attacks, the pressure to look pretty, be slim, fit in, appeal to boys—or girls—and the stress, always the stress, of trying simply to maintain her footing in the world.

The Woodsman showed no signs of disbelief.

"Explain how this came to be," he said.

Ceres did. She told him of the hollow in the tree, and the old dwelling on the grounds of the Lantern House. She told him of the speaking library, and the sentient ivy. She told him of the face she had seen in the attic room, and the voice she heard. She told him of *The Book of Lost Things*, and the stories she had found herself writing, stories that might have come from the book itself. She told him of Phoebe, and how she had become lost. And finally she told him of the Spirit of the Stream, the witches, and Calio—predatory Calio. It was a lot for one person to take in, and she felt bad about burdening the Woodsman with it, but he had asked.

"I'm of the opinion," she finished, "that I may be having a breakdown, and you're part of it. I'm sorry about that, for your sake, but since you're almost certainly not real, it's not as tiresome for you as it might otherwise be. For reasons I can't begin to understand, that novel, *The Book of Lost Things*, has become the basis for a fantasy world in which I now find myself stranded. But if I can locate the way out, meaning the key to the breakdown, then I'll wake up in a nice, clean hospital bed, and a nurse will offer me a cup of tea and a slice of toast, and all will be well, or at least back to normal. I'll settle for that."

"But why do you assume that this world is not as real as yours," asked the Woodsman, "if not more so?"

"It can't be. It just can't."

But as she spoke, Ceres again found herself willing something to be true while secretly recognizing that, unfortunately, it might not be the case. Everything here was *too* real: the sickness and discomfort from the poison, the sharp pain in her arm from Calio's sting, the taste of the soup, the heat of the fire, the smell of animal hides and lamp oil, even the sound of the Woodsman's breathing. No nightmare, no psychological or emotional collapse, could be so detailed. Could it?

The Woodsman was staring into the fire, lost in thought—or, as it turned out, memories.

"So he wrote a book," said the Woodsman to the flames. "Of course he did."

And Ceres saw such tenderness in his face.

"David," she said. "You're talking about David."

"Yes."

"Because he was here. You're the one he met, the same Woodsman."

She had surmised as much, but had not wanted to say so, not until she'd learned more.

"I met him," said the Woodsman. "I traveled with him, but he was not here, not exactly."

"You're speaking in riddles," said Ceres. "It's a flaw shared by a lot of the creatures of this world."

The Woodsman returned his full attention to her.

"This is not the same land to which David came," he said, "just as this cottage is not identical to the one in which I fell asleep. The world is similar, and will have retained some aspects of David's time here, of all that happened while he moved through it, but others will have altered. Some of what was once known will now be unknown, and the commonplace rendered foreign."

"Why?" asked Ceres.

"Because of you. If you are here, it is because you are meant to be here. No one finds their way to this place in error. It will have changed in anticipation of your arrival, and it will evolve further now that you have come. Everything that is you—your fears, your hopes, what you love, what you hate—will have its effect. This has become your story, and the world is creating the landscape in which it must unfold, just as it once did for David."

Ceres didn't like the sound of that. She didn't have enough confidence in her mental stability, even in better times, to want to spend very long in a world conditioned by it.

"He disappeared," said Ceres. "Did you know that?"

"He didn't disappear," said the Woodsman. "He returned—to this realm, and to everything he loved."

"That was the ending he wrote," said Ceres. "In his book."

"It was the ending he dreamed, and for him it became reality. It was his reward."

"For what?"

"For never losing hope."

"So he's here?"

"Somewhere," the Woodsman replied, "but remember, this is not the only version of the world, because there are others: worlds upon worlds upon worlds, some different in every detail, and some the same but for one. Spaces, doorways, connect them all."

"Could a tree be a connecting space?"

"When it wishes to be, or when it has to. It may be that David's old home in your world is another."

Ceres took all this in, or tried to, because it was a lot to grasp.

"But I didn't choose to come here," she said. "I was trying to escape the ivy, and the face in it, and by running away I was transported."

"I never said that you chose to come," said the Woodsman, "only that you were meant to—or were lured."

"Lured? But by what?"

The Woodsman added another log to the fire. From outside a howling arose, startling Ceres by the closeness of it.

"Only wolves," said the Woodsman.

"Only?"

"Once upon a time, there were worse-than-wolves."

"The Loups," said Ceres: the creatures in David's book, half-wolf, half-human, seeking to rule in place of men.

"They are no more, but the wolves still dream of them."

"In all those worlds of which you spoke, might there be one in which the Loups triumphed?" asked Ceres.

"If there is," answered the Woodsman, "I have no wish to visit it."

Or a world in which the Crooked Man had won, thought Ceres. *That, too, would be best avoided.*

"You were talking of how I came to be here," said Ceres, "and of lures."

"I can only guess, but you say that the house drew you to it. And what was in the house? An attic room, a library, books, *stories.* Then the presence manifested itself, the one in the ivy. From what you say, it may have been listening for you."

"But it tried to kill me."

"Did it?"

"It chased me. It wanted to catch me."

"Again, are you certain?"

"Of course I am."

"All that ivy—sentient in itself, but capable of being controlled by a superior consciousness—consuming a house inside and out, yet it couldn't stop one woman from escaping it?"

"It wounded me." Ceres lifted her trouser leg. "Look, you can see the marks where it tried to grab me."

"Grab you, or spur you on?" asked the Woodsman. "Ivy curls, sticks, chokes. It does not lash."

Ceres didn't want to accept that she'd been tricked into entering this world. She thought she'd evaded capture, and had at first congratulated herself on her speed and resourcefulness, if only for getting away from the house. But if the Woodsman was right, she had been neither fast nor resourceful, only the victim of someone much cleverer than she.

"I wrote stories about the Crooked Man," she said. "He was in my head. Could it have been he who—"

"The Crooked Man is gone," said the Woodsman. "From *all* worlds. He was already dying when David came, and he bisected himself when he could not have his way. He was the agent of his own destruction. Like the Loups, he has been reduced to a memory."

Ceres didn't argue. What did she know of this place anyway? Not as much as the Woodsman.

But it's not precisely the same world. He said so. What was once known has become unknown.

Ceres silenced the voice. Doubt wouldn't help her. She wanted to trust the Woodsman. She needed to have faith in his judgment, just as David once had.

"What about the dryad, Calio?" asked Ceres. "After all, they were the one who poisoned me."

"I saw no sign of any dryad when I came upon you," said the Woodsman. "There was a trail of sap, although I did not have time to follow it. But their kind has not been encountered for many years. The dryads, and those like them, are all but vanished from the world. If it truly was a dryad that attacked you, it must be very old, and very alone. But where has it been for so long, and why should it have reappeared at this time?"

The Woodsman examined again the sting on Ceres's arm. It was marked with six punctures: one for each fingernail, and the final one from the spur on Calio's wrist. It was this, the Woodsman explained, that had delivered the venom to incapacitate Ceres. There was a vertical cut through the center of the mark, where he had used a knife to make an incision in an effort to draw the toxin from it.

"But this, undoubtedly, is a dryad's work," said the Woodsman, "and the injury worries me. I didn't get all the poison out, or else you would not have been unconscious for so long. Someone with more expertise should examine it, but such people are few now."

"I have to get back to my own world," said Ceres. "My daughter is there, and she needs me. If there's a problem with the wound, it can be dealt with by doctors, but I can't stay here."

"It's dark now," said the Woodsman, "and even I would rather not travel through the woods by night. If the dryad is still out there, it—or rather *they*, whatever that might mean—will be nursing not only a wound but also a grudge. They will want their revenge."

"I hit them hard," said Ceres. "They may even have died."

"You won't have killed them, not with a rock. Dryads are beings of wood and bark. They can be struck by a stone, or pierced by nails, and it will wound them, but not fatally. Only fire will do that, because all living things fear it, and dryads more than most. This Calio may already have recovered from the blow, for dryads heal rapidly. No, we won't be venturing out until morning, and then only when we're sure it's safe."

"And how will we know that?" asked Ceres. "Calio was almost invisible to me until I hit them."

"There are ways," said the Woodsman. "Not all of nature will welcome the return of a dryad."

But Ceres was no longer listening. She had an overwhelming desire to see Phoebe again, to hold her hand and speak to her. She feared that if the routines she had established—the visits, the talking, the reading of stories—were not kept up, the fragile spark of her daughter's quintessence might be snuffed forever. Tears came, but Ceres brushed them away, fighting the urge to give in to grief, because she was afraid that if she started crying in earnest, she might never stop. She hoped the Woodsman hadn't noticed, although she suspected that he had. She imagined very little got past him.

"I have a story," he said, "if you'd like to hear it."

"Why not?" said Ceres. "Unless you have a pack of cards to pass the time."

"Actually, I do have gaming cards somewhere, if you'd prefer."

"No, I'd like to hear a story. Maybe I can share it with Phoebe when I return to her. Wait, is it a fairy tale?"

"Oh," said the Woodsman, "very much so."

"I've started to hate fairy tales."

"That's unfortunate."

"Why?"

"Because," said the Woodsman, "you happen to be in one."

THE WOODSMAN'S FIRST TALE

Once upon a time, there was a young woman named Morgiana who lived in a remote village by the sea. She was tall, but not too tall, and pretty, but not so much so as to be the object of envy to others, or of excessive vanity to herself. But like many of those who live in remote places, whether by the sea or far from it, she had an eye for distant horizons—although, as the wise will remind you, horizons always remain distant, no matter how hard you try to reach them, which is itself a lesson to be learned in life. Still, the girl did not wish to eke out her days in that village, married to some farmer whose enthusiasms extended no farther than the boundaries of his own land, or a fisherman more in thrall to the sea than to her.

One day, as she was walking on the beach, a rider trotted into her path. He was dressed all in white, his horse was white, and even his hair was white, although it was not the white of old age, because his skin was as young as hers. He was the most beautiful man the woman had ever seen: not handsome, but radiantly exquisite, like a statue carved from the purest marble. She had not heard his approach, and could see no tracks of his horse's hooves upon the sand. It was as though he had emerged from the sea itself, except he and his mount were completely dry.

"What is your name?" he asked, and the question was a melody, each word a note. Had anyone but Morgiana been present to witness the exchange, they might have heard only music from the figure on the horse; and if they were wary and shrewd, they might also have discerned some discord to it, like an instrument wrongly tuned.

"My name is Morgiana," she answered.

"And I am Faera."

Perhaps that was his name, but if he spoke the truth, an odd name it was, because its roots lay in taunting, and worse. Morgiana, having knowledge of no tongue but her own, thought only that it sounded sweet coming from his mouth, although every word, no matter how foul its meaning, might have dripped like honey from those lips.

"I have been watching you for many days," said Faera. "You walk each morning and evening on this beach, and always you stop and stare out to sea, as if in search of a ship that never comes."

"That is because I do not wish to be born, to live, and to die within a day's walk of the same village," said Morgiana. "There is a world out there to be explored, and already I feel time slipping through my fingers."

"Time is cruel," said Faera. "More than it gives, it takes: youth, beauty, even dreams. It steals them all, and consigns you to the dark at the close."

Morgiana, though already beguiled by him, noticed how he spoke of "you," not "us" or "one," and perceived how his skin glittered in the sunlight, and his breath perfumed the air. She knew him then for what he was: a fairy lord, a prince of the Fae, even down to his name. He was the first of the Fae she had ever chanced upon, because they kept themselves apart from men; some said from hatred, others out of fear, and still more because they were known to have little love for any creatures but themselves. Whatever the reason, it was better by far for men to have no dealings with them.

And women, too. Especially women.

"Does time not steal from you also?" asked Morgiana.

"Time steals from everyone, but some more languidly than the rest. Come with me, and you will not grow old like others of your kind. Come with me, and I will show you a greater world beyond these shores."

Faera extended a hand to Morgiana, but just as their fingers were about to touch, she hesitated.

"There are those here whom I love," she said. "I do not care to abandon them forever. Will I be able to return to visit my family and friends?"

"You may return at any time," said Faera, "and pay your respects to them. I give you my word. In return, you must promise always to come back to me."

Morgiana agreed, and their pact was sealed with a kiss. She took the Fae prince's hand, and he raised her easily to ride behind him. He faced the sea, rallied his mount, and he and Morgiana were consumed by the waves.

$\mathcal{H}$ere is a truth about the Fae: They may hate us, and they may fear us, but they also have a lust for humankind. They are fascinated by the flame of our being, which burns so fierce and fast. They like to hold it close, to watch—to feel—it fade, and even to consume it when the need or the mood takes them. While they may be deceivers, they do not lie, but rarely will the Fae make a promise capable of only a single meaning. One has to pay close attention during any discourse with them, and be certain of the nature of the bargain one is striking. But Morgiana, who was inexperienced and unwary—and in the way of youth, considered herself cleverer than she was—did not know any of this.

$\mathcal{F}$aera was true to his word. He took Morgiana to his own land, and for a while he treated her like royalty visiting from a far-off kingdom. She was given silk robes to wear, and diamonds, rubies, and emeralds as adornments. She ate the finest foods, wandered the peaceful Fae woods, and explored the splendid Fae palaces, but she was conscious always of laughter in her wake, and would turn to see a Fae princess smothering a smile, or a Fae prince observing her the way a fox might contemplate a fat, slow hen.

After only a few weeks Morgiana became restless, because despite the silks, the jewels, and the exotic dishes, and for all the quietude of the woods and the riches of the palaces, she was bored. The Fae led lives of lassitude and indulgence. Their existence had no purpose, or none beyond their own pleasure, but even this state they struggled to attain, and then only briefly. It is the curse of being long-lived: life ceases to hold many surprises, and only by giving oneself up to extremes can the monotony be broken.

And Morgiana was changing. At the end of her first day with the Fae, she discovered a gray hair where none previously was. The next day there was another, then more and more. Fine lines appeared at the corners of her eyes and on her forehead. Her skin, once tight, began to sag. The laughter of the Fae princesses grew louder and more frequent. Now they did not bother to hide their contempt, and few would even consent to speak with Morgiana. Faera, meanwhile, was absent, and no one would tell her where he might be.

But worse than all this, Morgiana glimpsed the truth of the Fae's appearance, disguised from her until now by the Fae glamour, like a mask modeled on a human face that ultimately failed to conceal the ugliness beneath. Sometimes, too, she heard what sounded like human infants crying deep underground, but only at night, and not for long. This, though, she kept to herself.

Finally, after a month had gone by, Faera returned, and Morgiana confronted him.

"I should like to visit my people," she said. "I miss them, and I am sure they miss me, too."

Faera tried to dissuade her, but Morgiana would not be deterred.

"You promised me," she said. "You promised that I would be free to return to my kinfolk, if I wished."

"And so you are," said Faera. "But remember, you promised in turn that you would always come back to me, and promises made must be kept, on pain of death."

Although Morgiana wished she had never agreed to join Faera, and wanted more than anything to have her old life restored to her, she was a girl of her word, whether on pain of death or not.

"*I will come back to you,*" she said, "*when I have walked among my own kind once again.*"

At this Faera lifted a finger in warning.

"*That, I'm afraid, you cannot do. You are now as much of our realm as we are, and your own land is rendered fatal to you, as it is to us. Were you to set foot on it, even for an instant, you would crumble to dust.*"

"*But you never told me that,*" said Morgiana.

"*You never asked.*"

"*Had I known, I would never have consented to go with you.*"

Morgiana was weeping, but Faera showed her no mercy. As he spoke, he seemed to her transformed, so that she saw him as he truly was. He was no longer beautiful, but blighted, his features more demonic than human.

"*That was your error, not mine. Do you still wish to visit your people?*"

"*More than ever,*" said Morgiana.

"*Then you must stay on the horse I give you, and neither your hands nor your feet may touch the ground. Do you understand?*"

Morgiana did, and better than she gave away.

"*I have a question for you, before I leave,*" she said.

"*Ask it.*"

"*My hair is now more gray than dark, my skin is looser, and I have lines like my mother's, yet I have spent only weeks here. How can this be?*"

"*I told you that you would not grow old like others of your kind,*" said Faera, "*and so it has come to pass. But I did not say that you would age more slowly than they. You should have listened more carefully, but you heard merely what you wanted to hear.*"

"*Oh, you are a vile creature!*" said Morgiana.

"*And you are a witless one, but the agreement was made, and you cannot renege on it.*" Faera touched a finger to Morgiana's hair, studying the new color to it. "*Unless, of course, you choose to die. You can cast yourself from the horse when you reach your homeland, and that will be the end of it.*"

He was daring her to kill herself, and Morgiana knew he would have been happy if she did. He was tired of her, like a pet that has ceased to amuse. Soon the beautiful lords and ladies wouldn't even bother to laugh any longer, so pitiful would she become, until finally she died, and her body was cast on the kitchen midden, there to rot with the half-eaten food.

But Morgiana was not witless, only hasty in the manner of the unseasoned, and too willing to trust, as is common to those with little experience of others' cruelty. Yet she had absorbed much and grown wiser in her time with the Fae, all lessons hard-learned, although the hardest was to come.

It was a bright winter's morning when Morgiana rode her horse into the sea at the border of the Fae realms. Behind her stretched the stone path that the Fae walked twice daily, because it was their habit to come to the beach to watch the sun rise and set, with mead for the dawn and wine for the evening. She wondered if she would ever see the place again, so tempting was the release promised by death. The waters closed over her head, and when they parted again she emerged into her own country. In the distance she could see her parents' cabin on the brow of a hill overlooking the ocean, and the rooftops of the village beyond, but when she reached her former home she saw that its thatch was gone, and the house was devoid of furniture and inhabitants. She rode on toward the village and passed an old man on the road.

"Do you know what has befallen the family that once lived in the cottage by the sea?" she asked.

"Why," said the old man, "that cottage has not been inhabited since I was a boy. The daughter of the house disappeared, feared drowned, and her mother and father never recovered from their grief. They died within the year, and the cottage was left to fall into ruin, because it was a place from which all luck but bad had fled."

Morgiana continued on the road, and saw that the village, too, was altered. It was larger, and filled with faces she did not recognize, or in which the shadows of lost youth were all that remained. But none of these older people remembered Morgiana, because the Fae had left their mark on her, disguising her from her own.

As the sun began to set, Morgiana rode back to the shore, and her heart was heavy with anger and loss. Her mother and father had departed this world in sorrow, believing their only daughter drowned, and those others she had once known were all dead or dying. She was a stranger in her own country, and had no place among the Fae except as an object of amusement while she wasted away before their eyes. In that moment, as the horse's hooves padded on the sand, and the waves broke before her, she came close to obliging Faera, and falling to the beach, there to die.

But as she was about to relinquish her hold on the horse's reins, and free her feet from the gold stirrups, she spied a boy on the shore. He carried two large sacks filled with the crabs and shellfish he had caught, the sacks so laden that he was forced to drag them along behind him. He paused before Morgiana, taking in the beauty of her and her mount, the detailing on the saddle, and the gold of the stirrups and bridle. The boy bowed, and Morgiana bowed back, all thoughts of dying banished for the present.

"I see that you've been busy," she said.

"The sea has been generous," said the boy.

"I should like to buy the sacks from you," said Morgiana, "but those alone. If you can find another way to carry your bounty, you may keep it."

The boy looked at her as though she were mad.

"But the sacks themselves are worth little," he said.

"They are worth this bridle to me," replied Morgiana. She removed it and handed it to the boy. She knew she could ride without it.

"But I'd be cheating you," said the boy, as the gold gleamed in his hands.

"I have been cheated before," said Morgiana, "but this is a deal I make willingly."

So the boy emptied the sacks and offered them to her.

"I have one more favor to ask," said Morgiana. "I should like you to fill the sacks with sand, as much as they can hold. Then find me some rope to bind them together, that I may hang them from my saddle."

The boy did as she requested. He filled the sacks with sand, bound them with a length of rope from a boat pulled up by the dunes, and placed them behind Morgiana's saddle. Morgiana thanked him, and prepared to leave her homeland for the last time.

"Will you tell me who you are?" asked the boy. "If I return to my mother with this bridle, and no clue as to its owner, she will accuse me of stealing it."

"Tell them that my name is Morgiana, and many years ago I lived in the cottage on the hill. Tell them that I made a bad bargain with the Fae, but I may have found a way to cause them to regret it more than I."

With that she spurred the horse into the waves and was swallowed by the sea.

The waters parted, and Morgiana came out of them. Before her was the path that led from the shore to the palaces of the Fae. Behind her, the sun was about to set in this world, too. As she reached the path, she took a pin from her hair and used it to pierce the sacks behind her saddle, so that the sands of one world scattered themselves on another, their alien dust indistinguishable from that of the Fae realm. Up and down she rode, up and down, until the sacks hung empty.

As the sun turned red, she went back to the beach, and waited for the Fae to come.

"What a horrible story," said Ceres, when the Woodsman was done.

"They're often the most interesting kind."

"My father would have agreed with you, and my daughter, too."

The mention of Phoebe caused her to well up again, but she pulled herself together.

The Woodsman took a pipe from the shelf above the fireplace, a sourced pouch of tobacco from his pocket, and began tamping the tobacco into the bowl.

"That's very unhealthy, you know," said Ceres.

"Is it really? I won't offer you any, then."

He produced a taper, lit it from the fire, and got the pipe glowing to his satisfaction, whereupon he puffed a thick cloud of smoke into the air. It smelled to Ceres like old socks smoldering over rotten wood. She folded her arms and glared at the Woodsman.

"Are you sure," he asked, "that you're not a sixteen-year-old girl?"

"Positive."

"Just checking."

Ceres got to her feet.

"I'm going to bed."

"That's probably a good idea. You've had a full day."

"But tomorrow you're going to help me get home, aren't you?"

The Woodsman poked at the fire.

"I'm certainly going to try," he said.

Which Ceres did not find completely reassuring.

XIX

Ealdor-Bana

(OLD ENGLISH)

Life-Destroyer

he dryad, Calio, regarded the cottage, the contours of it barely visible against the dark, and only the flickers of illumination through the slits in the shutters and the smell of smoke from the fire hinting at habitation.

Calio was seated on a rock, which was situated on a patch of bare, treeless ground. This was the Woodsman's domain, and he had corrupted its nature to his will, so that the bats and night owls acted as his eyes and ears, and the local ivy as his protector. Calio had felt the vegetation shift restlessly at their approach. If they tried to get closer to the cottage, it would seek to bind them until the Woodsman came, and Calio did not wish to be submitted to the Woodsman's justice.

But oh, how Calio suffered, and how they desired to inflict greater injury in return! The one called Ceres, the child-who-was-not-a-child, had wounded Calio. Their head smarted, they had been rendered blind in one eye, and their camouflage was sporadic, so they could blend in with their surroundings only for a short time before becoming visible again. Without their ability to conceal themselves, Calio was vulnerable, and exposure meant they were at risk of becoming easy quarry. Worst of all, they were weak, and the Returning Ones would not tolerate weakness. Dealing with Ceres would prove to them that Calio was still useful.

Yet the interloper was under the Woodsman's protection. He would not surrender her without a fight, and Calio was in no position to challenge him. Perhaps it might be enough to follow, to monitor, and then share with the others what they had learned. It would take their kin time to adjust again to the world, because it had changed so much since last they wandered it, and it was unlikely that they were aware of Ceres's arrival.

Yet why was she here? Everything in the world had a purpose, which meant that Ceres had one, too. Travelers from other realms were not unknown, but they were of two kinds: the ones who ventured into it unplanned, and the ones brought here by the memory of another. Calio adjudged Ceres to be among the former, because she seemed lost and confused. If she had journeyed from her world into this one, it was because something on this side wished it to be so, and there were few with that kind of power.

Calio's sole functioning eye settled on motion among the fallen leaves: a field mouse, looking for food while trying to remain hidden from night-hunters. The dryad's stillness, even without dissimulation, had lured the mouse into a false sense of security. Calio's left foot shot out, pinning the animal, and one of their long fingernails opened the animal from neck to tail, fatally wounding it.

Calio knelt beside the mouse, put their face close to its snout, and breathed in its essence as it died.

In the cottage, the Woodsman divided his attention between Ceres, who was sleeping curled up on the pallet bed, and the embers of the fire. He discerned faces in the flames: the one called Leroi, leader of the Loups— half-man, half-wolf, and the worst of both; he saw trolls and harpies, and the boy David; and finally there rose the Crooked Man, who had once ruled from the shadows, manipulating children drawn from their world to his, boys and girls tricked into becoming puppet kings and queens through fear and weakness.

But Ceres was not a child—in body she was less than a woman, but not in mind—and the time of sovereigns had passed. When the Woodsman had closed his eyes to sleep, this Elsewhere was already beginning to rewrite itself, and a new order of minor lords and ladies was on the rise, each with mandates delineated by rivers, mountains, and gorges, the boundaries decided by agreement between them. Much of the land, though, was set to remain a common expanse, open to all to cross, even to inhabit, as long as they weren't trespassing on the territory of a gorgon, a cyclops, or some other manner of bad-tempered creature. In that case, their journey was likely to be sharply and permanently curtailed, their fate becoming the subject of a warning tale to be shared with children; or their house would be reduced to rubble, with their remains left to molder in the middle as a reminder that just because you couldn't see something didn't mean it wasn't there.

So the Woodsman had left this world in a state of transformation, but not outright instability, only to return to find it under a cloud of unknowing. A dryad, a being not seen for centuries, had reappeared, and with the temerity to attack a person, a thing almost unheard of. The person in question, meanwhile, did not belong. She had not come willingly, but had stumbled into this world, or was pursued in such a way as to be left with no option but to enter it. So who wanted Ceres here, and to what end? Until this could be established, the Woodsman didn't think she would be leaving anytime soon. He took a last long draw on his pipe, and recalled the story he had told her, the tale of Morgiana and the Fae.

Now, the Woodsman reflected, *I wonder where that came from?*

The coming of the dryad offered a possible answer, but it was one he feared.

XX

Hleów-feðer

(OLD ENGLISH)

Shelter-Feather; A Protective Arm
Around Another

eres endured a miserable night. She became feverish, alternately so hot that she tried to tear off her clothing until the Woodsman intervened, and so cold that there were not enough furs and hides in the cottage to keep her warm. She was plagued by visions of beasts with two heads, many heads, and then no heads at all, and grew convinced that Calio was lurking in the gloom of the eaves, invisible to the Woodsman but present nonetheless, waiting for the chance to drag Ceres down into the dark. Her left arm grew so tender that she couldn't rest on it, and her neck so stiff that she was unable to move her head without yelping. The Woodsman gave up his own rest to sit by her, adjusting her bedcoverings according to the demands of the fever, and bathing her face with a damp cloth, while feeding her more of the infusion he had first used to tackle Calio's sting.

By the time dawn came, Ceres's fever had abated, but her arm remained swollen, and she could turn her head only with difficulty. She didn't think she could bear to spend another night like the last.

"I'm at the end of my knowledge," said the Woodsman. "I've kept the dryad's poison at bay, but ridding you of it is beyond me."

"Just get me home," said Ceres, "please. Once I'm back in my own world, there are doctors who'll be able to cure me."

The Woodsman's horse was whinnying in the stable, eager to be abroad again, although the morning was veiled by heavy clouds promising rain. When he checked the forest through the shutters, all was as it should be, but to make certain he left Ceres in the cottage and walked as far as the first trees. There he raised a hand to the ivy and allowed it to entwine itself around his fingers, interpreting with his skin the message it imparted: an interloper at the margins of the forest during the night, a creeping being, but gone now. And movement belowground, like the tremors of a distant earthquake or—

Digging.

The Woodsman flexed his hand, and the ivy released its hold.

Wrong, he thought, *all wrong*.

He returned to the cottage, his footsteps ringing uncomfortably hollow to him. From the topmost branch of a long-dead tree, a one-eyed rook stood sentinel until the door closed behind the Woodsman, before the bird took to the air and flew north. In its mouth, the button still shone: a treasure, and an affirmation.

The woman was here.

It took some time to prepare Ceres for traveling. She could not tie her own shoelaces, so distended was her left arm, and the Woodsman had to help her walk to the horse before lifting her onto its back. He equipped himself with the axe, Ceres seated between his arms. Ordinarily he would have made her sit behind him, but he did not want her to fall off should she be overcome by weakness. It meant that he was forced to ride with his left arm curled around her, his right hand holding the reins, and the axe across the saddle. If they were to come under attack, he would struggle to defend them, so he relied upon the ivy to test the safety of the way.

At Ceres's insistence, they went first to the stream. She dismounted with the Woodsman's assistance, and stared helplessly at the trees around her.

"It could be any one of these," she said, gesturing at dozens upon dozens of massive trunks. She progressed unsteadily from one to the next, knocking on the bark in the hope of detecting some cavity within, but they all sounded depressingly solid to her. She looked to the Woodsman, but he remained by his horse, stroking her neck.

"Aren't you going to help?" she asked.

"There's no point. Even were the coin still in place, I doubt the doorway would be. I told you: You didn't come here by accident. A tale is unfolding, and you have a part to play in it."

"But I don't want to be part of any tale," said Ceres. "I want to—*have* to—get back to my daughter."

"This world, like any other, doesn't care what you want. Whatever age you may be, you're too old for that mistake."

Ceres supposed the Woodsman was right. The new world didn't owe her any more than the old one, but it was still possible to feel shortchanged by both.

"Well, bother the bird that took my coin," said Ceres, returning to him.

"Are you sure it was the same one that led you to the house?"

"I haven't made a study of one-eyed rooks," Ceres growled, "so I couldn't swear to it."

She tottered, and used the horse to steady herself. The Woodsman handed her a flask, and she drank a mouthful of the infusion. She was growing sick of the taste, but when she drank it, she felt better.

"So what do we do now?" she asked.

"We have to get that sting tended to," said the Woodsman, "and along the way we may find out more about what's happening, which will give us some clue as to why you're here. When we know that, we'll have a better chance of figuring out how to get you home."

"And is something happening?" said Ceres, as he helped her back on the horse.

"Beyond your being here, which is troubling enough? Yes, something is happening."

He banged a heel against the earth, still damp with morning dew. The child-flowers scowled disapprovingly.

"I think," he said, "that there is an awakening."

At the cottage they stocked up on food, water, and bedding for the journey. Ceres, uncomfortable in her clothes after a night spent sweating in them, was advised by the Woodsman to search a small closet for suitable replacements.

"There's no point," she said. "Nothing of yours will fit me."

"Then just as well," he replied, "that there's nothing of mine in it."

Ceres opened the closet to find clothing of various sizes, and with some rolling up of sleeves and adjusting of trouser legs, she was able to assemble a passable outfit for herself. She also located a pair of short boots that fit her well, because her tennis shoes were now decidedly the worse for wear.

"Where did all this come from?" she asked. "Have you children of your own?"

"You're not the first to have passed this way," said the Woodsman.

"Not the first *what* to have passed this way?"

"Not the first anything."

"You know," said Ceres, "if I ever meet someone in this world who can give me a straight answer to a question, they'll have made a friend for life."

The Woodsman added more arrows to his quiver, and secured his scabbard to the horse's saddle. The axe he strapped to his back. After only a moment's hesitation, he handed Ceres a very short sword in a belted sheath. She tugged on the sword's hilt, revealing a clean, sharp blade.

"What am I supposed to do with this?" Ceres asked.

"The pointed end goes in first," said the Woodsman. "The rest of it will follow easily."

"I'm not going to stab someone. What kind of person do you think I am?"

"You were happy to hit a dryad with a rock."

"That was different."

"And how was it different?"

"I don't know." Ceres thought for a few seconds. "A blade just seems more intimate, and more final."

"It is if you use it right," said the Woodsman, before relenting. "Look, the sight of it will give pause to anyone who might wish you harm. Often, that can be enough."

By now they were outside, ready to depart, and to Ceres the cottage represented a place of safety that she was not certain she wanted to abandon.

"I meant to ask you before," she said, "but why did you add all those steel spikes to the walls and roof?"

"I didn't," said the Woodsman. "They were there when I woke up."

"So who did?"

"Not who, but what. The cottage decided they were needed."

"A cottage," said Ceres, "is just a cottage. It can't decide anything."

The front door of the cottage, which had been standing open, slammed shut, and Ceres heard the sound of the heavy timber bar being slotted into position from inside. If a dwelling could have harrumphed, this one would have.

"I take that back," said Ceres.

The Woodsman vaulted into the saddle with impressive energy for someone his age, and leaned down to give her a hand up.

"I can ride behind you," said Ceres. "I know why you were keeping me in front, but it's hardly practical, and not very comfortable. If I start feeling dizzy, I'll let you know."

A quick rearrangement of their supplies was necessary, but soon Ceres found herself seated behind the Woodsman, her hands holding on to his belt for added security.

"There are horses where we're going," said the Woodsman. "We can borrow or buy one that suits you."

"I don't plan on being here long enough to own a horse."

"Let me remind you," said the Woodsman, as he urged the mare on, "that you didn't plan on being here at all."

XXI

Stræl
(OLD ENGLISH)

Streak, or Flash; An Arrow

lthough she remained troubled by her inability to get back home, and the Woodsman's lack of an immediate alternative solution, Ceres couldn't help but take an interest in the landscape through which they traveled.

For the first few hours it was treescapes alone, with little indication of habitation beyond the occasional ruin: here a blockhouse overgrown with ivy, there a wooden dwelling slowly being repossessed by forest. They passed eel pools, traps decaying by their banks, the old fishermen's shelters barely distinguishable from the undergrowth. At one point they came to three small houses, the first consisting only of foundations made of bales of charred straw, the second a shell of burnt sticks, and the third formed of bricks, but the bricks were blackened, and the cottage exuded the unmistakable odor of barbecued pork.

"Never underestimate the resourcefulness of a bad wolf," said the Woodsman.

Later, as the sun reached its zenith, they heard a thrashing noise from the woods to their right, and the ground shook beneath the mare. The Woodsman was reaching for his axe when a mature yew tree yomped across the path, trailing dirt from its roots, without even acknowledging them. Seconds after, a smaller yew came running after, trying to catch up with its sire, pausing briefly to take in the riders before continuing on its way.

"Of course," said Ceres. "Walking yews." And for the first time since her arrival, she genuinely smiled.

At last they came to a colossal tower amid newer-growth trees, the trunks neither as thick nor as tall as those in the rest of the forest. Ceres dismounted to stretch her legs and used the opportunity to circle the building, monitored closely by the Woodsman. Ceres saw arched windows at the very top, but no door. The stonework looked recent to her—years old, rather than centuries—but she could not even begin to imagine how long it had taken to construct such a tower, or why it had been raised so far from anywhere.

"Coo-ee!" said a loud voice from above, and a head poked from one of the windows. It belonged to a young woman with blond hair piled in a high beehive on her head. She gave them a cheery wave. Ceres exchanged a glance with the Woodsman, who shrugged. Whoever this might be, he had no knowledge of her.

"Oh, hello," said Ceres, waving back uncertainly.

"You're not here to rescue me, are you?" asked the woman, and Ceres couldn't help but notice that a crossbow had appeared in her hands.

Again Ceres looked to the Woodsman, who called up, "Do you *want* to be rescued?"

Which struck Ceres as a silly question. Here was a woman stuck in a tower with no door, and with windows positioned so high that even a very tall ladder would have struggled to reach them, while any attempt to climb down unaided would have ended in death, the masonry being smooth as glass, with no visible handholds or footholds. Then again, the woman had inquired in a way that didn't exactly scream "Rescue me!," and there was the not-insignificant fact that she was cradling a crossbow. Her reply to the Woodsman decided the issue.

"No, I'm fine, thank you," she said. "I was just checking. Can't be too careful, you know."

"But . . . you're trapped, aren't you?" said Ceres. "Unless you built this tower for yourself, but then why not include a door?"

"Ah," said the woman, lowering the crossbow and seating herself on the window ledge, with one foot dangling, "that's an interesting story. You see, there was this witch, and you know how they can be: worryingly unpredictable, your witches, with a nasty way about them when they're crossed. Well, my mum and dad had a difference of opinion with this particular witch over her garden, which was right next to theirs, and whether or not they were entitled to help themselves to some of her salad leaves any time the mood took them. Mum loved a good salad. Lived for it. Would eat nothing else. Very thin woman. If she turned sideways, all you could see was her nose.

"Anyhow, over the years one thing led to another—or one salad led to another, if you like—and the witch got fed up with Mum and Dad 'taking liberties,' as she put it. I mean, Mum and Dad would always deny it was them doing the thieving, but it was hard to hide the extent of it after a while. Our whole house smelled of foliage, and you couldn't move for lettuce. Mum even started to look vegetal in a certain light. Finally, the witch caught them red-handed, or green-handed, and stuck me in this tower to teach them a lesson about respecting other people's property. They'd even named me Rapunzel, after Mum's favorite leaf, which was a bit of a giveaway. They hadn't really thought that one through."

"How terrible," said Ceres.

"I know!" said Rapunzel. "What kind of parents name their child after something that's half spinach, half radish? It's inhuman. There ought to be a law against it."

"I meant locking someone up in a tower is terrible," said Ceres. "Although the naming part isn't great either."

"Oh, I don't think the witch planned to keep me cooped up forever. It was probably meant to be a temporary thing—a year or so at most, just enough to put a scare into Mum and Dad. But next thing I hear, they've sold the house and gone off to become salad growers, although I don't imagine they'll have much luck with it, since Mum will just eat it all like the rabbity basket case she is.

"Then, as if that wasn't bad enough, someone only went and killed the witch. To be fair, she was a bit fractious, and it's an occupational hazard of being a witch, getting killed. It happens a lot, you know. It's not much of a job, witchery, when you think about it. You have to be very committed. I suppose it's more of a vocation, really. You do it for the love of it."

Ceres was beginning to regret starting the conversation. Rapunzel, whatever her other issues, was a competition-level chatterbox with a voice that certainly carried. If they weren't careful, the hind legs would drop off the Woodsman's horse.

"Perhaps we should just leave you to—" Ceres began, until the crossbow appeared again in Rapunzel's hands, its bolt pointing unerringly in their direction.

"Stay where you are," said Rapunzel, with deadly calm. "I haven't finished yet, and it's impolite to walk away from someone when they're talking, especially if you asked them to tell you a story in the first place. It makes a person twitchy."

Which was when Ceres noticed a man lying in the undergrowth. He was dressed in light armor: a breastplate, vambraces on the arms, and cuisses on the thighs, as well as a helmet with a narrow visor. He wasn't likely to be getting up anytime soon, though, because poking from the visor was the shaft of a crossbow bolt, which meant the business end was buried somewhere in his head. Ceres gave the Woodsman's leg a nudge to attract his attention, and indicated, as discreetly as she could, the presence of the corpse.

Ceres debated mentioning the dead man to Rapunzel, but it wasn't as though she was unlikely to be aware of him, since the chances were that one of her crossbow bolts had done the damage in the first place. Also, he wasn't exactly well hidden, but had been left to lie where he'd fallen. A couple of steps in the wrong direction, and Ceres might have tripped over him. Still, it was probably best to ask, just in case.

"Beg your pardon," she said, raising a hand to Rapunzel like a child seeking permission from a teacher, "you do know there's a body down here, don't you?"

Beside her, the Woodsman raised his eyes to the sky, and gave the sigh of a man who has ended up in the company of someone with a death wish.

"Oh, him," said Rapunzel dismissively. "I never got around to finding out his name. Some knight or other."

"Did you, um, shoot him?" asked Ceres.

"No, silly, I didn't shoot him. I shot *at* him. In his general direction, like. There's a difference. I was trying to discourage him, and I just turned out to have a better aim than I thought—or maybe a worse one. It depends on your perspective."

If discouraging the knight had been Rapunzel's intention, reflected Ceres, she had certainly been successful, because it was difficult to see how a chap could be any more discouraged.

"But what were you trying to discourage him from doing?"

Rapunzel tangled a lock of hair awkwardly around the index finger of her left hand while her right hand, Ceres noted, remained firmly fixed on the crossbow.

"You see," said Rapunzel, "I'd been up here for a couple of years, and to be honest, I was getting bored. The prospect of a walk in the woods, and the feel of grass against my bare feet, began to appeal. So when that bloke came along and said he might like to rescue me, I was all in favor, even though he didn't have much of a plan in mind. It wasn't like he'd brought scaffolding, or even a ladder. All things considered, I don't think he was very bright, because he spent a long time hemming and hawing, and scratching his chin, without making a great deal of progress on the rescuing front. He huffed and puffed for so long that I got disheartened, and started brushing my hair to pass the time, which was when he spotted how long it was, because it hadn't been cut in years, although I do keep an eye out for split ends—because you have to, don't you? In a flash he was all enthusiasm, and he shouted up:

" 'Rapunzel, Rapunzel, let down your hair to me.' "

" 'Are you sure?' I said, because it didn't come across as an especially good idea. Looking at him now, you wouldn't know it, but when he arrived he was carrying a few pounds, and I don't mean only his armor. There was a man who'd never met a pie he didn't like.

"So he said it again: 'Rapunzel, Rapunzel, let down your hair to me.' And he was so insistent that I thought, fine, we'll give it a try. I warned him that I wasn't convinced it would work, and he should let go if I told him to, but I don't know how closely he was listening to me by that stage of the proceedings. In my experience, once a man gets an idea into his head, it's very hard to shake it out of him; and the worse the idea, the more stubbornly he holds on to it. It would be funny if it wasn't so tragic.

"To cut a long story short, I let my hair down, and he grabbed two big handfuls and commenced climbing, but you can see where this is going: a big man, clad in bits of metal, hanging on to a woman's hair for support? It felt like my head was going to be pulled off my shoulders, and that was when he only had one foot off the ground. By the time he had both feet braced against the wall, I was set to be dragged out of the window. I told him to stop messing about, but he wouldn't, so I reached for the crossbow and"—she shrugged—"he stopped climbing. Stopped doing much of anything, really. I was sorry at the start, especially when the wind was blowing in the wrong direction and he began to whiff, but that was ages ago. To be honest, I'd sort of forgotten about him until you came along."

"Is that why you don't want to be rescued anymore?" asked Ceres.

"More or less. He reminded me of just how foolish men can be, so I decided I'm better off where I am. There's a well at the bottom of the tower, and I have a bucket I use to draw water, even if it does take a while to wind it up. I have a privy—okay, I have a hole in the masonry that drains out through the wall, but it does the trick. And I have plenty of books to read and food to eat, thanks to the rats. Very companionable animals, rats, and they can keep up their end of a conversation, unlike mice and voles."

Ceres was by now convinced that, even allowing for incidents of homicide, Rapunzel was quite mad. Ceres pictured her alone in her room at the top of the tower, nattering at length to a pack of rats who were staring blankly back at her while wishing they'd just kept walking.

"Excuse me, coming through," said a voice from below.

Ceres peered down to see a large gray rat dressed in a green-and-red waistcoat stepping gingerly between her legs. On its head it carried half a loaf of bread and a hunk of bacon, balanced on top of a slim, leatherbound volume.

Ceres stared at the rat. The rat stared back at her.

"What?" it said. "Do I have something on me? I hate it when that happens."

The rat carefully inspected its waistcoat, followed by its fur, its tail, and the pink soles of its paws. Once it was satisfied that it hadn't stepped in anything unpleasant, it returned its attention to Ceres.

"Right then," it said, uncertainly.

Another rat slipped by Ceres, carrying a small basket of blueberries. It was wearing a feathered cap, and juggled the basket so it could raise the cap politely to Ceres.

"Afternoon," said the second rat. "Pleasant weather, and all that."

"Yes, very nice," replied Ceres, after an awkward pause.

She continued to gape at the rats. She couldn't have said why she was so surprised by talking rats, not after all she'd already encountered, but she was. It might have been because rats were common in her own world, where they most definitely did not talk—or if they did, it was only behind people's backs, a possibility she now found disconcerting.

The two rats exchanged a glance. The first rat tapped a digit meaningfully to its right temple, the universal signal that they might well be dealing with an individual who was at least one slice of bread short of a sandwich.

"Ohhhhhh," said the second rat, as understanding dawned. "It takes all sorts, doesn't it?"

"Don't get me started," said the first rat, as they continued toward a small hole in the base of the tower. "Every family has one, and if you think yours doesn't, it's you."

"But I'm not mad," said Ceres to their retreating backs.

One of the rats raised a paw in acknowledgment.

"Course you're not," it said, before adding: "They all say that."

"First sign of madness," agreed its companion. "Or the second, after being mad."

Ceres gave up.

"We should be on our way," she called to Rapunzel. "It's been very interesting talking with you."

"Likewise, I'm sure," said Rapunzel. "You won't tell anyone you've seen me, will you? I'm rarely bothered, and I'd like to keep things that way. If knights and whatnot start coming around insisting on more rescues, I'm liable to become, you know—"

"Twitchy?" suggested Ceres.

"That's it exactly." Rapunzel caressed the crossbow lovingly. "Twitchy."

"If anyone asks, we never saw you," said the Woodsman, with feeling.

"That would be for the best," said Rapunzel.

They bade her farewell. Ceres remounted, and the Woodsman turned the horse away from the tower. They had just reached the tree line when a crossbow bolt thudded into a trunk barely inches from the Woodsman's head.

"You won't forget to forget, will you?" cried Rapunzel.

"No," said Ceres, frozen in the saddle, "I'm sure we won't."

"Just checking. Byeeeee!"

With a wave of a white handkerchief, Rapunzel retreated into her tower, but neither Ceres nor the Woodsman breathed easy again until they were safely out of range.

XXII

Völva

(OLD NORSE)

One Who Practices Magic Associated with Women

he tower receded from sight, which was certainly a relief to everyone involved. The forest thinned out, to be replaced by hills and meadows, the fields bordered by drystone walls, like the filaments of a net cast over the land. Dotted about were farmhouses, some close together, although nothing so large as to resemble a village or town.

"Apart from drawing attention to an act of murder," said the Woodsman, "you handled that well, all things considered."

"You mean considering we were dealing with a woman who really, really values her privacy?"

"Yes, considering that."

"Thank you. I noticed how you stayed very quiet."

"I deemed it advisable, given that the last man who spoke to her ended up being shot in the head."

"Not because he spoke to her," Ceres corrected, "but because he wouldn't listen. It's a common failing among men, I find."

"He wasn't given much opportunity to rectify it."

"If he hadn't learned to listen by that stage of his life, he was unlikely ever to progress."

"You strike me as notably unsympathetic to his fate."

"Not unsympathetic, just unsurprised. I've spent a lifetime dealing with men who declined to pay attention when I spoke, or dismissed whatever I had to say—not every man, but enough for a pattern of behavior to become apparent. Eventually, one of them was bound to push it too far. Stands to reason. I don't think men realize how much time women spend either being angry with them or trying not to be."

She was holding on to the Woodsman with only her right arm. It pained her to raise the left, and the stiffness in her neck was spreading to her back. She also wasn't used to riding on horseback, which didn't help. She didn't want to complain, but the Woodsman was too perceptive not to have noticed.

"How is that injury?"

Ceres saw no reason to lie.

"Not great," she admitted. "Tolerable. But then everything is tolerable, until it isn't."

"Use what's left of the infusion. We'll reach our destination before nightfall, and then you'll have no more need of it."

Ceres drank from the flask, but decided against emptying it out of caution, despite the Woodsman's assurances. It came from being a mother: never leave yourself and your child unsupplied, and always keep something in reserve. The effect of the concoction, combined with the motion of the horse, caused her to become drowsy, and much of the rest of the journey passed in a blur. But she saw—or dreamed she saw—a large black boot topped by a tin roof, with smoke pouring from a bowed chimney; and when they had to cross a river, their bridge was a giant glass slipper paved with thick timber planks.

At last, as the day was in decline, they came to the crest of a hill overlooking a wood cabin. Two adjoining fields were sown with crops, and enclosures for animals lay on one side of the main dwelling. Ceres saw chickens pecking at the dirt in one, and in the other a pair of pigs nuzzled in the mud. Beside the pigpen was a stable block, the head of a pony poking out from above the half door, and behind the stable was a pasture in which a cow was mooing plaintively. But all was otherwise quiet, and despite the cool of the approaching evening, no fire burned in the cottage, and its door stood ajar. The Woodsman nudged the mare on, but not before taking his axe from his back and laying it across his saddle.

"Hold tight to my belt," he said. "If we have to make our escape, it'll be fast."

They drew closer to the cabin, but no one emerged to greet them, not even when the Woodsman made their presence known.

"Mistress Blythe," he shouted, "the Woodsman calls."

Nearby, a rooster fought a hen for a single grain of corn, but that was the only feed that Ceres could spot in the dirt, because every other speck had been consumed. It made her curious as to how long it had been since the livestock were fed.

The interior of the cabin, or what little of it was visible through the gap in the door, looked very dark, but Ceres had no sense of occupancy. The Woodsman allowed the horse to continue into the dirt yard at the front before dismounting, axe in hand.

"Slip onto the saddle," he told Ceres, "and take the reins. At my whistle, the mare will break for open ground, and won't stop until she tires. Stay low, trust her, and you'll come to no harm."

"But what about you? We can't leave you behind."

"I can look after myself. Your care I'll happily entrust to this old girl."

He patted the horse's rump and it ambled away from the cabin. Using the wall to shield himself, the Woodsman pushed the door fully open.

"Hello in there," he called, and when no reply came, he entered.

The interior showed no indications of disturbance. The table was set for two, although a child's high chair stood between the two adult seats. To the right of the door was an alcove with a double bed, and a curtain that could be drawn for privacy, or to keep out the light. An empty cradle was positioned close to the bed, so that the infant's mother might easily reach out to tend to her offspring in the night. Herbs and plants hung drying from hooks on the ceiling, and those shelves that did not contain food held jars of unguents and potions. In the fireplace, a pot of stew hung over charred, cold wood. Next to it was a jug of cow's milk. The Woodsman dipped a finger in the milk and tasted it: a day old, he surmised, or more. He examined the bed, the clothing in an open chest, and what personal possessions he could see scattered about. Two adults lived here, one old, one younger, and a baby—a girl, judging by the wool doll in the cradle. But where were they?

He heard a sound behind him, and was ready with the axe, but it was only Ceres, standing in the doorway with her sword drawn.

"I thought I told you to stay with the horse," he said.

"You didn't, actually," said Ceres. She took in the room. "How many people live here?"

"Two, last time I visited: Mistress Blythe, and Golda, her daughter. Now Golda has a child of her own, and Mistress Blythe must be old. I see no evidence of a man in the household, though."

"So where have they gone?"

The Woodsman pointed to a staff by the fireplace. Beside it was a small sack made of patched leather.

"I don't know, but no aged woman would abandon her walking stick before embarking on a journey, and next to it is Mistress Blythe's healing bag. It's always with her when she travels. In addition, the infant's sling is still hanging by its cradle, there's food in the pot, and milk that's been standing for a day at least."

"Perhaps they had to leave in a hurry."

"Or were made to, against their will."

The Woodsman sniffed the air.

"What is it?" asked Ceres. "What do you smell?"

"Incense, or similar."

"I'm not surprised."

Ceres had begun to explore the shelves, with their jars of herbs and spices, of barks, oils, and resins. She inhaled deeply, drawing in the mingled scents. This was the stuff of herbal remedies. Some of the ingredients she could identify by sight, an inheritance from her mother: garlic, echinacea, feverfew, milk thistle; St. John's wort for ailments of the skin, motherwort for menstrual cramps, holly for the treatment of colic. No wonder the Woodsman had brought her to the home of Mistress Blythe. Unfortunately, the woman herself was nowhere to be found, but she'd left a notebook behind, its pages filled with drawings of plants, flowers, and roots, as well as lists of ingredients. It sat beside a bowl of rotting ink cap mushrooms, a jar of cloves, and a jug of water, the fluid from the mushrooms' decomposition ready to be mixed with water and cloves to make the ink for Mistress Blythe's quill, which lay along the spine of the open notebook.

In the women's small looking glass, its surface cloudy, Ceres caught sight of herself for the first time since the stream. Her initial thought was how strange it was for an older woman to be looking at her younger self in this way, and at this moment; but no stranger, perhaps, than for the child inside her to have watched itself grow older, year after year.

The Woodsman was now standing by the empty cradle, holding one of its blankets to his nose. When he set it down again, his face was even more troubled than before.

"We'll spend the night here," he said. "I doubt Mistress Blythe would have refused us a spot in her stable, but neither would she begrudge us a warmer place in her cottage while she and her family are absent."

"Shouldn't we look for them?"

"If they left on foot, it'll be hard to track them in the dark."

"You think some harm has come to them, don't you?"

The Woodsman headed for the door.

"The chickens have not been fed," he replied, "and that cow is lowing because it wants milking. Mistress Blythe would not have left her animals to suffer or starve. We ought to take care of them. Have you ever milked a cow?"

Ceres shook her head. She'd never even patted a cow, never mind milked one, and had been hoping to get through life without learning how.

"Then you can scatter feed for the poultry and check on the pigs. I'll stable the mare, tend to the pony, and after that we'll tackle the cow together. I don't want to leave you alone, not until we can be sure of what's happened here."

Ceres followed him out into the yard and watched as he led the mare to the stable. While he was making sure she was comfortable, and both horses had food and water, Ceres strolled over to the chicken pen. Hanging from a hook on one of the posts was a covered bucket containing vegetable peelings, apple cores, and more assorted leftovers from the kitchen, with maize and oats mixed in. She tossed half the contents into the pen, and the hens and the rooster descended on it. After her experience with the rats, she half expected one of the birds to say thank you, but the conversational skills of chickens appeared to be less highly developed than those of rodents.

She moved on to the pigpen, with its strong wooden fence. The two animals inside paid her no attention, so busy were they filling their bellies. Then Ceres saw what it was that they were eating, and suddenly she was screaming.

XXIII

Banhus
(OLD ENGLISH)

A House of Bones; A Body

he Woodsman held Ceres in his arms, her face buried in his chest. She had stopped screaming, but not shaking, and she'd been sick in her mouth. All that had spared her from making a bigger mess was her lack of appetite; she had consumed scarcely anything during the day apart from the infusion and a handful of nuts from the Woodsman's supplies.

Ceres found her voice.

"Is it . . . all of them?" she whispered.

"I can't tell," replied the Woodsman. "I want you to go into the cottage and lock the door behind you. Don't open it again until you hear my voice. Do you understand?"

But she held on even tighter. She did not want to be released, or to lift her face from his clothing. If she did, she might be forced to look again upon the bodies in the mud.

"What will you do?"

"I have to get them out of there."

He eased her back from him, turning her so that she was facing away from the pigpen, with the entrance to the cabin before her.

"Get a fire lit," he said. "It will be cold tonight, and we'll be grateful for the warmth."

Ceres weaved back inside. After what she had seen, talk of fires and warmth was inconsequential, even callous. She had only ever looked at one dead body before today, and that was her father's, lying peacefully in his hospital bed. The nurses had even combed his hair, a small act of solicitude for a man who had always been well turned out in life, and would have hated to be less so in death. No one had shown Mistress Blythe or her daughter such tenderness, instead casting them aside to be consumed by animals. As for the infant—

But Ceres did not want to think of that. To distract herself, she swept the grate clean and piled fresh wood and dry straw for a fire. In a nook in the stonework she found a wedge of flint and a piece of iron. After a few unsuccessful tries, and one grazed finger—all thanks to her weak arm—she managed to strike enough sparks to get a flame going, and soon the cottage felt less cold and empty. She waited by the window, but the Woodsman was not to be found in the gathering dusk. The cow, though, had stopped lowing, and Ceres could no longer hear the snuffling and grunting of the feeding pigs. She rarely ate meat, but even had she been more of a carnivore, she would never have touched pork or bacon again.

It was full dark by the time she heard a knock at the door, and the Woodsman spoke her name. She lifted the bolt to admit him. He was carrying a pail of milk, and although his hands were clean, his clothing was stained with blood and dirt, so she knew what it was that he had washed from his skin. On his back was one of the saddle bags containing their food, along with fresh clothes for himself. He set the bag down on the floor, then drew the curtain by the bed so he could change without embarrassing Ceres. When he returned, the soiled garments had been rolled up and secured with a strap. He set them aside and joined Ceres by the fire.

"What did you do with the bodies?" she asked.

"I buried them," he said. "There was only Mistress Blythe and her daughter. The child was not with them."

"Could she—? I mean, could the pigs have—?"

She couldn't bring herself to say it.

"No," said the Woodsman. "I think the child was taken from here after her mother and grandmother were killed."

"Who would do such a thing?"

"There's no shortage of cruelty in this world, no more than in any other."

He raised a hand to touch it to her forehead. She pulled back from it instinctively, recalling the task with which it had so recently been occupied, and then felt ashamed.

"I'm sorry," she said. "Please, go ahead."

He laid his palm against her skin.

"Your fever is up again," he said. "Show me the wound."

She pushed up her sleeve, exposing her injured arm. In the firelight, she could see how infected it had become. The flesh was puffy and red, with yellow streaks of pus running from her wrist to her neck, and she was struggling to move her fingers.

"Tomorrow we'll move on, and seek care elsewhere," said the Woodsman. "Until then, I'll make do with whatever Mistress Blythe may have left behind."

He took a mortar and pestle from the shelf and prepared a poultice from onion, ginger, garlic, and turmeric, along with eucalyptus and dandelion, before adding bread and milk to the mix. He applied it to the sting, and Ceres felt a coolness spread outward from the wound. After a few minutes she could stretch her fingers again, and the vivid redness had faded to a dull pink.

"Better," she said. "Thank you."

Together she and the Woodsman dug in the larder and discovered potatoes, turnips, carrots, and more onions, and from them they made a soup. The Woodsman threw out the stew from the pot, along with the older milk, just in case it had been tampered with by those who had killed the women. He refused even to give it to the animals.

They ate in silence. The soup was surprisingly good, helped by the herbs and spices that Ceres added from the cottage's store, but she struggled with milk fresh from the cow. It was too creamy for her taste, and so warm that it made her gag. She never kept anything heavier than low-fat in her fridge at home, and that was for Phoebe; she preferred skim herself. She decided not to attempt to explain either of these concepts to the Woodsman, who had moved on to his third mug of cow's milk, and showed no signs of stopping there. She wouldn't have put it past him to return to the cow, mug in hand, and drain the milk directly from the udder, like a man in a pub helping himself from the beer tap while the barman's back is turned.

The door was locked and bolted behind them. Ceres had spotted the big iron key on the windowsill, and the sight of it, this symbol of domesticity and security, made her feel heartbroken for Mistress Blythe and her family. Being in their home, surrounded by their handcrafted furnishings, their modest but treasured possessions, she thought she was beginning to know them, even as they lay buried in the earth they had once tended.

"What if the ones who did this should come back?" she asked the Woodsman, as he set down his empty bowl and searched in his pocket for the inevitable pipe and tobacco. It really was a very bad habit, but she couldn't begrudge him this time, not after what he had been required to do.

"They won't," he replied.

"How can you be so sure?"

"Because there's no reason for it. The women are dead, and they have the child. What else was worth taking, let alone returning for?"

"Money? Jewelry?"

"Mistress Blythe had no gemstones, and no need of them, and if the killers had been looking for gold and silver, they'd have ransacked the place before they left. If I did not know better, I would say murder was the only purpose here, but Mistress Blythe had no enemies, or none with such hatred, while Golda, when I knew her, was a mirror of her mother in disposition."

"What if it was the baby they wanted?" asked Ceres. "We can't leave her to people like that."

"Who said they were people?"

Ceres was about to ask what else they might be, but given that she had already met a water spirit and a dryad, as well as talking rats and fully mobile yews, the question was redundant.

"We still can't let them have a human child," she said, "whoever or whatever they are."

The Woodsman took a small metal tool, like a flattened nail, from his pocket, and used it to work on his pipe. He inserted the sharp tip into the shank and scoured it before blowing into the hole to scatter the debris dislodged. Then he took the flat end and scraped at the chamber to cleanse it of fragments of ash and burnt tobacco. This done, he commenced the process of filling the pipe afresh, using his finger to tamp down the tobacco. Ceres was tempted to dismiss it as a lot of fuss and bother for scant reward, but as she watched the Woodsman, she saw the comfort he took in all he did, with the smoking of the pipe as the final step. It was, for him, a form of ritual, a means of finding solace in a series of uncomplicated yet intimate routines. She used to feel the same way when she and Phoebe would share certain tasks at home: the shelling of peas (they both loved fresh peas, eating them like sweets); the making of bread; and the telling of stories at bedtime. Such small acts, such simple joys, yet they made day-to-day life more bearable, and so many of them had been taken from her since Phoebe's accident.

Now, as the Woodsman ignited a twig from the fire before applying it to the tobacco, Ceres accepted that if she were to persevere after what had befallen her family, if she were to live and not merely exist, she would have to find a way to gain fulfillment once again from rituals, including that of reading aloud. Once she was back in her own world, she would try to breathe new life into the old stories she read to Phoebe, but also discover new ones, so that through them they might embark on a different journey together. And if Ceres grew tired of the creations of others, she would make up her own. She knew she could do it now. She wasn't sure how it had come to pass, but she had already succeeded in creating two stories out of nothing. It was a kind of alchemy, inventing tales where none had existed before; and like all magic, it was better not to examine its processes too closely. Cutting the lark's throat to see how it sings, that's what her father would have called it: killing the very thing you sought to comprehend.

First, though, she had to find her way home, but they were now a day's ride from the great forest, and after the killing of Mistress Blythe and her daughter, it was likely that they would be forced to journey farther from it still. The Woodsman reminded her once more that he could only treat her wound, not heal it, and he remained convinced that Ceres would not be able to return to her own world until they discovered what had brought her to this one. There was also the fact of a missing child to consider. Ceres didn't quite know what she, or they, could do about this, only that they had to do something.

"You should rest," said the Woodsman.

"I'm not so tired yet that I want to sleep," Ceres replied. "Why don't you tell me another story? Although not a tale of fairies, not this time. In fact, why not share one about yourself? I know little about you beyond your name, and even that sounds more like an occupation than anything else."

She returned to her memories of *The Book of Lost Things*. One of its stories in particular had stayed with her, that of Red Riding Hood. Even as a child, it had always been one of her favorites.

"I know," she said. "Tell me a tale of you and the Loups."

After only the slightest of hesitations, one that spoke of old guilt, the Woodsman did.

THE WOODSMAN'S SECOND TALE

*O*nce upon a time, when I was younger and less afraid than I am now (because as we grow older we become more frightened, and so edge closer to the children we once were), a farmer arrived at my cottage to ask if I would help find his daughter, who had been missing for days. She had wandered into the woods to gather berries and not returned. The farmer and his wife searched for her, to no avail. They feared she might have been attacked by wild animals, but saw no blood, and nor could they spy the tracks of any rider who might have abducted her. Neither was she so unhappy with her lot that she would have left them without even a word of goodbye. All her worldly goods remained in their home, said the old farmer, and she was as beloved as any daughter could be.

So I went with him, because I could not turn my back on him in his *time of distress. To do nothing in the face of another's misfortune is to be no better than those who might have caused it to begin with, and the measure of the best of us is that we can correctly measure our own inconvenience against the weight of someone else's pain.*

I went to the village, and spoke to those who knew the girl, but all confirmed the truth of what her father had told me: this was a happy young woman, well liked by all, and as devoted to her parents as they were to her. The villagers, too, had aided in the search, but with no more luck than her mother and father. Their efforts might even have hampered any prospect of rescue, because in their clumsiness they could have obscured clues to her fate; a broken branch here, an imprint on moss there. On such small signs a life may hang.

At first light I entered the woods, and because my eyes were keener than those of the villagers, and this was not my first such expedition, I picked up the spoor of whatever had taken her. I spotted a dislodged stone by a rocky streambed, and part of a single print in the mud—deep, as though left by a heavy tread, or one carrying a heavy burden. But I was confused, because while it was as long as a man's foot, and showed traces of a bare heel and sole, it also displayed claw marks by the toes. If this was a man, then he was a queer one indeed, and if it was an animal, it had learned to walk on two legs, and was astute enough to use the stream to aid its escape.

But I had the scent now, and it could no longer hide from me. I came upon the place where it had left the stream, deep in the oldest, darkest reaches of that forest, and from a thorn bush I plucked a scrap of cloth: violet, like the dress of the girl who had been taken. Onward I went, even as night began to fall, until I heard the sound of weeping.

In a hollow were the entrances to five caves, and lying in the heart of the hollow were three girls, their hands and legs trussed with vines, and the youngest of them wearing a violet dress. Standing behind them were three figures, half-man, half-wolf. As I watched, one of them leaned over and licked the face of the girl in the violet dress, only to have another of the wolf-men, the biggest and strongest of them, slash at him with a paw, drawing bloody stripes across his rival's chest.

"Mine!" he said, and though the other snarled, he backed down.

Now a female voice spoke from the mouth of one of the caves, and into the light stepped a woman in a tattered red cloak. Beside her walked a massive gray wolf, and she trailed her fingers lovingly through its fur.

"Don't fight, my sons," she said. "We have one for each of you, and all will make fine wives—and if they don't, there are other appetites they can satisfy."

But there was in her tone a warning that, should they continue bickering among themselves, they would have her to reckon with, and would be the sorrier for it.

At this, her sons howled their approval at the moon.

"And what of me, Mother?"

Another of the beasts came forward, this one smaller than the others, and female.

"You must wait, my daughter," said the woman, "as men are harder to catch, but easier to tame. Your time will come, I promise you."

I stayed downwind of them, and tried not to move, for the senses of beasts are very acute, and here were wolves, and worse-than-wolves. I had heard of Blanchette, a girl in a red cloak who went missing in the forest years earlier, and of whom no trace had ever been found. Rumors had since spread from the south and east, talk of a figure in a red cloak glimpsed running between the trees, a wolf by her side; and of women whom she coaxed to join her with promises of the strange delights to be found in the company of wolves. Now it appeared that Blanchette had grown weary of trying to find mates for her sons with sweet words, and had resorted to abduction.

A young doe lay nearby, its throat torn open. On this animal Blanchette and her kin feasted, she, like her wolf husband and their hybrid sons, consuming her meat raw and bloody. I watched them reduce the doe to its bones, before these were broken and the marrow sucked. So sated was the pack by the time it was done that all its members fell into lethargy and were soon asleep. When I was sure they were dead to the world, I crept to where the girls lay, and enjoining them to be mute, cut their bonds and shepherded them from the clearing. They moved lightly, while it was I who stepped carelessly. An unseen branch snapped beneath my foot, and instantly the great gray wolf, Blanchette's mate, was awake. I nocked an arrow to my bow and loosed it at him, taking him straight through the heart. He died with a yelp, but his offspring had been alerted, and Blanchette too. My second arrow struck the middle son, the one who had licked the girl and suffered slashes from his brother for it. He stumbled, fatally wounded, and fell into the fire, where he met his end in the flames.

Now the chase was on, but I was not forced to fight alone. The girl in the violet dress joined me, and asked for the bow and arrow. I handed them over, to rely on my axe. Being young, she was not as skilled with the bow as I, but she possessed a good aim, and immediately Blanchette's daughter came to regret making herself a target. I heard her yip, and saw her snap the arrow's shaft against a tree while leaving the head embedded in her arm.

Meanwhile, the smaller of the two surviving males had loped ahead, hoping to come at us from behind, but another of the girls proved more able than he might have hoped, for she pulled a pin from her hair and stabbed him in the eye, forcing him to retreat half-blind. Yet we were tiring, and I could hear howling from all around, drawing closer and closer: more wolves, summoned to the fight by their half-breed cousins. Soon we would be over-run, the girls would be returned to their fate, and I would become food for the pack.

Then horns blew. I glimpsed torches burning in the dark, and the forms of men and women. The people of the village had followed my trail, and they would be our salvation. I let the girls run ahead to safety, while I stood my ground.

Before me stood three figures: a wolf-brother, his wolf-sister, and Blanchette. In their wake, whining and circling aimlessly, was their purblind sibling, but none came nearer. They knew their chance had passed. I waited for Blanchette to say something—a curse, a threat, a promise of revenge—but it was instead the unharmed son who spoke. His words emerged hesitantly, gutturally, but I could understand him well enough.

"I know you, Woodsman," he said. "You have killed our father and our brother, but you have not killed us, and we will not forget you. For every one of my family murdered here this night, I will claim a thousand lives, and their blood will be on your hands. A new order is emerging, an order of wolves. We will lead it, my clan and I, and in time we will rule *over all, because men will not be strong enough to stand against us. Look upon me. Remember my name. I am Leroi, and one day I will be king."*

Then all four fled, leaving me alone.

And that was the beginning of the Loups, and all that followed from them.

Ceres sat curled in her chair by the fire, lost in the story. Dreadful though it was, she had not wanted it to end.

"What of Blanchette?" she asked. "What of the sister and the purblind brother?"

"The sister was slain by Leroi," replied the Woodsman, "and the brother also."

"But why?"

"The sister—encouraged, it was said, by her mother, Blanchette—wished to be queen. Her weakened brother sided with her against Leroi, and they paid the price for it. There is only one rule in rebelling against a king, or against he who would be king: Do Not Fail."

"And Blanchette?"

The Woodsman took his pipe from his mouth. It had gone cold in the telling of the tale but he did not relight it. He stood. It was time to sleep.

"Dead, too," he replied. "By her son's hand, though she was more wolf than any of them."

XXIV

Oncýðig
(OLD ENGLISH)

To Suffer from the Want of Something or Someone

he sun brought scant warmth when it rose the next day. Ceres's arm had been tender rather than actively paining her during the night, and so she woke more refreshed, but the striations on her skin remained, and the stiffness in her neck and back was unrelenting. The Woodsman, who had slept by the fire, and kept it burning for warmth, pronounced himself cautiously pleased with his handiwork, and prepared a fresh poultice to dress the wound. Ceres, though, asked him to wait until after she'd had a chance to bathe, so he filled a metal basin with water, set it to heat over the fire, and when it was steaming, placed it on the floor before leaving her to her toilet.

Ceres located a cloth with which to wash, a rough towel with which to dry herself, and a bar of what she guessed was tallow soap—animal fat mixed with lye. From Mistress Blythe's store she added peppermint, lavender, and a hint of rosemary to the water. She then knelt on the towel, and bathed her face, hair, and torso before standing in the basin itself to take care of the rest of her body—except it was no longer hers, or not as before, just as she was no longer wholly in her own mind. She could perceive herself changing inside, reverting to a younger Ceres, as though her physical alteration were being reflected psychologically. She was surprised by how close to the surface the experiences of adolescence had remained, and how quickly they surfaced anew: the awkwardness and confusion; the sudden rushes of emotion, like fireworks exploding without cause; and the sense that her anatomy was in a state of turmoil and rebellion against her, that she did not even have control over her own corporeality. There had been swelling where all was once flat; hair where all was once smooth; even blood and pain, and the memory of the initial mortification that had come with them, because fertility had kicked in without a by-your-leave. No wonder that, when she was a teenager, she had briefly become enthralled by horror stories, and the grislier the better. When hair was popping up in unexpected places, and your own body was intent on mutation—a sometimes bloody one at that—why wouldn't you want to read tales of vampires, werewolves, and monsters, of creatures capable of transfiguration and metamorphosis? After all, they were your tribe.

So Ceres had left behind those years with gratitude—and the gruesome tales, too—rarely looking back on them with any affection. Now, returned to puberty, she was reminded not only of its difficulties but also its better aspects: the purity and ferocity of those feelings, how uncompromising they were, and the intensity of the friendships that formed out of them; or the pleasure of possessing a body that had not been marred by adult life, with no sore joints, no unwanted ribs of fat, and—mercy of mercies—no flattened arches or damaged pelvic floor from childbirth. She even stepped lighter; no surprise, she supposed, given that she now weighed considerably less than before.

But while her body was renewed, uncharted, her mind retained the discontents of adulthood: her betrayal by lovers, not least among them Phoebe's father, that childish, wasteful man; her grief at the passing of her father, the sight of his coffin being lowered into the ground, and the sound the dirt made as it landed on the lid; watching her mother grow older and weaker, and dreading what was to come—another funeral, and another grave; and Phoebe, her essence extracted from her body and placed out of reach of all. These were the burdens of maturity, and had made her who she was. She had to be careful not to let teenage Ceres sweep them from recall, even temporarily, and in doing so permit her younger self dominion. She had what some might have wished for—

an old head on young shoulders, the wisdom and experience of age combined with the strength and vitality of youth—but it wasn't sustainable.
The tension between them was too great. One or the other must win out,
and the struggle was already proving tiring.

Ceres stepped from the basin and dried herself. Her underwear was no
longer suited to purpose, being designed for a mature woman, but she'd
held on to it anyway, folding it into the pack given to her by the Woodsman. Now she washed the bra and knickers in the basin and placed them
by the fire to dry; she didn't like carrying around dirty underwear any
more than she liked wearing it. Searching through the possessions of the
dead women, she chose two shirts that looked like they might fit her with
some minor adjustments, along with a couple of pairs of handsome riding
breeches cut for a man—which might once have belonged to the absent
father of the missing baby—and a heavy cowhide jacket. Once more, she
rolled up a pair of trouser legs, passed a length of string through the belt
loops, and found that the result fit her well. In an alcove by the bed was a
comb with lengths of dark hair trapped in its teeth. Ceres did not remove
them, but left them in place as she disentangled her locks. From the mirror, her younger self, that familiar stranger, stared back at her.

"Mirror, mirror on the wall," she said aloud, "who is the fairest of
them all?"

Not you at sixteen, she decided. *You could have done with some feeding up,
and you didn't smile as much as you might have. You were also awkward and shy,
because nobody had informed you that you couldn't actually die of embarrassment.
Even if they had, you wouldn't have believed them.*

She set down the comb, strands of her hair now in intimate congress with those of another. She packed her things and went to find the
Woodsman. He was outside, scattering grain for the hens, but stopped as
she came up to him.

"You smell . . . *clean*," he finished, although she could tell he had been
trying to find another word, so doubtful did he sound.

"You should try it sometime," said Ceres. "You smell of horse, grease,
and sweat, with a hint of boiled cabbage for variety."

The Woodsman scowled, and dipped his nose toward his body. His
scowl deepened.

"I don't smell of—" he began, before catching the expression on Ceres's face.

"Got you," she said, "although you are sweaty, even after yesterday's rinse."

She lifted her left sleeve and showed him the fresh poultice.

"I think I've applied it right," she said. "It certainly feels good, and the swelling has stayed down."

The Woodsman checked the dressing and found no fault. Ceres rolled down her sleeve and began to pick wildflowers from the cottage garden.

"Where did you bury them?" she asked.

The Woodsman pointed out the grave, which he had dug close to the stable. Ceres went to it, laid the flowers on the fresh dirt, and stood with her head bowed. She was not very religious, or not in the sense of frequenting churches, but she believed in the possibility of a force or consciousness in the universe that was greater than humankind. Ceres might even have said that she believed in a world beyond her own, in a life after death—

She raised her head. The Woodsman was standing a respectful distance away, leaving one woman to commune with the souls of two others.

"Am I dead?" Ceres asked him. "Is that what's happening here? Did I hit my head when I burst through that doorway, and bleed out before anyone could get to me?"

"You don't look dead," the Woodsman replied. "You still feel pain, heat, cold, don't you?"

"I still feel everything."

"Well, then."

She saw the hint of a smile as he observed her mind working. Ceres returned her attention to the grave. The flowers added some color to the soil, but soon they, too, would be dead.

"You called this place Elsewhere," she said.

"Some call it that, but it has many names."

"I'm sure it does."

I think I have one for it, too. This is the space between.

This is Limbo.

XXV

Beorg
(OLD ENGLISH)

A Mound or Burial Place

rom a stand of long grass, the dryad, Calio, observed the girl cross the yard in front of the cabin to join the Woodsman by the stable, where a single mound marked the hole in which the two women were interred together. Calio had skulked nearby while the Woodsman dug it before carrying to it what was left of the dead and laying low their remains. He had wrapped each one in sacking from the stable, and their blood showed through, shadow upon shadow in the moonlight. Calio didn't imagine that the women weighed very much, not after the pigs had done their work; the Woodsman had been forced to fight the animals even for what little was left. Once he had placed the women together, one beside the other, he covered them with a layer of dirt before adding stones to frustrate any animal tempted to dig for their bones, then filled in the grave.

Calio was glad Mistress Blythe was dead, and her daughter with her. The crone was too immersed in the old lore, and had instructed her off-spring in it. That was why the Woodsman had gone to her in the hope of curing the girl, as Calio suspected he might, but he was too late. Now only a handful of others had the knowledge required to cure Ceres, and they, too, would soon be dealt with. By trying to aid the girl, the Woodsman would lead the way to their door, thereby contributing unwittingly to the end of human rule, and the restoration of a nobler dispensation, one in which Calio, by their actions, would have a place of honor and security. After that, they would no longer be so alone.

Calio didn't like the Woodsman. He was too capable, especially for a male; and he was old, far older than he looked, yet he would not die. Some whispered that he could not be killed, not unless time itself could be ended, but Calio knew of those who might be prepared to test the theory. His longevity notwithstanding, the Woodsman still needed to sleep, and any creature that required rest was not invulnerable.

Calio left the Woodsman and the girl, knowing that they could pick up the trail again later. They kept to the low places as they went. The damage caused by the girl could not be fully undone, and Calio's ability to disguise themselves was now permanently impaired. They could still blend into their surroundings, but only for a while, and the effort left them exhausted. Better, then, to use the gift only when absolutely necessary, and save their strength.

So Calio flitted and skulked, mile upon mile, until they came to a solitary mound in an untilled field, its sides inset with vertical stones of great antiquity. They circled the mound until they spotted a tiny breach behind the largest of the stones, a hole barely the size of their fist. Placing their mouth against it, Calio started to sing.

And from deep inside the mound, a voice sang back.

XXVI

Feorm

(OLD ENGLISH)

Food or Supplies for a Journey

he Woodsman ensured the cow was milked again before they left, and that there were sufficient scraps to keep the pigs and chickens satisfied for a day or so. He knew of some nearby farms that might be willing to add the animals to their stock. It was the kindest that could be done for them.

He saddled the Blythes' pony for Ceres. It was a little piebald, with a friendly disposition, and Ceres spent some time with it before mounting, feeding it pieces of apple from her hand and getting it used to her voice and presence. She had never been one of those girls who wanted a pony of her own—not that her parents had offered to provide one anyway, but whatever adolescent ill will she might have nursed toward them, refusing her a pony was not among its causes. Strangely, those teenage resentments were also coming back to her: how her father couldn't answer a question without turning it into a lecture, and the way in which her mother had tiptoed around his occasional solitary, melancholy moods; the conservatism of his tastes in music and film, combined with her mother's lack of interest in any popular culture whatsoever, game shows and soap operas apart; and their stubborn refusal, jointly, to see the world as Ceres did, and accept the wrongness of so many of their positions. Now she felt those old certitudes resurfacing. Even the Woodsman was beginning to vex her. God, he was so *smug.* . . .

"Are you feeling all right?" he said to her, as they prepared to depart.

"I'm fine," she replied, and heard the snap in her voice, like a trap closing on the neck of a mouse. "Why do you ask?"

"Because your expression suggests you've just licked dew from a nettle, and I was the one who advised you to do it."

She was embarrassed to have given herself away so easily. No wonder that, until she was almost twenty, her father in particular had been able to guess the direction of her thoughts at a glance. As a child, she'd been convinced he had magical powers, when instead he'd just been paying attention, and more of it than she had given him credit for. It was funny how few individuals, adult or otherwise, actually bothered to do that. Like listening instead of hearing, paying attention to others was an underrated and under-practiced art. Immediately her attitude toward both her departed father and the Woodsman moderated. God, these hormones! With them raging through her system, it was a miracle she'd reached adulthood without declaring outright war on half the people she knew, and here she was being forced to endure them a second time.

"I hate being sixteen again," said Ceres.

"I'm sure it'll pass," said the Woodsman. "I certainly hope so."

"Hey!"

But he had already given heel to his horse, so any clever reply would have been directed at his back. Ceres paid her final, passing respects to the grave marked with the flowers she'd picked. She realized that she had no idea what the Blythes might have looked like. In her own world, a home like theirs would have contained photographs, even paintings of the residents, possibly as adults *and* children, but of Mistress Blythe and her daughter there was no such record, only their store of herbs, spices, and medicines, a scattering of personal belongings, and an assortment of practical clothing. Ceres had taken something of each from the cottage: the ingredients for a fresh poultice, the comb she had used on her hair, and the breeches, shirt, and jacket she was wearing. It had not felt like stealing, not even from the dead. Rather, it was a way of commemorating them, of bringing a part of them with her on her journey. That way, they would not be forgotten by her.

Meanwhile, she and the Woodsman would also be searching for their missing child.

The piebald might have been smaller than the mare, but it was fast on its hooves and not as heavily laden, so she easily caught up with the Woodsman. Instead of immediately heading in the direction of the farms he had mentioned, the Woodsman made three circuits of the Blythes' property, each wider than the last, so that their progress took the form of a spiral. Ceres saw him checking the ground, trying to pick up the trail left by the killers, but he could find none and ultimately gave up.

"We have to move on," he said. "The dryad's poison will not long be held at bay, and even the poultices may stop working against it before the day's end. It's not like the bite of a spider or a snake. There's enchantment to that venom."

"But what about the baby?"

"We can't hunt what we can't locate. I see no boot prints, and no tracks of horses. Whoever took the infant may not have traveled on foot."

"Are you saying they flew?" asked Ceres.

"You read David's account of this place. There are creatures here that hunt and kill on the wing."

Ceres thought back to the book.

"Harpies?"

In the Greek myths she had read, harpies were half-woman, half-bird. The ones David had encountered were part woman, part bat, which made them even more fearsome, like vampires untroubled by light.

"It wasn't harpies that killed the Blythes," said the Woodsman. "They'd have fed on the corpses themselves, not left them for pigs. And if the killers had wanted the infant dead, she would have been slain alongside her mother and grandmother. It may be that we yet have some time."

But Ceres wasn't so sure. You could inflict hurt on a child without killing her, and no baby belonged with the kind of beasts, human or otherwise, that would murder their mother. Nonetheless, she did not see what choice she and the Woodsman had. They could only continue on in the hope that some greater knowledge might reveal itself.

XXVII

Eotenas
(OLD ENGLISH)

Giants

fter two hours, Ceres and the Woodsman arrived at a circular dwelling, its walls made of stone, its roof thatched. Lesser buildings of a similar shape had been constructed against it, like smaller bubbles adhering to the skin of a larger.

"I don't recognize this place," said the Woodsman.

But Ceres had seen structures like these before, if only as re-creations, or patterns uncovered during the archaeological digs her father liked to visit, and in which he would participate, if invited: It was a ring fort. The big one was the original house, and then, as the family grew, or as storage and livestock required, further rings had been added to the first.

A huge old man, nine or ten feet in height, and half as wide across, loomed from the main dwelling. He was so tall that he had to stoop low to avoid the head jamb, and so wide that he had to turn sideways to fit through the gap. Ceres could make out a horizontal cut healing on his forehead; obviously, he didn't always remember to duck when entering and leaving. A long gray beard hung to his navel, and his belly extended to his knees. He didn't look as though he'd be able to run very far or fast, but the muscles on his arms were to the Woodsman's as the Woodsman's were to Ceres's, and his hands were large enough to have enclosed her head. She wouldn't have said that his eyes were kind, but neither were they cruel. Here, Ceres thought, was a hard individual, but a fair one.

He raised his right hand, and only then did Ceres notice two younger giants, and a smaller giantess, all still in their teens, emerge from positions of concealment by the bushes and the walls. They were all over seven feet tall, but more slenderly built than the old man, if only relatively. Despite their size they had hidden themselves so well, aided by the color of their cloaks, that even Calio might have been impressed by their efforts. Each was armed with a massive hunting bow, and though they lowered them when instructed, they kept the arrows nocked and the strings half-tensed.

"Who are you, and what do you want here?" said the old giant, and his voice was so deep that it caused Ceres's insides to vibrate.

"We're travelers, on our way to a village on the other side of the chasm," answered the Woodsman. "I'm a woodsman, and this is my daughter."

But in the time it had taken them to approach the house, Ceres saw that he had once more unharnessed his axe and placed it across his saddle.

"You're well-armed for a woodsman," the giant noted, "and if you're going to lie about a child's origins, you'll have to do better than bathe her in herbs and dress her in borrowed clothing. I smelled her before I saw her, and knew she was not of these lands."

A finger as long and thick as a cucumber extended itself toward the Woodsman's axe.

"As for that plaything," the giant continued, "if we meant to kill you, you'd already be dead, and if we decide to kill you later, it won't avail you."

The Woodsman, accepting the logic of this, restored the axe to its harness.

"I remain a woodsman, but I am only the girl's guardian," he said. "Her name is Ceres."

"And I am Gogmagog," said the giant. "You are in my domain."

Ceres let out a little cry of delight: Gogmagog, the great giant of ancient Albion, one of the race of titans who, according to legend, had first settled Britain. In the stories her father told her, Brutus and his fellow warriors, fleeing the Trojan War, landed in Albion and fought the giants for the kingdom. Gogmagog, the last titan, was said to have died after being thrown from a cliff by the Trojans' champion, Corineus, although some versions spoke of him being brought in chains to London, there to serve as the city's guardian. Now here was an actual giant with the same name; not only that, Ceres was convinced he was *the* Gogmagog, for if Rapunzel could occupy a tower in the woods, why should Gogmagog not also have a role to play in her unfolding narrative?

"Do you know me, girl?" asked Gogmagog, noting her reaction.

"I have heard you spoken of," said Ceres. "Where I come from, your name is legendary."

Gogmagog preened with pride.

"You see, my children?" he said to his offspring. "I told you I was famous."

But they, in the universal way of children faced with an embarrassing father, remained visibly unimpressed.

"How long have you lived here?" asked the Woodsman.

"As long as I can remember," replied Gogmagog, but Ceres saw his face momentarily cloud with confusion. "As long as we all can remember," he added, and the younger giants' expressions mirrored his. Another individual now appeared in the doorway behind Gogmagog—a giant-wife, holding an infant in her arms, one almost as big as Ceres.

"This is my consort," said Gogmagog. "Her name is Ingeborg, with our little Goram in her arms, and these others are my sons Blundabore and Cormoran, and my daughter Gryla. The rest of my issue are out gathering wood."

As if in response, a tree crashed to the ground in a grove to the west, and the crowns of its fellows trembled fearfully in the aftermath. Ingeborg, all the while, smiled widely and welcomingly at Ceres, revealing teeth as big and square as bathroom tiles.

"What do you know of Mistress Blythe?" asked the Woodsman.

"She has been considerate toward us, and more," said Gogmagog. "She helped my wife with the birth of our new son, as it was a difficult labor. In turn, we have acted as good neighbors should."

Ceres sympathized with Ingeborg. Giving birth to Phoebe had been bad enough, thank you very much. She didn't even want to think about how much more painful it might be to push out a baby giant. Beside

Ceres, some of the tension eased from the Woodsman's body, but sadness took its place, the sorrow of one forced to share bad news.

"Mistress Blythe is dead," he said, "and her daughter, too. The child that was with them is missing."

"Dead?" said Gogmagog. "But how?"

Ceres could tell that his shock was real, and was mirrored by his family, with the children relaxing their bows completely.

"Murdered," said the Woodsman, "their bodies fed to pigs. I buried what remained, and now we seek the child, but those who took her left no trail that I can follow."

Gogmagog's wife touched his arm, and a look was exchanged between them. Gogmagog nodded in understanding.

"My wife has a better nose than I," he said, "and mine is a better nose than any hound's. We may have more success in searching than you. We will travel to the farm and see what we can discover."

"Their animals will need to be cared for," said the Woodsman. "Perhaps you could add them to your livestock."

"That we can do," said Gogmagog. Then Ingeborg spoke for the first time, her voice almost as deep as her husband's, to ask if there was anything they might require for their journey, but they had taken what they needed from the Blythes' store.

"Be careful after you cross the chasm," said Ingeborg. "There is discord on the other side, or so we have been told."

"The nobles are in dispute," explained Gogmagog. "We hear rumors of territory being seized and land despoiled. It is the way of men, because only men seek more than their share." He pointed to the tree line, from which two more of his huge sons had appeared, the first of them carrying a trunk on one shoulder, the other an axe that made the Woodsman's look dainty. "We take a single oak, but a man would covet the whole forest. It's selfish and rude."

"And even when he had that forest," said Ingeborg, "he would then set his eyes on his brother's, whether he had need of it or not, because it was not his to call his own."

"Which is why," finished Gogmagog, "we sometimes eat the rude."

Ceres wasn't sure what the appropriate reply to such an admission might be, so she elected, wisely, to say nothing at all, and was very glad that they had not been impolite to the giants.

"Ceres," said the Woodsman, "I hope you'll forgive me, but I'd like to confer with Gogmagog in private."

Ceres gave her assent. She didn't see much point in making a fuss, and whatever she needed to know, she'd discover in due course. But she doubted that the Woodsman would have done the same were she a man, or had she looked like the woman she was and not the girl she used to be. He certainly wouldn't have tried it with Rapunzel. He'd have been dodging crossbow bolts before he'd even finished the sentence.

The conversation didn't take long, and when it was over, Gogmagog's anger was obvious. But it wasn't directed at Ceres or the Woodsman, not that she could see, which meant that whatever might have been the cause of his unhappiness, they weren't it. The Woodsman rejoined her, and they thanked Gogmagog and his family for their assistance before continuing on their way.

"So the giant was not a stranger to you," said the Woodsman to Ceres, once they were out of earshot.

"I knew only his name. Where I come from, there really was a famous giant of legend called Gogmagog."

"Then that was he," said the Woodsman. "You did not bring Gogmagog here, but he is here because of you. As I told you, by your presence this world has been remade, and it has been preparing for your coming. Even Gogmagog was aware of it, because his memories, I think, rang untrue to him, like those borrowed from another. It may be that he has been in this version of Elsewhere for a long time without ever fully understanding why. I suspect that, having met you, he may now find himself less perplexed by it."

"And what about your memories?" asked Ceres. "Might they not also be borrowed?"

"No, my memories are my own."

"How can you be so sure?"

"Because," said the Woodsman, "I remember all my farewells."

XXVIII

Weem

(SCOTS)

An Inhabited Cavern or Pit

hey rode steadily, pausing only to eat and rest at an inn, where they were too much the objects of interest to want to remain long, especially since much of that interest came from the kind of men who meant nobody any good, not even themselves, and were likely to end up hanged by the law or skewered by someone more dangerous than they, when their luck inevitably ran out. In a glade by the inn, they met a man digging for mandrake with an iron spade and an ivory rod, aided by his deaf son, who would pull up the root once it was found, since the screams of a mandrake being plucked from the ground would kill any living thing that heard them. Later they passed a circle of standing stones, but Ceres was careful not to count them, even as a voice on the wind invited her to try.

"You hear it too, don't you?" asked the Woodsman.

"Yes, but I know better than to listen."

One shouldn't go counting standing stones, her father would tell her. They defied being counted accurately, and a person might go mad in the attempt; that, or dawdle too long while making the tally over and over, and come morning one more stone would have been added to the circle.

In the afternoon they reached the chasm. It was wide and deep, its base lost in mist. Ceres heard a harsh cry from below as a winged form took to the air from its perch and snatched a reckless pigeon in flight.

"Harpies," said Ceres. "I'm right, aren't I?"

"You sound excited," noted the Woodsman, "even pleased. You won't be so happy to make the Brood's acquaintance if they try to make a meal of you."

They followed the lip of the chasm south for a mile, the gap between the sides narrowing as they went, until they came to a bridge. It was made of wood and metal, with supports built into the rock at either verge, and an iron mesh to protect those crossing from attack. A high archway stood over the entrance, and from it, head down, hung the desiccated body of a harpy. Its torso had been pierced by a harpoon, the tip still protruding from its chest.

"A warning," said the Woodsman.

"To whom?"

"Other harpies, I should imagine. The trolls used to hunt them with harpoons, but the trolls seem to be gone. Still, someone was obviously paying attention to their methods."

A sign had been strung from the harpy's neck. It read BY ORDER OF BALWAIN, LORD PROTECTOR.

"'Lord,' indeed," said the Woodsman. "Who gave him such ideas above his station?"

"You know him?"

"I knew a Balwain once, but he was no lord, protective or otherwise."

To her left, Ceres spotted what appeared to be a pair of small stony hills. She guided her pony toward them, and discovered two ugly statues lying flat on the ground. The faces, grotesque and disfigured by nature, were additionally set in a rictus of agony. Strangely, the arms and legs were chained to stakes hammered deep into the ground.

"What are they supposed to represent?" she asked, as the Woodsman joined her.

"They are bridge trolls," answered the Woodsman, "or they were. At least we now know what became of them."

"You mean those were once living creatures?"

"Very much so, but it seems they didn't fare any better than that harpy under Balwain's new rule of law. He must have ordered them to be staked out, knowing that sunlight would do the rest. Trolls can stand a little sun, but not constant exposure. It turned these two to stone."

"What an appalling thing to do," said Ceres.

"If it's any comfort, Balwain would have lost men along the way. Trolls are not easy to subdue."

"I bet he didn't get his own hands dirty in the effort."

"If it's the same man, I doubt he even bothered to watch. For him, it would have been a purely practical matter, a problem to be solved as quickly and efficiently as possible."

They left the petrified trolls and started across the bridge. It groaned alarmingly under the weight of the horses, and Ceres had a premonition of the planks collapsing, and their bodies plummeting into the void; but they wouldn't perish by hitting the bottom as the harpies would have seized them long before then, which hardly counted as reassurance. Ceres tried to keep her eyes fixed straight ahead, focusing on the matching arch on the opposite side—also, she could see, adorned with a dead harpy. She had determined that she didn't like Lord Balwain. However dangerous the harpies might have been, they, like the trolls, were sentient creatures. Hanging the bodies of two of them from a bridge struck her as cruel—and unwise, because fear was very close to hate.

She soon had a chance to observe a living harpy at closer quarters when one of them ascended for a glimpse at the travelers. It had the wings of a bat, and the scaled body of a reptile, but its features were those of a woman, if a woman with the eyes of a snake and fangs to match. The harpy's hands and feet ended in black talons, and these it used to cling to the frame of the bridge as it landed above Ceres's head and set about shadowing her, its long silver hair billowing in the breeze. It smelled like a birdcage that hadn't been cleaned in years.

"What's it doing?" asked Ceres.

"Trying to frighten you," replied the Woodsman, "as a prelude to eating you."

"Well, it's succeeded with the first part, and I've no intention of obliging it with the second, so perhaps you could tell it to be about its business."

"It might be best just to ignore it."

Which was easy for the Woodsman to say, since he wasn't the one with a harpy glaring at him through a lattice of iron that no longer promised quite as much security as before. And the creature wasn't just hungry, but malevolent: hatred came off it in waves. Once again, Ceres would have debated with Lord Balwain the prudence of treating the harpies with such callousness, because this one didn't appear to have learned much of a lesson from the fate of its sisters, not unless vengeance counted.

Ahead of them loomed the far arch, and once they passed beyond it they would have no protection at all. But as they reached the end of the bridge, Ceres's pursuer took flight, returning to her sisters nestled in the cliff face. Ceres saw it dart into an opening, to be greeted with distant shrieks of inquiry.

"Why didn't it attack us once we'd cleared the bridge?" Ceres asked the Woodsman.

"The chasm is theirs, but nothing beyond," answered the Woodsman. "That's the spell that binds them. There was a time when to cross necessitated payment of a toll: generally food, depending on the size of the group. When the trolls took control, permission to pass required one to answer a riddle, or else risk falling prey to the Brood. Now 'Lord' Balwain has decided to fortify the bridge instead of permitting the harpies their due."

He paused to stare back in the direction they had come.

"Look," he said.

A dozen gaunt harpies now hovered by the lip of the chasm, kept in place by the updrafts. Floating higher than the rest was the silver-haired sister that had stalked Ceres. It scratched at the air, like a trapped animal testing the strength of its cage.

"Balwain has broken the old pact," said the Woodsman, "which means he may also have weakened the spell binding the harpies to the canyon. Their hunger could yet finish the job."

This time, when he urged his horse on, it broke into a gallop, and Ceres's little pony had to work hard to keep up.

XXIX

Venery
(MIDDLE ENGLISH)

Hunting, or the Pursuit of Sexual Desire

eres and the Woodsman kept always to the road that led from the chasm, avoiding the tree line in order to limit their exposure to predators. They saw only occasional signs of life, such as when, through a break in the woods, Ceres picked out seven small figures climbing a distant hill, each carrying a shovel or pick on his back. The last of them paused at the summit to look in their direction. He raised a hand in greeting, and Ceres waved back. Then the little man was gone, leaving her feeling unaccountably sad.

David, Ceres knew, had once traveled the same road: first alone, then with Roland, the knight errant. This was confirmed for her when, as day faded into evening, she spotted an abandoned tank in a field. David, in his narrative, had described finding a tank from the First World War, but this one was more modern, and marked with a painted Z, identifying it as Russian armor. It took Ceres only seconds to guess why: the First and Second World Wars were David's conflicts, one having ended less than a decade before he was born, the other being a part of his youth. Ceres's was a different war.

"Something else from my world," she informed the Woodsman.

"Do you want to take a closer look?"

"No," she replied, "quite the opposite."

From among the trees, a bird rose and circled, only to alight again within sight of them. Ceres half expected to see the one-eyed rook, but instead, on a branch of a beech tree, sat an owl with the head of a boy. Again, thanks to *The Book of Lost Things*, Ceres knew that these woods had once been the home of the Huntress, who fashioned new quarry for herself by fusing the bodies of children and animals, only to be killed by her creations after David's intervention. Either the owl-boy was very old, or the survivors of the Huntress's experiments had produced offspring.

The owl-boy left his perch to glide toward Ceres, before snatching the reins from her hands in an effort to draw her pony from the road. Ceres yanked the reins back, and a brief tug-of-war commenced before the owl-boy gave up and returned to his original resting place, there to hoot plaintively at her.

"He wants us to go with him," Ceres told the Woodsman, her pony now standing with its hind legs on the road and its front legs off it, looking as resigned as only a stranded pony can.

The Woodsman was in no hurry to comply.

"The woman who hunted here may be dead," he said, "but the memory of her evil persists—and more than the memory, I fear."

"You believe she haunts it?"

"Some badness does. I'd prefer to keep to the road, and you do not go where I do not."

Ceres thought he might be right about the haunted part, if nothing else. The trunks and branches of the trees in this part of the forest were so dark as to be almost black, like woodland purged by fire, and their leaves were a deep, dark green, tinged with red. They brought to mind the ivy that had begun to take over her cottage at home, and this in turn recalled to Ceres the face in the ivy of the attic room. It cautioned her, should she have required it, that other forces were at work here, ones that might well have liked to separate her from her guardian.

But she was also aware of a renewed surge of annoyance with the Woodsman. *You do not go where I do not. I mean, really!* Again, would he have been so condescending, so overly protective of her, if she were a boy? True, a young woman was vulnerable in ways different from a young man, but Ceres had long since refused to let this dictate how she lived her life. Next he'd be telling her to ride sidesaddle, or ensure that she didn't expose her leg above the ankle in mixed company.

The owl-boy was no longer alone, because other creatures were springing up from concealment: rabbit-headed girls, and a wolf-bodied boy; a bear with an old man's face, and beside him a badger-woman, her hair sharing the same mix of black and white as her fur; and a bobcat's body topped by the head of a girl about Ceres's age, her cheeks ravaged by claws, a souvenir of an old battle. All had lost the power of speech, if they'd ever possessed it, but the bear-man lifted one of his immense paws and beckoned to Ceres, making his meaning plain: *come*. None of the beasts struck her as hostile, only sorrowful.

"I don't think they mean us any harm," she said.

"They're not what I'm worried about."

"What if they need our help? You told me yourself: To do nothing in the face of another's distress puts us on the same level as those who cause it. If we turn our backs on them, how can we claim to be good?"

"But how do we balance our duty to others against a risk to ourselves?"

"Perhaps we shouldn't," Ceres replied, after taking a moment to reflect.

"Yet sometimes we must. There is no easy answer here, and conceivably not even a right one. You're correct, though: if we can help, we should."

So they left the road to accompany the beasts, the bear-man leading the way, scouting out the route easiest for the horses. Ceres was aware of the hush of the woods. She spotted birds amid the foliage, but they were all quiet, as though fearful of drawing attention to themselves; and while small mammals peered from burrows and bushes, they neither fled nor followed, but regarded the procession with sober curiosity, like passersby unexpectedly stumbling upon a stranger's funeral.

They came to a narrow dell, its borders thick with blackberry bushes. At the bottom of the dell was a stag, its coat a mix of red and silver, its head crowned by antlers of twenty-five or thirty points: a Monarch. The old deer lay dead in a wide, thick pool of its own blood, but no flies buzzed around it, and no carrion feeders had intruded. Circular wounds dotted its hindquarters, but its rear tendons had also been cut to prevent it from running away. She thought it must have taken the stag a long time to bleed out, a wicked end for such a venerable animal.

Ceres dismounted and touched a hand to its neck. Around the stag, the beasts had gathered, both ordinary creatures and hybrids. This was what they had wanted Ceres and the Woodsman to witness. The Woodsman, too, climbed down from his horse, but did not immediately approach the stag, instead investigating the margins of the glade, peering at the ground and touching his fingers to flattened grass, to the rotting stumps of trees, to a blackberry, half-bitten.

"They sat here to watch it die," he said.

"But it must have taken hours," said Ceres. "Who would let an animal suffer like that?"

"They wanted it to suffer. That was the point."

The Woodsman joined her by the corpse, kneeling to examine the incisions at its tendons, and the holes at its haunches and spine.

"No hunter, or no true hunter, would aim for this part of an animal. If they were hunting for food, or even a trophy head, they would try to take it down as cleanly and efficiently as possible. They would aim for the heart and the lungs, to make it a quick death.

"But all this"—he gestured at the trauma—"was meant only to inflict torment. Whoever did it had no need for food, or else the stag would have been butchered; and they were no collectors of trophies, since they left the head intact."

He placed the tip of a finger against one of the wounds, testing the diameter, gauging the size of the arrow that had made it, before comparing it with the puncture wound next to it. Even Ceres, who had never before beheld the damage a large arrowhead could cause to flesh, noticed they were different.

"Look in the bushes," the Woodsman told Ceres. "It may be that the killers dropped something that could give us a clue to their identity. But don't wander far."

Ceres did as he asked, even as she was sure that the Woodsman's keen eye would already have spotted any such items during his own inspection. She began a cursory search while keeping the Woodsman in sight, and caught him working on one of the arrow holes with the blade of his knife, cutting into the wound. Finally, he probed at it with the fingers of his right hand until they emerged bloody, but with a fragment clasped between them, which he palmed and pocketed before wiping his skin clean on the grass.

Ceres parted a thicket, leaving the dell behind. The reek of blood, the mingled scents of animals, living and dead, even the sweet aroma of blackberries, were combining to make her ill. She needed fresh air and a moment alone. She now knew that the Woodsman was intent upon concealing knowledge from her. He had not wanted her to witness his examination of the stag, or to see what he had extracted from its body, just as he had not wished her to overhear his conversation with Gogmagog. It was not that she didn't trust him—she wouldn't be traveling with him, or have shared close quarters, if she did not—but she was upset that he did not trust her, or not enough to be completely open with her.

Ceres paused. She could hear a voice calling. It was very faint, but she was sure it was crying out in distress. Her first instinct was to check if the Woodsman had heard it too, but when she looked back she could no longer see the bushes surrounding the dell, or any of the animals that had led them to it. They had to be nearby, because she knew she had not walked far. The voice came again, louder now. It sounded like a woman, and she was definitely calling for help.

Ceres walked on until she came to an old cottage. Its walls were thick with climbers, its windows concealed by brambles, and its condition spoke of long neglect, down to the door that dangled open on one hinge. The woman, whoever she might be, was inside, but her voice was weak, like one who had spent too long pleading to no avail.

Ceres advanced slowly, drawing her short sword as she went. She still didn't believe she'd be able to use it should she find herself under attack, and the thought of sinking sharp metal into yielding flesh increased her nausea. She had just been exposed to the devastation arrows and blades could wreak on tissue and bone. She did not wish to inflict any similar injuries on human or animal.

By now she was at the cottage door. An astringent, medicinal smell came from inside, recollected from days and nights spent by Phoebe's hospital bed, and a reminder of how desperately Ceres wanted to be reunited with her daughter. Here, in this place, she was no longer a mother; and if she was not a mother, what was she? All her old fears flooded back. Suppose even what little was left of Phoebe should be taken from her, what then? Was there a name for someone who used to have a daughter, who was once a parent?

What would I be without her? Nothing, nothing at all.

"Help. Me."

The voice was so faint that it was a wonder it had carried to Ceres as she walked in the woods. It was almost as though the connection had been more psychic than auditory, the consciousness of one troubled woman reaching out to another.

Ceres stepped out of the dusk, and into a nightmare.

XXX

Droxy
(COTSWOLDS)

Decayed Wood

y the bridge, the dryad, Calio, communed with the harpies, these sisters under the skin. Above Calio's head swayed one of the corpses hung from the arches by order of Lord Balwain. Tenderly Calio reached up a hand to run their fingers through the dead harpy's hair. The first of the moonlight caught the strands, and its radiance lent animation to a lifeless face.

"A man did this to you," said Calio, speaking, explaining, as they might have to a living creature, "because you would not bend to his will. We will make him regret it."

Before Calio, the silver-haired harpy, the oldest of the Brood, clung to the mesh of the bridge. So few of them remained now, and they were emaciated and weak, their bodies no longer even able to produce the eggs that would guarantee the survival of their species. The harpies bred parthenogenetically—that is, without the need for their eggs to be fertilized by a male—but it required them to remain in good health. Balwain, unable to strike at them in their caves, and having exhausted the efficacy of harpoons, had therefore elected to starve them to death, with the result that the species was now threatened with extinction.

The harpy recognized Calio as blood to her, but only through some old race memory, because many generations of the Brood had lived and died since a dryad last visited the chasm. She had shadowed Calio as they crossed, just as she had followed Ceres only hours earlier, but not with the hope of finding some weakness in the bridge that might have permitted her to attack. Instead she had tracked Calio because of the song they sang. This, too, was recalled by the Brood from ancient memory, when the world was old but men were young. It had not been heard for a long time, not since those who once sang it had fled before humankind.

"How many are you?" the harpy asked.

"We are every one that is and was," Calio replied.

Had Ceres been present for the exchange, even she might have felt pity for the dryad, so disconsolate did Calio sound, and so desolate was their expression.

"I hear it in your voice," said the harpy. "They are inside you, like a chorus, or an echo."

"As each one died, their essence came to us," said Calio. "We hold the memory of them within ourselves. So we are all, yet we are all alone. When we are gone, the dryads will be no more."

"How did they die?"

"Disease. Decay. Some we saw hunted down and burnt. The rest, we cannot say, because we did not witness their end."

"You seek revenge," said the harpy.

"We do. The Returning Ones will aid us, and give us shelter after."

"We, too, want revenge."

"Then take it," said Calio.

"We are bound to this place."

"Unbind yourselves. All that holds you is your own fear."

"We thought ourselves abandoned, forgotten."

"Not abandoned, never forgotten," said Calio. "But the time was not right."

"And what has changed to make it right?"

"The stranger who crossed before us, the one who travels with the Woodsman. She is part of it."

"A child," said the harpy dismissively.

"A child altered this world once before."

The harpy pointed to the corpse. "And are we the better for it?"

"The work was not completed. Bad rule was replaced by no rule at all. That must be undone. The stranger is the key. She is wanted, needed."

"By whom?"

"By the Crooked Man."

The harpy hissed her disapproval at the utterance of the name. Like all living beings, the harpies had suffered at the hands of the Crooked Man. The news of his passing had not been met with any great regret by the Brood.

"Gone," said the harpy. "Dead."

"No," said Calio, "not altogether."

XXXI

Chaffer

(MIDDLE ENGLISH)

To Haggle Over the Terms of an Agreement

ven with its damaged door to admit the gathering moonlight, the interior of the cottage was dim, shading to black in the corners and the eaves. It would have been murky even without the hindrance of nature, so small were the windows, and the dying of the day only added to the general air of decay. Ceres spied a bed covered in cobwebs, a long-disused fireplace, and a desk and chair, the latter lying on its side with its back broken.

In the center of the room stood two huge tables, stained with old blood that had faded to a dull brown over the years, and in the wood of each was embedded a blade, like the cutting edge of a guillotine. Next to the tables was a rack of knives and surgical implements, with more instruments scattered across the floor, browned also by rust and blood, and a variety of vials and tubes, all bearing a patina of dust. From the ceiling hung a system of ropes and pulley. The shelves, meanwhile, were stacked with glass jars and bottles of yellowing preservative, each containing body parts: a vessel of ears here, a canister of eyeballs there. In a third, a single, still heart.

And on the walls were mounted the heads of children and animals, the victims of the Huntress, she who had once called this charnel house home. Although their eyes were made of glass, they still seemed to Ceres to retain some memory of their final moments, haunted by all that was and all that might have been.

"Help. Me," called the voice again. "Please."

It was coming from the wall above the fireplace. One of the heads, set on a board apart from the rest, was speaking to Ceres. She crossed the floor to stand beneath it. This was not a child or an animal, but a grown woman, with long hair of black, white, and silver; and her eyes were not glass replicas, but her own. Her head had been neatly severed from her body at the base of the neck, and the exposed flesh glistened redly.

"What do you want from me?" asked Ceres.

"Water. Give me water."

Ceres spied a half-filled bucket by the fireplace. She tasted a drop of its contents on her finger, and found it brackish but not stagnant. She stood on what was left of the chair, placed the ladle against the woman's lips, and tilted. The woman swallowed the water, only for it to pour out from the severed end of her esophagus, but it was sufficient to wet her dry mouth and ease her speech.

"You're the Huntress, aren't you?" asked Ceres, stepping down.

"I was the Huntress," replied the woman. "Now I am nothing, just like you."

She heard me, thought Ceres. *She picked up on my thoughts. Be wary of her.*

"You shouldn't be so graceless, not after I gave you water."

"And what did it cost you?" replied the Huntress. "A moment of your time. But you're right: what I said was unkind, and I'm sorry for it."

"Who did this to you?"

"Who do you think? Those beasts beyond: my children, and theirs." Her eyes flicked to the left, where a bottle of clear salve rested on the stone shelf of the fireplace. "How clever they turned out to be, and how cruel. They severed my head from my body—I who gave them life, that they might become all that was best of both human and animal—and applied the salve to the wound, which is all that keeps me alive. Some curse has befallen me, for the bottle never empties, and so I cannot die, not unless they choose to permit it. And," she added, "they do not so choose."

"If they are cruel," said Ceres, "they learned it at your hand."

"That may be true. After all, if one creates monsters, one should not be surprised if they behave as such. But I was never as spiteful toward them as they are toward me, and this is a poor excuse for an existence. Their suffering was short, and when I killed, it was the work of a moment. But my persecution has been long, with no end in sight. Unless, of course, you decide to help me."

"And why would I do that?"

The Huntress smiled.

"Because, like any good hunter, I learned long ago to be cognizant of my hunting ground, to smell, hear, and feel its changes. The foundations of this cottage are deep and old. The brackets that hold my head in place are buried in its walls, and those walls are embedded in the earth. I know things that others do not, and I have heard your name spoken. Ceres: Is that not correct?"

Ceres did not deny it. "Who speaks my name?" she asked. "The one who brought me here?"

"Ah," said the Huntress, "so I have information you require, but what can you offer in trade?"

"I'm not bargaining with you," said Ceres. "You're not to be trusted."

"But you want to go home, don't you? You want to see your daughter again? Oh yes, I know about her as well. The longer you stay here, the more rapidly she fades. She does not have your voice to read to her, to tell her she is loved, to beg her to return to you. She thinks herself unwanted, an encumbrance that you would prefer to relinquish."

"That's not true!"

"I believe you," said the Huntress, "if others might be less willing. But who is to tell your daughter, trapped in a frozen body, that her fears are not real? With you gone, who can love her as you loved, and who will love you as she loved? In your world, you are a mother, and she is your daughter. Here, you are naught. It may be harsh, but it is no lie."

Every one of the Huntress's words cut Ceres. Were there no truth to them, they could not have hurt her.

"Then I ask again," said Ceres, "what do you want from me?"

"To be given the same chance that I gave my children of the forest," replied the Huntress. "To be fused with the body of an animal, and then set free. I will accept the hazard of becoming prey, of dying by tooth and claw, by arrow or spear, but I wish this misery to come to an end."

Ceres heard a noise behind her, and the Woodsman entered the cottage. With him were the bear-man and the badger-woman. But while the Woodsman was relieved to find her safe, the hybrids growled their displeasure at Ceres's intrusion, and more particularly her discourse with the woman who had made them as they were.

"I asked you not to wander," said the Woodsman.

"I didn't 'wander,'" replied Ceres. "I followed a voice. Her voice."

She pointed to the disembodied head of the Huntress, which had now fallen silent, waiting to see what unfolded and how it might be turned to her advantage.

The Woodsman took in the walls of the room, with their multitude of trophy heads.

"Is it not an apt punishment?" he said, lifting a hand to the sightless gallery of the lost. "Regard the anguish she caused, all in the name of the hunt."

It was not to him that Ceres spoke next, but to the bear-man and badger-woman, and through them to the rest. She addressed them respectfully, and with great sensitivity, but she did not falter.

"What this woman did to you was foul," she said, "and your ordeal continues. I can see it in your eyes, because I see it in my own every time I look in a mirror. A man did something awful to me. In a moment of stupidity and self-centeredness, he deprived me of my daughter, and took from her the life that should have been hers to lead. I cannot bring myself to forgive him for it, but for all the wrong that he has done, and the misery he has caused, I would not want him to suffer as my daughter and I do. I would not wish that on anyone. If I did, what kind of person would it make me?

"As long as you keep the Huntress in this condition, as long as you prolong her agony, you remain her captives. Each day you are forced to listen to her cries, and each day you apply the salve so her pain will continue. But by inflicting this torture, you compound your own. What you're doing, however justified it may appear, is not so very different from what she did to the animals and children she brought here, those who were forced to feel the bite of her blade and the sting of her arrow. But you are not her. You are better than that. Do not let her corruption cause you to forget it."

The bear-man was silent, the badger-woman too. Ceres feared she had overstepped the mark, and immediately began to regret opening her mouth. What right did she have to tell them that what they were doing was wrong? Admittedly, she could point to her own distress, but it was not the same as theirs. That was one of the curses of misfortune: every living thing was destined to suffer, because to suffer was part of life, and no one could ever completely comprehend the suffering of another, because each of us suffers in our own way. But that did not mean we should not try, and even in failing, seek to console.

"We heard the end of your conversation with her," said the Woodsman. "She offered to help you only if you would help her in return."

Ceres's shoulders sagged. She was weary, but it was a weariness beyond the physical, an exhaustion of the soul. It was unfortunate that part of her exchange with the Huntress had been overheard, but only because she had already moved beyond it.

"I don't care about her promises of help," said Ceres. "I stand by what I said, even if she never speaks to me again. This has to end. It is wrong."

"What would you have them do?" said the Woodsman. "Make her like them, and hunt her to death? Cause an animal to be put to the blade, in order to forge a new incarnation of the Huntress?"

"No, but I would ask them to destroy the bottle of salve. Whatever good it might once have done, whatever power it had to cure or heal, is forever blighted by what happened here. Without the salve, the Huntress will die, and this will be over—not forgotten, nor should it be, but ended at last."

The old bear-man brushed past the Woodsman to rear up before Ceres, and she saw what big teeth he had (all the better to bite her with), and what big claws he had (all the better to rend her with). The Woodsman gripped his axe, because even he was uncertain as to what might happen next. Ceres backed away from the bear-man, but he stepped past her, and with a sweep of a paw knocked the bottle of salve from the fireplace to shatter on the floor. From high on the wall, the Huntress released a long sigh. Instantly, the wound on her neck dried up, and her skin began to wrinkle and her flesh decay. Her eyes became albuminous, and all her hair turned white before falling from her head.

"The Crooked Man," she said, before her tongue was stilled forever. "He has returned."

XXXII

Galstar
(OLD HIGH GERMAN)

A Song or Incantation

he passing of the Huntress freed from her thrall the creatures she had birthed. With the help of Ceres and the Woodsman, they reverently removed the heads from the walls of the cottage, and by the light of burning torches buried them in a freshly dug grave beneath a willow tree. The body of the old stag was laid to rest with them, that he might watch over them, and they over him. In a second grave were interred the organs and limbs from the Huntress's collection, because these, too, were parts of people and animals. The head of the Huntress, now reduced to a bare skull, was tossed in a hole in a patch of wasteground behind the cottage, the spot destined to lie unmarked, eventually to be covered by grass and briars. Her instruments of torment were inhumed alongside her, those blades, saws, and scalpels. Finally, the Woodsman's axe chopped to pieces her operating tables, and the wreckage, along with all the furniture from the cottage and everything else it contained, was burned in a pit. The roof was removed, and fast-growing ivy was transplanted, so that the forest might reclaim the cottage, hiding it from view forever.

All this required Ceres and the Woodsman to work well into the night, giving them little time to talk. When they eventually did speak, it was alone and by the warmth of a fire far from the pit in which the Huntress's possessions had been burned. That pyre had smelled foul, and Ceres thought she could descry ghosts in the flames.

"How can the Crooked Man be alive?" Ceres asked the Woodsman. "David saw him destroy himself."

"The Huntress might have been lying."

"But she had no reason for it."

The Woodsman did not disagree, although it was clear he would have liked to. The possibility that the Crooked Man had survived was not one he was eager to entertain.

"But what can he want from you?" asked the Woodsman. "I can't see you consenting to be made queen, if that's his plan."

"Queen Ceres. It doesn't sound so bad, now that you mention it."

The Woodsman crooked an eyebrow at her.

"I'm joking," said Ceres. "Being royalty always struck me as hard work, when it wasn't just dull."

She nibbled on a wild strawberry. The creatures of the forest had brought them nuts and fruit, and the bear-man had produced a fresh trout from the river that ran to the south. Around them, animals and hybrids slept in the firelight. Only the bear-man remained awake, the fire reflected in his dark eyes, although the Woodsman had assured Ceres that nocturnal creatures were alert, and moving among the trees, led by the badger-woman. They were being well guarded.

"You still haven't told me what killed the old stag," she said.

"Because I am unsure."

But he would not meet her gaze.

"Didn't the others see what happened?"

"From what I can establish, they woke to the body."

"But they can't have slept through the stag's death. You said yourself that there are night creatures here. Surely they would have been awake, even if it happened after dark."

"Yet somehow they slumbered," said the Woodsman. "Whatever tortured the Monarch to death did not wish to be disturbed."

"A spell?"

"More than a spell, or no common one."

"Spell or not, could the Crooked Man have been responsible?"

"It wouldn't be beyond him," came the neutral reply, causing Ceres to fling the last of the strawberry into the fire, where it dissolved with a sizzle.

"Why are you lying to me?" She was trying to keep her voice down so as not to disturb the sleepers, but it was a struggle. "Why can't you just be honest?"

"I'm not lying to you," said the Woodsman evenly. "I have suspicions, but I don't want to share them until I can be sure I'm right. For that, I must consult with someone wiser about all we've seen so far: the deaths of Mistress Blythe and her daughter, the disappearance of the child, the killing of the stag—and the injury to your arm, because that, too, is part of what is happening here."

Ceres touched a finger to the wound and felt pressure, but little pain. She had applied the poultice, and so far it was working. The memory of her speech to the bear-man and badger-woman returned. She felt like such a hypocrite, because she would happily have stuck Calio's head on a wall and left it there to rot, given half a chance.

Ceres lay on the ground, with a saddlebag for a pillow, and showed her back to the Woodsman.

"Fine," she said. "Have it your way. Keep your stupid secrets to yourself."

She could not recall when last she had sounded so childish.

XXXIII

Sefa

(OLD ENGLISH)

Mind, Heart; Understanding

eres and the Woodsman said goodbye to the denizens of the forest. The bear-man clasped Ceres to his chest, and the badger-woman nuzzled her. The owl-boy sat on her shoulder and hooted his soft goodbye, and a sloth-girl curled around Ceres's feet and immediately fell asleep, requiring her to be woken by her comrades and lifted away, whereupon she promptly dozed off again. A retinue of beasts escorted them to the road, where they resumed their travels. Ceres had managed a few hours of sleep, but had woken in discomfort before dawn, the poultice completely dry, and she was sore and mildly feverish once more.

"It won't take us long to reach our destination," said the Woodsman.

They had barely exchanged two words since starting out, even if Ceres had once more given up being angry with the Woodsman. There was no point. The ire of others just washed over him. It was like arguing with a portrait on a wall. But she was quiet also because it hurt her throat to speak, and even her stomach was at war with her. Calio's poison seemed to be attacking Ceres's system with renewed vengeance to punish her for her temerity in trying to fight it. Ceres wavered in her saddle, and did not protest when the Woodsman lifted her from her pony to his horse, seating her sidesaddle in front of him. Once he was satisfied she was secure, he extended the pony's reins and tied them to the pommel of his saddle, so it could trot alongside them.

"It hurts," Ceres whispered. "It hurts so much."

Her eyelids flickered, and he could see she was fading.

"I know," said the Woodsman.

But it was not alone the pain of the dryad's sting to which she referred.

"I want her back," said Ceres. "I want her with me again."

The Woodsman gathered Ceres closer, but did not reply, because there was nothing to be said that would make this better. Then she clutched at his shirt, and her eyes were panicked.

"He's supposed to be dead. The book said so!"

Then the book, the Woodsman thought, *may have been wrong*.

Ceres relaxed against him, and her eyes saw nothing.

"Hold her still!"

"I'm trying to."

Ceres drifted in and out of consciousness. A beautiful woman with very dark skin was staring down at her, her face contorted with effort. The pain in Ceres's arm immediately sharpened. She tried to find the cause, and saw that her forearm had been sliced open, exposing the redness within. The dark-skinned woman was working at the flesh with a pair of tweezers, pulling at a dark thread that writhed like a worm in the grip of the metal.

"Stop it," said Ceres. "Please stop."

"She's awake."

It was the Woodsman's voice.

"Then dose her again," ordered the woman.

"Are you sure?"

"Do it!"

Another voice: older, male. "Too much and we'll lose her."

"Too little," said the woman, "and the surgery will kill her."

A damp rag was placed over Ceres's mouth and nose. It smelled sour, and she struggled against it, because it made her feel as though she were suffocating.

"Breathe," said the Woodsman. "Just breathe."

Ceres did, and was gone.

Light, but a faltering kind: shimmering, faint, fighting the shadows.

Fighting, failing.

Dying.

Ceres was in a tunnel deep underground. The light was coming from a grotto ahead of her. Now there was noise: the crying of a tiny child, and the child was the light. Shapes shifted around it, distorted by the glow. They were singing, singing to one another, singing to calm the infant on whom they fed. So beautiful they were, beautiful like spiders, beautiful like sharks.

Beautiful like Death Herself.

Calio was there, too, standing apart, watching but not participating, and Ceres was aware of the dryad's feelings of hurt and rejection. Something had happened, something that had left Calio forlorn, but also intensely, viciously angry.

The singing ceased. All changed. These feeders were alert, aware of an interloper, searching for whomever it might be; Calio also, seeking to locate some unseen, half-sensed presence as the child died. Ceres tried to make out faces but could not. The death of the baby meant also the end of the light, but before the descent into utter darkness Ceres picked up on difference, rage, hate.

These beings were vengeful. And they were coming.

"Ceres. Ceres, wake up."

"She's not moving."

"She's breathing, though. I'll settle for that."

"I warned you that the dose was too high. She's just a girl."

"No, she's more than that. Ceres! Ceres!"

Ceres sat in the bough of a tree. Beside her was a night heron, and on the forest floor below was Calio, cleaving to the dimness. Ceres could make out the injury to their head: a concave depression in the dryad's skull, marked by an open wound still wet with sap. Calio paused by the tree and peered up, their gaze alighting on the heron, but not on Ceres.

Ah, I see you but you can't see me. Your intuition is strong, but not strong enough to make visible what is invisible, or not yet.

The heron took flight.

Very wise. They'd have killed you, given the chance. Killed you to watch you die, and then fed on you as your life leached away, just as the others did with the child, and the old stag as well—because that was their handiwork, wasn't it?

Calio shook their head, as if to free it of an unwelcome buzzing, and continued on their way.

Except they're not like you, are they, Calio? That's why they rejected you. That's why you're so bitter. They're different, superior, and they decided to remind you of that fact. But in reality they're no better than you—distinct, maybe, but not better.

No, they're much, much worse.

"Ceres." It was the Woodsman. "Ceres, you need to come back to us."

One moment more. I like this.

A labyrinth, and a library. An intricacy of books, of stories told and wait-ing to be told. Great shelves of them, towering into obscurity, and they're always being added to, because each person's life consists of stories: sto-ries upon stories upon stories. We're not creatures of flesh and blood alone, no more than a book is just ink, paper, and card. We're beings of tale and fable. We exist as narratives. This is how we understand the world, and this is how we must be understood.

Through the labyrinth—not a maze, because a maze has many choices of direction, while a labyrinth has only a single route to its heart—a spirit moved. It had no form, or no permanent one, not any longer, yet it persisted. It was as real as the labyrinth, which was a reflection of its mind, and the books were the embodiment of its memories.

You can destroy a book. You can burn it, you can tear it to pieces and scatter them to the four winds, you can soak it until it reverts to pulp or the ink turns the water black, but you can't destroy the contents of the book, or the idea of the book, not as long as there are those who care, who remember . . .

Who read.

Neither can you destroy stories, not unless you destroy people—and some have tried.

A labyrinth of stories: stories told, stories unfolding, stories about to be born.

I see it now, Ceres thought.

"And I see you," said the Crooked Man.

Ceres came awake to the sight of the Woodsman. He smiled at her, and clasped her right hand tightly, grateful for her return. Ceres's left arm, lying outside the sheets of the bed on which she lay, was bound with white linen as far as the elbow. It pounded dully, but bearably. With the Woodsman was the dark-skinned woman. She looked almost as weary as Ceres felt. In her hands she held a bowl, covered with a cloth stained red and black.

"Welcome back," said the Woodsman.

Ceres asked for water. The Woodsman helped her sip from a clay cup, then wiped away the spillage.

"I saw them," said Ceres, when she had drained the cup dry, "below-ground. I saw a child, too, and heard its cries. They fed on it, sucking the life from it until it had no more left to give, and then it died. What are they?"

The Woodsman's smile vanished, and he exchanged a glance with the woman.

"Rest for a while longer," he said. "Then we'll talk, I promise."

He tried to release her hand, but she would not let go.

"I will rest," said Ceres, "but first, answer me. What are those things?"

Her tone brooked no argument.

"The Fae," the Woodsman answered. "The Hidden People have returned to the world."

XXXIV

Dökkálfar

(NORSE)

Dark Elves

 eres, as a little girl, seated in her father's lap, the fire burning before them, a pipe fixed in his mouth, puffs of smoke signaling his contentment. She had relished the smell of his tobacco smoke when she was young, loved how it permeated the room and infused her clothing so that she brought something of him with her wherever she went. He was a confident figure, as at home outdoors as he was among library shelves, and his scent provided her with some of that strength and confidence in turn.

Only later, when the sickness took hold of him, did she become more ambivalent about tobacco smoke. The pipes—he smoked six or seven a day, and more if he was working on some project that required especial concentration—gave him cancer of the mouth and pharynx, first stealing away the voice of this man who loved sharing stories, before slowly, inexorably claiming the rest of him. After his death, even as some childlike part of her still associated a hint of tobacco smoke with him, and always would, the memories were complicated by anger and loss. Funny how so much of her life had been tainted by those emotions. Funny, and not funny at all.

But, for now, she was back with him at five or six years of age; and he in his prime, dressed in his favorite pants and sweater: the latter less an item of clothing than a series of holes held together by threads, like a spider's conception of what a sweater might resemble; and the former made of brown moleskin, a miracle of the tailor's art—or, more likely, testament to her mother's labors, for no matter how stained or muddy the pants became on one of his trips, they would be restored to her father a day or two later as pristine as when they had first been purchased; and he would comment on how no one made trousers like these anymore, and remind Ceres and her mother that he wanted to be buried in them, and in the sweater, too, because he couldn't imagine a more appropriate costume in which to commence his study of the next world. Oh, and they should make sure that he had on his feet whatever pair of boots he had most recently broken in, as he didn't want to spend eternity in uncomfortable footwear. And they might see about including his old leather knapsack as well, along with an unused notebook and a couple of boxes of mechanical pencils. At which point Ceres's mother would suggest that, at the rate he was going, there wouldn't be any room left for him in the coffin, and they'd have to bury him with it strapped to his back. But in the end they found space for everything, and for him, because illness and death had made him so much smaller.

Stop pulling me forward to that time. Let me remain with him as he was, if only for a while.

The fire. A pipe. His slippers on his feet, and a dog's head resting on the slippers. This one is Coco, who took a year or more to learn how to bark and, once she got the hang of it, felt moved to indulge herself at every opportunity, in perpetual awe at the ability of her modest lungs to produce such a spectacular sound, and always destined to be lauded for it by her fond owner, for whom she could do no wrong. No dog of his could, nor anyone else's dog either, because any fault lay with the person, not the animal. To her father there was no such thing as a bad dog, and he could point to a succession of beloved mongrels to prove his point. If, in his favorite poem, J. Alfred Prufrock had measured out his life in coffee spoons, her father measured out his in dogs. When each passed, he would mourn it deeply and unashamedly for a day (and remember it for a lifetime) before venturing out the next morning to adopt another, invariably returning with the right one—or the right one for him, at any rate, Ceres and her mother being obliged to accommodate the quirks and foibles of whatever previously stray, abandoned, or rejected waif her father elected to take to heart and hearth.

"You have to love not one dog, but all dogs," he would explain to Ceres. "You only have them for a short time, you see. To them it's a lifetime, while for you it's never long enough. So you love each of them for what they are, because no two are ever the same. But you also love *dogness*, the fact of them in your life and the world, so they become individual chapters in a book that spans your days, and you name that book *Dog*." Dogs, too, were a story to him, one to be recorded and recalled, even as he was required to watch them grow old too fast.

Like the Hidden People watching us, marveling at how quickly we age.

"Tell me about fairies," says Ceres.

"I've told you about them a hundred times," he replies, which is a lie. He has told her about them ten times that, and more, but she never tires of hearing it, because he makes them real to her. He makes them real, because they are real to him also.

"I've forgotten," says Ceres, and he pantomimes horror at this lapse.

"But you mustn't forget!" He draws her closer, and lowers his voice, for fear they might be overheard. "You must never forget, or doubt their existence, because if you do, they'll—*come for you!*"

He grips her swiftly, tightly, and she squeals with the fright of it, the delight of it. But quickly he is serious again.

"We don't call them fairies, though," he says. "They don't like it, and if they don't like something, it's best to pay attention and act accordingly, so as not to provoke them. You don't want to be one of those foolish children who hear the word 'fairy' and picture tiny creatures with wings like a dragonfly's: tricky by nature, but benign, even helpful, when they choose—waving a wand to produce a pair of glass slippers, or granting Pinocchio's wish to become a real boy—but without any harm to them. No, that's none of them that has ever lived, or would ever wish to live. They're not like us, don't think as we do, and don't like us, not one little bit. That's why they kill us when they can.

"So we don't say 'fairies,' just as there's no call to make distinctions among elves, brownies, hobgoblins, or whatever, because they're one and the same, all facets of the same race, or that's my thinking on it. Those who want to stay on the right side of them refer to them as the 'Good People' or the 'Gentle Folk,' as if calling them what they aren't might make them so, or placate them into kindness. I've always favored 'Hidden People,' or better yet, 'Fae.' But it's wiser not to name them at all, or have cause to name them, because they may take it as a summons, and you'll have to deal with the consequences."

The pipe glows, the smoke rises. He is both with her and far away, walking the byways of the Secret Commonwealth.

"Some scholars believe them to be elementals," he says, "made of water and air, fire and earth, but if they are, there's blood in them, too, though it runs cold and blue. Others say they are old gods, gods of nature, but no gods of the natural world would be so cruel to living creatures. And then there are those who consider them to be the spirits of the first men and women ever to die, ghosts so consumed by envy of the living, and fury at what has befallen them—this shadow never to have touched another before—that they refused to accept their fate, and contrived to rebel against it. I'd submit in qualification that the Fae preexisted men, but otherwise I'll accept the very spirit of death abides in them. The dead are dwellers under the earth, and the Fae, in their own Hades, are half in love with death, which may be why they favor the dark so much—and why they're so hard to get rid of, except with fire and steel."

"Why fire and steel?" she asks.

"Fire, because all living things fear it; and steel, because it is man-made, not of the natural world. The Fae, they hunt with weapons of bronze and silver, flint and gemstone. A man will never die at the point of a more beautiful weapon than one made and wielded by the Fae, if that's any comfort as the life bleeds out of him."

The dog stirs, running in her sleep; pursuing, or being pursued.

"Did I ever tell you the tale of the Knight and the Pale Lady Death?" her father asks.

Ceres shakes her head. She knows all his stories, or thinks she does, even those she has heard only once. This one, by contrast, is new to her.

Her father checks over his shoulder, but her mother is absorbed in a conversation on the telephone. Ceres's mother worries about some of the stories her father tells her. She thinks they may give her nightmares, but Ceres's nightmares are mostly about school, or a time when her parents may no longer be with her. The terrors of the real world, potential or actual, are far worse than any folktales her father might choose to share with her.

"Well," he says, "you're old enough to hear it now. If the Fae were the first self-aware beings to die, then Death may have formed herself in their image. That's what people don't realize, you see: the Fae are death to us, but Death, too, is Fae."

And so he begins to speak.

THE FATHER'S TALE

Once upon a time, there was a knight who was returning to his own land after years of fighting abroad. He had journeyed far to win honor and glory on the field of combat, only to learn, like so many before him, that there was little of the first to be found, and none of the second, honor and glory being the myths old men peddle to the young to make them fight their wars for them. The knight had left blood on the field—his own, along with that of others—and the body of his squire, but he had also consigned a little of his soul to it, for he was less than the man he once was, and this world had become spectral to him.

After many months of wayfaring he reached a lake, with ice at its margins, where a woman sat alone on a rock, running a comb of yellow bone through her long red hair. At first he thought her young, certainly younger than he, but she had old eyes, like one who had seen too much too soon, and he suspected that his own eyes might have resembled hers. She wore a blue dress overlaid with a green cloak, and he could make out her reflection on the still surface of the lake, her dress and cloak echoing the tones of the waters and the weeds, so that she might have been a creature of that stygian, rimy place, constructed from whatever she could source or salvage from its depths.

She was beautiful, but so pale. Had he not witnessed the movement of the comb through her hair, he might have taken her for a body pulled from the lake and left to rot, thus to be returned to nature. She was unadorned, except for her clothes: no rings on her fingers, no pendants around her neck, and no jewels in her hair. The more he stared, the more the knight accepted that she had no need of them. They would not have enhanced her beauty, because it required no embellishment, and neither did she desire to add the treasures of this world to her wealth, because she was not of it. This, the knight fancied, was one of the Hidden People, the Fae.

The comb paused in its work, and her eyes found his. He saw that they were of no fixed color, but instead were in a state of constant transformation, their color alternately fading and deepening, like the sea responding to the play of sunlight. He had listened to poets speak of drowning in a woman's eyes, and believed it to be a figure of speech, but there, in that place, he understood for the first time its true meaning: a sound like the breaking of waves came to him, and concealed within it was Death's whisper.

Her lips moved, and she spoke to the knight; but the shapes made by her lips did not match the words he heard, confounding his perception, and her voice evoked the tinkling of distant bells, so that there was no distinction between utterance and melody. This was the glamor of which the old tales warned, the spell of speech woven by the Fae to bind men to their will, strong and sticky as spider silk.

"Don't be afraid," she said, and in the knight's head, a voice of warning said Be afraid.

"I'm not afraid," replied the knight, and she heard I am afraid.

She beckoned him closer, tugging on the unseen threads that were slowly winding around him, and he came to her.

"I should like some gifts from you," she said, *"and I will give you gifts in return."*

"I have none to offer," replied the knight, *"since I am not long from war. I have my horse and a small purse of gold coins. I have a sword and a strong arm. Are any of these the gifts you seek?"*

"The gifts I seek are none of those. I ask only for a garland of thorns for my head, a choker of vines for my neck, and a bracelet of buds for my wrist."

"And what will you give me in return?" asked the knight.

"Two gifts," she replied. *"The first will be my love, for a single night; the second will be an escape from this world, for I can tell that it has caused you great anguish, and you wish to forsake it, just as it has forsaken you."*

This the knight could not deny. All that was best of him lay buried in the filth of foreign fields, never to be restored. What manner of living was left to him now?

"I will bring you the gifts you desire," he said, "in exchange for yours."

So the knight collected the thorns, the vines, and the buds, and he worked with them as the sun began to set, until he had made a garland for her head, a choker for her neck, and a bracelet for her wrist. These he placed on her, and while at first her skin was chilly to the touch, it grew warmer as he fixed the garland, tied the choker, and bound the bracelet, so that a glow rose to her cheeks, and a pulse, undetected until then, made its beating felt against his thumb.

She drew the knight to her and kissed him.

"Here is my first gift," she said, as night enveloped them both, and clouds hid the stars from sight.

When the knight woke, he was standing on a desolate hillside, but he was not alone. Before him stood serried ranks of pale kings and princes, with starving lips and haunted eyes, and by his side was his lover transformed, the color gone from her, the warmth, the life, this pitiless ruler over all, the Pale Lady Death.

"Here," she told the knight, "is my second gift."

And the knight advanced to take his place among the damned.

XXXV

Cumfeorm

(OLD ENGLISH)

Hospitality Offered to a Stranger

 table had been laid with food: roasted vegetables; long-grained rice dotted with blackened onions; salads of green and purple leaves; and at the heart of the feast, a pot filled with thick stew that, from its smell, Ceres knew must be based on mutton or goat. She was seated at one end of the board, beside the Woodsman, while the remaining chairs and benches were taken up by family members and other guests. Occupying the position of authority was the dark-skinned woman who had treated Ceres's injury, and whom she now knew to be called Saada. She was the head of the village, although so far Ceres had seen no more of it than the interior of the house in which she was recovering.

From the Woodsman Ceres had learned that the village consisted of about four hundred souls. Judging by those present at the table, the inhabitants were mostly Black, with a smattering of other races, and all deferred to Saada—not least her husband, Thabasi, who had supervised the cooking and serving of the meal, assisted by their children, a son named Baako and a younger daughter called Ime. Thabasi barely touched his food, electing instead to monitor his wife closely, and respond to whatever it was she required by providing it as soon as she reached for it, or even before, with what approached a near-telepathic grasp of her needs. A slight movement of Saada's left hand saw a slice of bread appear on her plate, and a gentle inclination of her head resulted in her cup being refilled with water.

But Thabasi's actions and attitude, Ceres noted, were not in any way dutiful or fawning. They were those of a man who realizes that his wife has more important things to consider than an empty cup, or where the bread might happen to lie. If the power in the village resided in Saada, Thabasi was the one who enabled her to wield it with greater focus.

Conversation ebbed and flowed throughout the meal, all of it led by, or filtered through, Saada, but much of it in a language unknown to Ceres. Apart from seeking confirmation that the food was to their satisfaction, Saada left Ceres and the Woodsman to eat and drink undisturbed, although Ceres could tell by the frequent glances in their direction that they were the subject of discourse among the guests.

"Can you understand any of what they're saying?" whispered Ceres.

"All of it," replied the Woodsman, "and they know I can, but it would be rude, as well as tedious for both of us, to start translating everything for your benefit. Anyway, you can guess the substance of it—us, and why we're here—but the detail will become clearer after the meal."

Ceres wished everyone would hurry up and eat, then, instead of talking all the time. Her mind was filled with thoughts of the Fae and the Blythes' stolen daughter. The longer they delayed taking action, the poorer the infant's chances of survival—if she were not already dead, because Ceres couldn't be sure that this was not the child she had seen being consumed. She glimpsed again those shadowy figures sucking tendrils of light from the swaddled form. As though guessing the direction of her thoughts, the Woodsman touched her left arm.

"Patience," he said. "Progress is being made here, and more rapidly than you might think."

Ceres noticed that he had deliberately placed his fingers directly against the bandaged site of Calio's sting, but she barely flinched. The swelling and marbling were gone, aided by an ointment prepared by Saada, and her head was clearer than at any point since the dryad's attack. She was not yet fully herself—a vague feeling of intrusion and contamination lingered, along with a slight tenderness around the site of the wound—but she did feel much better.

If Thabasi devoted his attention to his wife, then his son's scrutiny of Ceres was no less intent. In fact, so disarmed by Ceres's presence was Baako that he managed to miss his mouth with his spoon on more than one occasion, and consequently his shirt was stained with stew.

"I believe you have an admirer," said the Woodsman, indicating Baako with his spoon. Baako, realizing he'd been spotted, found something interesting but elusive to pursue in his bowl.

"Oh, gross," said Ceres. "He can't be more than fourteen."

But Baako's ears were as sharp as his eyes.

"I'm fifteen," he said. "Nearly sixteen."

Ceres contrived to take in this information while simultaneously ignoring its source, a teenage skill that had apparently lain dormant while awaiting the perfect moment to be pressed into service again.

"Yuck," she said, keeping her eyes fixed on the table and away from the young man. "That makes it even worse."

"Perhaps he likes older women," whispered the Woodsman.

"You're disgusting. I'm embarrassed even to be sitting next to you."

But she couldn't help but grin. It would be hard to spell out to the boy why his attentions were unlikely to be reciprocated, although she didn't want him making cow eyes at her for the duration of their stay, however short she hoped it might be. If he persisted, she could say something to his mother, woman to woman, and let Saada take care of the explanations, because the Woodsman had revealed Ceres's predicament to her. Saada could then try to explain it to her son. Mind you, what if that succeeded only in fanning the flame? Ceres didn't even want to think about what the inside of the average fifteen-year-old boy's head might be like—"grubby" was probably the kindest word—but it wasn't beyond the bounds of possibility that the idea of a mature woman trapped in the body of a girl roughly his age could be catnip for him.

As soon as everyone had finished eating, Thabasi and the two children cleared the table, wiped it down with hot water, and dried it with a cloth. When they were done, the water was replaced by jugs of a mildly alcoholic, slightly fizzy beverage made from—the Woodsman informed

Ceres—fermented mare's milk. Baako and Ime were instructed by Saada to depart once the drinks had been poured, although Ceres could tell that the former wasn't happy to be excluded from whatever discussion was to follow, and Ime didn't look overly impressed either. The siblings were probably irritated that Ceres—who, to their eyes, was only marginally older than they—was permitted to remain while they weren't. Baako even opened his mouth to protest, until a killer stare from his mother sent him on his way.

Tough, thought Ceres. *Take it up with the boss later, and I wish you luck.*

Once the door had closed behind Baako and Ime, Saada and the rest of the guests turned their attention to the Woodsman.

"Some of us," Saada began, gesturing to the men and women at the table with her, "are reluctant to accept that the Fae might have returned. A dryad is one thing—we thought them extinct, although the evidence of the sting is irrefutable—but the Hidden People have been gone for more than a thousand years. There was a time, long ago, when they might have been observed moving between mounds at the start of each season, because it was said that they were restless beings, but no more. Most here believe them to be dead, having long withered away in their burrows, too fearful of men to show themselves, and too weak to confront them."

Saada's tone, and her expression, suggested she was not among the doubters, or was prepared to countenance more than others at her table. It caused Ceres to speculate on the kind of history shared by the Woodsman and Saada. There was some intimacy there, an old respect, even affection, but not of a kind to arouse jealousy in Saada's husband, or none that Thabasi was willing to acknowledge openly.

"The Fae were never afraid of humankind," said the Woodsman, "or no more than was prudent. They hated them, and did not wish to share the world with them, but they were not frightened. Their retreat from sight was not a surrender, or a sign of weakness, but a deliberate strategy; and if formerly they were unsettled, they may be so no longer. Theirs is a long strategy, and always has been."

"But too much time has passed," said one of the men at the table, smiling. "The strategy has failed."

His hair was white, and he was close to blind with cataracts, but he could still see well enough to pick up and drink from his cup of fermented milk without spilling a drop. It was with him that Saada had spent much of the meal quietly debating. If there was a leader of the opposition, it was he.

"You're thinking like a man, Abansi," said the Woodsman, "not the Fae. You are eighty years old, and in this place you are a respected elder, but to the Fae, you're less than a child, lately departed from the womb. Time moves slowly for them, and they are very patient. Ten, even twenty generations of men is barely enough for one of the Fae to progress from infancy to the first bloom of maturity."

"Even if that's true," argued Abansi, "it is a big leap from a few killings, and a woodland spell, to the reemergence of an ancient threat."

In reply, the Woodsman opened his right fist and placed on the table what he had been holding. It caught the torchlight, dispersing splinters of light across the wood, but transformed to green: a jade arrowhead, roughly cut and polished. Ceres had no idea what it might have been worth back in England, or even here. She knew only that she had never seen a gemstone as big in her life.

"I found that embedded in the hip of the old stag," said the Woodsman. "There's no doubting it's of Fae construction."

The Woodsman passed the arrowhead to Saada via her husband. Saada examined it, being careful to avoid the tip and edges, before placing it on the table and sliding it toward Abansi. The old man picked it up and held it close to his right eye, like a jeweler making an appraisal.

"It is the work of the Hidden People," conceded Abansi, albeit reluctantly. "It holds their chill."

He set the arrowhead down and pushed it away from him, reluctant to keep it too near.

"Perhaps someone else used it to kill the Monarch," said a young woman seated next to Abansi.

"Really?" asked the Woodsman. "Since when have hunters become so wealthy that they can afford to use jade weaponry, only to bequeath it to their quarry when they're done? As for spells, it's one thing to bewitch an individual animal, or a single man, even an entire household; but to cast much of a forest under enchantment—a host of different creatures, each with their own capacities—requires charms of a very potent kind."

He produced a second arrowhead, this one made of flint, like those her father sometimes unearthed on his digs to be added to his private collection.

"This, too, was in the old stag. His killers didn't distinguish between the stones. Each was of similar value to them, and therefore each was equally valueless. No man would think that way."

The second arrowhead he slid directly to Abansi, who set it beside the other. Ceres could tell that the old man's doubts were under siege.

"Did the Fae kill Mistress Blythe and her daughter?" asked Saada.

"And took her child, too, most likely," replied the Woodsman.

How long had he known? Ceres pondered the question. At least since he had dug the arrowhead from the old stag, but he must already have been entertaining suspicions. She brought back to mind the story he had told her on that first night in his cottage, of Morgiana and the Fae lord. Perhaps from the moment Calio had made their presence known, the Woodsman had feared what the dryad's coming might augur.

"A woman in a village a day's journey from here had her child stolen a month back," said Abansi. "A search revealed no trace of the boy."

"They hanged two men for the crime," said Saada. "Wanderers. They may have been innocent."

Abansi shrugged. "They were ne'er-do-wells. If they didn't take that child, they'd done something equally bad in the past. I was present when they were hanged, and one could tell they had blood on their hands. In the end, they deserved to dance."

There was a general murmur of approval. Ceres, who was a member of Amnesty International, and wrote letters to newspapers protesting the death penalty, forced herself to hold her tongue. She could tell she wasn't going to alter anyone's mindset here.

"If the Fae have resurfaced," said Saada to the Woodsman, "why now? What has changed? They would not return unless it was advantageous to them."

Abansi's chin indicated Ceres.

"This one," he said. "She is the change." It didn't sound as though it was one of which he greatly approved.

The Woodsman placed a hand on Ceres's shoulder, making the significance of the gesture obvious to all. She was under his protection.

"Ceres may be part of what is unfolding, but she is not the cause. Her arrival was sudden. I doubt the Fae could have anticipated it."

"Unless it was the Fae who brought her here, or are allied with the one who did."

This time, it was Thabasi who spoke. Until now he had only nodded and smiled, leaving the talking to his wife. His voice was soft—not the kind of softness that caused a person to be ignored, but a studied mildness that would lead a shrewd listener to lean closer in order not to miss what was being said. The Woodsman didn't show any surprise or disapproval at his contribution, nor did Saada, although Ceres caught a trace of amusement on her part. Ceres, who had spent enough of her adult life with couples to be able to spot their dynamics, identified this, too, as an element of the relationship between Thabasi and Saada: he might sometimes say aloud what she, out of caution or diplomacy, could not, so versant was he with the workings of her mind.

"What has been the most significant development in this realm since last I came to you?" the Woodsman asked.

"The end of the Crooked Man," answered Saada without hesitation, to nods of agreement from the rest.

"Even the Fae did not dare move against him," added Abansi. "He alone exceeded them in cleverness and cruelty."

"So it was as much from the Crooked Man as mankind that the Fae retreated," said the Woodsman, "two enemies they did not wish to challenge, or not at the same time. But with the Crooked Man gone, they may have perceived a shift in their favor, enough to risk sorties to determine if a greater campaign might succeed."

"Which is why they took the children," said Saada. "Dormant in the dark, the Fae would require little sustenance. Moving in the open, they have to feed."

"That's certain," said the Woodsman, "but it may be that they, or we, are mistaken in one important regard."

"Which would be?"

"The Crooked Man endures."

These four words provoked an uproar at the table, one that Saada struggled to subdue. Eventually she was forced to hammer a fist on the wood, restoring order.

"The Crooked Man is dead," she said, "ripped apart by his own hands. The boy David witnessed it, and we saw the evidence with our own eyes: the fallen castle, the collapsed tunnels, the spirits released from captivity to find peace. More than that, the Crooked Man was not seen again thereafter. Had he lived, he would have sought to regain power, and begin anew, but he has not troubled this world since I was a girl."

To Ceres's eyes, Saada looked to be in her late thirties, and eight decades had passed since the events described by David in his book. Maybe Saada was older than she appeared, or it was not for the Fae alone that time passed differently.

"What evidence do you have for the survival of the Crooked Man?" asked Thabasi.

"I will let Ceres tell you," said the Woodsman. He gestured for her to contribute. "Describe for us, please, how you came to be here."

Ceres did. She told them of Phoebe, the old house, and the face in the ivy. She shared with them the final words of the Huntress, and described the labyrinth of books she had observed while under the influence of Saada's narcotic, and the voice that had spoken to her there. When she was finished, the gathering weighed her testimony, making her feel like the accused awaiting the verdict of a hostile jury.

"The Huntress might have lied," said Abansi, the first to comment on what had been heard.

"To what purpose?" asked Ceres. "There was no benefit to her in being dishonest."

"Because she was wicked?" suggested Saada.

"That she was," replied Ceres. "I saw the evidence. But I think she was just relieved to be dying at last."

"I agree with Ceres," said the Woodsman. "There was no deception to the Huntress in her final moments."

"But what could the Crooked Man want of her—of you?" Saada corrected herself, redirecting the question from the Woodsman to Ceres.

"I don't know," Ceres admitted. "But I'm convinced I crossed his path while my mind wandered. He could see me, even if I could not see him, and the voice was the same as the one I heard at the house."

"If this is true," said Abansi, "he may wish to install a new queen on a different throne, and rule again through the puppet."

"I think this world has moved on too far for that," said Saada. "The Crooked Man might have been as old as the land, but everything he built during his existence fell to pieces when David defied him. If his intention is to make Ceres queen, she will be a monarch of nothing, and how would that serve him?"

Ceres didn't very much like the idea of being a pawn in conspiracies, particularly when nobody was able to figure out just what those conspiracies might involve.

"His ways are devious," said Abansi. "*Were* devious, because I still struggle to accept that he may be stalking the land once again."

"Nevertheless, we must assume that, somehow, he lives," said the Woodsman, "and we have to be vigilant. If we are wrong, and I hope we are, we will have expended energy only on being cautious; but if we are right, we will be better prepared for whatever he is planning—and it will also serve us against the Fae."

"Assuming you are correct," said Abansi, "this may be only a party of Fae scavengers, weary of the underworld and intent on making mischief."

Yet Ceres noticed that he kept his impaired gaze away from the arrowheads on the table before him. Abansi, she surmised, was a man whose sight was both willfully and physically impaired.

"The killing of women, and the abduction of children, however few, is more than mere mischief," Saada countered.

"I did not mean to sound dismissive," said Abansi, "but there is a difference between an incursion and an existential threat."

"The first can quickly become the second, if it is not dealt with," said the Woodsman.

"What would you have us do?" asked Saada.

"We all have a part to play. Ceres and I must alert Balwain to the danger. If he aspires to lead, and his protectorship amounts to more than slaughtering emaciated harpies, we'll offer him the chance to prove it. As for here, in this place, it is you, Saada, who are the priority."

"And why is that?"

"I think the Fae killed Mistress Blythe and her daughter because they were among the last adepts of the old medicine, capable of countering Fae poisons and spells. You are another, as you have proven with Ceres, which means the Fae will be safer if you, too, are dispatched. I gave a similar warning to the giant Gogmagog and his family, because it has long been known that steel forged by giants has a particular power, and the Fae would be happy to see his fires go cold, and his body with them."

"How long do we have to prepare?" asked Thabasi. "Days, weeks?"

The Woodsman shook his head.

"Hours."

XXXVI

Frumbyrdling

(OLD ENGLISH)

A Young Boy Growing His First Beard

aada's village was known to its inhabitants as Salaama, "the safe place." It was protected to the north by a steep, rocky hillside, covered with loose scree that was treacherous underfoot, alerting the inhabitants to any approach from that direction; and to the south, east, and west by a deep, fast-moving river, across which even the stoutest of horses would struggle to swim without being swept away. A bridge, wide enough for a single cart, forded the river, and was guarded on both banks. A road led from the bridge to the main gate of the village, set in a wall of stakes and thorns. The gates were closed at night, when the guards on the bridge withdrew behind the security of the walls.

But Salaama had not been attacked since the days of the Loups, and enjoyed good relations with its neighbors. As a consequence, its residents had grown comfortable, even incautious, and the watch were not above napping at their posts.

Salaama was a fortress waiting to be breached.

Ceres was taking the night air, while the debate about how best to counter the Fae went on without her. While Saada might have been the head of the village, Abansi, near-blind or otherwise, was responsible for much of its day-to-day running, including maintenance, supplies, and security. In other words, he had power and influence, even if the final decisions lay with Saada. Anything that needed to be accomplished had to be done with Abansi's cooperation; without the latter, the thing would be done badly, if it were done at all. As long as he remained unpersuaded about the Fae—and, indeed, the Crooked Man—any efforts to counter the threat they presented were destined to be undermined.

The air smelled of burning from the torches that lit the village, and the fires that provided warmth for its roundhouses, which were not wholly dissimilar from Gogmagog's ring fort. Built from stone, or wood posts, joined by panels of wattle and daub—or, in some cases, walls of straw bale and cordwood—and topped by conical thatched roofs, they resembled the houses that had provided shelter to the people of Britain until the Iron Age. Ceres could picture rainy weekend afternoons spent with her father visiting facsimiles of primitive dwellings on windswept moors, while her mother either remained huddled in the car listening to Radio 4 or, location permitting, took shelter in the nearest pub. How her father would have delighted in Salaama, Ceres reflected, the smoke seeping through the gaps in the thatch, and the small stones of its main metaled road catching the moonlight like shards of fallen stars. As a teenager she often thought it sad that he spent so much of his life immersed in yesteryear, trying always to imagine and re-create what once had been. It was leading him, she feared, to miss much that was good about the present. Then, as she grew older, and more of her own life began to stretch behind her, she recognized the importance of reaching an accommodation with the past, because there would come a time when the most precious things she possessed were her memories. Ultimately, were they not now all she had of Phoebe, and maybe all she would have?

A noise disturbed her, and she discovered Ime, Saada's daughter, observing her thoughtfully.

"Hello," said Ceres, the first word she had spoken to the girl.

"Hello," replied Ime. "What are you doing out here alone?"

"Thinking."

"About what?"

"About my home, my father, my daughter."

Ime wrinkled her nose in puzzlement.

"You're very young to have a daughter," she said.

"I'm older than I look."

"And how old is your daughter?"

"Not much younger than you."

"No, that's not true. It can't be."

"It is. I wouldn't lie about something so important."

Ime drew nearer.

"What's your daughter's name?"

"Phoebe."

"It's a nice name. What does it mean?"

"It means bright, like a light shining."

"And who is looking after her while you're away, her father?"

"I don't live with her father anymore. It's just the two of us."

"What about your own mother and father? Are they taking care of her?"

"My father is dead, and my mother lives in another country."

Ime, part of a community in which virtually every family member, and every friend, was no more than a stone's throw away, struggled to imagine such a situation. She sighed in exasperation.

"So who *is* taking care of your daughter?"

"Phoebe is sick," said Ceres. "She's in a hospital—a place where children are cared for by people like your mother. They're watching over her for me."

"And will she get better?"

"I don't know."

Ceres's voice faltered, but as it happened, Ime's interest had jumped to a more pressing subject.

"My brother likes you," she said.

"Really? I have bad news for him on that front."

But Ime was not to be so easily discouraged.

"He wants to marry you. He is planning to speak with the Woodsman about the arrangements in the morning."

"He's *what*?"

"There are some details to be worked out before an agreement can be reached, but my brother is sure that this won't take very long. He thinks the Woodsman may value you at eight cows, but he doesn't want to pay more than six." Ime nibbled on a hangnail. "Six cows is still a lot. I think he should offer four."

Ceres was affronted.

"I'm worth more than six cows," she said.

Ime shrugged, indicating that, as far as she was concerned, Ceres was overvaluing herself considerably on the cattle index.

"I'll like being your sister," she continued. "When you have your first daughter together, you can name her after me."

This conversation, Ceres decided, had taken a disturbing turn, and needed to be brought to a halt.

"That's not going to happen," said Ceres.

"Why not? Ime is a nice name."

"It's a lovely name, but I'm not marrying your brother, so the issue won't arise. Have you ever heard of the patriarchy?"

"I don't think so."

"Well, let me tell you, it's alive and well in your brother's mind. The Woodsman isn't in any position to offer me as a bride, not for all the cows in Christendom, so Baako will have to look elsewhere for his marital happiness. And when he decides he's found it, I'd strongly recommend that he first approach the young woman in question to determine if she feels the same way about him, before he begins haggling over cattle behind her back."

"That'll never work," said Ime. "It's doing things the wrong way round."

"What about your mother? Surely she can't be willing to go along with that kind of nonsense."

"When it comes to questions of marriage, she is very traditional. Also, she knows the value of a cow."

The "unlike you" remained unspoken.

"Good grief, just because you live in Bronze Age houses doesn't mean you actually have to live in the Bronze Age," Ceres finished angrily—if, admittedly, also somewhat lamely.

"What's a Bronze Age?"

"Oh, it really doesn't—"

Which was when all the torches were extinguished, plunging them into blackness.

XXXVII

Wæl

(OLD ENGLISH)

Slaughter, Carnage

ater, after the killing had stopped, Ceres would have to force herself to piece together all that had occurred, so alien was it, and so bloody. For now, in the dark, she felt the cold gust that suppressed the nearest torch, putting out the flame with a single puff, like a candle being extinguished on a birthday cake. The wind brought with it a scent of clove, incense, and—yes, she was sure of it—saffron, but overlaying a nastier aroma, the stink of decay, as if someone were trying to conceal spoiled meat by smothering it with spices before serving it to an unloved guest. She thought, too, that she had been correct to associate the loss of the light with a breath sent forth, because she heard inhalations and exhalations from close by, the sounds moving from left to right, as whoever or whatever was making them circled the two young women.

Ceres pulled Ime to her, and drew her sword from its scabbard. She hoped that some of the villagers might have noticed the torches going out and come to investigate, but no one was about. They were all safely in their houses, warming themselves by their fires. Ceres squinted into the shadows, trying to identify the threat lurking in them, but the night was growing increasingly murky, dingier than it should have been even without the torches to light it. Coils of shadow rippled through the gloom, deepening it as they came, and she was reminded of ink in water: altering, clouding, colonizing. Here, she sensed, was true dark, the kind untouched by sun, moon, or stars; the dark of the pit, of the grave.

Ceres opened her mouth to shout a warning, but no words would come, no matter how hard she tried. It was a recurring nightmare from her childhood made real, one in which she woke to an intruder in her room, a wraith that could neither be seen nor touched but was present nonetheless, and wished her only harm. Yet when she tried to summon help from her parents, she could produce not even a whisper, as the entity drew nearer and nearer, a being without shape because it represented all that she feared, terrors named and yet to be named: the pain of life, and losses still to come.

Ime was clinging to her. Ceres risked a glance down, and saw that Ime's mouth was open wide in a silent shriek. The watcher was making themselves known at last.

It was a man, or like one: very tall, with his black hair tied in a topknot, revealing an absence of external ears. Instead of being front-facing, his slitted, catlike eyes were positioned closer to the sides of his head, so there was also a hawkishness to his aspect, like a predator composed of the aspects of multiple beasts. He was dressed in a tunic of forest green, trousers of moss and brown, and leather boots without a heel. He wore no adornments, and his clothing contained no metal buttons or clasps, nothing that might alert his prey by making an unwanted noise or catching the light. Even the long sword in his hand was a dull gray, its hilt wrapped in black. The fingers that gripped it were concealed by gloves, with only the tips uncovered. As he advanced, Ceres could see why: his fingernails were long, black, and very sharp, weapons in themselves.

But he was also beautiful at first glance, even as there was a dread to it, just as there was a lethal grace to his movements. Then, as his breath came to her again, all spice and corruption, and he approached within touching distance of her, Ceres saw more plainly the nature of his ruin. His face was lined with tiny fissures and wrinkles, like an old oil painting of a young man, the aging and drying of the varnish causing the portrait to crack and warp, creating a curious hybrid of the handsome and the ugly. She caught the yellowing of his sclera, the retreat of the gums from his teeth, and the patches of skull that showed through the thinning of his hair. He resembled the animated corpse of one who had died in his prime, an extinct thing fighting its inevitable rot. Her father's words came back to her—*they're half in love with death*—and she knew she was in the presence of the Fae.

And still Ceres could not scream, but she could not move either. The sword, heavy in her hand, was frozen in place. She could only blink and breathe—and soon, if the Fae had his way, even those actions would cease. She heard him speak, though his words were incomprehensible to her, and she thought that she had probably been hearing him ever since the torches went out, and his glamor descended on her and Ime. Whispers flowed like melodies, his dark-red lips—oddly plump, like leeches that had recently fed—forming sounds in a language exotic and entrancing, even as she gleaned their purpose: to hypnotize her so she would be easier to kill.

Yet it was not Ceres for whom the Fae reached, but Ime. He gripped the child by the hair, yanking her toward him, and his sword rose to deliver a fatal strike to her neck. He drew in a deep breath to power the downward thrust, and a strange tongue popped from his mouth; not an organ of muscle and blood, but cedar and steel. The arrow had penetrated the back of the Fae's head with such force that its tip protruded some six inches from between his lips, dripping blue-black blood. The Fae remained upright for a moment, his expression briefly betraying bewilderment, before he collapsed to his knees and fell face-first to the dirt, the feathered flights of the arrow vibrating with the force of the impact, as though haunted by some final, fleeting memory of the bird of which they were once a part.

With the Fae's death, the glamor faded, and the cry of warning that had been sealed in Ceres's throat was released.

"They're here!" she screamed. "The Fae are here!"

Only as Ime added a second voice to hers did Ceres notice the bowman who had saved them. He was nocking another arrow, seeking a fresh target. He looked younger than in his final photographs, but she recognized him instantly.

"David?"

"Not now," he replied. "Can you use that sword?"

"I don't know," said Ceres. "I haven't tried yet."

"Well, you'd better get the hang of it fast."

Before she could say anything more, he was off. All around them villagers were rushing from their homes, bearing whatever weapons they had to hand, others following with torches to light the dark. From the central roundhouse appeared the Woodsman, closely followed by Saada, Thabasi, and Abansi. The Woodsman carried his axe, while the others held spears with footlong steel tips. More men and women loomed behind them, all armed.

The Woodsman rushed to Ceres and Ime, Saada and Thabasi at his heels.

"Are you hurt?" he asked.

They shook their heads as Thabasi turned the dead intruder onto his back, the shaft of the arrow snapping in the process.

"Definitely Fae," said Thabasi. "But this isn't one of our arrows."

"David killed him," Ceres told the Woodsman.

"David is here?"

Ceres had no opportunity to elaborate, because a choked cry came from next to her as Abansi began to ascend. His feet left the ground as the rope around his neck drew him toward the roof, where a stooped, shaggy figure squatted, barely visible against the enchanted Fae blackness. Some of the men below tried to grab Abansi's legs, but he was already beyond reach, his top half disappearing over the edge of the roof. Someone shot an arrow into the gloom, but Saada warned them to stop for fear of hitting Abansi, until the issue was put to rest by his body falling back to earth, minus its head. With no danger of causing him further harm, a flurry of spears and arrows was launched, but whatever had killed Abansi was already on the move again.

The Woodsman grabbed Saada.

"We have to get you back inside," he said. "You must be kept safe."

"But these are my people. I can't hide while they fight and die."

"The Fae have come to kill you. If they succeed, it won't be your people alone who will suffer in your absence."

"He's right," said Thabasi. "Without you, we are all lessened—and I," he added, "will be lost."

Saada, accepting the wisdom of the first argument, and the depth of feeling behind the second, nodded her assent. Instantly a phalanx of warriors surrounded her and Ime, spears and swords at the ready, and they retreated in battle order to the safety of the main house.

"You should go with them," the Woodsman told Ceres.

"No, I'll stay out here with you," she replied, and gave the sword an experimental swish. "Otherwise, this is only good for decoration."

The Woodsman didn't bother disagreeing. There was no time for it. Villagers were dying at the hands of the Fae.

"We can't fight them in the dark," said the Woodsman to Thabasi. "We need more light."

"Bring torches!" ordered Thabasi. "All you can find."

Within moments, fresh flames were igniting around them, and the Fae darkness shied from them, like a creature that feared being burned.

"Keep to small groups," ordered the Woodsman. "Remember, those torches are as good as steel to you. Fire is a weapon, and its light is your advantage."

A pile of unlit torches was deposited beside Ceres. She picked one up and lit it from a brazier. All around them came shouts of confusion and panic, the sources lost in the Fae murk. A shriek came from somewhere to their right, followed by a woman crying "No! No!" It sounded very close. Ceres looked to the Woodsman, and together, with Thabasi and another man behind them, they went to the woman's aid. The sinewy blackness retreated before them, and once or twice Ceres heard a distinct hiss as a tendril failed to react quickly enough, to be scorched by the flame, leaving behind a smell like ignited gunpowder.

An elderly man lay half in, half out of the doorway of a hut. Over im towered one of the Fae, this one smaller and fairer in color than the one who had confronted Ceres, with both male and female characteristics to their face and body. In their right hand they held, by one leg, a baby, the infant's face already turning purple from the blood rushing to its head. The Fae was trying to break free from the grip of a woman, most likely the child's mother, who had thrown a fishing net over the left side of the Fae's body, entangling them in the mesh from shoulder to leg so they could not easily use their sword. At the same time the woman was trying to hold on to the Fae's sword arm with her left hand while slashing ineffectually at the leathered armor with a small knife, but the Fae managed to twist the blade of their sword to slice through the mesh. They shrugged off the net and brought the sword around in a sweeping, underhand movement to eviscerate their tormentor—

Ceres, swinging her own sword with two hands, hacked with all her strength, severing the Fae's arm at the wrist. The Fae let loose a screech of agony, like an orchestra of detuned violins trying to play the same note, but the noise was silenced by the *snick* of the Woodsman's axe, and Abansi's death was appropriately avenged with another headless corpse. In death, the Fae released their grip on the baby, and its mother, now lying on the ground beneath it, caught it in her arms. Ceres checked on the old man in the doorway, but his suffering was almost at an end, and the dirt would soon be welcoming him. The woman, her baby held close, went to his side.

"I will stand sentinel over him," she said. "Go now. Others need your help."

Ceres rejoined the rest, their attention already fixed on a group of women who had cornered one of the invaders by the steep edge of the hillside, keeping it at bay with sticks, pikes, and pitchforks. The Woodsman pushed his way through the crowd, and Ceres saw that the villagers had trapped a crouching, hairy beast, easily the size of a mountain gorilla, with shaggy brown fur topped by a pale, hairless skull, its features distorted by tumorous growths.

"It's a rawhead," said the Woodsman to Ceres, "a hobgoblin."

The hobgoblin's eyes were yellow, lending it a curious, blank malevolence, but lest there had been any doubt about the matter, it held in one paw Abansi's severed head, a prize it was loath to surrender, even though it was surrounded by hostile women. Ceres could understand why: The hobgoblin's armor had blackened human skulls for epaulettes, and the leather had been inset with what at first glance resembled a multitude of pearls, but on closer examination were revealed to be human teeth. Draped over its shoulders was the thin cord with which it had snared

Abansi, while in its right hand it held a wooden mace studded with jagged spikes of quartz and jade.

As the Woodsman closed in on it, the hobgoblin bared its fangs, recognizing a new and more dangerous enemy, but the Woodsman was merely a diversion. As the hobgoblin turned its attention toward him, lifting the mace, it exposed its vulnerable underarm. Thabasi, stepping from the crowd, pierced its side with a spear, pushing the weapon through until steel found heart, and the hobgoblin shuddered and died.

"They're leaving," shouted someone in the distance, and Ceres noticed that the night was growing brighter, the darkness dissipating. The Fae were in flight.

"Hold the gates!" said another. "They've taken children."

Ceres became part of a rush of villagers to the walls, but the warning had come too late, and the damage was already done. The gates stood open, leaving the villagers to stare into the night, their faces lit by the bridge, which had been set alight by the departing Fae to secure their withdrawal and now burned with a cold blue fire.

But of the Fae themselves, and the children they had stolen, there was no sign.

XXXVIII

Wæl-Mist
(OLD ENGLISH)

*A Haze That Covers a Battlefield
and the Bodies of the Dead*

 alaama was in turmoil. Seven people were dead, and twice as many injured, while two infants, a boy and a girl, were missing. Some of the villagers were already preparing boats to cross the river in pursuit of the Fae, though the Woodsman was trying to dissuade them.

"You can't hunt the Fae in the dark," he said. "Even by daylight, they're hard to track, and if these are the same ones who killed Mistress Blythe and her daughter, they may leave no trail at all. They can also see and hear better than any of you, so you'll be easy pickings."

But they would not listen, especially not the families of the stolen children. Ceres could hardly blame them. These were mothers and fathers whose babies had been taken from them. It was unthinkable to them to do nothing more than wring their hands while they waited for dawn to come, knowing that, all the while, the Fae and their captives would be receding into the distance. Even Saada could not convince them of the wisdom of holding off.

"Let them go," she told the Woodsman sadly. "We can't make them stay."

"*You* can," the Woodsman corrected her. "You can order them to be held until sunrise."

"And do you think they'll ever forgive me for it, should their children be lost to them as a consequence?"

"The children are in no immediate danger," said the Woodsman. "The Fae will want to keep them alive, to feed on their light a little at a time. They are provisioning themselves so they can stay on the move."

"But what if they choose to gorge?" asked Saada. "What then?"

"They won't. Those children were hard-won, and cost the Fae casualties. The attack also failed in its objective of killing you, and they have sacrificed the element of surprise."

"Nevertheless, I will not prevent the families of the children from going after them immediately."

So they stood by as three boats, filled with armed men and women, crossed the river to the far side. The villagers clambered out, climbed the bank, and were swallowed by the night. Saada and the others retreated behind the walls to tend to the wounded and bury the dead, leaving the Woodsman to mutter his frustration.

"You don't understand," said Ceres quietly. "You don't have children of your own."

"What do you know?" replied the Woodsman, and the flash of anger took Ceres by surprise. He was on the verge of saying more, but managed to bite his lip before stomping back through the gates, his demeanor making it clear that he did not care to be followed.

Another voice spoke up.

"You're wrong," it said. "They're all his children."

It was David. Ceres had not talked with him since the killing of the first Fae, although she had watched him engage in a brief, close conversation with the Woodsman. David was currently sitting on the riverbank, binding a small wound to his left hand. Ceres joined him.

"What do you mean by that?" she asked.

"He's the steward of this place—of all these places, because I think it's just one world of many, or more correctly, one variant of the same world. He feels every loss."

"But it's not the same as being a mother or father," said Ceres.

"Isn't it?" David tied a knot in the bandage, and tested the binding by clenching and unclenching his fist. "Perhaps you're right. It may even be harder for him."

"Why?"

"Oh, I'm just thinking aloud. You know the line from the Bible, 'Greater love hath no man than this, that a man lay down his life for his friends'? I've always thought it was wrong. The greatest love is to lay down your life for someone you don't know. We love our children because they *are* our children. We feel for other people's children when they suffer, but in a different way. It's not as deep. It can't be. But the Woodsman isn't like that, or us. To him, all are equal."

"Except the Fae," said Ceres.

"Even them he would prefer not to hurt, but he won't stand aside and let the strong persecute the weak."

David took a flask from the pack beside him and offered it to her.

"What is it?" she asked.

"Brandy, of a kind. We make it ourselves at home. It's not bad. Burns a bit at the start, but you quickly stop noticing."

"I don't like brandy."

"Drink it anyway. You've been running on adrenaline, and soon your system is going to punish you for it. The brandy will help."

Ceres accepted the flask and sipped tentatively. David wasn't lying. The liquor tasted of cherry, which she didn't like, and scorched her throat as it went down, but she had to admit to feeling warmer and calmer as a result, although she'd have preferred a cup of sweet, strong tea. She and Phoebe shared that fondness.

"My name is Ceres, by the way," she said.

"So I've heard. How old are you, sixteen?"

"Thirty-two. I have an eight-year-old daughter."

David laughed, but not in disbelief.

"You changed the first time you came through?" he said. "That must have come as a shock."

"I hate being sixteen again. I think it was the worst year of my adolescence."

She took another mouthful of brandy, and this time managed to swallow it without spluttering.

"You've been here far longer than I have," said Ceres. "Where is this, exactly?"

"Exactly? It defies that kind of certainty. When I saw my wife and child again, I thought it might be heaven, but it's far from it if it can accommodate killers like the Fae. Still, it may be where some of us, if we have suffered deeply, and dream hard enough, can come to experience a version of the life that was denied us. Or it may be that it *is* the dream, the final firing of all those little neurons in our brain as death approaches, but that's a lot less fun to imagine, isn't it? I mean, I don't expect you're in a hurry to accept that you may be dying, are you?"

"Not really," said Ceres, "although I had wondered."

"Just as I once did. But no, this isn't death. It's close to it, though, closer than ordinary life, and if you misstep, you'll quickly find out what dying is like. And it's not eternal either. I'm growing older, just like my wife and son. A day will come when we'll have to leave here, and go to wherever is next. We may get to choose that day for ourselves, or we may not, but either way, it'll arrive when it's meant to, and I hope it'll be fast, and without pain. But there won't be any regrets. I had regrets and sorrows in my old life, but not in this one. I've loved every moment of my time here."

"Where are your wife and son now?"

"My wife is at the cottage, where she's safe. The forest will make sure of that. My son has commenced his own story, with a woman who loves him and a child on the way. I left them all when the world shifted. It shimmered for me, and I felt your arrival, so I came looking."

"Why?"

"Curiosity, and unease. I've had a shadow over me in recent weeks, one I can't identify or explain. Call it a foreboding, and it's not only that I can sense my days drawing to a close. The Fae, I think, are part of it, but it's not them alone. There's more to it."

Ceres considered how strange her life had become, that she should be having a conversation with a man who, by any reasoning, ought to be dead, and might well be, whatever theories he offered to the contrary.

Now she was about to return him to an ordeal from his youth. But then, had David not recorded a truth at the beginning of his book? We carry our childhood, the good and the bad of it, into our adult lives. In that way, we're never very far from the children we once were.

"I may know what it is," said Ceres. "It's the Crooked Man."

XXXIX

Choss
(MOUNTAINEERING)

Loose Rock, Dangerous to Climb

he Woodsman was trying to tamp tobacco into his pipe, and failing in the effort—a sure sign that he was unsettled.

This realm, like every other, was made up of a near-fathomless number of individual consciousnesses, each forced to negotiate the consequences not only of their own free will but also that of others, both known and unknown. Few wished active harm on their fellows, but sometimes, whether out of love, fear, jealousy, anger (righteous and otherwise), or shame—whatever emotion might briefly govern their actions—they managed to do them an injury. It was impossible to live a full life, to interact with people, and not occasionally hurt or be hurt. Hearts were tender, and bruised easily, although they recovered faster than some would have you believe.

Rarely, though, did one encounter active, premeditated malevolence: evil done for its own sake. It existed, but it was the exception, not the rule. Even the Fae, the Woodsman knew, were not by nature evil, although they were capable of committing evil acts. They believed the world was rightfully theirs, and they were better stewards of it than men—and who was to say they were wrong? Saada had told him more of Lord Balwain's denuded forests to the east, of the pits dug by him to extract fuel for his furnaces and gold for his coffers, and the filth he poured into rivers and streams. The Woodsman himself had stood before the harpies killed by Balwain, among the last of a race at least as old as men, slaughtered because one upstart noble refused to commit to a venerable pact that did not suit his purposes. Yes, the Fae took children, and fed on them, but they viewed humankind as an inferior species, just as human beings barely gave a second thought to the animals they slaughtered and ate.

Now men and Fae were set on a course that could lead only to further bloodshed unless some truce could be reached, though the Woodsman doubted that any such compromise might be possible. The Fae were too ancient, their belief in their superiority too established, too integral to their notion of themselves, to concede any ground; but men, though younger, were little different in that regard. In addition, they outnumbered the Fae, and were spreading farther afield every day. The Fae's time had passed. All logic and reason said so, yet something had convinced them that this might not be the case.

Why, he worried, had they given up their assault on the village so easily? True, they had left with captives—and those children would have to be recovered; their light could not be allowed to die just to feed the Fae—but their main aim had surely been to eliminate Saada, and her daughter, too, just as they had the Blythes. In this they had failed. In fact, they had barely exerted themselves in the effort . . .

The Woodsman ceased his tamping. He could see Saada, with Thabasi by her side. Both were anxiously seeking a face in the crowd that they could not discover, and searching among the dead for one they feared to find. He heard the name of their son being spoken. Baako was missing.

The Woodsman shivered. Peril was close. Above him towered the slope behind the village, and his eyes now swept its sheer face of scree, up and up, until they came to an unnatural darkness, one that concealed the peak from sight. He detected a cadence from within, like drumming, and he knew then why the Fae had terminated their raid before achieving their goal: because, where Saada was concerned, theirs was not the main force.

"Saada," he shouted, "get inside!"

Three forms dropped from the dark of the mount, swift as arrows.

Two peeled off to draw away the warriors surrounding Saada, leaving her isolated, while the third, the old, silver-haired harpy who had confronted the Woodsman and Ceres at the bridge, aimed straight for Saada herself, her approach like the stoop of a falcon, her speed astonishing. The harpy's feet impacted with bone-shattering force, the claws digging deep in Saada's flesh as she soared again, barely impeded by the weight of the dying woman, the murk descending to meet them. The remaining harpies retreated to follow their sister, the shadows accepting them also, enfolding them as they rose toward the summit, where the gloom turned to tendrils before melting into the night sky.

XL

Aelfscyne
(OLD ENGLISH)

Beautiful Like the Fae

 aako had been walking alone, lost in thought, when the Fae came. He was musing on the girl, Ceres, who had dismissed him so precipitously at the dinner table. He might have been irritated by her rejection of him, but he was not yet prepared to give up hope. Arranged marriages were common among his folk, and he knew of many couples who had been mismatched at the start only to find common ground over the years that followed; or unions to which one of the pair had initially proven resistant before coming to love—or tolerate, anyway—their partner. Of course, he was also aware of marriages in which both parties were unhappy without respite, their misery growing more pronounced with each day they spent together, but it was better to look on the bright side: those relationships were in the minority, so the odds favored a happy union for him and Ceres.

Baako, it should be noted, had been spending too much time in the company of the soon-to-be-deceased (indeed, soon-to-be-headless) Abansi, a man who was of the opinion that he—in common with most, if not all, of his sex—knew better than women, and part of the male burden was the occasional necessity of steering females in the right direction, even as their obstinacy dictated that they should take another path. Once women realized the error of their ways, Abansi counseled Baako, and the correctness of the male guidance they had received, they generally settled into a state of placid contentment, and were frequently less restive when similar situations arose in the future.

Abansi was a widower and lived alone. His wife had died many years previously, and no other woman had shown any inclination to take her place, despite Abansi's wealth and position of authority. In addition, Abansi's resentment of Saada was known to all, as was his lack of respect for her husband, whom Abansi viewed as a worm wriggling under his wife's thumb. Baako was at that awkward age when some young people resent both their father and mother, and was therefore susceptible to the influence of the crafty elder, not recognizing that he was being manipulated by Abansi in an effort to undermine Saada's authority.

For the present, though, Baako's attention was fixed on securing the strange, otherworldly girl as his bride. If the Woodsman could be persuaded to cede Ceres to him, Baako knew that his finer qualities—of which, he was satisfied, there was no shortage—would rapidly become apparent. His deliberations took him beyond the gates of the village and past the dozing guards. He crossed the bridge, attracted by the scent of the night-blooming flowers on the far bank. He thought he might pick some of the sweetest for Ceres, and lay them at her door. Should the opportunity present itself, he might even offer them in person, although from bitter experience of village life he knew that the moment one tried to do something requiring a degree of privacy, every individual in the vicinity would immediately arrive on the scene. Small communities, he reflected, had a bottomless capacity for mockery, and the memory to match.

Baako walked along the bank, plucking moonflower and jasmine, catchfly and evening primrose. When he had assembled the makings of a suitable posy, he sat by the water and began arranging them in a manner that would make them easy to transport without being damaged. After some consideration of the outcome of the guards waking just in time to see him carrying a large bunch of flowers, he removed his cloak and prepared to conceal the blooms in its folds.

At that moment a shadow moved across the water, and Baako sniffed incense and rot combined. A primitive survival instinct cautioned him to remain very still, and not for the first time, he was grateful for the color of his skin as an aid to concealment by night. Crouched in the tall grass, with the current of the river and the action of the moonlight on its surface as added distractions, he would be difficult to spot by all but the keenest eye, and then only if he moved. Even his natural body odor was masked: he had spent so long in the dining hall of his mother's house that he smelled mainly of woodsmoke, and the air around the village was always thick with it at this time of night. Without stirring, he tried to pick out what it was that had thrown its profile on the water.

Baako, like all his generation, and many long deceased, had never set eyes on one of the Fae. His childhood, however, had been filled with tales of them, told as much to discourage bad habits as to thrill or entertain. Don't go taking food from the larder after dark, or the Fae—night eaters that they are—will sniff it out, and you along with it. Don't tell lies to your mother and father, or the Fae will snip off the tip of your tongue. Don't leave chores unfinished or undone, or the Fae—who detest the incomplete—may finish them for you, before stealing you away and making you their slave, to teach you a long, hard lesson about laziness. Don't, don't, don't: if his mother and father were to be believed, the Fae spent so much time correcting misbehaving children that it was a wonder they managed to get anything else done at all.

As he aged, Baako began to question whether the Fae might ever have existed, although even the most skeptical and daring of the village youths refrained from stepping into mushroom rings, or interfering with the old mounds under which the Fae were said to sleep. But thanks to the stories, they all knew how the Fae were said to look, with their side-mounted eyes and their absence of outer ears. This one's head was completely bald, but adorned with intricate tattoos of distorted visages. So close was the Fae warrior that Baako could make out the details of the design by the light of the moon, and some trick of it animated the faces, so that their eyes rolled in their sockets and their mouths opened and closed. By a willow tree the Fae paused, a long black bow in his hands, a stone-tipped arrow nocked. Neither was he alone. He lifted a hand from the bow string and signaled with his fingers, whereupon two more Fae slipped by, making for the bridge. Alongside them ran a pair of hunched figures with distorted skulls, and of these, too, Baako had heard stories: rawheads, hobgoblins, collectors of men's bones.

Baako knew he had to warn the village. If he hollered loudly enough, he might be able to wake the sleeping guards, and even be heard by someone beyond the walls, should they be taking the air. But there were two problems with this. The first was that, so frightened was Baako, he wasn't sure he'd be able to find the strength to emit more than a croak; and the second was that as soon as he made a sound, the Fae would be on him. His choice was to stay silent and live, but only by sacrificing everyone and everything he loved; or speak, and sacrifice himself.

Baako, after only a little hesitation, made his choice. He waited until the bald Fae was some way distant before shifting position to ease the pressure on his lungs, allowing him to take the breath he needed to call out across the river. He drew that breath, but before he could release it he heard a single note of music, sharply and discordantly struck. Ahead of him, the bald Fae stopped dead: one of the faces tattooed on the back of his head had sung out a warning, and was staring directly at Baako. The Fae pivoted on his heel, and in the same movement loosed an arrow, but the slipperiness of the bank betrayed him, and the arrow missed its mark by an inch, embedding itself close to Baako's left foot. As the Fae drew another arrow from the quiver, the boy seized his opportunity.

"Th—"

A whisper, barely a syllable. The rest was smothered by an icy hand clasping itself against his mouth, and a strong arm embracing him from behind.

"Hush, child," said a woman's voice, and Baako had never heard a sound so terrible, for it held within itself the echoes of every last cry of the dying since the coming of men. The chill expanded across his face and neck, spreading swiftly over his shoulders and chest, closing on its prize.

"Shut your eyes," the woman ordered. "Don't look upon me."

Baako's eyelids fell, as much in response to her will as his own.

I failed, thought Baako. *When it mattered, I failed.*

The woman, seeming to read his mind, said, "Yes, child, you did," as a fierce, cold burning seized Baako's heart, slowing its beat and plunging him into insensibility.

It was almost a kindness.

XLI

Uht

(OLD ENGLISH)

The Period Just Before Dawn

 habasi's sword was in his hand, for all the good it might do. Around him armed men and women had assembled, poised to act, even as they continued to stare at the mountain, its peak like an incision in the sky. One of the women closed on Ceres and the Woodsman, her features contorted in grief. The front of her dress was stained with blood, but it was not her own.

"You did this," she said. "You brought the Fae down on us. They pursued you here, and now we must bury our dead because of you."

The Woodsman did not reply. He was too wise, and too filled with pity, to respond. It was left to Thabasi, who was dealing with his own loss, to speak.

"No, Rehema," he said. "They came only to warn us. Whatever came after should not be laid at their door."

The woman named Rehema looked ready to argue until she resigned herself either to the futility of it or the truth of Thabasi's words. Whatever the cause, her face emptied as all the fury departed her body. So sudden was the alteration that she almost fainted, and only Ceres's intervention prevented her from dropping. Rehema recovered herself and stared at Ceres's right hand on her forearm, appalled at the temerity of this young woman whom she had, moments earlier, been blaming for her grief.

"I'm sorry," said Ceres, and pulled her hand away. Rehema was immediately enveloped by a group of women, their cloaks closing protectively around her like the petals of a flower, shielding her from further distress.

"We have to get Saada back," said Thabasi, but Ceres heard in his voice a fracture born of despair.

"Saada is dead," said the Woodsman, as gently as he could.

"We don't know that."

But Ceres thought he did. They had all witnessed the light being extinguished from Saada's eyes as the harpy raised her up, squeezing the last of the life from her. There might even have been a dull crack as Saada's back broke, but Ceres could not be sure of that, or told herself so.

"Thabasi," said the Woodsman, "look at me."

The grieving husband turned to him.

"She is gone," the Woodsman continued. "And what was said before still stands: to venture into the night with Fae and harpies at large will only bring more deaths."

"I hear you, Woodsman, but I have to be sure," replied Thabasi. "If Saada is dead, her body must be retrieved and given a proper burial. I will not let her bones be cast into the chasm. But I will wait until first light."

Ceres had no idea how Thabasi proposed to retrieve Saada's remains from the caves of the Brood. Even with ropes, a descent would be hazardous, and that was before the harpies began defending their territory. But Thabasi needed to try, even if all he brought back were fragments. It was horrible, just horrible.

"Let's recover our strength," said the Woodsman. "I would advise setting watchers, though I doubt the Fae will return."

He did not need to add that, thanks to the attack by the harpies, the Fae had partly achieved what they had set out to do. Neither did he mention the harpies themselves; they, too, would have no need to come back to the village, not with a corpse to occupy them.

"And Baako?" said Thabasi. He glanced around, seeking his son among those present and failing to discover him. "Has he not yet been found?"

There was a general shaking of heads.

"He, too, we will search for come light," said the Woodsman.

"I want to kill them," said Thabasi. "I want to kill them all."

The Woodsman did not reply, but it didn't take much effort for Ceres to read his thoughts: *Then you and the Fae have that much in common.*

Nearby stood David. How could he love such a place, when it was so dangerous, so filled with misfortune? But then Ceres remembered her own life back in—she was going to call it the "real" world, but who was to say any longer what was real or unreal? Call it the "old" world then, with her old life. That world also contained more than anyone's fair share of misery: Phoebe was proof of that. There were some people for whom it all became too much, and Ceres herself had come close to feeling that way. What kept her going was her love for her daughter, and a duty not to abandon her, but also those instances of peace and beauty that were given to everyone, those occasions of joy, however fleeting, that made life bearable, and enabled us to carry on. David had learned to accept the horrors of this place, this Elsewhere, because it allowed him to be with his wife and son again. If you concentrated only on the worst aspects of existence, they became all you saw, but they were never all there was, even when everything was at its bleakest.

As Thabasi stood desolate and distraught, Ime arrived, weeping for her lost mother. The man embraced the child, and the anguish of two became one. Ceres walked away, leaving them alone with their heartbreak, yet not utterly alone.

We go on, she thought. *It's not the only thing to be done, just the best we can do.*

As Ceres was trudging to the bedroom that had been set aside for her by Saada, seeking to snatch even an hour or two of sleep before they set out again, cries arose from outside.

"Baako! It is Baako!"

Ceres joined a throng, led by Thabasi and the Woodsman, that was making its way to the river. There, on the opposite bank, by the ruins of the burned bridge, stood Baako. A boat crewed by four villagers—

two to row and two to watch for trouble—was already making its way across the water to retrieve him. Quickly Baako was helped inside and brought back. His father was the first to greet him as the prow of the boat touched the bank, wading into the water to hug his son, but Baako barely responded to this show of emotion, and his arms hung limply by his sides. He appeared to Ceres to be in a state of complete shock, if otherwise unharmed. A blanket was produced to warm him, and helped by his father, Baako walked blankly to his home, the retinue following. When they reached the main house, Ime was waiting. She called her brother's name, but he did not respond.

"He is disordered," explained an old man to Ime. Ceres thought they might be related, because she had heard Ime call him "uncle" during the meal, although the Woodsman had explained to her that in the village words like "uncle" and "aunt" were used as terms of endearment by the young to the old, even among those who were not kinsfolk. "He has seen something so frightful that it has caused him to take leave of his senses. He needs rest, and the security of home. With these, his senses will return."

But Ime didn't look convinced, and neither did the Woodsman, who was observing Baako with apprehension—even, Ceres might have said, suspicion. As Ceres, barely able to keep her eyes open, prepared to make another attempt to reach her bed, the Woodsman took her by the elbow and led her to a corner so that they could speak without being overheard.

"Is there a bar on your door?" the Woodsman asked.

"I think so."

"Then use it," he said.

XLII

Utlendisc
(OLD ENGLISH)

Strange

t was still dark when Ceres woke to a scratching at her door. She didn't know how long she had been asleep, but it felt like she had just laid her head on the pillow. As instructed by the Woodsman, she had barred the door before going to bed, leaving open only the room's small window to admit some air.

"Let me in," said a girl's voice. It sounded like Ime. "Please, Ceres, let me in."

Ceres told Ime that she was on her way, but not before unsheathing her sword and holding it by her side. She pulled the bar, but braced her right knee and foot against the door as she opened it, thereby making it marginally harder for anyone outside to force their way in. But when she looked through the gap, there was only Ime to be seen. Ceres pulled the girl inside, and closed and barred the door again behind them.

"Ime, what's wrong?"

"It's Baako," she said. "He's not the same."

Ceres knelt before the girl.

"We don't know what happened to him by the river," said Ceres, "or what he might have seen there. Baako's not himself, but that will pass."

"You don't understand," said Ime. "He's not Baako."

Ceres stared at her in confusion.

"What do you mean, he's not Baako? He's in a stupor, but that doesn't mean he won't recover, given time."

"You don't understand. Baako is left-handed. He does everything with it. But this Baako, he uses his right. I saw him as he was going through his things in his room. He was lifting them with his right hand, and gaping at them like he'd never seen them before."

Ceres was somewhat versed in trauma from her time spent discussing Phoebe's care with doctors and therapists. Sometimes, after a head injury, people developed new abilities, and she supposed it could involve, in certain cases, a change to the way in which they used their hands. But Baako, as far as anyone could tell, had suffered no injury; and after all that had taken place, it was no surprise that Ime might also be struggling to adjust. She had been spared the sight of her mother's abduction, but that was scant comfort. Here was a traumatized young girl.

"We'll talk to the Woodsman about it," said Ceres. "But I need to lie down for a while longer. I'll fall apart if I don't. Would you feel safer sleeping in here with me?"

Ime nodded. The bed was big enough to take both of them, with a bit of a squeeze, because Ime was a small child. Ime curled herself around Ceres, her head resting on Ceres's chest, and was soon asleep. Ceres remained awake, but not because of what Ime had said about Baako, perturbing though it was. She wanted to enjoy the feel of the girl against her, because it reminded her of Phoebe, and how she, too, used to love sharing a bed, falling asleep with her head against Ceres, lulled by the sound of the heartbeat she had known from the womb.

So Ceres imagined that this was Phoebe, with her once again. She hummed to the sleeping girl a refrain of her own creation, a wordless air of love and loss, and to Ceres her own voice sounded sweeter and higher than she remembered. She had never been a particularly good singer, and never in tune, but she was both now. It reminded her of the Fae glamor.

Beside the bed lay her short sword. She thought about returning it to its scabbard, as the Woodsman had instructed her to do ("Unsheathe a sword," he had advised, "only if you intend to use it. Otherwise, keep its steel concealed."), but there came to her an image of Baako, blank-eyed in his room, picking up objects that should have been recognizable to him and examining them anew, all with the wrong hand.

"He's not the same . . . He's not Baako."

Ceres left the blade exposed and tried to rest.

XLIII

Cræft

(OLD ENGLISH)

Skill

eres saw herself in the bed, Ime beside her. She stood apart from her own slumbering form so that she was both watcher and watched, and she walked through her dreams as a detached observer.

Or not dreams, because they were too real for that. She was again in the vision state she had occupied during the surgery to remove Calio's poison from her body: drifting, espying, discovering. She glimpsed Baako, deep belowground, and with him was Calio, and more of the Fae, but their attention, even Baako's, was elsewhere, directed at a figure Ceres could not make out, obscured as it was by a mist that, even as she slept, caused goose pimples to rise on Ceres's skin, her breath to cloud, and her lips to turn blue. All the Fae genuflected before it. Baako, too slow to follow suit, was struck a blow that forced him to his knees.

But Baako could not have been belowground, because Baako was here, in the village.

In the vision, Calio frowned. Their shrewd eyes searched the shadows, and Ceres thought she saw the dryad's lips whisper her name.

XLIV

Hamfaru

(OLD ENGLISH)

To Attack an Enemy in His House

ord, Ceres had forgotten what it was like to share a bed with a child! Ime tossed, turned, and thrashed, throwing out random fists and feet that struck Ceres in the face and body. It was more like negotiating a boxing ring than a bed. Her earlier yearning for such closeness might almost have amused Ceres, had she not been so weary. At last she gave up on getting any kind of rest if she remained next to Ime, and seized a pillow to try to make herself as comfortable as she could on the floor—in other words, not particularly so, but sufficient, combined with her exhaustion, to enable her to drift off.

What woke her was not a noise, because no noise was made, nor was it a stimulus to any other senses, or none that she could have named. But the moment she opened her eyes, she knew danger was close. Ceres had positioned herself between the bed and the nearest wall, with her feet toward the door. She was facing the bed when she woke, a blanket covering her from head to toe to keep out the cold so that, even close up, she might have been mistaken for discarded linen.

Beyond the bed itself, and high on the wall, was the room's window, barely eighteen inches in length and a foot in width. But despite the narrowness of the gap, a man was forcing himself through. A pair of hands gripped the wall, followed by a head and shoulders. It seemed impossible to Ceres that he should be able to enter without breaking or dislocating bones, but she heard no fracturing, or any grunts of effort or discomfort. Rather it was as though his body was either boneless, in the manner of a worm, or what bones he possessed were soft and adaptive, as with some fish. The frame of the window compressed him, but as soon as he was free of it, his body expanded once again. Now his bare torso was visible, hanging downward as his muscles continued to enlarge and contract, inching the rest of him into the room. He was smooth from the navel down, so that only his face and torso gave any clue to his sex.

But he did not drop, not even when gravity should have taken hold. Instead his body stuck to the wall, so that he clung, head down, to the dry, painted mud. His gaze twisted toward the bed, but by then Ceres already knew him, had known him as soon as she first caught sight of those long fingers clutching at the window frame: Baako, and not Baako. His eyes were greenish-black, like the surface of polluted ponds, and had migrated from the front of his face to the sides. His mouth had widened so that the corners were halfway up his cheeks, and the teeth revealed by his grin were long and yellow, the gums having receded so far as to expose the roots. He did not show any surprise at finding Ime alone in the bed. If anything, that awful grin grew wider, and his focus was solely on the child as he slid silently to the floor before rising up beside her, the fingers of his right hand splayed, the nails extending to grip and pierce.

At that moment Ceres cast aside the blanket, her sword poised in her right hand. Baako, or the entity that had assumed his appearance, paused in his attack, and for the first time he made a sound, a snakelike hiss of warning and dismay that was suddenly joined by a second sibilance, as Ceres's sword swished through the air barely inches above Ime's face, and sliced off those long stiletto fingers at the knuckles. Baako's hiss turned to an appalled howl, waking Ime, who immediately crawled away from him, falling off the side of the bed to land on the floor beside Ceres.

Baako's mutilated limb dripped blue-black blood, and the stubs of his fingers bubbled and smoked. He slashed at Ceres with his uninjured left hand, but it was a defensive move, designed to keep her and her steel at bay: he was already backing off, seeking a means of escape. His left arm grew longer and longer, stretching to twice its previous length, as he reached for the window frame to draw himself up, but Ceres jumped onto the bed and chopped at the arm, severing it just below the elbow. Again Baako howled, as fists banged at the bedroom door; although doubly wounded, he was still dangerous. Accepting that retreat was no longer an option, he decided that if he was going to die, it would not be alone. He sprang, his mouth gaping, his teeth ready to gnaw their way through Ceres's face. He was fast, so fast that, in the blink of an eye, his jaws were an inch from Ceres's nose, his breath moist against her skin.

But that was as close as he got, and the breath was his last. Ceres's sword had buried itself to the hilt, stabbing his heart. As he died, all vestiges of Baako fell away like a snake shedding its skin, revealing the Fae beneath. A pale light sparked briefly in those rapacious eyes. At first Ceres thought she was seeing her features reflected in them, but the face, though female, was not her own. It was older, cleverer, deadlier: another presence briefly inhabiting the doomed Fae to peer out at his killer. Then, as quickly as it had manifested, the image was gone, and the last of the Fae's life departed with it. Ceres released her grip on the sword, and the Fae collapsed on the sheets, his head coming to rest on the pillow.

The bedroom door exploded inward and the Woodsman came with it, Thabasi and his warriors bunched behind. Ime ran to her father, who entrusted her to the care of two of his men, still wary of the creature on the bed.

"It's all right," said the Woodsman. "It's dead."

He turned his attention to Ceres.

"I'm fine," she told him.

But her eyes were fixed not on the Woodsman but on the dead Fae. She had done this.

And I would do it again: for Ime, for any child.

With the tip of his axe the Woodsman raised from the corpse a gray-black membrane, bearing about it traces of the lost boy.

"It looked like Baako," said Ceres, "right until the end."

"A changeling," said the Woodsman, "sent to murder Ime."

Thabasi examined the residue on the Woodsman's blade.

"Now we know they have Baako," said the Woodsman, "and he is alive. The changeling could not have assumed his form otherwise. The Fae cannot mimic the dead."

"But will they let him live after this?" asked Thabasi.

"He's more use to them that way. For better or worse, he is still young, as much child as man."

"So they'll feed on my son?"

"He's strong, like his mother and father. He can survive their predation."

"But for how long?"

"With luck," said the Woodsman, "until we find him."

XLV

Skyn
(OLD NORSE)

Perception

alaama was a scene of great activity, some frenetic, elsewhere more subdued. The hunting party that would attempt to retrieve Saada's body was assembling food and equipment, while other villagers were preparing the bodies of the dead for burial.

Ceres took it all in. Thabasi was ensuring that Kaya, the woman appointed to replace Abansi as senior advisor, would keep the watch vigilant and assign trustworthy personnel to the task of ensuring Ime's safety in his absence. The guards who had fallen asleep at their posts the previous night, thus permitting the intruders entry, had died by Fae blades, so their punishment was complete and absolute. But had they survived, Thabasi would not have disciplined them harshly; he, Saada, and Abansi were as responsible as anyone for allowing the defenses to lapse over the years. Many was the night Thabasi and his wife had left the village, slipping past snoozing sentries, to walk by the river. They might have had words with the watch upon their return, or made some remark to Abansi the following day, but that was the limit of the action taken. They had all grown too complacent, and the Fae, aided by the harpies, had made them pay.

A decision would have to be made on a replacement for Saada as the head of the village, once her death was confirmed. Thabasi had no right, even by marriage, to succeed his wife, since the community had always functioned as a matriarchy. He thought it likely that Kaya would be the villagers' choice, and a good one, but for the present she deferred to Thabasi.

A runner had returned, sent by the villagers who had left in the night to track the Fae. While the Fae could travel on foot without easily being detected, a human like Baako had a heavier tread. His footprints had been discovered close to the river, and by following them for a few hours, it had been determined that the Fae were heading toward the chasm. This gave hope to Thabasi and the rest, Ceres and the Woodsman included, that Baako might yet be rescued, and it was with a greater sense of purpose that the search party at last set out, intent now on joining up with the first group, which was waiting for them, and taking on the harpies and the Fae with a larger force.

David elected not to join them. He had been subdued ever since Ceres spoke to him of the Crooked Man, and was now committed to his own path. He patted Ceres's pony as she sat mounted before him, the Woodsman alongside. To his stock of supplies and weapons the Woodsman had added a cloth bag containing a single item roughly the size of a melon. The bag was tied to his saddle, and Ceres was doing her best not to let it touch her.

"Where will you go?" Ceres asked David.

"Where it ended," he replied, "or where I thought it had ended. Back to the castle. Back to where I saw the Crooked Man die."

And the Woodsman did not attempt to dissuade him.

Within hours the two bands of villagers had met up, the combined search party numbering about forty in total. A council was convened, because at the spot where they came together, it looked like the Fae might have split into two groups, one moving northeast, and the other—with Baako—continuing in the direction of the chasm, although the first set of tracks petered out after only half a mile.

"We continue west," Thabasi told his people.

"But what about the children," said the Woodsman, "the ones from your village? We can't know that they're with the Fae making for the chasm."

"I would split our force, if there was another trail to follow, but there is none."

Which seemed unarguable, if only because, as Thabasi had pointed out, there were no options to distract them.

"So where did the rest of the Fae go?" Ceres inquired of the Woodsman.

"The harpies might have aided them," he replied. "Or—"

He shook his head, reluctant to finish, so Ceres did it for him.

"Or they left the trail they wanted us to follow."

"We may be attributing more deviousness to them than we should," said the Woodsman.

"Is that possible where the Fae are concerned?"

The villagers were already on the move again. The Woodsman tapped his heels to the mare.

"There's always a first time," he said.

They kept behind the trackers, just in case the latter should lose Baako's spoor and need to retrace their steps; by not deviating from the trackers' path, they would not risk erasing any signs. Only Ceres and the Woodsman were on horseback. The rest proceeded on foot, but they ran ceaselessly, and even as the hours went on, and the sun passed its zenith, they did not tire. The terrain was hilly, and devoid of trees, but the grass was long, and the ground sometimes muddy, so that Ceres thought she might have been able to follow Baako's movements herself, so clear was his imprint. The residual pain from Saada's surgery on the sting was easing, but it had been joined by another, one that Ceres had been brooding on since the day's mission had commenced, just as she had been mulling over the images in her dreams.

High above them, a bird flew alone, but too distant to make out the species. Whatever its purpose or destination, it, too, was heading west. Just as Ceres was about to return her attention to the ground, a larger bird—a falcon or hawk—broke from altitude, using the sun to mask its descent as it targeted the solitary traveler. It dropped so fast that Ceres could barely follow its trajectory, its wings folded tightly against its body, the better to counter the resistance of the air. Only at the final moment did it alter its pose, its wings spreading and its talons extending to strike at its prey—

But the first bird was no longer where it once was. It had darted aside at the final moment, and it not only had evaded death, but was now also hovering above the raptor. The predator, weakened by its failed strike, had become the prey. As the entire party stopped to witness the outcome, the smaller bird pounced on the larger, and a brief struggle ensued. It ended with the raptor plummeting to earth not far from where they stood. Ceres guided her horse over to examine the body of the bird. Its breast had been punctured repeatedly by a sharp beak, its neck was broken, and it had lost both eyes. Above Ceres, the victor circled, but still too high to make out.

"It's a raven, or a rook." Thabasi had come to join her. "But I've never seen one best a hawk before, or not alone. Even in greater numbers, they will succeed only in chasing off a hunter, not killing it."

Ceres said nothing, but contemplated the circling bird as she and Thabasi returned to the rest. Only when she was alone with the Woodsman did she speak.

"It looks like my spying friend is back."

"You think it's working on behalf of another?"

"Don't you?"

The Woodsman glanced at the sky.

"I wouldn't assume anything," he said, "about so resolute a creature."

In the early afternoon, Baako's footprints ended, and no matter how hard the trackers searched, the trail could not be picked up again. While the others rested and ate, the Woodsman and Thabasi, along with the head scout, Mosi, consulted together, Ceres seated alongside them.

"I smell harpies," said Mosi. "It's faint, but their odor is most particular."

"It would explain the disappearance of the prints," said the Woodsman, "and why the tracks have been leading us in the direction of the chasm."

Thabasi was unhappy, as well he might be. He had already lost a wife to the Brood, and might be about to lose a son, too.

"Then we double our pace," he said. "We no longer need to travel slowly, because we know where they have taken Baako."

Ceres intervened.

"I don't believe the harpies have Baako."

Mosi smiled indulgently, but it was obvious that he was offended by her suggestion.

"Harpies were here," he said. "I am not mistaken."

"I don't doubt that," said Ceres, "and neither do I mean to slight your abilities. I've seen how you picked up tracks and signs invisible to me in order to get us this far. I'm amazed at your skill."

The Woodsman's mouth twitched in approval at Ceres's diplomacy. It would do them no good to alienate the tracker, and Ceres had smoothed his ruffled feathers.

"Then why do you say we are on the wrong trail?" asked Thabasi.

Ceres gathered her thoughts before speaking.

"First of all, we know the Fae can imitate Baako. They've done it once, and may have done so again in order to trick us into believing that we're following in his footsteps. But also, ever since Calio stung me, I've been having visions of the Fae. The strongest of them came when Saada was removing the poison from my body, but I've had others since then, the most recent last night. I saw Baako, too, but he was underground, and the other children, the stolen ones, were with him."

Ceres waited for Mosi and Thabasi to dismiss this as foolishness, but they were listening to her seriously.

"I think," Ceres resumed, "that when they stung me, Calio left something of themselves in me, and now there is a connection between us."

"Second sight," said Mosi. "It is not unknown among those who cross the Fae and their kin and live to tell of it."

"If that's the case, then Calio has it, too. I know they feel it when I'm close, but either they don't fully understand what's happening, or they don't know what to do about it. Whatever the reason, Calio could be reluctant to admit this to the Fae. The dryad made an error in poisoning me but failing to steal me away, and I sense they're worried that the Fae will make them pay if it's discovered. So Calio wants to keep that from the rest, which is to our advantage."

Ceres paused again. Even speaking about Calio made the site of the sting throb, and she wondered if the dryad, wherever they might be, endured their own version of that pain whenever they uttered Ceres's name.

"There was a game I used to play—*that* I play—with my daughter," said Ceres. "It's called Hot or Cold. You hide something, and the other person has to find it, but the only clue you can give them is to tell them that they're growing colder when they walk away from it, and warmer when they get nearer. Ever since we left the village, I've been growing more distant from Calio: colder, if you like. We're farther from them, and wherever they are, so too are the children and Baako. The harpies and the chasm may lie to the west, but I'm convinced that Calio and the captives are elsewhere."

"Do you think you can locate the dryad this way, like in the game?" asked the Woodsman.

"Yes," said Ceres, "I'm sure I can."

Thabasi looked to Mosi for guidance.

"Whatever decision you make involves some risk," said Mosi. "If we give up the race to the chasm, we may be abandoning Baako and the rest to the harpies; if we choose to go on, we'll need as many fighters as possible. Already we have barely enough to hold off the Brood while we attempt a rescue."

"Mosi is right," said the Woodsman. "Speaking plainly, Thabasi, even if Saada is dead, you have a duty to retrieve her body; and if Baako is with her, you may yet be able to bring him back alive. Should you change your plans because of what Ceres has said, you will have doubts, and you would be right to have them. Therefore, Ceres and I will travel alone, and try to find Calio together."

"And if you do," said Thabasi, "what then? Two of you against the Fae: What hope do you have?"

"We will find help, if we require it."

"You sound very sure of that."

"What is right draws rightness to it, and it has always been the way. What else is hope, but the belief that rightness can prevail?"

Their farewells were short but heartfelt. Ceres and the Woodsman turned back east, while Thabasi and his people resumed their trek west, but faster now, so that after only a few minutes they were no longer in sight.

"Are we headed in the right direction?" the Woodsman asked. "Even a slight deviation may cost us valuable time."

"I'll know," said Ceres.

Peculiar though it was, while separation from Calio might have eased her physical pain, it caused her a form of emotional discomfort. She was reminded of how she felt when Phoebe was away from her for more than a night. A sleepover at a friend's house, a single absence, was as much as Ceres could take before she began to miss her daughter, especially the sound of her voice. That silence was what had made the months since the accident so difficult.

And Ceres knew something else. Had a tree revealed itself before her at that instant, its bark separating to expose a doorway back to her own world, and to Phoebe, she would not have entered, not yet. She might not have been able to bring her own child back, no matter how hard she tried, or how much she wished and prayed, but perhaps she could, by her actions, rescue the children of others, so that their parents might not suffer as she had.

With the sun setting behind them, Ceres and the Woodsman rode on.

XLVI

Attercope
(OLD ENGLISH)

Poison Head; Spider

hey journeyed until evening teetered on the brink of night, even though Ceres did not need daylight to track Calio. Now that she understood the nature of her visions, and the ebb and flow of the throbbing at the wound site and in her heart, she felt a confidence that she had not experienced for a long time. What Ceres regarded as her failure to protect her daughter had transformed her view of herself, and not for the better. Now she had a sense of purpose, of mission. Perhaps *this* was why she had been called here: to recover lost children, and know that she could do so, that she had the capacity to rescue, to restore—

No, she was getting carried away. While some of it might be true, she had not arrived in this place by choice. If the Huntress was to be believed, Ceres's coming was the work of the Crooked Man. But as the days went by, and the more imminent, physical threat posed by the Fae took precedence, that of the Crooked Man had faded. Was he really out there somewhere? If so, why had he not made his presence known to her? Assuming he was alive, he must want something from her, otherwise he would not have pursued her from her own world into this one—forced her, in fact, to flee from one to the other, if the Woodsman was correct.

The first drops of rain, cold and hard, fell on her face. They had left the plains behind and were once more in woodland.

"We should take shelter," said the Woodsman.

"I'm not tired," said Ceres, "and I can locate Calio in the dark."

"You may be able to hunt the dryad, but we are both blind at night to other threats, while they may not be so blind to us."

He drew up his horse in a sheltered clearing and dismounted. Ceres did the same, and they tied the mounts to a tree before hobbling their front legs. Neither had any concern that the horses would wander, but it was a precaution in case they should take fright during the night and run off. An unseen bird rose into the dimness. Ceres followed the sound, trying to descry the source, but failed. She summoned the image of the dead hawk, and the rook that had bested it. The rain clouds had begun to gather an hour or so after she and the Woodsman had gone their own way, but she thought the bird had stayed with them, only to be hidden from view as the sky grew overcast.

"Let's not jump at shadows," said the Woodsman, "or every beating of wings."

"The sound of these particular wings is growing unpleasantly frequent," said Ceres. "I'd ask if it was unusual to be pursued by a rook, but we're currently hunting murderous fairies in a land in which Rapunzel shot at us with a crossbow, so it hardly begins to qualify."

"Rooks, like ravens, have been known to track quarry for wolves in return for a share of the prize," said the Woodsman. "The Loups used them, once upon a time, and I've met men who've tamed them for the same purpose. I even knew an innkeeper who claimed to have trained a crow to play cards—and to cheat, too, as it happens. Someone killed him for his troubles."

"The crow?"

"The innkeeper. The crow flew off, wise bird that it was."

"Well, once again, if you have your bow to hand, and the opportunity arises, I really do think you should bring the rook down," said Ceres, "whatever your views on its intelligence."

"But how will I know it's the same bird?" asked the Woodsman.

"Because," Ceres replied, "it will only have one eye."

❧

In an old place, deep and dark, through caverns measureless to man, the entity waited. It haunted these grottos and galleries, these subterranean tunnels sealed off from the world above, even as it knew the places where the walls were fractured, where the rubble sat in such a way as to permit the comings and goings of small, scurrying creatures, where the surface layer was thin enough to be broken by the determined scratching of a mouse, a weasel—

A rook.

There should have been no light down here, the network of shafts and hollows being too convoluted to permit its passage from the surface, yet light there was, of a cheerless kind: a gift to the entity from the Fae, an acknowledgment of a pact agreed. And so, had an intrepid prospector found a way into this underground expanse, this place of a thousand rooms, all with their own stories, they might have been permitted to bear witness to a hidden history of the realm, one written by the Crooked Man. But there was no traveler, only a one-eyed rook following wonted paths.

The rook glided through a crypt filled with glass cases, each containing a cloudy, yellowing preservative, with corpses discernible in the murk. The chemicals had begun to lose their efficacy years earlier, and so the bodies were decaying, but their faces were still visible, and remained distinctly human, even if their identities had long been erased from memory.

Close by was a cave heavy with dusty spiders' webs, and on the floor, the withered remains of the arachnids that once spun them—if remains they were, because one could never be sure with spiders. North of their lair, a shaft led to a dressing room, furnished with a chair upon which sat an ornate bone comb made from the femur of a child, and a pair of mirrored spheres just large enough to fit into the sockets of a skull. The chair, along with the tiles beneath, was covered with a layer of powder and ash, all that was left of the woman for whom the orbs had once served as eyes. There was power in them still, and to look into them would be to see oneself reflected at the instant of one's death, making one cognizant of the moment and manner of it, a shadow to be cast over the years, months, days, and minutes that remained. Did the woman, then, have knowledge of her own death? Who could tell? Not her, at any rate, the Crooked Man having deprived her of her tongue as well as her eyes. It might have been a blessing for her when she finally crumbled to dust, although she was known to smile as the Crooked Man forced his victims to gaze on her, so possibly not.

In the next room the accoutrements were even sparser, consisting only of a mirror, now lying shattered on the stones. This one had revealed lies and deceptions—not of the ones who looked into it, but of those they loved, and thus that love was poisoned. The Crooked Man had always liked reflective materials, whether formed of glass or still water. He understood that a reflection could be a world unto itself, and a mirror's facade, or the surface of a pool, might serve equally as a window or a door. That was why one of his favorite halls had been filled only with pools, each reflecting a different part of the kingdom, and by diving into one, the Crooked Man could emerge at that spot. But the pools were stagnant now, and thick with mats of scum.

The rook was approaching the heart of the catacombs. It paused, though, in a chamber adorned with the small skulls of lost children, a name carved on each, because even the Crooked Man had found it hard to distinguish one from another, and it was important that he should be able to recall them. The torment of his victims was like nectar to him, but that of children was particularly sweet. The rook was standing on one such skull, and not for the first time, as its sharp claws had left a graffiti of fine scratches on the bone. Why this skull, above any of the others? It was not that it offered a particularly useful vantage point, being tucked away on a low shelf. The name etched into its frontal bone—*Peter*—was hardly uncommon, and even the Crooked Man might have struggled to bring to mind anything exceptional about the boy and his demise.

But the rook remembered: kindness, companionship; words taught, words spoken. The rook was very old. It had outlived its parents, its children, their offspring, their offspring's offspring, on and on: eight lifespans or more, and still it refused to die, or this world had decided not to allow its death, not yet. Down all the years, it had not forgotten the boy, who had raised it from an injured fledgling: nothing to the Crooked Man, but everything to the rook.

The bird roused itself—from rest, from reflection—and continued into the hall dominated by the great hourglass that had marked the days of the Crooked Man's life. The bottom bulb was shattered, spilling the skulls that had served as its grains, and erasing their potency along with it. Even were the glass to be replaced, it would have served only as a monument to what once had been. This was a place of dead things.

For the most part.

The rook alighted on a stack of yellowed bones. Before it stood a wall of ivy, its foliage more red than green. Ivy should not have been able to grow down here without sunlight, but grow it had, fueled by the same glow that lent illumination to the cave walls.

The branches rippled and twisted, forming a face from their leaves.

"Speak," they rustled, and the rook croaked its report.

XLVII

Draumur
(OLD NORSE)

Dream

he Woodsman had set a fire and was roasting a coney over the flames. Ceres had marked his killing of the little rabbit, the arrow taking it in mid-leap so that it was alive when it left the ground and dead when it landed. It spasmed just once, and its nose gave the slightest of twitches, as though to smell the world one last time before departing it forever. Although she was hungry, and the fragrance of the meat made her mouth water, Ceres stuck to fruit, along with some of the bread and boiled eggs with which they had been provisioned before they left the village. The coney had not suffered long, but its death weighed on her because she had looked on death too much in recent days.

From deep in the forest came the clamor of foxes mating. It resembled the wailing of a child, and Ceres, in an instant, was a young mother once again, caring for Phoebe alone and wishing, praying, that the infant would Just. Stop. Crying. How exhausted she had been during that first year or more of motherhood, how hard she had found it to connect with the tiny, squalling being she had birthed. There were nights when had some stranger, whether blessed or cursed, materialized on Ceres's doorstep and offered to take the baby away in order to let her mother rest,

Ceres would have consented in a heartbeat. She understood how prisoners in cells, deprived of sleep for days, could sign confessions falsely admitting to murder. They would put their name to any avowal, any at all, if only they might be permitted to close their eyes.

But what would she now have given to hear Phoebe cry again? What would she *not* have given?

Sometimes Ceres feared that, in even imagining such a thing—surrendering Phoebe to another in return for a good night's sleep—she might have sown the seeds of what came later: the accident, and the loss of her child to a slumber without end, like Briar Rose in the fairy tale, her bed cloistered by thorns. Was there a force in the universe that heard our darkest wishes, only to grant them with an added twist of malice? *You wanted your daughter to be silent? Here, then, is your silence.* Was that not another convention of the fairy tale? Be careful what you wish for, and phrase it well, like a lawyer drafting a document that leaves no loophole to be exploited, and no clause whose meaning might be open to dispute or used against you. Beware of Fae bargains, in other words.

But surely that was only how stories worked. A wish, whatever form it might take, did not constitute a contract, and it was in our moments of doubt that we were most human. There was nothing fair about what had happened to her and Phoebe, but nothing unfair either. Raging against it, or despairing, would not change anything. The past does not imprison us. We may offer ourselves up as its captives, but equally, we can choose to open the cell door and walk free. Even if it's locked, the key is nearby, because we keep it with us, always. It's just a matter of finding the right pocket.

"You look like you're in another world," said the Woodsman, breaking the spell of remembrance.

"Is that supposed to be funny?" It came out sounding terser than intended. "Sorry," she added, "but I *am* in another world, aren't I? And—"

She paused.

"Go on."

"I think I'm slowly losing myself—my old self, I mean. The longer I stay here, the more distant it seems to me, but I'm no longer frightened of losing it, if that makes any sense. The old me was on the verge of giving up. I was visiting Phoebe less often. I'd drink a glass or two of wine, and use that as an excuse not to drive to the hospital. Sometimes, when I was very low, I would imagine an existence without her, where I could grieve, but in which both of us would no longer be trapped by fate. Now I've glimpsed a version of what that existence might be like, and I don't want it. Even if I never hear Phoebe's voice again, I have to believe she can hear mine. I don't want her to be alone, and I don't want to be without her, either.

"So when I get back to her—*if* I get back—I know what I have to do. Strange though it may sound, I think I've found a kind of peace through my time here. Some might call it resignation, but it's more than that. I'm not angry anymore, or bitter. I'm still sad, but that's okay. It would be odd if I weren't, and I can live with sadness. But anger, bitterness, regret? I think they would have destroyed me in the end, and my daughter would have suffered for it."

The light of the fire flickered on the Woodsman's face. The coney being cooked to his satisfaction, he had retreated for his meal to the comfort of some moss. His distance from Ceres, combined with the fluttering of the flames, served to cast him into semi-obscurity, so that his features appeared to her altered, and in them she once again glimpsed traits of one beloved in another life.

"This world is no different from any other," said the Woodsman, wiping grease from his mouth, "in that the most valuable lessons are often the hardest learned. Are you sure you don't want some of this? It's exceptionally tasty."

"I've just opened my heart to you," said Ceres, "and you're offering me rabbit?"

"Very good rabbit."

"This is why you have no friends."

"I'm hurt," said the Woodsman, although he clearly wasn't. Ceres threw a nut at him, which missed. Not only did it miss, it also adjusted its trajectory to avoid hitting him, because Ceres could have sworn that it had been well on its way to bouncing off his forehead. To crown the trick, the Woodsman opened his left fist, revealing what Ceres was fairly sure was the same nut.

"How did you do that?"

"It would be telling." He tossed the nut back to her, set aside a stripped rabbit thigh, and grew serious. "What of Calio?"

Ceres raised her hand and pointed east.

"Over there, somewhere, judging by how much more insistent the throbbing in my arm has become since we turned back. I'd say a day away, no more—or I hope not, because this blasted sting has caused me enough discomfort already."

"Be careful how you dream of them."

"I can't control my dreams."

"In this case, I think you can, and must. If there is now part of Calio in you, there is also, as you surmise, part of you in Calio. Your blood has mingled with theirs, and when they are revealed to you, you also reveal yourself to them. They will use that against you if they can."

Ceres was ambivalent about her insights into Calio. They were uncomfortably vivid, and the fading life essence of the captured infants brought the same sense of righteous anger that she experienced upon viewing news footage of starving children, or refugees fleeing war zones. On the other hand, the link meant that she was not powerless to intervene. It was a matter of finding Calio and the Fae in time to save the captives, Baako among them.

"Would you think me foolish," she asked, "if I said I have pity for Calio?"

"It would take a lot to make me think you foolish about anything," the Woodsman replied.

"I feel their loneliness, and I'm beginning to grasp why they speak of themselves in the plural, not the singular. Calio contains multitudes, or the memory of them, like someone carrying ghosts. Every dryad who has died is in Calio, but those spirits can't speak, so they can't explain what happened to them. They're like little bubbles of hurt, all held within one body, but those bubbles have punctured and leaked over time, and the hurt has infected their host. I think it's driven Calio insane."

"Don't let your compassion blind you to the danger they represent," said the Woodsman. "Calio has allied themselves to the Fae, and the Fae mean only harm."

"No, Calio is no longer their ally. Calio is furious at the Fae, too. Calio is furious at everyone and everything."

"Then Calio is unreasoning, which makes them more lethal."

"And what of the Crooked Man?" asked Ceres. "Why have we not yet seen him?"

"It's true that in the past he would have made himself known before now. David would tell you as much, if he were here. But if you're right about the rook, it may be that the Crooked Man has been monitoring us all along, and waiting."

"For what?"

"For the right moment, when you're at your weakest, angriest, or most frightened. Those are the instances when we can be exploited, and bent to the will of others. I think that may be why you left your world an adult, but entered this one as a youth. The Crooked Man wants you to be confused, half-formed, your identity in flux, which is why it's so important to hold on to the best of what you are. Remember, though: if you do find yourself in his presence, he will hide a single lie in a bushel of truths, because that is what the cleverest liars do."

"And if he offers me a way home?"

"Then it will come at a price. It will be for you to choose whether to pay it. I can't make that decision for you."

While Ceres mulled over what he said, the Woodsman removed what remained of the coney from its spit, filled a battered metal bowl from the leather water bag on his saddle, and set it to boil over the fire. As it began to bubble, he added a dark powder to the water and stirred it with a stick. When he was satisfied that the mixture had dissolved, he asked Ceres for her cup and shared half the brew with her. Ceres sniffed it suspiciously before drinking, then sighed with pleasure. It smelled like hot chocolate, and tasted close enough to make no difference. It was bitter, and could have done with some sugar—marshmallows wouldn't have hurt either, and a dollop of whipped cream—but it warmed her, and reminded her pleasurably of evenings spent at home as a teenager, because it was only then that she had developed a taste for hot chocolate. And here she was, a teenager once again, seated by a different fire, and remembering a time when she used to be as she was now. The complexities of it made her head spin.

She finished drinking, set aside her cup, and lay down. The ground was hard, and a saddle and folded blanket didn't make for much of a pillow. In addition, she feared her dreams, and what she might see in them, so she didn't hold out much hope of rest.

With luck I may doze, she thought. *That would be better than no sleep at all.* And instantly she was asleep.

Ceres saw Calio standing over five infants. One of the children, its sex impossible to determine, now resembled an old person, so shriveled and wrinkled was its face, like a piece of fruit sucked dry of juice. Flakes of skin were peeling from its forehead and cheeks, and its breathing was very shallow. It evanesced amid the shadows, but only faintly. Ceres thought that this might be the child of Mistress Blythe's daughter, or one of the babies stolen from the other village, the one close to Saada and Thabasi's—the act of theft for which two men had been hanged unjustly. The remaining little captives looked healthier, and their radiance was largely undimmed, but it would only be a matter of time before they began to resemble the first. Among them drifted the Fae, pausing sometimes to sup, inhaling worms of light from the children, diminishing their prey with every breath.

Calio was moving away, and Ceres followed them through underground tunnels until they emerged in a corridor lit by torches, the walls decorated with tapestries and artwork. Ceres heard voices, and watched as Calio ducked into an alcove to avoid detection. Three servants arrived, speaking among themselves, and carrying jugs and bowls on silver trays. Only when the servants passed did Calio continue on their way, and Ceres was party to their feelings of relief. *They've been having trouble with concealment since I hurt them, but it's coming back now.* Calio gave no sign of being aware of Ceres, perhaps because they were too distracted by their purpose. *No, they can feel me near. They're just pretending not to. It's as if they want me to see this.*

Calio paused before an alcove containing the life-sized portrait of a man. Dressed in black and gold riding clothes, he was depicted against a backdrop of blood-red drapes. Between the drapes a window could be glimpsed, open to the evening. As Ceres watched, a pair of hands appeared at the windowsill in the painting, followed by a head with dark eyes set into its sides. The Fae—female, and slim and dangerous as a stiletto blade—climbed into the room behind the man in the portrait, slipped past him to advance to the edge of the frame, and stepped from it into the hallway. Only then did Calio look over their shoulder, seeming to stare directly at Ceres.

Calio clicked their fingers, and the vision ended.

By the tree, the Woodsman also slept, but did not dream. His slumber was not deep, and he was ready to wake to any sound beyond the nickering of the horses, or Ceres's soft breathing. The movement of leaves, though, was not likely to disturb him, not unless it was accompanied by footsteps, or the beating of a harpy's wings, so he did not see a face form from the ivy that blanketed the tree beneath which he lay, nor its leafy eyes gaze past him towards Ceres's still form.

The entity, using some of its precious reserves of strength, had come to confirm for itself the approach of the girl-woman.

XLVIII

Leawfinger
(OLD ENGLISH)

Forefinger, or Betray-Finger

ere is something that is important to grasp in order to understand people and their motivations: in stories, as in life, there
are no secondary characters. Each of us is the center of our
own universe, and other people are the planets and moons
that orbit us, the heavenly bodies that are variously repelled or
attracted by our gravitational force, and—occasionally—the bright stars
that become, either temporarily or permanently, our twins.

Shift the focus of a tale—this one, for example—and it becomes about
another person: the giant Gogmagog; Ime, daughter to the lost Saada; the
benign, dedicated Spirit of the Stream; or even the Huntress. To them,
the Woodsman and Ceres were minor figures passing through their lives,
incidental presences in a drama in which they alone occupied the leading role. It is an error to assume those around us are not as significant as
ourselves, or that their fears, aspirations, and desires are not as worthy
of attention as our own. This is how our best-laid plans may be undermined, because they are based on a premise that is false from the start:
I am important, other people less so, and everyone involved accepts this
version of affairs.

So let us leave the sleeping Ceres, the dozing Woodsman, even the

watchful presence in the ivy, and travel through the night, like our kindred spirit the one-eyed rook, to a dungeon below a castle. The dungeon
was no longer in use. The floor was unstable, and the walls and ceilings
cracked. It belonged to an older incarnation of the stronghold, one built
by a queen dead so long that nothing of her remained, not even her name.
The dungeon was used by her successors until—thanks to David, the
hero of his own story—the line of kings and queens came to an end, the
Crooked Man was vanquished, and the great fortress to which each of his
puppets had added during their reigns finally fell asunder.

But the dungeon, being set far underground, survived, along with
some of its sister chambers, and was sealed off, if imperfectly; a locked
and barred door, neglected by those who put it there, can be made to
open again with a little ingenuity and application by others who should
not be granted such access. The trick, of course, is to make sure no one
else knows that you happen to have a key.

One of the flagstones of this dungeon concealed the entrance to a
tunnel, though even the most desperate of prisoners would have struggled to find it when the cell was in use, and after discovering it would
have failed to open it, so intricate were its devices. It was the work, like a
great deal else in these depths, of the Crooked Man. When he vanished,
all knowledge of the tunnel should have departed with him, but the damage to the dungeon's structure during the destruction of the old castle had
caused the secret flagstone to rise by an inch. Decades later, this enabled
determined fingers to explore the underside, discover the nature of its
mechanisms, and disable them, making the tunnel easily reachable—and
undetectable again, once the flagstone had been restored to its previous
position.

In the dungeon, its darkness lit only by a candle, now sat Calio: so
venerable, the last of their species, abandoned by their close kin, the Fae,
when the Fae turned their backs on the world and retreated to the safety
of their mounds. There they held themselves between sleeping and waking, venturing out only to snatch a child, for one among them always
acted as a sentry, listening for the unwary tread of the young in the fields
above, or the cries of an infant on whom a distracted mother had turned
her back for a moment. Best of all, though, were the newborns abandoned

by parents who could not afford to feed them, or by adolescent mothers who had hidden their pregnancy from their family. Fearing disgrace or banishment, they gave birth alone amid tree and stone, a stick clenched between their teeth to stifle the pain of delivery, and left the babies to the elements. Such foundlings were easy pickings for the Fae. Occasionally, if they were young and exhausted enough, so too were their mothers.

Calio, also, had stolen children, but just for company. They had not consumed them like the Fae, because they did not like to feed on human-kind. Doing so felt wrong to them. They suckled milk from cows and brood mares when their strength was very low, calming the animals with their song, and in times of desperation or sickness would draw the life from a rat or field mouse, but that was as far as their predation went.

When it came to the children they took, Calio had tried to tend to their needs, and feed and water those little ones as they would a plant or flower, a delicate organism requiring care to flourish. But the first of them died, no matter what they were fed, leading Calio to conclude that human infants were harder to grow than shrubs. Their deaths made Calio sad, and so after that they kept the children only for a while, before leaving them where they might be stumbled upon again by their own kind.

But eventually even such short-term borrowings became too danger-ous. Calio did not want to be captured by men. It was better that dryads, like the Fae, should fade from human recall, lest men decide to hunt them down. Anyone, or anything, connected to the Fae aroused feelings of dread and anger in human hearts, and among Calio's worst memories was watching from a place of hiding as one of their sisters was burned alive by villagers with torches. Calio had been too terrified to intervene, knowing that if they did, they too would be put to the flame. The humans laughed while the dryad burned, and then, after far too long, another spirit was added to Calio's burden of souls. Perhaps that was the moment madness overcame them—and if so, who could blame them for it?

At the risk of repetition (but what is important must needs be re-peated), here, then, is a reminder of another lesson to be remembered: few beings—human or dryad, faun or Fae—are entirely bad. They may do awful things, some of them even unforgivable, but a difference exists between what someone *does* and what someone *is*. In the end, if we were all judged only by the worst things we did, many of us would be behind bars, and the rest would have no friends.

This was crucial to any understanding of Calio. The dryad had been alone for too long. They had witnessed the gradual eradication of their race, both directly at the hands of humans, and indirectly through the latter's desecration of the environment of which the dryads were a party. The Fae, who should have been Calio's allies, had discarded them, viewing them as inferior, leaving them to survive as best they could in a world in which they were surrounded by enemies. There was much good in Calio—so much tenderness toward the natural world, so much solicitude toward the spirits they carried inside—but grief, loneliness, terror, bitterness, and dread had served to poison this last dryad, turning sour what once was sweet, and foul what was once fair.

In the dungeon, Calio counted off their enemies on their fingers. First came mankind, although they were too many to number, so one finger would have to do for them all, except those who deserved a digit of hate all to themselves. This brought them to finger number two, and Ceres, who had hurt them so badly, when all Calio wanted was to spend time with her belowground, because Calio thought the girl might survive longer down there than an infant. Rightly or wrongly, Calio had since reached the conclusion that Ceres resembled one of the young women who had turned their sister into a screaming, flaming figure of heat and light. To Calio, all humans were alike, and therefore all were equally to blame for the hurts inflicted on the dryads. If Calio could not punish the girl who had helped to kill their sister, Ceres, who took after her, would make a fine substitute.

Next on their hand of antagonists were the Fae themselves. To Calio's eyes, the Fae were barely better than humans. Men might have destroyed the land Calio loved—cutting and burning its trees, digging deep holes in its earth to mine for wealth, turning rivers and streams to dead zones with their filth—but the Fae had allowed it by not making a stand, electing instead to shrink from view. The Hidden People might have convinced themselves they were awaiting the right opportunity, but they had delayed too long for Calio's liking, and the damage caused by their hesitation could not easily be undone. Calio suspected it was already too late, and men were bent on the world's ruination. It would recover, but only after it had turned against humans, erasing them forever from its annals.

Perhaps more importantly—although Calio was reluctant to concede this even in the quiet of their own heart—the Fae had forsaken *them*, and on returning had continued to view Calio as a menial creature, one to be used and dismissed as conditions required. But what the Fae did not know was that Calio was dying, and was aware of it even before they had crossed paths with Ceres. The blow from the rock had not only injured them, but also hastened their end, so any chance they might have to avenge themselves for all that was done to them and their kind needed to come soon.

One of the Fae glided past, a being so decrepit that the skin of his face had withered away from his cranium, the exposed bone coated in greenish skull-lichen. He did not even deign to acknowledge Calio, although he knew they were present. His dismissal of them made Calio seethe. It was Calio who had brought the Fae to this point, Calio who had whispered in human ears, Calio who had prepared the way. But all the Fae cared about was assassination and destruction.

And so Calio came to the final finger, and the final enemy: the Crooked Man. Like all creatures with an instinct for self-preservation, Calio had tried to avoid him during his domination of the land. His evil was without bounds. He lived only to create stories, and manipulated others for the purpose of his narratives, but each tale had a hollow core and ended badly. Calio knew that others had believed him dead, but the dryad, rooted in the natural world, had identified a recurrent disturbance, like the distant shifting of tectonic plates, and anomalies in the behavior of small, creeping beasts and banks of ivy, as though, if only for a few seconds, they displayed unsettling signs of self-awareness. Calio gave no indication of noticing these changes, only storing them in their memory, but in these changes they detected some echo of the Crooked Man. Now here, in this dungeon, his presence was so immanent that had Calio woken to find him standing before them as he once was, they would not have been surprised.

Calio did not know why the Crooked Man wanted Ceres. Whatever his reasons, it suited the Fae to ensure that the girl became his, which was why orders had been given that she should not be hurt during the attack on the village. But Calio intended to spite them all: humankind, Fae—and the Crooked Man, once they could discover what he desired, and why.

Best of all, Calio had plans for Ceres as well. When all the dryad's aims had been achieved, Calio would return to their little hollow to die, but they would not do so in solitude. They would have company as they faded away, to be returned to the soil. Ceres would be with them, and Calio would wait for her to expire before closing their own eyes for the last time, leaving their pain behind forever.

XLIX

Herrlof
(OLD NORSE)

A Trophy of War

eres and the Woodsman rose early, ate quickly, and resumed their search for Calio. Ceres had told the Woodsman what she had seen the night before. The image of the Fae emerging from the painting haunted her. She didn't think she'd ever feel comfortable again in an art gallery, and as for the pictures on her walls at home, she might have to get rid of those, too.

"But I can't swear that the Fae actually climbed out of the picture," Ceres finished. "It was like I was being presented with something that wasn't really happening, but contained a truth nonetheless: a metaphor, of a kind."

"And Calio wanted you to witness it?" said the Woodsman.

"They've guessed that I'm the one haunting them."

"Yet they aren't trying to hide from you, or find a way to block you."

"Not that I can tell. Calio may want me to find them."

"If that's the case, they could be laying a trap for you."

"We don't have a choice but to keep going," said Ceres. "Calio showed me the children. They're dying . . ."

Shortly before midday, they saw a rider approach. Even before she could make out his face, Ceres knew him to be David, if only because of Scylla, the beautiful white horse he rode. According to *The Book of Lost Things*, Scylla had once belonged to a knight named Roland, a heartbroken man who finally found peace, after which Scylla became David's mount. Ceres and the Woodsman were glad to see David, and paused to stretch their legs and exchange news.

"There was nothing more to be done in the village," said David. "The dead have been buried, the watch has been doubled, and Ime is being well guarded, with bread scattered around her bed at night, and a protective steel choker fastened at her neck. I was on my way to the site of the old castle and spotted you from a distance. I thought you'd be with Thabasi and the rest, yet here you are, riding in the opposite direction from the chasm."

"Ceres is of the opinion that it was all a diversion," said the Woodsman, "and Baako is still with the Fae, along with the rest of the stolen children. She can lead us to them."

"And how will you do that?" David asked Ceres.

"Because of Calio's sting," she replied. "It hurts me more the closer I get to them. And I see them in my dreams, except they're more than dreams. I walk with Calio. I see what they see."

"I've heard stranger," said David.

Ceres didn't doubt it. By the standards of *The Book of Lost Things*, a telepathic bond formed with a tree spirit barely counted as worthy of mention.

"The problem," said the Woodsman, "is that Calio may also be aware of Ceres. A game is being played here, but at least we see it for what it is. There's a difference between playing and being played."

Ceres wasn't sure she completely agreed with this. It was hard to play a game if one wasn't familiar with the rules, although where Calio was concerned, Ceres didn't think there were any rules.

"Calio hates me," she said. "They radiate hostility, and not only because I hurt them. It's like an old enmity, though we'd never met before."

"You represent humankind," said the Woodsman. "The antagonism between humanity and the Hidden People is as old as any, and Calio is kin to the Fae."

"But Calio's ill will feels specific, not general. It's me they hate, not what I represent, or not that alone."

The discussion came to an end, unresolved. It was time to go on, but now as three. The Woodsman went ahead, leaving Ceres and David to get to know each other better. Ceres tried to explain to David the ways in which their world had changed in his absence, but he showed the barest of interest. This was his world now, even as he remained convinced he would soon depart it.

"The Woodsman once told me," said David, "that most people come back here in the end. It took me a long time even to learn what he meant. He didn't just say they *came* here, but that they came *back*. They returned. It may be that we all have our origins in this place, but how, I don't pretend to know."

"Have you tried asking him about it?"

"Of course."

"And what did he say?"

"He told me that a dull life is one in which every question has been answered. He can be very gnomic when he likes. It's not one of his more endearing qualities."

Ceres wasn't sure what gnomic meant, exactly, but judging by what David had just told her, it involved giving a skewed answer to a straight question, which she had grown well used to since her arrival.

"Does it mean there are others like you—like us—wandering this world?"

"Not necessarily this world, but worlds not dissimilar from it. Once, not long after I returned, I went exploring with my wife and son, to find out more about what was around us. We set up camp by a lake on the first night. While they were sleeping, I stood by the water, watching the moon. But when I knelt to drink, it wasn't my face I saw reflected, but those of two others: a pair of young women, both in their late twenties, I should have thought. They were holding hands, in the way that lovers do, and crying, but with joy, and I guessed they had just been reunited in their rendering of Elsewhere, the version of it they had dreamed into being; that one of them had died too young, and now their lost years together had been restored to them, just as mine were to me.

"We'd all arrived at a place where the wall between worlds was thin, so fine as to be transparent, if only fleetingly. They looked at me, and I looked at them, and we smiled at one another, because we were alike, and we knew we were. All the pain we'd endured, all the grief, was forgotten, and the days that should have been were ours. They waved goodbye, and I never saw them again.

"I think that's how it works here. What was lost is found, and the years of sadness are wound back. Some, like my family and me, receive decades, some just an hour, or a few moments, but always enough for what was done to be undone, or what was unsaid to be said at last."

"And then?" asked Ceres.

David spread his hands in a gesture of unknowing.

Ceres peered at him. Even in the short time they'd been apart, his hair had grown sparser and whiter, and the fine lines around his eyes and mouth had deepened. The final grains of sand were slipping through his hourglass, but he showed no fear. He had been reunited with his wife, and together they had watched their son grow up. Soon they would go on together, leaving loss behind. But first David would do what he could to ensure that this odd, ever-altering world remained, if not safe, then at least secured. The Fae, and what they, at their worst, represented—predation, the rule of the powerful over the powerless, and the belief that one race might be superior by reason of color or blood—could not be allowed supremacy.

The landscape altered. They arrived at a wide road on which they became three among many, barely noticed amid carts, riders, and men and women on foot. Smoke drifted across fields that were untilled or overgrown, and whole sections of forest lay denuded, the bases of their trunks left to rot. A foul smell, which reminded Ceres of the cities of her childhood with their air polluted by coal smoke and factory chimneys, overcame all else, and she noticed that the brook by the side of the road no longer ran clear but was sullied by a dirty yellow froth. She doubted that anything could survive in that water, and she thought again of the first creature she had encountered, the cheerful Spirit of the Stream. This contamination would have made him miserable.

They reached the brow of a hill. Below, and to the south, stood a citadel, its high castle keep resembling the center of a target, with a series of concentric walled rings extending from it, each section accommodating its own gardens, stables, homes, and businesses, the satellite regions growing more crowded the farther they were from the castle. To the north was a huge mine, with smoke and fumes pouring from furnaces and chimneys, and channels and pools gouged in the earth to take the runoff from the operation. A strip of woodland, combined with the hilly terrain, served to conceal the workings from the residents of the castle. The Woodsman looked appalled by it all, although Ceres thought he might have been more troubled by the existence of the citadel than the mine, even though the former was quite pretty, she thought. David, too, appeared taken aback.

"Of course," said the Woodsman. "What else would Balwain have done?"

Ceres asked him what he meant, but it was David who answered.

"Balwain has built his city on the site of the old castle, the one through which the Crooked Man once ruled in secret. When last we saw it, the castle lay in ruins, but a new stronghold has taken its place."

"Why waste good stones?" said the Woodsman, before adding, "Or bad ones."

Trumpets sounded behind them, and voices ordered that the way be cleared. Two companies of riders advanced, each wearing different insignia, but both equally impatient and heavy-handed with their fellow travelers on the road, whipping recalcitrant cart horses to force them onto the verge, and nudging women and children aside with their mounts. After them came a pair of armored coaches, their curtains drawn to conceal those inside from the envious gaze of the common folk, as well as to protect the occupants from the sight of the masses—and, most likely, their odor too, because even Ceres had to admit that some of those around them smelled pretty ripe. Then again, she had now been traveling on horseback for nearly two days, so she wasn't sure that she'd be unreservedly welcomed into polite society either, or not until she'd had a bath and a change of clothes.

Ceres, David, and the Woodsman let the coaches go by, followed by more soldiers, before resuming their journey. As they descended, they saw further riders and coaches approaching the castle from the north and east.

"This Balwain must be very popular," said David.

"It looks like a council of the local oligarchs has been convened," said the Woodsman.

"Because of the Fae?" asked Ceres.

"A lord who permits infants to be stolen by old enemies won't be in charge for much longer, not unless he does something about it. That's good news for us, because it means we won't have to waste energy convincing Balwain and his allies to act."

A small troop of filthy miners, their clothing and skin blackened with coal dust, came trudging up the hill. Some were men, but most were dwarfs, the two species intermingling with no hierarchy or division, although nobody was whistling a marching song. They were all too exhausted for that. Ceres saw David examining the faces of the dwarfs, hoping, or not, to spot among them those whom he had once known, but none was familiar to him, and they reacted hostilely to his attention.

"What you lookin' at, then?" asked a dwarf. His hat had a bell on the end, but it was dented and didn't jingle—or, indeed, jangle.

"I was searching for friends," David replied.

"You'll not find friends here. Brothers, if you get enough coal dust in your lungs, but no friends."

"If'n you're looking for work," said another dwarf, "there's always room for one more in the pit. We've three dead today already, so if you lot sign up, you'll even the score."

"But I wouldn't recommend it," said the first dwarf, his attitude softening at the sight of Ceres. "If you put your mark to the contract, there's no rubbing it off again. It's a bad life, and leads to a worse death."

"Then why do it?" asked Ceres.

The dwarf checked around to ensure that he wouldn't be overheard, but just as he was about to resume, one of the men placed a warning hand at his back and inquired, "On your way to see his lordship, are you?"

"We are," answered the Woodsman.

"Acquaintances of his?"

"We haven't yet had the pleasure."

"Well, when you do, be sure to give him our regards. Tell him there are only happy workers here."

But his tone, and the weariness on his face, sent a different message.

He patted his dwarf companion, and the miners resumed their journey—to food, and rest.

"Forced labor?" asked David of the Woodsman once they were gone.

"Reluctant, at best."

By now they were caught up in the throng trying to gain entry to the city, men and women carrying their possessions on carts, on donkeys and horses, or, in the absence of any of the former, on their own backs. Many had children with them, or herded cattle, and kept dogs on lengths of rope. Here and there Ceres heard talk of the Fae. This was an exodus of frightened people, all seeking the protection of high walls. Each was questioned by the guards before either being admitted or advised to try their luck elsewhere. Not having a place to stay was the main reason given for rejection. Those who were refused permission to enter joined a growing community camped outside the walls, some of whom had already lit fires over which to cook, or by which to warm themselves.

Ceres caught herself scratching at the wound on her arm, raking at it hard enough to draw blood.

"Calio?" asked the Woodsman.

"It's itching and smarting like crazy, which means they must be very close. If it gets much worse, I've half a mind to chop my arm off."

"Let's hope it doesn't come to that," said the Woodsman. "You have ointment should the discomfort become too much to bear, but use it sparingly. If you numb the pain too much, we'll have no way of tracking the dryad."

"They're somewhere in that city," said Ceres. "They have to be, although I confess, I can't see how. It's so tightly sealed, even a rat would struggle to get through the walls."

Ahead of them the guards were ordering all riders to dismount. Ceres and the others got down and led their horses over the drawbridge.

"Unless Calio didn't bother trying to get through them," said David, as they reached the other side of the moat.

"What do you mean?"

David tapped his foot on the dirt. He knew better than anyone the lay of this land, this hollow place.

"It might be," he said, "that the dryad went under."

When they reached the gates, they found their way blocked by a wooden barrier studded with rivets, which had been lowered to seal off the entrance to the citadel. Eight guards were on duty, supervised by the castle's marshal, who was in charge of its men-at-arms.

"No more inside for today," said the marshal. "Turn back and return tomorrow."

"We're here to see Lord Balwain," said the Woodsman.

"You and everyone else," replied the marshal wearily, but not unkindly. "Go and find somewhere to rest, and ask again come morning. But I can tell you now, you won't be gracing his lordship with your company, even if we do consent to admit you. And if you try to bother him, you'll be back on the wrong side of the walls quicker than you can say his name."

"Oh, I think he'll want to see us," said the Woodsman.

"And why is that?"

"We have something to show him."

"You can show it to me first, and I'll decide whether it's worth his lordship's time."

The Woodsman untied the sack that had been dangling from his saddle since departing Salaama, and drew from it the severed head of the Fae changeling who had, for a time, assumed the form of Baako. The head still smelled mildly fragrant, and was uncorrupted by decay.

"So," asked the Woodsman, "do you think Lord Balwain will see us now?"

The marshal took in the grisly trophy. Ceres supposed it was the first physical evidence he'd been offered of the Fae's existence. He peered at it closely, simultaneously fascinated and repelled by the sight. He made as if to touch it before reconsidering, as though, even removed from its body, the head still had the power to harm.

"Since you put it like that," the marshal said, "I suppose you'd better come in."

L

Wyrmgeard

(OLD ENGLISH)

An Abode of Serpents

hey were escorted through the city by a quartet of guards, led by the marshal, who introduced himself as Denham. He was an old soldier, with the scars to prove it, and walked like one whose injuries had healed imperfectly, so that he was reminded of his mortality with every step he took.

While there was an air of activity inside the walls, Ceres did not notice any particular preparations to repel an attack, although the number of troops increased as they drew nearer the castle itself. Their horses were taken from them and brought to a stable, where hay and water would be provided, while they were guided to an antechamber off the main hall. Food arrived a few minutes later: cold meats, grapes, bread, sweet cakes, and a carafe of wine. In addition, three bowls of hot water and a single bar of fresh soap were placed by the window so they could wash before being admitted to Lord Balwain's presence. The men stripped to their waists, but Ceres wasn't about to do the same, regardless of how much time she'd spent with them, or how comfortable she'd become in their company. She bathed behind a curtain, and changed into her last set of clean clothes; she didn't want to put back on the dirty ones now that she was feeling more human. She also applied a thin layer of ointment to her wound, just enough to take the edge off the soreness and irritation.

When she was done, she and the Woodsman ate, but David did not. Their eyes followed him as he walked around the chamber, his fingers tapping distractedly at the walls. Finally, he returned to the window, but left it unopened, and his gaze was directed inward, not out. Ceres set aside her plate to join him.

"Are you okay?" she asked.

"This was my bedroom," he replied, "when I first came here long ago—or rather, the room where this one now stands was mine. Who knows, some of the stones in the walls may be the same. The lancet windows are similar. It's even possible they survived the collapse."

He looked past Ceres to where the Woodsman sat listening.

"I don't think we should stay here," said David.

"I wasn't planning to make a home of it," said the Woodsman. "We have to locate Calio, and convince Balwain to help us recover the children. Once that's done, we'll be leaving."

"I'm not sure I want to remain even that long. Don't you feel it?"

The Woodsman studied him carefully.

"Feel what?" he asked.

"You were right. These stones ought not to have been reused. They should have been left where they fell, and nature could have taken care of the rest. Instead, all the badness that once infused them has been allowed to thrive again. I can smell it, and taste it on my tongue, because I remember its smell and taste from before. How long has this castle been standing?"

"Decades, judging from the size of the citadel."

"And during all that time," said David, "the inhabitants have been breathing its air, their skin brushing its walls, its poison seeping into their pores. Even had the Crooked Man really died, I still wouldn't have wanted to live in a place built on what used to be his lair. But the fact that something of him may persist makes me worry more."

A knock came at the door, and it opened to reveal a retainer standing in the hallway, two guards alongside him. The guards were tense, each with a hand resting on the pommel of his sword. The retainer, meanwhile, was a thin, gloomy man with rheumy eyes, who looked as though he didn't eat enough, or if he did, took no pleasure from it. His clothing was drab, which made the ornate chain of office around his neck all the more incongruous, and even that seemed to weigh heavily on him, since he carried himself with a pronounced stoop. He didn't bother to share his name, either because he was not important enough, or more probably because he fancied himself too important. What mattered were his title and his position in the household hierarchy, not any social niceties.

"I am Lord Balwain's steward," he said. "He has agreed to see you now. You should bring along the—" He paused, and his right hand, the index finger extended, made a gesture, a conjuration of the correct word, before finally settling on "remains."

The Woodsman picked up the head in the bag and extended it toward him.

"Would you care to carry it?" asked the Woodsman.

"I'm sure you're more than capable," said the retainer, eyeing the bag with disgust, but not that alone. There was a distinct wariness to him that Ceres hadn't noticed in the marshal at the gates; and she intuited, with a certainty born of decades of dealing with men, of being forced to nego-tiate a world in which they always held the upper hand, that the steward was hiding something.

Without further conversation, Ceres and the others accompanied the steward, a guard before and behind, into the heart of the castle. As they progressed, its environs became more and more identifiable to Ceres, down to the very color of the stones in the walls, the shapes of the win-dows, and the sconces for the torches. She knew she was following in Calio's footsteps, and that the castle, and all who resided in it, was at the mercy of the Fae. As if to confirm this, her injury began to pulse with an insistence that brought to mind the sharpness of the initial sting. Calio was near.

"This is the place," she whispered to the Woodsman. "These are the halls I saw Calio walk."

The Woodsman gave a small nod, and Ceres noticed the steward tilt his head toward them in an effort to hear her words. *Not to worry*, she thought, *you'll find out soon enough.*

They came to a door flanked by two more guards, which was opened to admit them to Lord Balwain's receiving room, with a long table at one end for meetings, dominated by a large, elegantly carved throne at the head. A less formal area, consisting of couches and rug-covered chairs, surrounded a huge fireplace, where three hounds dozed in its warmth. Illumination came principally from the torches on the walls and the candles on the mantelpiece and tables. Because the room was at the base of the castle, it received little light, so its windows were more decorative than functional. This struck Ceres as odd. Had she been in Lord Balwain's position, she might have preferred a chamber higher up, from which to view her lands. Perhaps there was, in fact, a similar room in the upper reaches, and these were temporary, secondary quarters, put to use because of the threat from the Fae. It would be harder to flee from the upper levels without being seen or captured, and Ceres thought that concealed within these walls might be another door, and an escape route.

By the largest of the windows a man stood with his back to the visitors. He was imposing—tall and broad—with long black hair that brushed his shoulders. He wore a velvet tunic and trousers, over which hung a short surcoat of scarlet, while worn boots of black leather came up to his knees. His hands were clasped behind him, the bare fingers intertwined. He did not turn to face them until they were announced, and then only slowly, as though reluctant to give up a vista of stones. Ceres recognized him as the man in the portrait, however crude the representation might have been. She half expected to see a Fae warrior begin climbing through the window behind, but it remained closed, admitting trickles of diffused light through its clouded glass.

Lord Balwain was in his late forties, with some gray to his dark locks and trimmed beard. He was undoubtedly handsome, but gave the impression, even at first glance, of being too pleased by it, and his eyes, although bright, held no perceivable warmth. In Ceres's world he might have been a captain of industry, the head of some multinational company that would make thousands unemployed at the stroke of a pen or the push of a button, all to add a few pennies to the price of a share.

Ceres had never been in the presence of a lord before, and wasn't schooled in the etiquette. Did one bow, kneel, shake hands? She decided to take her lead from the Woodsman, but he was studying Balwain skeptically, like someone being offered a horse for sale who suspects that it might keel over as soon as he is out of the dealer's sight. Ceres didn't consider it appropriate for her to follow suit by eyeballing nobility, and so seized the opportunity to take in the décor of the room. She was drawn by a vast wooden carving that occupied a wall to the left, and she noticed that David, too, was interested in it. The carving depicted the routing of the Loups and their wolf allies, in a battle that had taken place on this very site when David was a boy. The latter, though, was notable by his absence, while the lead horseman scourging the enemy bore a striking resemblance to a younger Balwain. History, it was often said, was written by the victors, but it was also written by those with enough wealth and power to create their own version of it, with truth as collateral damage.

Balwain spoke, and Ceres had a vision of someone pouring syrup over a sharp knife.

"The Woodsman returns," he said, with a touch of mockery, and more than a touch of displeasure. "Always a sign of trouble in the land. One might conclude that you bring it with you, so surely does your presence confirm it."

"You've come far, *Lord* Balwain," replied the Woodsman. "When last I knew you, you held no title, and your surroundings were more modest—although you were always ambitious, so your elevation comes as no surprise. Did you choose the title yourself?"

Balwain was not used to being put on the back foot so quickly, or being reminded of his humbler roots, and plainly didn't relish it. A man with thicker skin might have ignored the thrusts, but Balwain, for all his power, was both too proud and too insecure to let an insult, whether actual or perceived, pass unremarked.

"My title was agreed upon by my fellow nobles," he said. "A new hierarchy was required after the fall of the last king."

"And did those who labor in the mine have a say in the formation of this distinguished caste?" asked the Woodsman. "Because I assume that filthy hole in the ground is your handiwork."

"The Pandemonium mine is jointly owned by the six nobles," said

Balwain, "each with a share commensurate with their power and level of investment in the project. As for the workers, they are paid for their efforts. There are no slaves here."

"But are they paid well?"

"They are paid enough," which Ceres took to mean enough for the liking of Lord Balwain and his confederates. How the workers themselves felt about the situation had been made clear by their brief encounter with the exhausted miners.

"And what are they digging for?" asked Ceres.

If Balwain was displeased to be questioned so directly by the Woodsman, and without the usual formalities, he was more unhappy still to be interrogated by a girl, although Ceres suspected that she could have come before him as her thirtysomething self and still have been on the receiving end of a dose of superciliousness from his lordship. He might have been tempted to ignore her completely, but she was in the company of the Woodsman, and whatever Balwain's reservations, anyone in the Woodsman's company carried a measure of authority by association.

"Gold, copper, and iron," he replied, before adding, after a pause, "The open pit you saw is just one part of our operations. Close by are a number of secondary underground mines, from which we're beginning to extract coal and diamonds. But unless you've come here with an investment proposal, or to make a purchase, then the finer points are irrelevant."

Balwain's focus shifted to David, who had yet to speak.

"You were once the boy David, vanquisher of the Crooked Man," said Balwain. "Older now, but with the child about you still."

"I like your carving," said David. "It's very dramatic, although I don't recall your involvement in the events of that day."

Balwain walked swiftly to the wall that held the woodwork, positioning himself as though to obstruct David's view, which was, Ceres thought, futile for a piece so large.

"You would have preferred to see yourself depicted in heroic mode?" asked Balwain.

"Only in the interests of accuracy. To be honest, I've tried to forget what happened here. If this were my castle, I wouldn't like to be reminded of its history."

Balwain gestured to the chairs by the fireplace, inviting them to sit. This would also, Ceres noticed, require them to turn their backs on the carving. She tried to spot what it was about it that Balwain might be anxious to hide, but could not—unless, of course, he was just embarrassed to have been caught in a lie.

"But it's not your castle, is it?" retorted Balwain as they sat. "And what you began, the rest of us were forced to complete. After the fall of the Loups, we slaughtered every one of their wolf brethren we could find as punishment for their insurgency. Only a few packs survived, and they retreated to the old forests. But we will find them, however long it takes, and drape their carcasses along the walls."

"Just as you hang harpies from bridges," said the Woodsman, "and stake out trolls for petrification?"

"Trolls can't be reasoned with: It's kill or be killed. As for the harpies, they are a threat to all who try to cross the chasm. Until we can find a way to wipe them out, they must be kept in check."

"It was an unnecessarily provocative act, a breach of an accord, and it has freed the Brood from the chasm. The harpies only ever attacked those who failed to pay the toll, and those instances were rare. Now they want revenge. They were part of the order of this world, an order you seek to usurp, and there will be consequences."

"The *old* order of this world," Balwain corrected, as he clicked his fingers to summon a servant bearing a tray of wine and sweetmeats. "As you note, a new order is taking its place."

"If I recall correctly, the establishment of a new order was also the aim of Leroi, the Loup king. One might suggest that one pack of wolves has replaced another."

This time Balwain did not take offense. If anything, he was flattered by the comparison.

"I admired Leroi's ambition," he said. "He, too, had grown weary of the older dispensation—of which you, Woodsman, are a remnant."

Balwain took a goblet of wine from the tray, but he was the only one who did.

"You're not thirsty?" he asked.

"We prefer to keep clear heads," replied the Woodsman.

"Speaking of heads," said Balwain, smiling at his joke, and indicating the bag by the Woodsman's feet, "I believe you have something to show me."

Using the toe of his boot, the Woodsman nudged the head toward Balwain, who didn't pick it up, but waited for a servant to do it for him.

"Take it out," Balwain instructed. "Display it for me."

The servant did as ordered, although not with any enthusiasm, and blanched as the head was revealed. Balwain, by contrast, contemplated it at length, as though it had offered up some conversational nugget worthy of consideration.

"Your handiwork?" Balwain asked the Woodsman.

"I would have preferred to have seen it buried with the rest of him, but I thought you might need to be convinced of the reality of the Fae's resurgence."

"I'm already aware of the return of the Fae, and steps are being taken to deal with them. I've summoned the nobles to a meeting, to take place this evening. By the end of our session, I'm confident that a strategy will be in place for going forward."

Once more, Ceres was reminded of obnoxious businessmen she had known. All Balwain lacked was a BMW and a set of golf clubs. The Woodsman, in turn, remained unconvinced by his bluster.

"I doubt the Fae have much respect for human strategies," he said.

"Then so much the worse for them. The realm has been transformed in their absence. It contains more steel, and more men, than they could ever have imagined."

"They have not been absent," said the Woodsman. "They were here all along."

"Slumbering in their mounds," said Balwain dismissively, "just a step away from death itself."

"*Listening* in their mounds," the Woodsman countered, "because their sleep is not like ours. Even then, they take turns to wake and to watch. To remain unseen is not to be unaware, or unprepared. And," he added, "the Fae are not the only danger we face. The Crooked Man has returned."

At this Balwain laughed aloud.

"You have grown old, Woodsman, and like the Fae, I fear you've been snoozing too long. The Crooked Man? The Crooked Man is no more. Your companion here will testify to the truth of it. After all, he was the one who drove the trickster to self-destruction."

Balwain waited for David to confirm this, but he did not.

"It may be that he was harder to get rid of than we thought," said David.

Balwain shook his head. "No, I won't be diverted by phantoms and old wives' tales, not with the Fae on our doorstep. Is there something wrong?"

It took Ceres a moment to realize Balwain was addressing her, and that she had been rubbing at her sore arm.

"A recent injury," she said. "It still bothers me."

"I can have my physician examine it, if you like."

"No, thank you. It's healing slowly."

"How did you come by it?"

But it was the Woodsman who answered, after a sharp glance that warned Ceres to leave the talking to him.

"She was attacked," said the Woodsman. "By a dryad."

"A dryad?" said Balwain. "How curious. I thought they were all dead."

"This one was very much alive."

"Maybe it didn't like strangers." Balwain eyed Ceres over the rim of his goblet. "Because you are a stranger, aren't you? Where do you come from?"

"Far away," said the Woodsman.

"The girl has a tongue of her own," snapped Balwain.

"I come from far away," said Ceres, "like the Woodsman said."

An awkward pause followed, during which Ceres saw herself, under different circumstances, being tossed into one of Balwain's prison cells to teach her some manners.

"Then," said Balwain, "you would be well advised to return there, and take him with you." He flicked a finger at David. "Your foreignness makes me tense. As for you, Woodsman, you've said what you have to say. The rest is in my hands. Leave the head. I'll make sure it's disposed of. While I'm tempted to turn you out on the road and lock the gates behind you, it will soon be dark, and the Fae are abroad. The steward will have beds prepared for you, and you can spend the night as my guests."

He placed his goblet on the tray and got to his feet, David and Ceres following suit. Their audience with Lord Balwain was over.

"One more thing," said the Woodsman, who remained seated.

"What is it?"

"The Fae have taken children. They must be rescued."

"I can't spare men for a search, not at this time."

"You may not have to, or not many of them. We are convinced the children are nearby."

Balwain registered this information without any change of expression. They might have told him that trees have leaves, for all the shock he displayed.

"What makes you think that?"

"Do you doubt my skills?"

"Not when it comes to hunting humans or animals," Balwain replied, "but the Fae is different. They leave no trail, unless they choose to, and then only a fool would follow it. Are you a fool, Woodsman?"

"Sometimes, like all men, but not on this occasion. You should be worried, Balwain. If the Fae are abroad, then you, as the power in this part of the land, may be foremost in their thoughts. That, I would venture, is a dangerous place to be."

"I don't fear them," said Balwain. "All our intelligence indicates that we're dealing with a small band of troublemakers. This isn't an army, or an invasion, just the final kicks of a dying race."

"They're feeding on children."

"They've always fed on children. That's all they are: child-stealers. They prey on the most vulnerable because they don't have the courage or the numbers to stand against men. But a handful of children won't be enough to sustain them for long, and the more the Fae expose themselves, the easier they'll be to kill. As for the infants, they're likely already dead. Even were they not, and we were somehow able to locate them, the Fae would finish them off to spite us, and leave only skin and bone to bury."

The words came out of Ceres's mouth before she could stop herself, thought and speech functioning in unison.

"If they were your children, you might be more eager to save them."

"But they're not, are they?" Balwain instantly looked much older than his years. "My daughters are dead, and my wife too. The caravan in which they were traveling was attacked by bandits. My family managed to flee into the forest, but then the wolves came, led by a luna who had stirrings of the Loup in her. I think she might have been shadowing the caravan all along, waiting for her chance. After all, I had slaughtered her mate and cubs, and she was intent on doing the same to mine. She's out there still, but I'll put an end to her before I die."

Ceres watched anger and sorrow combine to alter his features, revealing both the man he was and the one he might have been. What she saw didn't make her like him any better, but she did understand him more.

"Did you think you knew me?" asked Balwain. "You're just a child. What can you know of adult grief?"

"More than you might think," said Ceres. "And I'm sorry for your loss, truly I am. We'll find those missing children without your help, but I think your wife and daughters would be ashamed of you."

Balwain lifted his right hand, and Ceres readied herself for the blow. The Woodsman stepped between them, and Balwain backed down.

"Get out," he said, "and I look forward to not seeing any of you again."

The steward scurried forward to usher them to the door, which opened at his hiss. Before it closed behind them, Ceres risked a final peek at Balwain, but he was staring at the carving on the wall, lost in dreams of the death of wolves.

LI

Ofermod
(OLD ENGLISH)

Pride, Overconfidence

he visitors did not talk again until they were safely back in their quarters, where they discovered that three simple beds had been brought, each with a hard mattress, a harder pillow, and a single blanket that might have been made of paper for all the warmth it was likely to provide. Once they were alone, the Woodsman raised a finger to his lips, indicated the walls of the room, and then touched the same finger to his right ear. He walked to one of the windows and opened it, admitting noise from the courtyard below. When he spoke, it was in a whisper, and Ceres and David responded in like manner.

"Balwain is, in some ways, a much changed man," said the Woodsman. "Unfortunately the changes in him are for the worse. This land has a bad custodian in him."

"He was hiding something," said Ceres, "and so was the steward."

"Balwain's nature is always to conceal more than he reveals, although that hardly makes him unique. At the very least, he will be trying to find a way to turn to his advantage the danger posed by the Fae. We have one night under his roof to discover what we can, and hope that, in the meantime, you can lead us to Calio and those children."

Ceres flexed her arm.

"It hurts less now that we've left Balwain's presence. For a while I had to bite my lip so as not to scream in there."

"We were at ground level," said David. "Any lower, and we'd have been in the cellars and dungeons—or worse." And Ceres knew that he was remembering again his hours walking the byways of the Crooked Man.

"If Ceres was more sensitive to Calio, it would seem to confirm that the dryad has discovered a way to move under the castle," said the Woodsman. "And if Calio is down there, so are the Fae—or some of them, anyway."

"I have no idea how deep the Crooked Man's tunnels might have gone, or how extensive the network was," said David, "but there must have been miles of them under the castle alone. Its destruction would have caused some to collapse, but more may have survived intact."

"Then we need to find a way in, and allow Ceres to do the rest."

"But why would they come here?" asked Ceres. "Surely there are safer places for them to have taken the children. This castle is full of guards and soldiers, all armed with steel. It must be the most perilous of places for the Fae."

"Because if they can kill Balwain, they'll sow terror and confusion," answered David. "The other nobles will jostle for power, squabbling and fighting among themselves. A divided enemy is easier to conquer."

"Balwain must have taken that possibility into account," said the Woodsman, "yet he showed no signs of worry. It may be that power and greed have clouded his judgment."

"His mind struck me as pretty unclouded," said Ceres, "except by thoughts of killing wolves. Why didn't you mention to him that we were using Calio to track the Fae?"

"Why didn't you?" the Woodsman countered.

"Because I didn't trust him. More to the point, I didn't like him, and therefore I didn't *want* to trust him. But that's wrong, isn't it? You don't have to like someone to have faith in their abilities. There are all kinds of unpleasant people who are very good at what they do, even if what they do best is be unpleasant."

"So if we accept that Balwain is clever, unpleasant, and not to be trusted," said David, "the question remains: What exactly is he playing at?"

LII

Screncan

(OLD ENGLISH)

To Cause to Stumble, To Deceive

alwain was alone in the receiving room. His steward and household staff were occupied elsewhere, ensuring that the final preparations for the meeting of the nobles were in train. Six places would be set at the table in the Great Hall, with Balwain to be seated at its head. No guards, and no advisors, would be present. What would follow was only for the eyes and ears of those with the bluest of blood.

"Show yourself," said Balwain, and there was a stirring on the carving. The body of the largest wolf became swollen, like an animal about to give birth, before a section of wood fell to the ground in a shape that was vaguely human. A shimmering, and Calio was revealed.

For a few moments the dryad remained curled on the floor by Balwain's feet. The effort of extended concealment had cost them: bloody sap flowed from their nose and mouth, and dripped from the nail beds of their fingers and toes. Finally, as they began to recover their strength, Calio got to their knees, but could rise no further, and so stayed low before Balwain, like a supplicant.

"Well?" said Balwain.

Calio elected to lie. Unlike their Fae kindred, they were good at lying.

"It must be as the Woodsman said: my cousins, journeying in haste, left tracks, and he followed them."

Calio was not about to share the truth with Balwain—this short-lived being, this mayfly creature—that it was they who had lured Ceres here, and the Woodsman and David with her. Neither could the Fae be permitted to know it. If any of them suspected, it would be the death of Calio.

"That was negligent of them," said Balwain.

"If you wish to express your unhappiness in person, an audience can be arranged," said Calio. "I'm sure the Pale Lady will prove a sympathetic listener."

Balwain doubted that, but he didn't like being mocked by a tree spirit, another throwback to a bygone age. The Fae were worthy of respect, but this wight belonged only on a fire. Once his business with the Fae was concluded, Balwain might seek to seal the pact with a sacrificial offering, and Calio would do nicely. It would give him no small satisfaction to finally render the species extinct, and soon after the dryads would be joined in annihilation by wolves, harpies, and, ultimately, the Fae themselves. A new age had dawned, the Age of Men, and there could no longer be coexistence with the old races.

"Just be sure your kith are ready," said Balwain, "and their aim is true. I don't want chaos on my hands."

Calio noticed that Balwain didn't say anything about his conscience. His list of victims might be short and selective, or long and exhaustive, whatever his ambition required, but each person on it would be dispatched quickly, cleanly, and quietly. Balwain did not want anyone to suffer, and had no desire to make a public spectacle of murder. He was not a cruel man, just a practical one. Besides, there were children among the doomed.

"The Pale Lady is waiting," said Calio. "I must be gone."

Balwain indicated the sack containing the severed Fae head.

"You can take that with you. Give it a proper burial, or whatever it is the Fae do with their dead."

"They rest among them," said Calio.

Calio had been inside the Fae mounds, and had witnessed for themselves the great mausoleums of bone.

"Whatever for?" said Balwain.

Calio shrugged.

"So that when they die, it will not seem so strange."

Balwain's nose wrinkled in disgust.

"That explains why, beneath their perfume of spice, they stink like a charnel house—and you can tell your Pale Lady I said so, not that she'll be bothered by the comparison."

"The Fae think you also smell of death," said Calio, "every one of you. You're transient, barely born before you expire. A whole human life is like the passing of a day for them. They blink, and you are gone."

"But we walk in the sun, while they cower beneath the earth."

"They are cowering no longer."

"No," admitted Balwain, "but this land will not be theirs again. They can have their mounds, and we will leave them to lie undisturbed with their ancestors, their vaults inviolate, until sleep becomes death. If they want to feed, they can limit themselves to the weak. They'll make for poor pickings, but better than nothing."

"The Pale Lady understands the terms of the contract," said Calio. "Peace for the Fae, untroubled by men, while you—"

"—get Pandemonium for myself alone," finished Balwain. "And the Pale Lady surrenders the she-wolf who killed my family."

"The Pale Lady has the luna wolf ready for you. I have seen it caged."

Calio touched a stone on the wall. It withdrew under the pressure of their hand, and a cabinet shifted position, revealing a doorway behind. As the dryad prepared to leave, Balwain asked a final question.

"What the Woodsman said about the Crooked Man, is there any truth to it?"

Calio shook their head, as another lie came easily to them.

"None," said Calio. "None at all."

LIII

Heortece

(OLD ENGLISH)

Heartache

eres was weary, but the Woodsman discouraged her from lying down just yet.

"If you sleep," he said, "you may glimpse Calio, but it will be useless to us. There are too many people milling about, and we'll attract attention if we try to move with any urgency. It would be better to wait until the council of nobles is about to begin, because all interest will be focused on the meeting place. You can close your eyes shortly before then, and wait to see what is revealed to you. My hope is that, if Calio is close, you'll be able to find them, and we can make our move. For the present, I suggest we explore as much of the castle as is open to us. You may get to know places you later see in your dreams."

Beyond the door, although not stationed directly outside, a pair of bored guards loitered. The Woodsman called to them.

"My young companion, foundling that she is, has never visited such a great castle before," he explained, patting Ceres on the head in a way that came close to earning him a kick in the shin. "Might we be allowed to stretch our legs—under escort, of course—and take in our surroundings?"

The guards consulted briefly, after which the older instructed the younger to stay with their "guests," but not to interfere with them unless they tried to enter any private chambers. Ceres, David, and the Woodsman were therefore relatively free to wander, which helped to shake off some of Ceres's tiredness. The guard maintained a discreet distance, and seemed equally happy to be walking instead of standing in a windowless corridor watching dust motes drift by.

They began with a circuit of the castle's exterior, although the air wasn't exactly fresh, filled as it was with the smells of horses and soldiers, since the nobles' escorts had all established informal camps in the courtyards. Armed men and women lounged, snoozed, or sat in small groups around fires, eating and smoking, but not drinking anything stronger than water and small beer, and all their talk was of the Fae. The different camps did not mix, though, and their attitudes toward one another ranged from casual disinterest to barely concealed hostility. If this was a reflection of how their lords and ladies felt, Ceres thought the imminent council was set to be a lively affair. On more than one occasion she caught soldiers staring at her without embarrassment, stripping her with their eyes despite her apparent youth. She wondered how many of them had wives, sisters, and daughters of their own, and how much cruelty they might have inflicted on the wives, sisters, and daughters of other men.

Ceres gave an area of honeysuckles a wide berth, as the Woodsman had informed her that the shrub was traditionally used to mask the smell of shared latrines. The bush was also present in the water closets inside the castle, where it had some effect, but so many people used the outside toilets that whole groves of honeysuckle wouldn't have been enough to hide the stink. If the sight of the bushes was insufficient to encourage Ceres to keep her distance, along with a warning blast of foul air caused by the wind temporarily changing direction, there was also the insistent buzzing of flies. Ceres wouldn't have entered those toilets for a bag of gold, no matter how much she might have needed to do her business. Frankly, she'd rather have burst.

From the rampart, Ceres could see more campfires burning beyond the main walls, where those who had failed to find safety within were doing their best to make up for it with flame and numbers without. She knew that this scene, or some lesser version of it, was being reproduced all over the land, as villagers sought security behind fences, walls, and gates, their doors and windows barred, and their children forbidden from venturing outside for fear of the Fae. But it might have been that even the most poorly defended hovel was safer than Balwain's great fortress, built as it was on false ground through which, if David's suspicions were correct, enemies were moving.

Unnoticed behind her, and concealed by shadows cast by the setting sun, the ivy on the castle walls moved. A face peered from the greenery, its hollow eyes regarding Ceres before shifting to David. At the sight of him the mouth opened, ready to consume him should he have ventured close enough to be taken. Then the face disappeared, and once again all was as it had been.

Rain started to fall, forcing the trio and their escort back inside. Now they took in as much of the interior as they could, the guard having scant interest in their activities, since they showed no sign of doing anything they shouldn't, and were careful to seek his permission before trying any closed doors, or venturing down interesting passageways. They arrived at the castle's kitchens, where a banquet—potage, roasts, pies, pastries, and tarts—was being prepared for the nobles in the lord's kitchen, while in the common kitchen great cauldrons of meat bubbled for their retinues. The staff, Ceres noticed, were all male, the alewives apart, and the smells of cooking were underpinned by those of fermented yeast, pickling vinegar, and blood.

They didn't stay long, because wherever they stood, they managed to get under the feet of a cook or pot boy. Before they left, one of the alewives, fresh from delivering yeast to the bakers, pressed hot scones on them, which made the guard even more relaxed in their company. Ceres was still munching away happily when she turned a corner and stopped, the pastry turning to dust and gravel in her mouth. Before her was the portrait of Balwain, one hand on a book, the other on his sword, with the open window behind him.

"This is it," she whispered to the Woodsman. "This is the picture I saw in my vision."

She stood in front of the painting, and stretched out a hand to touch it, half anticipating her fingers being subsumed into the scene, but the canvas remained rigid.

"Don't do that," said the guard, the first words he had spoken, otherwise limiting any expressions of approval or disapproval to nods and shakes of his head.

"I'm sorry," said Ceres. "I was curious."

"This is his lordship's most precious possession, even if he can hardly bear to look at it these days."

"Why is that?"

"Because his late wife was the artist."

So this was how she saw Balwain, Ceres thought: handsome but austere, even threatening. His drive was evident in the set of his jaw, and the steeliness of his eyes, while the open book upon which his hand rested contained lines of numbers: accounts, not poetry. Unusually, he was not depicted staring directly out of the frame, but looking down to one side, implying that the artist—and, by extension, his wife—was of less interest to him than the figures in his ledger. Here was the story of a marriage, and not a happy one.

Behind the figure of Balwain was the open window, with darkness beyond: the night from which the Fae warrior had emerged. But the Fae couldn't really climb out of a painting, could they? Then again, if one of them could take the form of an adolescent boy and wriggle like a serpent through a narrow gap, all to kill a girl, who was to say that manipulating a work of art was beyond them?

"You should be getting back to your quarters," said the guard. "The council is about to be convened."

He led the way from the kitchens, taking back stairs and quieter, less traveled hallways. Ceres suspected he might now be regretting having allowed them such free rein, and he didn't hide his relief when they arrived at their room without incident, although Ceres still made a point of thanking him for his assistance. The door closed behind them, and once again they went to the window to talk.

"Well," said the Woodsman, "that was useful, especially the return journey. There are ways to move about unnoticed."

"We'll have to get out of here first," said David.

"Soon everyone in this castle will have their hands full with the council. They'll also be watching out for the Fae, which means they'll be looking beyond these walls, not inside them. But should I prove to be mistaken, I'm more than capable of creating a distraction."

The Woodsman turned to Ceres.

"Now it's time for you to sleep," he said. "To sleep, and to dream."

LIV

Hel

(OLD NORSE)

The Goddess of Death

eres, lying on one of the beds, drowsing, willed herself to come upon Calio and the missing children. She summoned the hallways through which they had earlier walked, and the interiors of chambers glimpsed through open doors, mapping the castle in her mind. But when she finally began to dream, the visions took her not to stone corridors or earthen tunnels, but to a bedroom in the Lantern House, with the curtain on the window drawn against the waning of the day. Phoebe lay unmoving apart from the soft rise and fall of her chest. The lamp by the bedside was lit, the one Ceres used for reading to her at night. It was the only illumination in the room, casting the rest into obscurity.

And in that dimness, a figure prowled: a woman, visible only as a silhouette, a shadow composed of other shadows, pieces of darkness pressed into service, compacted to lend substance to that which did not belong. The top of the woman's head was deformed, so that shards of glass or splinters of wood might have pierced her skull. It took Ceres a moment to identify it as a jagged crown growing out of the bone.

"Do you know me?" the woman said, as the room grew colder. "Because I know you, and the child. You're not the only one who can cross between worlds."

"You stay away from her," said Ceres. Like the woman, an aspect of herself was in the room, like the spirit of one not yet deceased, so Ceres knew that she had agency here. Unfortunately, so also did this predatory female.

"Why?" said the woman. "She is more dead than alive, and therefore more mine than yours, so close that the distance between us is barely a step—or a breath. There is so little life left in her that it's hardly worth the effort of taking it."

"Then leave her be."

"Are you begging me?"

"No, I'm telling you. Keep away from her."

The woman's laughter sounded like ice shattering.

"And what will you do? What can you do, where countless others have tried and failed? Have you any conception of how many have pleaded or blustered when the end came—when *I* came? At least your daughter will expire in silence."

"I will fight for her."

"But you summoned me. You willed me here. You wished her dead—and yourself, too. You despaired, and I am the inevitable coda to that song."

"That's not true. I wanted only for this misery to cease, and at a moment of weakness, when I thought I couldn't go on."

"Such sophistry. Nevertheless, I heard, and I answered. Now, speak my name. Acknowledge me."

"I will not."

"Because you're afraid of what might happen if you say it aloud."

"Yes."

"Don't be. She will feel just a sting, even as you did, and what follows will be a mercy for both of you. I am always merciful, if only at the very last."

"I see no mercy in you," said Ceres, "only hunger."

"Your fear blinds you to the first, and overstates the second. But I won't deny that my appetite is my affliction. It's never sated, nor would I wish it to be. I am that which comes to all things, because it must come. I am in them and of them from the moment of their birth. I walk beside them all their lives, and mine is the final face they see."

"You enjoy death."

"No, I *am* Death."

The woman came forward, shedding the dark as she came, blackness falling from her like charred leaves as she drew nearer the bed: the Pale Lady Death, revealed in all her glory. Her lips parted as she leaned down to kiss Phoebe.

"No!" said Ceres. "I will not allow it."

And she flung herself at Death.

On the pallet bed, watched by the Woodsman and David, Ceres cried out in torment. David leaned forward as though to wake her, but the Woodsman stopped him.

"Don't," he said.

"But she's in pain."

"She was in pain when she arrived, and long before that, just as you were when you came here for the first time. You were a child searching for his lost mother. She is a mother searching for her lost child."

Reluctantly, David stepped back. Ceres's teeth were gritted, and the tendons in her neck stood out as her body contorted with the anguish of what she was enduring. On her bare left arm, the site of Calio's sting had become red and angry once more. The lump distended visibly before their eyes, rising to a whitish head of infection.

"But she may be dying," said David.

"There was a time when she might have been glad to die," said the Woodsman. "Now, I think, she wants to live, whatever distress it may bring."

He laid his hand on Ceres's forehead, and she gave a cry that was both agony and release, like the final effort of parturition, the last desperate push that had brought her daughter into the world. The mass of swollen tissue on her arm burst, exuding a smell like sour milk, with a flood of pus that was followed by a stream of bright red blood. Ceres's body relaxed, and she breathed out a single soft sigh. A minute passed, and then she spoke.

"Balwain," she said.

Ceres was standing once again before the portrait of the castle's lord, hidden away by the kitchens. She had little memory of what had happened after she put herself between Phoebe and the Pale Lady, but she was no longer immediately concerned for her daughter. Death had been kept at bay, if just for a while.

She heard movement above her head, and looked up to find Calio clinging to the ceiling, their attention focused on the passageway ahead, and the retreating backs of Fae warriors armed with longbows. Calio crawled after them, leaving Ceres alone.

Sometimes, in life as in dreams, the world tries to communicate a truth to us, but in a manner so subtle that it takes us time to figure out.

The portrait, she thought. *They climbed out of the portrait.*

Now I understand.

Ceres opened her eyes to the Woodsman and David. Her arm was bandaged with a fresh length of torn sheet, stained red, and she felt cleansed.

"I know how to get to the children," she said. "But first you have to warn Balwain. The Fae are here."

LV

Swicere
(OLD ENGLISH)

Traitor

he nobles had convened in the Great Hall of the castle, which was a more modest affair than the name might have implied. It could have accomodated fifty people for a banquet in some degree of comfort, but it had not witnessed any such celebrations since the death of Lord Balwain's wife. Now it was used solely for the business of ruling: meetings, tribunals, and the settlement of grievances in a civilized manner; or, where a grievance had been settled in a manner that was most certainly *not* civilized—as with a sword, a dagger, or an axe—the dispensing of punishment, should it be required or demanded. Thus it was that the Great Hall had more than once heard a sentence of execution being passed, although only on those without wealth or power. Justice may be blind, but her robes have hidden pockets, and they can hold a lot of money. The poor and the vulnerable, meanwhile, have to make do with the law, however harsh and unyielding it may be.

Currently the Great Hall contained only a single table surrounded by six chairs. Two candelabra had been lit, as well as the torches in their sconces, and a fire burned in the stone hearth, the latter tall enough to accommodate a grown man standing upright without his head becoming lost to sight in the chimney. The nature of the lighting meant that a ring of darkness surrounded the central table, and the minstrels' gallery, which had not been troubled by music in many years, was in shadow.

The table was laid only with two jugs of red wine, and simple goblets from which to drink. Much in Balwain's castle was plain. Balwain enjoyed being wealthy, because wealth meant power, and power meant survival, but he distrusted vulgar displays of material possessions. They communicated insecurity, since only those who were secretly vulnerable felt the need to show off what they owned. Also, in an often violent world, people with expensive rings on their fingers were asking for those rings to be removed, and the fingers along with them.

Currently seated around the table, waiting for Balwain to make his entrance, were the five nobles who ruled this part of the realm with varying degrees of fidelity, envy, and smothered resentment toward their overlord, depending on their levels of ambition. The most competent, and therefore the most dangerous, was the Countess Christiana, reputed to have poisoned her husband, Earl Hans—who was also her nephew, a complicated arrangement that suited no one, least of all the countess, which was why she had seen fit to dispose of him. To her left was Baron Wilhelm, and beside him his younger sibling Jacob: greedy, idle men, but easily manipulated, although they had recently expressed dissatisfaction with their share of the proceeds from the Pandemonium mine, and were seeking a renegotiation of their contract with Balwain. Both were married to equally greedy, similarly idle women, and had begun siring children who showed no signs of being any different from their parents.

Across from Jacob sat Charles, Duke of Perrault, half brother of the late and generally unlamented Earl Hans, who regarded Christiana as a murderess, but chose to keep this opinion to himself because he had no desire to be poisoned in turn, and currently employed a team of tasters to sample his food before he sat down to table. Last, beside Charles, was the Marchioness Dortchen, Balwain's sister-in-law, and the noble theoretically most closely bound to him by ties of blood and loyalty, although neither counted for much where the nobility was concerned, blood being something to be spilled when required, and loyalty an asset to be traded for advantage.

"He's late," said Christiana. "Punctuality is the politeness of kings, or hasn't he heard?"

"Balwain is no king," said Wilhelm, "not even in his dreams."

Beside him, his brother snickered.

"The last king was eaten by wolves," said Jacob, "while Balwain just fed his family to them. Perhaps he misunderstood the requirements of royalty."

"That's a poor joke," said the Marchioness Dortchen, "and in worse taste."

Jacob ceased his snickering, although he had no fear of Dortchen making unfavorable reports to her brother-in-law, as she had no more love for him than anyone else. Dortchen had expected to receive a further share of the mine upon her sister's death, since Balwain's wife had been endowed with a portion of it as a wedding gift, and her will stipulated that, in the event of her demise, all her wealth should pass to Dortchen, who would hold it in trust for the children. When those same children were consumed by wolves along with their mother, Balwain and his lawyers decided that the terms of the will no longer applied, depriving Dortchen of her additional percentage. So, while Dortchen continued to stand by Balwain, she did so because the alternative—namely, an alliance with one or more of the other nobles—did not appeal, or not yet.

Only Duke Charles remained silent. He owned the smallest share in the mine, and might have preferred to hold none at all, but it was better to be involved, and have some say in the running of it, than to be without influence. Privately, Charles viewed the mine as a blight upon the land, especially because his territories were low-lying, and the runoff from the operation was slowly poisoning his rivers and the surrounding fields and forests. His tenants had begun to complain, because the pollution impacted directly on their yields, and what affected their income had a bearing on the rents Charles could charge. So far, though, his petitioning of Balwain to do something about the situation had fallen on deaf ears.

And now there were the Fae to be considered. Charles didn't imagine that they would look very favorably on the mine's existence. The Fae were acutely sensitive to changes in the environment, and regarded its protection as a duty, not least because its purity was integral to their survival. There were stories from olden days of the Fae torturing to death farmers who did not treat nature with sufficient respect, and drowning landowners who permitted waste to sully their streams. In the safety of his own house, and the privacy of his own mind, Charles speculated that the mine itself might have drawn the Fae from their mounds and burrows. If this was the case, he was fully prepared to advocate its closure rather than risk an escalation of hostilities, but he doubted that his business partners, and Balwain in particular, would be as willing to walk away from so much untapped wealth.

"Damn the man," said Wilhelm. "Where is he?"

Which was when Balwain appeared in the minstrels' gallery, a single candle in his right hand. The gallery took up three sides of the Great Hall, and Balwain was positioned at the midpoint, peering down on his guests with neither gratitude nor affection, but something closer to disdain.

"I am here," said Balwain, "and have been for some time."

If any of those who had spoken out of turn were ashamed or concerned, they hid it well. With the return of the Fae, Balwain needed them as much as they needed him. If he chose to take offense, that was his business. They all had bigger fish to fry.

"I don't mind you occupying a bigger chair at the table, brother," said the Marchioness Dortchen, "but having to stare up at you for the duration of our meeting will rapidly prove wearying."

"You needn't worry yourself on that front, sister," said Balwain. "The deliberations won't take long. In fact, you could say they were concluded before you arrived."

Dortchen scowled. Jacob and Wilhelm giggled, which they did at times of stress or uncertainty. Christiana looked as though she was considering getting back into the poisoning business. Only Duke Charles, whose instincts for self-preservation were highly developed, reacted with speed and purpose. He was already on his feet, making for the door and the promise of safety, when a stone-tipped arrow took him in the small of the back. The impact sent him staggering on for a few more steps before he fell, when a second arrow put him out of his misery.

By the time the last breath left him, most of his fellow nobles were dying too.

LVI

Dern

(MIDDLE ENGLISH)

Hidden, Secret

he young guard who had chaperoned them during their tour of the castle was now the sole sentinel in the hallway when Ceres, David, and the Woodsman left their room. The guard was propping up the wall, his arms folded and his legs crossed, since there was no one around to chastise him for it, and the stone floor, combined with the curvature of the walls, meant that he'd be able to detect the approach of one of his superiors by sound long before they came in sight. Still, the sudden appearance of his charges surprised him enough to cause him to stand up straight and seek out his pike.

"You have to stay in your quarters," he said. "Lord Balwain has ordered that the castle be secured while the council is in session."

"The castle is not secure," said Ceres, "because the Fae are already inside."

"That's not possible," said the guard.

"It is, because I've seen them."

This caught his attention, even if Ceres decided not to add that she'd seen them only in a vision, which was likely to undermine her credibility as a witness.

"She's telling the truth," said the Woodsman. "They're using the old tunnels beneath the castle, and a hidden entrance by the kitchens."

The guard listened to the Woodsman with less doubt than he'd directed at Ceres. *The patriarchy grinds along,* Ceres thought. If she ever managed to get back to her own world, she would never again vote for a male politician.

"What harm can it do to check?" asked David. "It'll take only a few minutes. We're not armed, so we can't pose any threat."

"And if we use those back stairways," said Ceres, "no one will be any the wiser."

"I'm not supposed to leave my post," said the guard. "I'll be put on report."

"If the Fae get to Balwain," said the Woodsman, "there'll be no one to report you to. But later, if it's discovered that, by your actions, you failed to prevent some harm from coming to him—"

The guard quickly agreed that it couldn't hurt to be sure, although he insisted on searching them for hidden weapons—well, he searched the Woodsman and David, but contented himself with a visual inspection of Ceres, because her expression left him in no doubt that he would be unwise to lay a hand on her. When he was as satisfied about her as he was going to be, the guard indicated that they should walk ahead while he followed, his pike at the ready. They descended through the same dusty stairways and corridors they had so recently explored, avoiding all but a handful of servants, who were too busy with their own errands to be more than mildly curious, and so they reached unchecked the portrait of Balwain.

"So, where is this hidden entrance?" said the guard.

Ceres tested the frame, inserting her thin fingers behind the gilt, pushing and probing at the ornamentation.

"I told you," said the guard, "you're not supposed to touch that."

"It's just the frame," said Ceres. "I'm not exactly ripping up the canvas." She glared at the three men. "Well, don't just stand there gawping. There has to be a device of some kind. Look for it."

The Woodsman and David commenced an examination of the walls, pressing at the stones, the sconces, even applying heavy pressure to the tiles on the floor. The guard stood aside until, accepting that this was no ruse, he felt obliged to assist, but to no avail. The portrait remained in place, and no concealed entrance revealed itself. Ultimately, Ceres was forced to admit defeat.

"I was sure," she said. "I was so sure—"

Which was when they heard a distinct *click*. Behind Ceres, the portrait of Balwain came away from the wall, like a door opening on its hinges. They stepped back, so that the painting hid them from whomever might emerge.

The Fae warrior who stepped into the hallway was heavily scarred, and missing her right eye, which meant that Ceres and the others remained unnoticed by her for a few crucial seconds. It was enough to allow the guard to ready his pike, but not to use it, because the Fae reacted instantaneously to the scrape of wood against stone. A thin, lethal shape shot from her right hand: a dagger with a smelted iron blade, and a hilt carved from yellowed bone, edged with silver. Ceres got a good look at that hilt, because the dagger was instantly buried up to its crosspiece in the guard's neck. His pike dropped to the floor, and he followed, taking Ceres with him as he fell, even as the Fae drew a sword, ready to strike at the next most imminent threat. This she took to be the Woodsman, the largest and strongest of the trio, who was closing in on her.

The Fae, though, was mistaken. Like the guard, she had underestimated Ceres, who had left the room with her short sword tucked into the back of her trousers, hidden by the folds of her shirt. As the Fae turned to face the Woodsman, Ceres drew the blade and buried it so deep in the warrior's right thigh that the tip popped out the other side. The Fae shrieked, her flesh sizzling from the touch of steel, and the leg collapsed, unable to bear her weight. She tried to stab at her tormentor, but Ceres was too quick, and the sword struck only sparks from the floor. Behind the Fae, the Woodsman hefted the pike and impaled the Fae on its spearhead, killing her instantly.

Ceres got to her feet, braced the sole of her boot against the Fae's body, and pulled her sword free. In death the Fae's dark eyes turned gray, and Ceres watched as her reflection in them slowly vanished, like a moon obscured by clouds.

"Her brothers and sisters will have heard that scream," said the Woodsman. "They'll come to investigate."

Before them yawned the gap revealed by the hinged portrait. The opening was not of recent construction, which meant the Fae weren't likely to have been responsible. Instead, it looked as though the painting had been made to match its dimensions, or vice versa: another escape route for Balwain, should events have someday conspired against him.

"It's odd that this should have been their way in," said David. "Through a painting of Balwain, I mean."

"Or not just through his portrait," said the Woodsman. "Only a handful of people must know of this doorway, and Balwain is certainly one of them. What if it was he who invited the Fae to enter?"

"Why would he do that?"

"Because they could offer him what he wanted, as long as he promised them something in return. Everything is a transaction with them."

Steps led down from the opening, lit by a pink luminescence from within the rock walls: hackmanite or similar, Ceres guessed, a mineral that glowed in shadow but showed plain in daylight. The tingling had returned to her arm. Calio was to be found in the tunnels, and likely the abducted children as well; but also another, because whatever remained of the Crooked Man would be found in those regions, along with the reason she had been brought here.

Ceres hesitated. She never liked being underground for long, not even on the Tube in London. It wasn't claustrophobia—she didn't become frightened, or start to panic; she just felt uncomfortable—but it was enough to count as an aversion. The Woodsman took her hand. He looked sad, and she knew what he was going to say before the words left his mouth.

"I can't go with you," he told her. "Whatever you have to face down there, you must face it alone."

"I understand."

And she did. It didn't mean she wasn't scared, but she was stronger now, altered forever by this journey. The Ceres who had first arrived would not have been capable of walking through that doorway—or more correctly, would not have believed herself capable of it, which was not the same thing. That Ceres was lost, and melancholic, but had forgotten for a while that this was the human condition: often to be lost, confused, or anxious, but finally to comprehend that, at crucial instances, we will find ourselves lost *precisely* where we were meant to be; that there is little of use to be learned from the familiar—one may gain comfort from it, but not knowledge—only from what is strange and new; and that everything worth experiencing or embracing is, because unknown, first touched by fear.

"I can go with her," said David. "After all, I once stood at a doorway not unlike this."

"You can stay with her some of the way," said the Woodsman, "but the ending will still be hers to write. While you're gone, I'll do what I can up here. It may not yet be too late to stop Balwain from making a grave error—and the Fae, too."

The Woodsman kissed Ceres softly on the head.

"I will see you again," he said, "whatever happens."

Then Ceres, aided by David, advanced into the unknown.

LVII

Selfæta
(OLD ENGLISH)

Self-Eater, Cannibal; One Who Preys on His Own Species

 n the Great Hall, six Fae archers were lined up along two sides of the minstrels' gallery, nocking fresh arrows in case they should be required. Christiana was lying facedown on the table, an arrow through her neck, her poisoning days now behind her. The brothers, Jacob and Wilhelm, had each been hit in the chest. Curiously, Wilhelm was still giggling, as though the arrow had merely tickled him instead of fatally nicking his heart. His brother was dead, the draw on the bow so heavy that the arrowhead had gone straight through his torso, pinning him to his chair.

Only Dortchen, Balwain's sister-in-law, so far remained unharmed. As blood spilled across the table, she lifted her wine goblet from the gore, and moved her chair to avoid getting her dress stained. They were actions of surprising calm, the trembling of her hand offering the sole clue to her true state of mind.

"Well," she said, "it seems the balance of power in the land has shifted conclusively."

Balwain remained where he was, staring down at Dortchen, flanked by the Fae. He had barely blinked during the slaughter.

"It was said by many that I should have married you," he said, "if not by my late wife. She respected your determination and guile, but she did not love you."

"Nor I her," said Dortchen. "She was too gentle, too yielding. Had I been the one cornered by wolves, with my babes in my arms, I think you might have been a husband and father still."

"There's truth to that. I'd give wolves poor odds against you, not to mention a lot of men. You were born in the wrong body. Your soul was meant for a different vessel."

"I have long suspected as much," said Dortchen. "It may be why I never took a husband, and there were too many eyes on me to take a wife, although neither would have sufficed to make me happy. I was better off alone."

She drank a mouthful of wine. The quivering of the goblet caused some of the liquid to dribble down her chin. She wiped it off, glancing at the redness on her fingers before taking in, once again, the bloodshed around her. Despite her fear, she was calculating, seeking a pathway to survival.

"After this butchery, instability will ensue," she said. "I can provide a calming influence, a voice of reason. Many will be angered by what you've done. You will require allies."

Balwain spread his arms, taking in the Fae at either side of him.

"I have allies," he said.

"I meant human ones."

"They will follow. I plan an orderly transition, and those who prove resistant to persuasion will have to accept the consequences."

"From your scapegoats, the Fae?"

"Certainly not from me."

"Not directly, although I doubt anything done in your name will trouble your sleep. What have the Fae promised you, for conspiring in this betrayal of your own kind?"

"What do you think? A consolidation of my authority, and an end to allegiances of inconvenience with treacherous women and indolent men. Wealth that I won't have to share with those who would waste it on fripperies. And revenge: the Fae have captured the she-wolf, the luna who led the attack on my family. I plan to spend a long time killing her. I believe I could make the pleasure last for years, if I set my mind to it."

"And what have you guaranteed the Fae in return?"

"The sanctity of their mounds. A limit to the intrusions of men. Peace."

"Peace?" Dortchen almost laughed. "Do you really think there can be peace after this, for you or them? Even if some accord could be reached, are you so deluded as to believe that they will keep to their side of the bargain? Or"—she took in the impassive visages of the Fae—"are they so naive as to believe that you will keep yours?"

"The Fae cannot lie. What they promise, they must deliver. And I am an honorable man."

"Honorable? You call *this* honor? As for the Fae, nothing they promise is ever what it seems."

"Which is why our arrangement is simple: Pandemonium shall be mine alone, and the she-wolf will be set before me. Their room for maneuver is minimal, as is yours."

Balwain spoke as though he were not surrounded by Fae, or they were deaf to his words. In a way they were, since the contract had been agreed with the Pale Lady Death. The dryad, Calio, had acted as intermediary, Balwain not being permitted to look upon the Pale Lady's face— not that he had been eager for the experience. His time would come, as did all men's, but there was no need to be in a hurry about it.

Dortchen, having exhausted transactional politics, had only an entreaty left.

"Is there no chance," she asked, "that an accommodation might be reached between us, for the sake of the one whom we both lost?"

But even as she spoke, she knew the answer, because it could be read in Balwain's face. Some forms of lunacy are easily identifiable. They may involve the rending of garments, the abandonment of all pretensions to cleanliness, and the loss of rationality and reason. But there are other types of lunacy so close to sanity as to be almost indistinguishable from it, especially in those who have set aside morality and compassion. This was Balwain's particular madness, and like all who are mad, he failed to perceive it—or perhaps he did, to a degree, which made his actions all the more unforgivable.

"I'm almost tempted to let you live," said Balwain, "but you're too wily to be trusted, and too ruthless for me to be able to turn my back on you. So I am afraid, sister, that the time has come for us to part. You stepped blindly into this trap, so it seems apt that you should enter the next world in the same manner. Farewell."

He twisted a hand in the air, as he might have dismissed from his presence an unloved courtier who had brought mildly disappointing news. Six arrows pierced Dortchen: one to the womb, one to the heart, one to the neck, one to the forehead, and one for each of her eyes. The Fae's aim, Balwain reflected, was positively uncanny, especially since Dortchen had visibly jerked with the impact of each arrow. If it had not been for their unfortunate vulnerability to fire and steel, the Fae might have been the ones consolidating their hold on the land. Balwain took this as another sign that it was men, not Fae, who had always been destined to rule here.

And by "men," he meant himself.

LVIII

Beáh-Hroden
(OLD ENGLISH)

Crown-Adorned

he Fae archers lowered their bows as, from a hidden doorway behind the fireplace, Balwain's steward emerged, accompanied by four rough-looking hirelings, men who had no compunction about dumping corpses—or, when required, creating corpses to be dumped. At the steward's signal, the hirelings commenced carrying out the bodies: the women first, then the men. Jacob took longer to remove than the rest, because the arrow skewering him to his seat had first to be broken, and Fae weaponry was remarkably resilient. Balwain supervised the whole operation from the gallery, down to the washing of the more obvious blood from the table. When all was accomplished to his satisfaction, he joined the steward below.

What came next would have to be accomplished delicately. Balwain's intention was to reveal only that the nobles had mysteriously vanished before the council could be convened, and a subsequent search would reveal bodies pierced by Fae arrows. An announcement would follow that the lands of his former allies were to be annexed, and overseers loyal to Balwain appointed to manage them, while the realm united to face the common threat represented by the Fae, all under Balwain's banner.

"The retinues of the five nobles should continue to be watched," Balwain instructed the steward, "but make no move against them. When the time comes, they'll be offered the chance to serve me, and swear an oath of allegiance. We'll send to the dungeons those who refuse, to allow them an opportunity to reconsider. Now I should like to be alone with my grief. I've just lost my sister-in-law, and a number of very old acquaintances."

With one final apprehensive glance at the Fae in the gallery, the steward slipped away. Balwain took his place at the head of the table, in the single chair untouched by blood. He tried to explore his feelings, but there were none to explore: not pleasure or relief, and not shame or disgust. There was only a disappointment occasioned by his inability to take joy in the furtherance of his ambitions, which slowly became a broader depression that clouded his thoughts, so that for a while his surroundings were forgotten. He hoped that when the she-wolf was brought into his presence he would find himself capable of a deeper emotional response.

A sound from nearby—stone grating upon stone, as of one of the room's hidden doorways opening—summoned him from his melancholy. The Fae archers had now joined him on the floor of the Great Hall, even though he had not requested their company; had, in fact, assumed they would return to make their report to the Pale Lady. In this, as in so much else, he was mistaken. The Fae had no need to go to her, because she was already with them.

The temperature plummeted around Balwain, but before he could determine the cause, cold lips touched the back of his neck, succeeded by a sharp sting, like a needle being inserted into the base of his skull. A chill entered his chest, rapidly spreading to his limbs. He tried to call for help, but his tongue was turning to ice, and his breath plumed silently from his open mouth. Even the moisture in his eyes froze, so that his vision became blurred, and the Pale Lady Death, her skull crowned with spurs of bone, was barely a mist among mists, an agent of the dark.

"Balwain," she whispered, "let us conclude our bargain."

The steward did not get far. As he scurried down a hallway, he was intercepted by the Woodsman, accompanied by a troop of palace guards who had been shown the dead Fae and their fallen comrade by the kitchens. The guards were led by the marshal, Denham.

"Where is Balwain?" the Woodsman asked.

"He has convened the council of nobles," replied the steward, "and is not to be disturbed."

"Circumstances have altered. Take us to him."

Protesting all the way, the steward led them to the main entrance of the Great Hall, and prophesied dire consequences once his lordship learned of how his steward had been manhandled. The Woodsman knocked hard on the door and shouted Balwain's name, to no response.

"Your lord isn't answering," said the Woodsman to the steward, "and his nobles either. If they're in there, they're dead. If they're not, you should be anxious to find out what's happened to them."

The Woodsman turned to Denham.

"Do you have the authority to break down the door?"

"I do, but I'd prefer not to."

"Damage can be repaired. Death is permanent."

"So I've heard."

The marshal summoned the strongest of his men, who commenced forcing the door. Soon they heard cracking, as the wood began to give under the press of bodies.

"One more effort," said the Woodsman. "Push!"

The guards retreated, gathering their energy for the final attempt, before slamming their combined weight against the door. The inner bar snapped, and the door opened, revealing the emptiness of the Great Hall: no Balwain, and no nobles. The guards drew their swords and spread out to search. The Woodsman entered last. He walked to the table, rested his hands on the wood, and felt them stick, even as the steward scampered for the door.

"Hold him," the Woodsman ordered. Two guards intercepted the steward, and hauled him kicking and complaining to stand before the Woodsman and Denham.

"You have no power here," said the steward. "In his lordship's absence I—"

"In his absence," said the Woodsman, "you'll answer our questions, the first of which is"—he raised his stained hands before the steward's face—"whose blood is this?"

LIX

Beheafdian

(OLD ENGLISH)

To Decapitate

eres and David were negotiating a network of very old tunnels, only one of which—the main, illuminated shaft—was in regular use. Some of the rest had collapsed, making them partly or wholly impassable, reduced to little more than indentations in the stonework, but at least one of these would prove lifesaving.

As the Woodsman predicted, the Fae had heard the cry of their sister, and Ceres soon picked up on their coming. While the Fae were capable of moving silently, they had no need for stealth in these depths. But even had caution been advisable, the urge to help one of their own in peril forced them to move speedily. The soft padding of their feet, and the jangle of their weaponry, gave them away, allowing Ceres and David to seek shelter in a side tunnel. Nevertheless, so shallow was the one they chose that Ceres could have reached out and touched the three Fae as they passed, and only when she could no longer hear them did she allow herself to breathe out. Beside her, David did the same, then whispered:

"They seem so few. What can they hope to achieve when men vastly outnumber them?"

"Maybe it's just better than doing nothing, whatever it is."

They resumed their expedition, plunging deeper and deeper, guided by the knowledge that they were following the tunnel from which the Fae had come, and further aided by the nagging pain of Ceres's injury. For all the suffering Calio had caused her, it was proving invaluable in their search. But once the children were found, the dryad could wither and die for all Ceres cared, or be broken up and used to make matches.

"Did you hear that?" said David.

Ceres listened.

"I don't hear anything at all," she said.

"Hush!"

Ceres glowered at David. She didn't like being ordered about by a man, no matter what the reason, but since the light was so dim, her death stare was wasted on him.

"There's no need—"

There it was: the wailing of a baby, barely audible. These were the cries of an infant so feeble or exhausted that it could hardly summon the strength required to make the sound. Ceres and David traced the sobs to a room filled with mirrors, each glass containing the final moments of someone enduring a painful death, their faces twisted in torment, the end replayed over and over. Every mirror was similar in shape—an oval of about eighteen inches in diameter—but every frame was unique, just as every path to death is different, but the destination the same.

"One of the Crooked Man's chambers," said David. "It has the feel of his amusements."

But Ceres was intent on a corner of the room, where a quintet of wicker cots sat around a brazier of glowing coals. Above one of the cots crouched a Fae, his head low as he breathed in tendrils of white vapor, feeding on the life force of some mite. It was from this child that the cries were coming, even as they began to fade into a final silence. Ceres thought that she had never felt such fury, perhaps not even at the man who had robbed her of her daughter. The driver hadn't set out to hurt Phoebe. There was no malice to his actions, and had he been given any inkling of what was about to happen, he would immediately have set his phone aside and returned his focus to the road. But this: to feast on a child, to consciously deprive it of life in order to extend one's own—

and that a life already long-lived, centuries upon centuries, while this tiny being had barely been given time to feel the sun on its skin.

Before David could stop her, Ceres was running, sword in hand. So absorbed was the Fae in his meal that he did not spot the threat until Ceres was almost on top of him, and by then it was too late. The sword had already commenced its swing as the Fae raised his head, and the blade struck as he turned, so that Ceres was able to see the look on his face as his head was separated from his body, to land hissing among a cairn of small bones that shattered with the impact.

"Look what you made me do!" cried Ceres, addressing herself to the mutilated corpse, its sundered head, and perhaps also to this world and the world left behind, each a distorted reflection of the other. "Look at what I've become!"

Because this killing was different. Back in Salaama, the Fae changeling had pounced at her, and the sword was in him before she knew it, so she could not have said with any certainty whether she had intended to dispatch him or not. This time, though, she had set out to put another being to death, and the rage behind the fatal blow was a cold one. She had not been overcome by it, but had channeled it.

Then David was beside her, holding firm to her sword arm, just in case the adrenaline coursing through her should cause her to take a swing at his head as well. In her words he heard an echo of his own many years earlier, when he also had taken a life, and he wondered if it was a price that had to be paid for the lessons learned in this place, and the true death was, in reality, his own: the passing of the old self, and its replacement by another, one that was wiser but sadder. He didn't try to tell Ceres that it was okay, because it was not, nor would it ever be.

"It's done," was all he said, "and it had to be done."

Of the five cots, three were occupied by infants, none above a year old. A fourth cot was empty, and the last contained only the shell of a child, like one of the preserved bodies retrieved from bogs that had so fascinated her father and so disturbed Ceres. The faces of the living children were thin and hollowed out. They would be frail for a long time after, and she thought they would always bear the marks, both visible and hidden, of what they had endured in these tunnels.

Any further reflections were cut short by a groan from among the bones. For a second Ceres feared that the Fae had somehow survived his decapitation and was about to begin shouting for help. She didn't think she had it in her to begin hacking at a head disunited from its body. Her sanity wouldn't be able to stand it. But drawing closer, she saw a pair of hands manacled to a loop in the wall behind the cairn, and a near-naked male figure curled in on itself. She placed a hand on the man, and he pulled away as though her touch burned.

"Baako," said Ceres, for it was he, "don't be afraid."

Baako reacted to the sound of her voice, and Ceres could not help but wince at the sight of him. His eyes were sunk deep in their sockets, his cheekbones were sharp beneath the skin, and there were gaps in his mouth where some of his teeth had fallen out. Most of the flesh was gone from his bones, and even his hair was touched with silver. This was what the depredations of the Fae had wrought on him.

"How bad do I look?" he asked, responding to Ceres's expression of horror. "Because I feel very bad."

She struck at the chains with her sword to avoid answering the question. They were old, forged by the Crooked Man himself, and resisted her efforts, so that Ceres was breathless by the time she managed to break them.

"We'll make you well again," said Ceres.

"*That* bad."

"If it's any comfort, I wasn't going to marry you anyway."

She and David helped Baako to his feet. He tottered at first, but was soon able to stand unassisted. Whatever the damage to his body, he still had his spirit, and a core of deep strength on which to draw. Ceres knew he would grow up to be a man worthy of respect.

"What about my mother and father?" he asked. "And my sister?"

Ceres was careful not to give anything away.

"Your father and sister were fine when I left them," she said. "Your sister was in the village, and your father had gone in search of your mother. She, like you, was abducted. I don't know anything more."

Which was true, if only up to a point, but it wasn't for her—and this wasn't the place—to inform Baako that his mother was certainly dead. He had suffered enough for the present, and she didn't have time to spare comforting him.

"We should leave," said David. "We can carry a child each, and leave our sword arms free."

There came the beating of wings from above their heads, and the one-eyed rook alighted on an empty torch sconce by the smallest and darkest of the shafts leading off the mirror room. It cocked its head at Ceres, and croaked.

"I can't," said Ceres to the two men. "I have to go on."

David took in the tunnel mouth, as though by penetrating its gloom he might spot a waiting presence within. Beside him, Baako had made a pair of papooses from the thin sheets in the cots, and was using them to secure one child to his chest and the other to his back. The remaining infant he held in his arms.

"I'm too weak to be much use in a fight," he told David, "but I can free you to do what you can."

David hugged Ceres.

"Remember," he whispered, "if it is the Crooked Man, he'll promise you something, something you really want. He's a tempter, and a trickster, but what's on offer will be real. That's the hard part. You'll desire it, and he has the power to grant it."

"At a price," said Ceres.

"Yes, there's always a price," said David. "But it may be a price you're willing to pay."

He released Ceres and went to join Baako, who was waiting by the main passage. Ceres removed a torch from the wall and ignited it from the brazier, to light her way. Nothing more was said, and the three parted company, leaving the room of mirrors still and quiet, filled only with the dead, both recent and ancient, or so it seemed.

But high on the ceiling came movement, as though a section of the rock were about to calve from the whole, except that it had arms, legs, and a head, and it did not fall to the floor but crawled, in defiance of gravity, across the mirrors, its shape becoming gilt and glass as it went, before finally reflecting stone again when it reached the cavern floor. It shimmered, and Calio was revealed in their true form. They waited until the light from Ceres's torch had disappeared before trailing her deeper into the underworld.

LX

Gwag
(CORNISH)

A Hollow Space in a Mine

alwain came awake suddenly. He was shivering uncontrolla-
bly, the cold having settled into his flesh and bones. Around
his neck was a metal collar, which bit despite the deadening;
and though his eyes were open, he could see nothing, so absolute was the dark. He was sitting on, and against, stone, and
when he tried to move, a chain jangled—a short one, too, since he was
pulled up after shifting position by only a few inches.

He knew he wasn't alone. Deprived of a pair of crucial senses—sight
and touch—the others sought to make up for the deficiencies, and so his
hearing, always acute, had become sharper still. The sound of breathing
came from two directions.

"Who's there?" he asked. "Why have you done this to me?"

Which were, under the circumstances, very good questions, although
the immediate response wasn't one he might have wished to receive, because Balwain heard snarling, and picked up an unmistakably animal odor.

Light bloomed in the dark: a blue glow, although Balwain couldn't yet
determine how distant or near it might be. Only as it grew, and the lin-
eaments of the woman holding it became apparent, did he see that it was
about twenty feet away from him—almost the same distance as the massive

she-wolf chained by the neck to the wall of the cave, so that the three presences formed the points of a roughly equal triangle: man, woman, wolf.

But no, not wolf, not fully; and not quite woman, either. The luna, gray of muzzle, gnarled of body, was the offspring of a purebred wolf and a half-human Loup, and contained aspects of both. The hominid was noticeable in the structure of her skull; in the size and shape of her ears; and most strikingly in her eyes, which were a bright green and disconcertingly human. The cave's other occupant raised the light, the source of which was a large insect, housed in the bulb of a clear jar. The insect's abdomen grew brighter the more agitated it became, but the narrowness of the jar's neck prevented it from escaping the vessel in which it had been born and raised. Now its luminosity revealed a long, ashen face with uncommonly bright red lips, and a hairless pate from which grew the spurs of bone that encircled her skull completely, forming her crown. Her eyes were set closer to her nose than those of the Fae, so that, like the luna wolf, she showed traces of two distinct species, and her teeth were pointed and white, with a bite like a closed trap.

Balwain knew her for who she was. This was the Ageless Queen, the Pale Lady Death. He wished he had not looked upon her, but to stare Death in the face was not the same as to embrace her.

"You made a bargain," said Balwain, "a sworn pact."

"And we have kept to it," said the Pale Lady. "We rid you of your rivals. The mine, in whose lowest reaches we now speak, is yours alone. And we have delivered the luna wolf to you—and you to her, of course. One accord does not necessarily preclude another."

"No, that is not what we agreed—"

"It is *precisely* what we agreed, but the spirit of an agreement and the letter of it may not always be one and the same. As for you, you would have reneged as soon as it suited you. We cannot lie, or fail to adhere to the terms of a contract, written or verbal, because our essence forbids it. But only morality and honor would have prevented you from breaching the terms, and you possess neither, although whether by nature or inclination is unclear, and is destined to remain unknown. As for the luna, she desired only to confront you at the last, so that she also might have her revenge. She is near to death, and has watched too many of her pack die at your hands, or by your order."

"Because she killed my wife and children," said Balwain.

"Oh, but your hunt had commenced long before then," replied the Pale Lady, "and her violence was a response to yours. You impaled an entire litter of her cubs on spikes, and left them to rot at your gates. Why would you assume that she did not love her offspring as you loved yours, if not more? Because I fear your disposition, Balwain, was never inclined toward the devotional. Prideful, yes, but absent of affection."

The luna's low growl had persisted throughout this exchange, her gaze never deviating from Balwain, but she had remained otherwise unmoving. At the mention of her cubs, she leapt, a response to a stimulus so undeniable as to be virtually involuntary, except the chain around her neck permitted her as little freedom as Balwain's restraint, and she was stopped before her rear paws could leave the ground. But the attempt forced Balwain to retreat to the rock face and stay there, because what he noticed, if the luna as yet had not, was that her effort had caused her chain, rising from a hole in the rock, to lengthen by a single link, which shone silver where the rest was red with rust. If she continued to exert herself, the wolf might well be able to reach him.

"What game is this?" he asked.

"One you can win, if you try," replied the Pale Lady.

She directed a gust of breath at the cave floor—although unlike Balwain's, and the luna's, the Pale Lady's breath did not show white, so cold was she inside—causing a cloud of black dust to rise and reveal a dagger, housed in a jeweled scabbard. It lay between the wolf and Balwain.

"Your chain, like hers, is controlled by a mechanism in the rock face," said the Pale Lady. "I saw you notice what happened when she tried to reach you, so you're already aware that the chains are not fixed. But she's a clever creature, and will spot that the distance between you is capable of being closed. If you can reach the dagger before she gets to you, you may be able to kill her. Then you'll be free."

"And you'll let me live if I succeed?"

"Any thoughts of revenge would surely lie with you. If you survive, you'd be wise to consider it a lesson hard-learned, or you can seek me out, and we'll speak again."

With that the Pale Lady departed, leaving Balwain and the wolf alone.

LXI

Scomfished

(SCOTS)

The Feeling of Being Suffocated
While Underground

he rook guided Ceres through the ruins of the Crooked Man's domain. Here were debris and rockfalls, but here too were rooms undamaged, as though awaiting the return of their occupants. A few of the chambers were recognizable to Ceres from David's account, and the knowledge of what they had once contained caused her to become more and more nervous, for fear that her presence might awaken memories better left undisturbed.

Sometimes places in which great harm has been done to others, or much suffering has been inflicted, are haunted by it forever, just as a person may be damaged, physically or psychologically, by trauma. We may sense this haunting should we be forced to spend time in these locales—a wrongness, a dread—leaving us eager to be gone. Even then, it may take hours, a day, or a lifetime to shake off the miasma of what we have encountered. The Crooked Man's lair had witnessed every harm that could be inflicted on another being, in body or spirit; every cruelty, however monstrous or small; every betrayal, grievous or venial; and just as an echo may persist after the cry that caused it has ceased, or ripples continue to disturb the surface of a pond after a pebble has sunk, so too these spaces resonated with old grief.

Ceres stopped by the entrance to a bedroom dominated by a carved wooden bedstead. The sheets were flung back from its mattress, which still bore the imprint of two bodies; and not alone their imprints, but their shadows also, or so she thought. Puzzled by the sight, she pushed her torch farther into the room, and saw that the mattress was blackened by a dual charring, and the air, even after so long, held the smell of roasted meat. She drew nearer, unable to understand why the whole mattress had not gone up in flames, filled as it was with straw that poked through where the silk overlay had begun to rot. The toe of her right foot caught on a flagstone, causing her to stumble. She reached out to steady herself, her hand grasping one of the bedposts—

And saw two people on fire, a man and a woman, their arms wrapped around each other, unable to break free. The burning would not stop, but went on and on, because it gratified the Crooked Man, who had been rejected by one or the other of the pair. "So you burn with passion? Well, let me show you what it truly means to burn . . ."

Ceres jerked her hand away, and mercifully, the image faded. If that was the horror a bed could hold, she didn't want to think of what she might have witnessed had she touched the spiked chair in the dusty cell next door, or the iron boot that lay amid the long-cold ashes of a fireplace, a pair of tongs hanging from a hook so that the boot could be placed, red-hot, on a bare foot.

Although she was very frightened, Ceres did not consider turning back, and not only because she was certain that the way home lay through these tunnels. At the end of the same side passage that housed the bed-chamber and the cell, she had discovered the rook perched by the lip of a well filled to the brim, not with water, but with discarded children's shoes. These she did not touch. She didn't think she could stand the hurt—of the infants themselves, but also of their parents, she whose child was both present and absent, alive but not living. If the being responsible for all this evil had somehow survived, then he had to be confronted, just as David had once faced him down, because otherwise she would be complicit in whatever further pain he might cause. But she had to force herself not to think about the layers of rock above her head, the absence of sunlight, the staleness of the air, and the blackness that would consume her should her torch sputter and go out, leaving her to die alone down here—or worse, not alone.

The rook scrutinized her with its single eye. She was tempted to find some missile to fling at it, this servant to a master who would do such things, but the rook flew on before she could lay a hand on a suitable object. It was only as Ceres trudged after it that she began to understand the rook had brought her to the well, a detour requiring them to leave the main conduit. The rook had *wanted* her to see the shoes, just as it had not tried to prevent her from entering the room with the burnt bed, and had not ushered her away from the cell with its chair and boot. It could easily have discouraged her, had it chosen to—it was a large bird, with a sharp beak and long claws—but instead it was going out of its way to share with her the worst aspects of the Crooked Man's decayed kingdom. Of course, the rook might have been trying to scare her, to soften her up for what was to come, but that would have been pointless, as she was scared enough already.

An unfaithful servant, then, she thought, *or an unwilling one.*

The blackness behind her was so complete as to be almost tangible, and Ceres could pick up no sound beyond the spitting of her torch, but she was convinced that she and the rook were being watched. Nearby, the bird preened itself without anxiety, since what could be worse than its master? The rook concluded its grooming and fluttered ahead, although it was careful not to fly beyond the torchlight.

Ceres went with it, and Calio followed.

LXII

Andsaca

(OLD ENGLISH)

Adversary

n their stone arena, Balwain and the she-wolf were inching toward a final confrontation, lit only by the agitated fluttering of the insect in the jar. The wolf had figured out that she could expand her reach by putting pressure on the chain, but not consistently; only short, sharp jerks worked, and then not every time. Balwain was in a similar quandary: on occasion the chain might yield an extra link or two, while subsequent efforts would prove futile. Once, he had even felt himself being drawn back an inch or two, undoing the painful progress he had made—because it *was* painful: the collar choked him, and he was forced to strain against the chain in order to advance. Either the mechanism was flawed, Balwain thought, or it had been constructed that way. The latter struck him as likelier, since it would make the contest more interesting for any spectators. Perhaps the Fae, clustered around the Pale Lady Death, were watching to see how the issue was decided. Well, Balwain would give them a fight to remember, once he reached that knife. He planned to gut the she-wolf, and then he'd do the same to the Fae, once he'd returned to the surface and gathered his troops. The Fae he couldn't lay hands on, he would burn by pouring oil into their warrens and setting it alight, before razing the mounds and sowing the soil with salt.

The she-wolf, meantime, recognized the threat posed by the blade. If she could get to it before Balwain and paw it away, he would have no hope of prevailing against her. The wolf's oh-so-human eyes had looked on the heads of her dead cubs, and seen the corpses of her pack piled up and incinerated on pyres by Balwain's hunters. She intended to eat Balwain slowly for his crimes, starting with his fingers and toes before proceeding with the rest of him. His head she would save. She had trailed her scent through these dark places, and was certain she could find her way out again. She would retreat to the woods with Balwain's head in her jaws, and make a totem of it by hanging it from a branch above the entrance to her den, where she could look upon it as she died.

So Balwain strained, and the wolf tugged, and the insect in the jar fluttered with increasing distress, for despite its size and situation it was an observant creature and had witnessed the preparations of the Pale Lady Death. It knew what was coming, and wished only to escape from its prison before it was too late.

LXIII

Dreor
(OLD ENGLISH)

Blood, Gore

he steward was initially reluctant to speak of what might have transpired behind the closed doors of the Great Hall, but the application of the tip of Denham's poniard to the soft underside of his jaw, and the accompanying threat to pull his tongue through the hole it would make if he didn't start talking, convinced him to be more forthcoming. The continued absence of Balwain decided the issue, since the steward feared that the Fae had proven cleverer than his master, and his best chance of protection and survival now lay in coming clean. The fate of the five nobles was thus known, as was Balwain's alliance with the Fae, and his reasons for it: a consolidation of his wealth and power, and the promise of the she-wolf being delivered up to him. Wherever he might be, Balwain was undoubtedly ruing the deal he had struck.

"So they betrayed him, just as he betrayed the nobles," said Denham, as he walked the rampart with the Woodsman that they might speak privately. Denham might have been Balwain's marshal, but he had not signed up for murder or a pact with creatures that fed on children. Also, as the captain of the guard, he was responsible for the safety of everyone inside the castle walls. The murder of guests was an affront to him.

"The Fae don't betray," said the Woodsman. "They deceive, but only those who aren't paying close attention. The prudent don't fall prey to them, only the ill-advised, or the blindly ambitious."

"But what did they hope to get from Balwain? The deaths of a few nobles—and even Balwain's, too, damn him—won't change things for long. Kill a lord or lady, and another one takes their place. There's no end to them."

"Spoken like a true disappointed revolutionary," observed the Woodsman. "You could be in the wrong line of work."

"Since people I was sworn to protect have been killed," said Denham, "you may be correct. But you still haven't answered my question: What do the Fae want?"

Through the open window behind them, distant fires lit the night sky as the mining went on. Balwain had spoken of digging ever deeper, but also of expanding its operations, and mapped on the wall of his chamber, alongside the great wood frieze, the Woodsman had seen sites marked for further exploitation.

The Fae did not like men to dig. The Fae did not like men at all.

"Access," said the Woodsman. "I think we need to clear that mine."

LXIV

Hell-Træf
(OLD ENGLISH)

Infernal Temple

eres and the rook had arrived at the chamber containing the broken hourglass, its floor littered with shards and grain-skulls. This had been the heart of the Crooked Man's kingdom. When the last skull dropped, it should have marked the end of his life. Why, then, had it not?

The rook was waiting by a hole at the base of the wall. The hole resembled the entrance to a drain, and indeed a gutter in the floor ended there, the channel stained black in the torchlight.

But red once, Ceres thought. *That's old blood.*

She knelt before the rook, which responded by hopping into the gap.

"I can't fit in there," said Ceres, though she probably could, with a bit of a squeeze; but she didn't want to. Even after all this time, it smelled like the runoff from a slaughterhouse. But the rook met her objections only with a caw, which seemed to settle the matter. If a shrug had a sound, it would have resembled that caw.

Ceres leaned back, took a deep breath of marginally cleaner air, held it, then began to wriggle through, the torch extended before her, revealing a burrow in the rock that sloped gently downward. The opening was tight at her shoulders, and she had a premonition of becoming jammed there for however long it took her to free herself, or to lose enough weight from starvation to enable her to go on. Ceres willed herself not to panic, even though this was the stuff of nightmares. Not only was she deep underground, she was also at risk of becoming trapped there, compounding an already bad situation. She did not want this to be how she died.

At last, with considerable squirming, and the scraping away of some skin, she was through. She was forced to continue slinking on her belly for about fifteen feet, which was the point at which the tunnel started to widen, eventually permitting her to walk, first in a crouch, then fully upright. The rock face also changed, its surface becoming more uniform, but rifled like the barrel of a gun. Ceres puzzled over how the tunnel had been constructed, so sleek was it. The answer came as she entered the largest of the grottoes she had encountered so far, its ceiling as high as the greatest cathedral, and lit, like the shaft nearer the castle, by soft illumination from within the stone itself, assisted by torches set in sconces. Before her lay the desiccated membrane of an enormous worm or serpent, its skin, even in decay, bearing markings similar to those in the shaft. How long it had been dead, Ceres could not begin to guess, but this was a creature that had once dug through rock. She could see more tunnels of comparable size bored elsewhere in the chamber walls, and very much hoped that they had all been created ages ago. She had no desire to encounter one of those worms in its full bloom of health, whatever its diet. Close to the corpse ran an underground stream, following a course first cut when the world was still young.

Unlike the tunnel walls, those of the chamber were irregular. It was only as Ceres shone her light on the nearest section that she discovered the reason why. She was standing in a hall embellished with bones, thousands upon thousands of them. They formed pillars and arcades, corbels and lintels, even ornamental balconies and stairways. A bone throne stood on a raised dais, and a bone table was surrounded by thirteen chairs, each topped by a single human skull surrounded by femurs, like the rays of the sun that would never shine on this place. On the table sat a whole roast chicken, a bowl of apples, pears, and grapes, and a jug. A place had been set for one, with a wooden plate, a silver knife and fork, and an empty glass.

"Eat," said a voice that came from everywhere and nowhere at once. "You must be hungry."

Ceres peered around, but failed to locate the speaker.

"Who are you?" she asked. "Where are you?"

"I think you know who I am, as otherwise you would not have followed the rook. As for where I am, well, I am here—in spirit, if not in body."

What might have been a breeze passed before Ceres's face, bringing with it the scent of old books.

"I can't speak with someone I can't see," said Ceres.

"You do it all the time, in your world. Why should this one be any different?"

"Then let me put it another way: I can't negotiate with someone I can't see."

"Ah," said the voice, "is that what we are engaged in, a negotiation?"

"You must have a purpose in bringing me here. You want something from me, which means you have something to offer in return, otherwise you're hardly starting from a position of strength, are you?"

Ceres heard laughter.

"Even I occasionally forget that you only look young and callow. So, a negotiation it is."

"Not until you show yourself."

"Don't overplay your hand!" snapped the voice. "You're stuck belowground, far from your friends. Just because I might be inclined to strike a bargain doesn't mean I'm not prepared to hurt you, if only to confirm who is in charge here."

Ceres relented. There were ways to deal with difficult men. All women learned them.

"Will you show yourself?" she asked. "Please?"

"Are you sure that's what you want?"

"I'm sure."

"Then, since you asked so politely—"

Ceres heard movement from all about—scuttling, clicking, skittering— just as a large millipede scurried across her boot. She flicked it into the shadows, only to see it immediately reappear, this time surrounded by its brothers and sisters, as well as beetles, cockroaches, ants, centipedes, earwigs, silverfish, bristletails, scorpions—hundreds, thousands, tens of thousands of multilegged beasts—all converging on one spot. They came together, and Ceres saw the mass form a torso and arms, and a neck and head, topped by a crooked hat made of plump black spiders, beneath which holes in the face roughly approximated to eyes and a leering mouth.

And lo, the Crooked Man was restored.

"Are you happy now?"

Though repelled, Ceres did her best to hide it.

"It's better than talking to thin air," she said, even if it wasn't.

"We should shake hands," said the Crooked Man, "as a sign of good faith." He proffered a hand forged from five fat scorpions, their tails its digits, their stingers its fingernails.

"I don't think that will be necessary."

The Crooked Man laughed again.

"I like you," he said. "If we can't come to an agreement, I may keep you just for amusement value. And when I cease to find you funny any longer—which I fear might come to pass sooner rather than later, for I suspect that, like many youths, you harbor recalcitrant tendencies—I'll add your bones to my collection, and your skull can grin back at me for eternity."

A scorpion finger indicated the food.

"The invitation to eat still stands."

At the table, any number of insects had decided to ignore the Crooked Man's summons in favor of feasting. The chicken was proving particularly popular.

"I've lost my appetite," said Ceres, although she had also read enough fairy tales to know that only the very foolish would agree to sample such a feast, for fear of some enchantment.

The beetles responsible for the Crooked Man's lips reassembled themselves into an expression of disappointment.

"And the cockroaches stole it all from the kitchens specially," he said. "Not that it will go to waste, as you can see, but I wouldn't want my confederates to begin expecting cooked meat at every meal."

While he spoke, the Crooked Man's body was in a state of constant motion, but Ceres thought it was not alone the restless natures of the insects and arachnids that accounted for the instability of his appearance. She could see the effort it was costing him to maintain this physicality, to corral these lesser minds into participating in the embodiment of a consciousness, all while the lower half of him remained a congregation of crawling, confused, combative creatures, into which the top half was only a moment's inattention away from collapsing.

"If the niceties have been concluded," said Ceres, "we can get down to business. What is it you want from me?"

"Release. An escape from this world."

"And what will you give me in return?"

"A happier ending to your story," replied the Crooked Man. "This is my promise: I will restore your daughter to you."

LXV

Coffen

(CORNISH)

An Open Mine, Deep and Narrow

alwain was closing in on the knife. It was almost within reach now, so near that his fingertips had brushed its hilt, but two steps forward cost him a step back, so it was beyond him once more. The she-wolf, on the other hand, was growing increasingly frustrated by the chain. The beast in her was overruling the human, reason being subdued by instinct, so that she had resorted to trying to bite through the metal, causing her teeth to break and her mouth to bleed.

Balwain tested the chain, and felt one link release, then another, and another. For a second time, his fingers touched the dagger. He drew a breath, relaxed his body, and inched forward. This time, the chain did not recoil, and Balwain's hand seized the hilt. In the jar, the motions of the insect became a panicked blur, its light turning from blue to blazing white.

Balwain lifted the dagger, still sheathed in its scabbard. It felt surprisingly heavy to him, but only as he held it up to his face did he spot that the scabbard, too, was hooked to a chain, one that disappeared into a hole in the rock floor. What he had felt was not weight but resistance. He wrenched the dagger free, thinking no more of the anchor, as hidden devices and unseen instruments were activated.

The Fae had been preparing for this moment for years by the reckoning of men—seeking out weak spots belowground, and preparing charms—although to the former, for whom time ticked slowly, their actions might have been considered hurried, even impulsive. The collar around Balwain's neck came apart, freeing him, but so also did that of the she-wolf, as deep in Pandemonium a rumbling commenced.

The Woodsman, aided by Balwain's soldiers, had succeeded in clearing only the upper levels of the mine when the first vibrations began to be felt, and many of the workers, summoned by a relay of horns, were still trying to escape the lower reaches. Some were making their way on foot along the pathways that curled around the mouth of the works, while others were climbing systems of tall ladders, or being winched up in cages pulled by horses and oxen. As cracks appeared in the rock face, and rubble fell, the animals were driven to redouble their efforts, and the miners started to panic.

"We're not going to get them all out," said Denham, who was standing by the Woodsman's side, watching the disaster unfold.

"We might not have managed to get any of them out," said the Woodsman.

"So you're saying it could have been worse?"

A huge section of black rock separated from the whole. It plummeted past the ascending miners, dropping deep into the workings, taking walkways and gantries with it, along with the men, dwarfs, and animals using them to flee.

"No," said the Woodsman sadly, "only better."

LXVI

Angenga
(OLD ENGLISH)

Lone Wanderer, Solitary Being

alio had passed through the drain and followed the worm hollow to its mouth, where they now crouched, listening to the conversation between Ceres and the old monster.

The dryad knew the girl considered herself clever, but the Crooked Man was crafty, and crafty outdid clever every time. He was more artful even than the Fae, in whom cunning ran like blood, which was why the Pale Lady Death hadn't attempted to frame a contract with him that might be open to manipulation. The pact between them was a simple one: The Crooked Man would leave Elsewhere, and the Fae—whom he had persecuted, just as he had men, Loups, and every other creature—would not try to stop him or seek to punish him in his weakened state for his many crimes against them. With the Crooked Man gone, the Fae would have only humankind to contend with.

But for the Crooked Man to depart, fulfilling his side of the bargain, it seemed that he required the cooperation of Ceres, and she could not assist him if she was dead. Calio's poison sac was heavy with fresh venom, enough to subdue Ceres before stealing her away to a nice, dry den, thereby avenging themselves on both the Fae and the girl with a single act, as well as thwarting the Crooked Man, who had sometimes come hunting for Calio when the mood took him, wielding a burning torch and calling their name, so that more than once they had only narrowly avoided immolation at his hand.

Such fury contained in this once gentle being, and also such sorrow, because the two are often linked, and one nourishes the other. Calio had not been made this way. They were not a dryad begotten of rotten wood, but had been birthed, in the first days of the Fae, from a young poplar, a tree associated with resilience; this may have been why they had survived for so long, when the rest of their kind had perished. But to be the last of a species is to be cursed with loneliness, since there is a price to be paid for endurance. Calio had felt their kind fade from this plane of existence, one by one, and with each loss this oldest of dryads was further diminished, even as the spirits of the departed came to reside in Calio's small, sad heart. Turning in upon themselves, alone with their thoughts, regrets, and longings, Calio had forgotten all they—or, long ago, she—had once been.

But try as Calio might to shadow the Crooked Man and the girl, seeking their moment to strike, they were distracted from the task by an odor close at hand: the smell of scorched wood, accompanied by a whistling that, the closer they listened, resembled the distant echo of screams.

To their left was another worm tunnel, its mouth curtained with cobwebs. The smell and screams were coming from inside it. While they were reluctant to leave Ceres and the Crooked Man alone, the lure of the unknown was too great. All things have a purpose, and just as it was part of Ceres's finally to confront the Crooked Man, so also had Calio journeyed to those lower reaches for a reason. Calio might have thought it was to stymie the hopes of so many—even as they entered the tunnel, this remained at the forefront of their mind—but their story was destined to have a different ending.

So down Calio went, the smell and noise growing stronger and louder, until they arrived at a room resembling a chapel in size and structure, but bare of furniture. Calio stepped inside, and froze where they stood. Slowly, softly, their eyes began to shed tears of sap.

For Calio now knew why they were alone of their kind.

LXVII

Wrecan
(OLD ENGLISH)

To Avenge

n the cave, the contest to the death between Balwain and the she-wolf was about to be decided. Both had incurred grievous wounds. The she-wolf had been stabbed half a dozen times, yet still she stood, and still she threatened. Like the marshal, Denham, she was a veteran of many battles, and her visible scars were only a fraction of those concealed by her fur. But one of Balwain's thrusts had penetrated her right lung, and she was finding it hard to breathe. She did not have much time remaining to her.

Balwain, though, was incapacitated on one side. The luna's jaws had savaged him so badly that his left upper arm was raw meat from shoulder to elbow, and both major bones in the lower arm were broken. He had also suffered a bite to his left thigh that had excised a chunk of flesh the size of a fist, and the wound was bleeding profusely. He could now barely stand, but if he fell, the wolf would be on him, so he was trying to support himself against one of the walls while keeping his ruined parts from touching it.

From all around came the tumult of catastrophe, leaving both combatants covered in a fine layer of dust. Distantly, Balwain thought he could hear the shouts and screams of men and dwarfs, and the cries of animals in distress. He knew what was happening: The mine system was collapsing, and its destruction had been precipitated by his actions, both in that cavern—the pressure on the chain, the picking up of the anchored dagger—and before, when he had believed himself devious enough to manipulate the Fae, only to be manipulated far more deftly in turn. Even now, he could not claim that they had not given him what was promised: They had removed the five nobles, offered up the she-wolf, and the Pandemonium mine was his alone, and would serve as his tomb. But if he had to die, he would do so knowing the luna had predeceased him.

"Come on," he goaded. "Are you just going to let me bleed to death, or will you finish what you started?"

The she-wolf's jaws dripped blood and saliva. She tried to get closer to him, but she was as wary of the blade as Balwain was of her jaws, and so each was staying out of range of the other. The she-wolf drew back and appeared to stagger, as though tripped by her own feet. Balwain saw his chance. He launched himself at her, the dagger raised to strike at her heart—

But the stumble was a ruse, and Balwain stabbed thin air. Off-balance, and believing that he had been about to be cushioned by flesh and fur, he landed instead on stone. The pain was indescribable, rendering him momentarily unconscious with its ferocity, as his mind tried to shield him from the hurt.

Balwain lay on his back, afraid to move, afraid even to open his eyes, while warm droplets exploded on his face. Finally, open his eyes he did, to discover the luna standing over him. Balwain tried to use the dagger, but the wolf shifted her left paw, pinning his right hand to the cavern floor.

All the fight left Balwain. It was done.

"They tricked us both," he told the wolf. "Take your victory, for what it's worth."

The luna lowered her head, opened her jaws, and slowly, tenderly, tore Balwain's throat apart.

LXVIII

Eaxl-Gesteallas

(OLD ENGLISH)

Shoulder-Friends, Dearest Companions

eres could not bring herself to speak. The Crooked Man would give Phoebe back to her?

"You doubt me," said the Crooked Man, "and I don't blame you. You see, her story is still being written, as is yours. The physicians, her friends—even you, in your moments of desperation—have forgotten that, and given her tale an ending in which she never wakes up, in which no prince breaks the enchantment by falling to his knees before her, or indulging in actions a little more intimate."

The hole that was the Crooked Man's left eye contrived a lewd wink, aided by the actions of a cockroach. Without thinking, Ceres slapped him, but her hand passed harmlessly through a mass of legs, carapaces, and antennae which re-formed behind her, though not before gifting her a few bites and stings for her trouble. The Crooked Man scuttled back, his hands raised in apology.

"Forgive me," he said. "I overstepped the mark, much like any number of handsome princes have done when confronted with a sleeping girl. Nasty creatures, men. When your daughter wakes, assuming our bargain is concluded satisfactorily, you'd do well to warn her against them. I can assist her in that regard."

"And how do you propose to do all this?" asked Ceres, finding her voice at last.

"Let me show you," said the Crooked Man. He moved toward the oldest, deepest, and darkest of the wormholes. "Come and see what no one else has ever seen."

Calio, too, was bearing witness to something of which previously only the Crooked Man had knowledge, because it was he who had created it: a chapel decorated with warped, blackened wood, each misshapen piece a dryad consumed by fire. Some Calio recognized, despite the ravages: here was Acantha, whose bark had bloomed with pink roses in summer, and Daphne, of the laurels; there Elodie, from the marshes, and Orea, of the mountains. Many were old and mature, but others were newly formed, dead so young that their fingers were barely buds. Each had been carefully positioned so they faced outward, their limbs intertwined so that not even an inch of the wall behind them was visible, and thus the chapel might have been constructed entirely from scorched wood. Even that would have been an affront to Calio—trees were living organisms, and deserving of respect, in death as in life—yet this was not wood alone, but the remains of ancient souls intimately connected to the land. And here was their fate: to be burned alive for the amusement of an entity that had lived too long, before being used to adorn one of the rooms of the labyrinth in which he dwelt, where he could relive, at his leisure, the moment of their destruction.

Whatever there was in Calio that remained unbroken, whatever it was that had enabled them to endure alone for so long, was finally sundered. For an instant they were nothing at all, as the last glimmer of their old self spun away and a new selfhood prepared to take its place, one devised from absence, darkness, death: things that are not. When the transformation was complete, Calio was no longer simply themselves, but every being that had ever suffered at the hands of one stronger and more ruthless than they; every animal hunted and killed for pleasure; every woman violated by a man; every child preyed upon by an adult; every infant starved; every life impoverished by the cruelty of another. Species was no longer of consequence because pain was universal, and harm done to one was harm done to all. To Calio's wrath there was a purity, even a grace, and an incandescence as terrifying and all-consuming as the greatest of infernos.

Calio looked to the torch hissing beside them on the wall. Throughout their life they had fled from fire, just like their brothers and sisters, although it had caught and annihilated them all in the end, each and every one. Even in their new form, it took all Calio's courage to do what they did next.

They grasped the torch.

LXIX

Ærgewinn
(OLD ENGLISH)

Ancient Enmity

avid and Baako reentered the castle through the doorway behind the painting. On their journey they had encountered no
more of the Fae, which was fortunate because the infants had
not enjoyed being carried along the tunnels, and expressed their
unhappiness through ceaseless, low-level wailing.

They paused at a window, and watched by moonlight as a stream of
people and animals—workers, their families, and what horses and oxen
they could save—sought to escape the impending disintegration of Pandemonium and its sister mines. An inconstant drumbeat reached them,
and the castle walls vibrated in sympathy. They had felt the quaking in
the tunnels, but had not known the cause. Now they did.

Nobody paid them any mind as they moved from the lower reaches to
the upper. Everyone was too concerned with the mine, and the possibility
that its destruction might spread to the castle and its environs. Although
Pandemonium lay some way distant, it was common knowledge that the
land was riddled with tunnels and caverns from the Crooked Man's time,
only some of which had been discovered during the mining operations and
the construction of the new castle. So just as the miners were fleeing Pandemonium, so also were many residents of the citadel in exodus, seeking to

put as much distance as they could between themselves and the area at risk. In the castle itself, panic had not yet set in, but David could tell it was not far off. All it would require was the appearance of one crack in a wall, or one small sinkhole in a courtyard, for alarm to become hysteria.

It was with some relief, therefore, that they came upon the Woodsman, who had also returned to the castle in the hope that they might have found their way back. He was delighted to discover them safe, and with infants recovered. As for Ceres, he had not expected, he admitted, to see her with them, which was not to say he had not wished for it.

"The castle remains standing, for now," he told them, once servants had been found to take care of the children. "But it all depends on how the Fae have engineered the ruination of the mines. My guess is that they've weakened the excavations at key points, but they may have got their timings wrong. There has been loss of life already, but had the collapse been more sudden, the death toll would have been much greater. As things stand, a lot of the miners have been evacuated, and the rest are close to salvation. But the destruction of the mine was the Fae's priority, not the deaths of miners."

"If that was the case," asked David, "why murder the Blythe woman and her daughter, or attack Baako's village?"

"The purpose was to wipe out those adepts with the skill to counter Fae magic, which suggests that this is but the first move in a longer campaign. The loss of such knowledge is more damaging than the collapse of any mine."

"What of my mother?" asked Baako.

"I wish I had news to share with you," said the Woodsman, "but you'll have to wait for word from your father and his people. They were the ones who went searching after the harpies abducted her."

Baako nodded.

"What will be, will be," he said.

Then, exhausted by his efforts and the rapacity of the Fae—and, it may be, by some intuition that his mother was now beyond pain—Baako slumped to the floor. Aided by the Woodsman, David got him back to his feet, although he remained unconscious, and together they went to saddle the horses. It was time to leave the castle. As for Ceres, they could only hope.

LXX

Scima
(OLD ENGLISH)

Light, Brightness

he worm tunnel down which the Crooked Man led Ceres grew wider and wider—twenty, thirty, finally forty feet in circumference—before ending in front of a pair of colossal wooden doors. To Ceres they appeared taller than the height of the tunnel roof itself, as though they occupied a plane different from the rest of the Crooked Man's lair.

"Do you love books?" asked the Crooked Man.

"Yes," said Ceres. She saw no reason to dissemble. "I've spent my life surrounded by them."

"Stories, too? Because they're not one and the same, you know."

The Crooked Man sounded eager, like a child. It made his appearance all the more obscene, this writhing swarm of creeping, stinging, biting things.

"No, I don't suppose they are."

"A book is like a house," continued the Crooked Man, "and stories are the souls that inhabit it. A book without a story has no soul. You must understand that, or else what I'm about to show you will have no meaning, and our discussion, and your life, will be at an end."

"I do understand it," said Ceres. "I've always liked stories."

"As have I," said the Crooked Man. "You could say they're my life's work."

He briefly lifted a finger, composed of a tangle of centipedes, and touched it ever so softly to one of the doors, which opened slowly and soundlessly before them.

"Enter," he said. "Know the world."

And Ceres entered.

If the doors had seemed impossibly tall for the tunnel, what lay beyond them confounded all conception of distance and volume, because stretching as far as the eye could see, and farther still—laid up and down, sideways and diagonally—were shelves upon shelves of books, but contained in a room no bigger than Ceres's childhood bedroom. In fact, it *was* her childhood bedroom. She could see its walls, its worn carpet, its wardrobe, its dresser with her great-grandmother's mirror on top, and the single bed in which she had slept throughout her childhood and adolescence, until she left home to attend university. It even had the same posters tacked above and beside the bed: pretty pop stars who were now fathers, and handsome actors now dead. But when she tried to brush her hand against the wall, it remained beyond reach, and when she took a step forward, it receded. An infinite room, containing infinite, or near infinite, numbers of books.

"Every book a world," said the Crooked Man, as though reading her thoughts. "So many worlds, enclosed in so small a room."

"But it's not my room, is it?" asked Ceres. "It's just an illusion."

"Would you prefer this?" said the Crooked Man. He snapped his fingers, decapitating a pair of beetles in the process, and the room became the local library to which her mother had brought her as soon as she was old enough to join. Two little cardboard tickets had been handed to her with her name on them, into which the slips from borrowed books would be placed: a reminder that those volumes had, for a time, gone to live with her, to share a shelf for two weeks with the handful she owned. But even after they were returned, something of them remained with her, for Ceres, like all readers, was altered by every book she read, and so her life became a record of their consumption. Were an ultraviolet light to be shone on her in a darkened room, their titles might have been written on her skin, so many as to be as tangled and intertwined as the insects and spiders the Crooked Man had called upon to lend himself shape.

"Or this?"

Another click, and Ceres was in the reading room of her university library, so much larger than the one in her hometown, and musty with the scent of old paper; still, in its way, so very small (because how could it accommodate more than a tiny fraction of the books that had been written?), but when she went in search of a title, magically it would be there, or could be produced from hidden stacks within hours. Individual existences, worlds, universes, more of them than she could ever hope to explore in a lifetime, or a thousand lifetimes, all in that single building. Even her childhood bedroom, by the time she left it, had housed hundreds of books, every one a macrocosm, stored in an area that would not have facilitated a second bed. The Crooked Man's library was not beholden to physical laws, for what library or bookshop really is?

A final click, and she was once again back in her bedroom, or this version of it. Unable to reach the walls, she settled instead for stroking the nearest books, and felt them pulse beneath her fingertips. The binding on each was leather (*or skin*, she thought) and warm to the touch. She drew one from its shelf. On the cover were runic symbols, used to signify both numbers and letters: a name, or a title. As she held it, the book's pulse faltered, then stopped. Ceres smelled burning, and on the cover fresh runes appeared.

"A death," said the Crooked Man. "A life ended, the date recorded."

"What do you mean?"

"Every life is a story, and therefore fit to be commemorated between covers."

"So these are all—?"

"Accounts of lives: some complete, others just beginning, and a few paused, in stasis."

Ceres restored the book respectfully to its place on the shelf, and wished Godspeed to its soul.

"Is Phoebe's story here?"

"All stories are here."

The shelves shifted, although Ceres experienced the brief nausea of sudden, unanticipated movement, and suspected it might be she who had altered position, not the shelves. When it ceased, Ceres was standing beside the bookshelf from Phoebe's bedroom, filled with the titles she loved—and one additional volume, with pale blue binding, that pulsed faintly when she took it in her hands.

"This is her story?"

"She *is* her story," replied the Crooked Man. "It is your daughter that you hold."

Ceres lifted the book to her face, breathed in deeply, and smelled Phoebe, as assuredly as though she had leaned in to kiss her as she lay in her sickbed. She even picked up the antiseptic tang of the hospital.

"Can I look inside?"

"If you wish."

Ceres opened the book and saw page upon page of runes, written in a reddish-brown ink like dried blood. She turned to the last page containing any script, and saw that the final rune was incomplete, as if the scribe had been called away on some pressing business.

"Yours is nearby," said the Crooked Man, "if you'd like to see it, although it makes for dull reading since your daughter was taken from you."

"And you, is your book here? Because your life must also be a story."

Again she felt movement, but for a longer time. When it stopped, they were standing before a thick volume set alone on a lectern, a book thousands and thousands of pages long, with intricately decorated silver clasps and corner pieces to protect the leaves and binding. It lay open on bare facing pages. As they watched, a series of runes burned themselves into the blank space, leaving behind an acrid smell. Surrounding this inner sanctum was a shape Ceres remembered from her father's shelves: a huge dodecahedron, each of its open sides a window on a landscape, the views constantly altering. Ceres caught glimpses of her world—war, fires, conflict, hate, but moments of joy and tenderness also—and other worlds, too: suns being birthed, planets dying; nothingness, a void, the first darkness from which sprang all life; then a glimmer of light, and the light began to form letters, because in the beginning was the Word.

"This is my story," said the Crooked Man, "my book."

"It's very long."

"Well, I'm very old." He gestured at the volume in Ceres's hands. "Your daughter, meanwhile, is very young, and that binding will accept many more pages."

Ceres clutched Phoebe's story to her breast.

"How do I make it resume?" she asked.

"Through me," said the Crooked Man. "She needs just a little life, and I have some to spare."

Ceres frowned.

"I don't understand," she said. "You'll *give* her life?"

The Crooked Man paced a circle around her.

"I want to leave this world," he said. "It has no love for me or my tales. Here is where stories are formed, but your world is where they live, where they're told, shared, written, *remembered*. I wish to live there. I'm tired of this realm. I once ruled it through runaways from your world, but that time is gone. I always envied those children, however lost they might have been among their own kind. With each of those that came to me, my envy grew. Now I no longer care to exist in the shadows of one world, when I can walk in the light of another.

"But I cannot do that without a body, so here is what I propose: Give me your daughter, for a few seconds, and I will leave some of my life force with her in return. Permit me to go back with you, to pass into her when the doorway opens again, and I will remain in her only until another comes near, someone into whom I can jump, someone young. If they're sick, I will heal them. If they're dying, I will give them new life. I will save them, and your daughter too."

"You promise you'll surrender her? You won't take her for yourself?"

"I give you my word."

"The word of a creature with a heart made of spiders," said Ceres, who could see the black mass of them beating in the Crooked Man's breast. "The word of a creature who has tortured and killed for his own amusement."

"No, the word of a creature who lives to create stories," said the Crooked Man, "and some of the most memorable stories are cruel. Show me a story without anguish, and I will show you a tale that's not worth the telling."

"And where there was no pain, you supplied it."

"Because the story was all that mattered. The greater the strife, the greater the story, but I am not averse to happy endings. What better ending than to return your daughter to you, after all you have been through?"

Beneath Ceres's feet the ground shook. She had been aware of the clamor for a while, like shell impacts and explosions from a battle occurring miles away, but this quake was the strongest yet.

"Time is running short," said the Crooked Man. "The Fae wanted the mine gone, and soon they'll have their wish. When it falls in, you'll be entombed down here with me, and I guarantee you won't like what happens after."

"But you'll be trapped too."

"Except I won't die, unlike you. My story will go on, until I find another person with whom to negotiate, someone who will accept my offer—and I *will* find them. It's a question of need, or love, because they're both the same, if you take the time to look. Perhaps you just don't love your daughter enough, don't need her enough, to allow me to help her."

"Or poison her. Why would I want anything of you in her?"

"What choice do you have?"

"I have hope," said Ceres.

"Hope?" The Crooked Man's amusement was awful. "Look around you. This is the end of hope. This is where your hope comes to die, and you with it. But it doesn't have to be that way. Once more, and for the last time, I invite you to take my hand. Shake it, then speak your daughter's name aloud to me, and we are agreed. If not, even your broken bones will never again be warmed by sunlight. I work better in the dark, and suffering brings its own illumination."

The ground shook again, and on their infinite shelves the books huddled together for consolation. The torches on the walls began to extinguish themselves, one by one, and Ceres was truly afraid. She did not want to die down here with this monster, and in that moment, she was tempted.

A warm orange radiance flowered on the wall behind her, slowly seeping into her peripheral vision. Ceres turned to see a burning figure approaching fast, making directly for the Crooked Man. As it drew nearer, its face became visible, even amid the blazes. It was Calio. All living things fear fire, but, like pain, some choose to embrace it at the last.

The components of the Crooked Man's body scattered, disintegrating around Calio, even as insects popped and scorpions ignited, and the Crooked Man re-formed behind the dryad.

"You'll have to do better than that, nymph," he said, "if you want your revenge."

But Calio did have something better in mind, even as their skin burned, their vision clouded, and their consciousness faded. The Crooked Man was not their prize: his book was. With a final effort, Calio threw themselves upon it, and instantly it ignited. The Crooked Man barely had time to scream before his invertebrate form burst into flame, the larger bugs struggling as they died, the smaller ones shriveling directly to cinders. As they fell away, they left behind a ghostly imprint of the Crooked Man, like a brand scorched on the air, his mouth gaping in a scream that had no voice to give it sound. His eyes opened in a kind of wonder as he watched his book combust, and the story of his long, wicked life ended in fire. Calio's body had already become one with the burning volume, barely distinguishable from it. The dryad had stopped moving, their loneliness at an end.

Ceres stepped away from the sight, as the biggest tremor yet rocked the depths. By the light of the burning book she found the door and made for the tunnel, but no sooner had she left it for the central grotto than it caved in behind her. Around her the remaining tunnels were also giving way, although the hall of bones itself remained intact—not that this would do her much good, as being buried alive in a big room was no better than being buried alive in a small one.

And Ceres was not alone. A presence was seated on the throne of bones, a woman with pale skin, a hungry mouth, and a misshapen crown on her head. The Pale Lady Death had come for her, as she came for everyone.

"No," said Ceres. "It's not fair. I wouldn't let you take my daughter, and now you want me instead? Haven't you had enough killing for one day? Why can't you just let me go? After all this, to have come so far—"

The Pale Lady Death rose and advanced, stilling Ceres's tongue. She was so very thin, and so very hungry. She had come into being with the first living creature, and would not cease to exist until the last was gone, the world turned barren, and the universe grown cold.

Then, from the cavern floor, a voice said, "This way, and be quick about it, if you'll pardon the informality."

Ceres was standing so close to the bank of the underground brook that her heels were overhanging it. From beside her left foot, the Spirit of the Stream peered up at her.

"Got promoted," he said. "Spirit of *All* Streams. Lot of responsibility, but you can't rest on your laurels, can you?"

A pair of watery hands extended themselves toward Ceres.

"Just lean back into my arms," said the Spirit of All Streams. "I'll catch you, I promise."

The Pale Lady Death continued her stately approach. The appearance of the Spirit of All Streams did not cause her to rush, and she showed no anger at his intervention.

Because her chance will come again, Ceres thought. *Someday, when I'm too sick, tired, or old to escape, it will be her and me alone, and I'll accept her kiss, just as I invited it once before. I might even welcome it, but not today, so let her be patient.*

Ceres closed her eyes and allowed herself to fall.

LXXI

Anfloga

(OLD ENGLISH)

Lone Flier

he current was warmer and faster than Ceres had anticipated, and more buoyant, like a watercourse heavy with salt, although she suspected that the Spirit of All Streams had something to do with this, protecting her from both the cold and complete submersion. She lay on her back as they passed through crevasses so narrow that her already skinned shoulders were abraded again, and through gaps in the rock so low that her nose was only an inch away from receiving a skinning of its own. Even so, she was not afraid. The reverberations grew fainter and fainter, and the water warmer and warmer, so that she began to feel sleepy, and came to know how someone lost at sea might surrender to the allure of drowning. They emerged into the dark of night, and the Spirit of All Streams brought her to rest on a small stony inlet. Now that she was out of the water, Ceres started to shiver.

"You need to stay warm until I can bring help," said the Spirit of All Streams. "Gather some wood for a fire."

The riverbank was littered with branches, as well as smaller sticks for kindling. Ceres piled the latter, and formed a pyramid of branches around them, but she had no way to ignite it. Even when she had camped with her family, she always struggled with starting a friction fire, and once watched her father—during one of his occasional back-to-nature experiments—spend an increasingly frustrating thirty minutes messing about with a spindle and a piece of flat wood before giving the whole business up as a waste of time and using a lighter instead. Unfortunately, Ceres didn't have a lighter. Neither did she have the energy to try friction, and the Spirit of All Streams had temporarily abandoned her, so it wasn't like she could ask him for advice.

Then fireflies came, seemingly mobilized by her presence, and as they danced, the kindling came alight. Ceres added more branches, and soon she was seated before a steady blaze. But as she gazed into it, she witnessed once more Calio's death throes, and saw their delicate body consumed by the conflagration.

Ceres ran her fingers over the site of the sting. It didn't hurt anymore. It didn't even itch. Ceres didn't know what had made Calio act as they did. She knew only that the last of the dryads was gone, and she welled up with grief. Exhausted, she curled up by the fire and was taken by sleep.

The one-eyed rook watched the stream carry the girl to safety before returning to the hourglass room, where it alighted beside the skull of the boy. It placed its head under its wing, and did not look up as the woman's footsteps approached. The boy's voice called to it, a chill touched its feathers, and its heart stopped.

But by then the rook was with its beloved again.

LXXII

Unfaege
(OLD ENGLISH)

Not Doomed or Fated to Die

nly when Ceres's breathing had grown deep and regular did the pair of Fae stragglers show themselves. The mines were gone, the castle's foundations eroded. Six nobles had been killed, the rule of humankind had been destabilized, and, perhaps best of all, three wise women—the Blythes and Saada—were dead, all for the loss of a handful of warriors. More importantly, the Fae had learned that the land would soon be theirs again. If the mine was anything to go by, men were intent on laying waste to the world, and themselves along with it; but the world would recover, even if men would not. When it did, the Fae would return to claim it.

Now here was a sleeping girl, filled with succulent life. The two Fae thought they might feast one more time before returning to their mounds. They didn't even bother to unsheathe their blades as they descended on her. They would have no need of them. Physical strength would be enough to overpower her.

The Fae were nearly upon Ceres when they were lifted bodily from the ground, each with their arms pinned to their sides in a massive, meaty fist. Before they could cry out, they were pierced through the heart by a forefinger tipped with a steel thorn, and both died with the same final thought in their minds: *Giants*.

Gogmagog and Ingeborg, his wife, settled back down to watch over the girl. But they had traveled far, and were hungry, so they nibbled on the Fae, nibbled on them until they were gone.

The Spirit of All Streams located David, Baako, and the Woodsman where they had set up camp by the water, and told them about Ceres. David and Baako immediately set off to find her, leaving the Woodsman behind. He declined to go, claiming that he preferred to keep an eye on the horses while they were gone. The Spirit of All Streams also stayed. Only when David and Baako had left them did it speak again.

"The Lady is near," said the Spirit of All Streams.

"I thought as much," said the Woodsman.

"But it's not you she wants."

"No, I'm beyond her reach."

The Woodsman trailed his fingertips across the surface of the stream, as he might have stroked a faithful hound.

"Thank you for helping Ceres," he said.

"It wasn't her time."

"But without you, it might have been."

"Perhaps," said the Spirit of All Streams. "I'll leave you now, for you have business to conclude."

The Spirit of All Streams vanished beneath the water, and the Woodsman was alone. He remained by the fire, warming his hands, until the Pale Lady Death showed herself.

"You've feasted richly today," he said.

Her reply was a whisper, and her breath raised goose pimples on the Woodsman's skin, fire or no fire.

"I could have eaten more."

"Why didn't you? Why stop at the mine? The castle still stands, if barely. Why not take that, too, and all who live there?"

"The mine was an abomination."

"They will dig another, and greater besides. The Hidden People can't destroy them all, no more than they can kill every man and woman, even with you at the head of the host."

The Pale Lady Death did not reply, and the Woodsman regarded her carefully.

"Ah!" he said, "but they've figured that out for themselves, haven't they?"

"The Fae can wait. They will sleep in their mounds for as long as it takes."

"For as long as what takes?"

"For this world to purge itself of mankind, to be made clean again. Then the Fae will emerge to reclaim it."

The Woodsman, who could see so much, past and future, offered no dispute.

"And find you," he said, "standing amid the bones."

The Pale Lady Death dipped her chin in agreement, and the tip of her tongue licked her ruby-red lips.

"The woman, Ceres," said the Woodsman.

"What of her?"

"I want you to give her more time."

"I don't give time. I only make it stop."

"This is not a contract to be twisted to your will. She has made her choice."

"She once made a different one."

"No, she came close, and only of weariness. There is a distinction."

The Pale Lady considered this. Shadows billowed around her, the darkness cleaving to accept her.

"I can wait," she concluded. "For her, at least."

The Woodsman nodded his acceptance. He knew how it must be, as it had been before, and would be again, ever and ever, as long as there was living, dying, and the space between.

"Be gentle with them," he said.

Something that might have been benevolence showed briefly on the face of the Pale Lady Death. Pain was integral to her, but so also was the ending of it.

"They'll feel nothing," she said. "They will not even hear my footstep."

Then there was only the night, and the fire. The Woodsman put his face in his hands and wept.

LXXIII

Cossian

(OLD ENGLISH)

To Kiss

eres, David, and the Woodsman accompanied Baako back to his village. They brought with them two of the infants, each of whom bore the tattoo of Baako's people. The third child they had entrusted to the marshal, Denham, who assured them he would do his best to locate her parents.

Already lesser nobles were jockeying for power in order to fill the vacuum left by recent events, and two rival claims had been made on Balwain's castle and lands, including the site of the Pandemonium mine. There was talk of civil war.

"What will you do?" the Woodsman asked Denham.

"I'm a soldier," he replied. "I will choose a side and fight."

Ceres listened and despaired. Only men, she reflected, spoke this way, but it was beyond her power to change them.

As they reached Baako's village, a procession came out to meet them, Thabasi and Ime among its number, dressed in the white of mourning, and it was confirmed to Baako that his mother was no more. The harpies had left her body untouched, and did not try to prevent its retrieval: Saada's lore had suffused her flesh and bones, making her unpalatable to them. Thabasi, in a fit of rage, had killed their leader, but resisted the urge to visit further vengeance on the rest of the Brood, leaving them to dispose of their sister's corpse as they saw fit.

Ceres and the others stayed long enough to pay their respects, and watch as Saada was consigned to a pyre, now that her son was present to say goodbye to her. Afterward, they rode without incident to the chasm, where people had again begun to leave gifts of food for the harpies before crossing. They did the same. By the time they reached the other side, the food was gone.

Not far from the Woodsman's cottage, they parted ways with David. By now his hair was completely white, and he resembled the final photographs Ceres had seen of him. She did not comment on the change in his appearance, and neither did he mention it, except at the last, as she hugged him in farewell, and found herself crying for him.

"Don't," he said. "I knew it couldn't be forever, nor did I wish it to be. I just wanted time with them, and that I was allowed."

They kept him in sight as he rode away, and did not resume their journey until the horizon took him.

The Pale Lady Death was waiting for David at his home, but he did not see or hear her, and so that it might be the last word on his lips, she permitted him to call the name of his wife—although by then she was already beyond all care—before touching her lips softly to the base of his neck.

The world melted away, to be replaced by light, and so David's story came to a close.

LXXIV

Hyht
(OLD ENGLISH)

Hope

eres stood by the tree trunk, the skin of its bark and the flesh of its sapwood and heartwood stretched open to the pith to receive her. She allowed herself to be gathered into the Woodsman's arms, and when she freed herself from his embrace she was altered: older, heavier, wiser, the child inside cloaked by adulthood once again. She gazed on the Woodsman with grown-up eyes, and saw in him the spectre of her father, just as David had once looked at the same face and glimpsed the shadow of his own parent. *They are all his children,* she heard David say.

No, she thought, *we are all his children.*

Only then did she tell the Woodsman of the Crooked Man's offer.

"I was close to accepting it," she said. "Had Calio not intervened, I might well have."

"Then I, too, have an offer," said the Woodsman. "I am obliged to make it, if only for the sake of my conscience."

"What is it?"

"You can stay, if you choose," he said. "Again, time here is not time there. In hours, or days, your daughter will join you. Like David and his family, you can live out your lost years together, however many they might be. You can spare yourself whatever hurt awaits you if you return to your own world: those painful pilgrimages to her bedside, those nocturnal vigils."

"Because Phoebe may not recover."

"Who can tell? Not I."

Once more, Ceres was tempted: to be disencumbered of all that heartache, to be reunited with her daughter as she once was, all in a matter of days at most. Yet for Phoebe they would not be days but years, and spent without her mother to watch over her, whether she was aware of her presence or not; or the sound of Ceres's voice reading to her, whether heard or unheard. The doctors could not know what was going on inside that effigy, but whatever it was, Ceres would not leave Phoebe to endure it alone, not even if she had to wear out the sum of her years by that bedside.

"No," said Ceres. "I can't do that. I have to be with her."

"Because there's always hope?"

"Even if there isn't."

"Then it may be that I'll see you again," said the Woodsman, "with your daughter."

"Don't be offended if I say that I'd prefer a different outcome."

"I won't be offended at all."

They embraced one last time, and Ceres, without looking back, and without regret, stepped into the heart of the tree. It closed behind her, and she was in darkness.

Ceres was wandering through woodland, her head hurting, and her shirt covered in blood. She was trying to walk in a straight line, but her feet wouldn't do as they were told, and finally they wouldn't do anything at all. Her legs tangled around themselves, and she staggered in a circle before falling to the ground. The back of her head hit damp earth, but before her eyes closed she heard voices, and someone spoke her name.

"I came back," she said. "Tell her I came back."

Ceres woke, not in the woods, but on a gurney in the care home, with a sore head, a drip in her arm, and a nurse fussing over her, monitored by an anxious Olivier.

"Welcome back," said Olivier. "You had us worried there."

"My head hurts," said Ceres, then: "Is Phoebe okay?"

"She is as she was when you left her earlier today. I just looked in on her, because I knew you'd ask as soon as you came to. As for your head, you're almost certainly concussed, and Elaine here will have to put some stitches in your scalp. You may be sorry you went exploring, if you aren't already, because you're going to be sore for a while."

"Am I in trouble?"

"Well, we figured out where you've been, so trespassing, property damage? They'll throw the book at you. Six months hard labor, on bread and water."

The nurse hushed Olivier.

"Don't mind him," she told Ceres. "You're just lucky that place didn't fall down around your ears while you were inside. Maybe it'll convince them to fix it up at last."

She filled a syringe and gave it a squirt to remove any air bubbles.

"Now I really do need to deal with that cut. This will sting a bit."

Ceres yelped at the first jab of the needle, and the second. By the third, though, her head was numb.

"Right," said the nurse, "what pattern should we stitch into your scalp? I prefer love-hearts myself . . ."

Ceres was permitted to look in on Phoebe only briefly, as the on-call doctor at the Lantern House insisted that Ceres should be reviewed at the local emergency room as a further precaution. She was eventually released after a few hours, and took a taxi back to the Lantern House. Olivier escorted her to Phoebe's room, and left them alone together. When he was gone, Ceres cried as she hadn't cried since the accident.

"I thought I'd never be able to hold you again," she told Phoebe. "I thought you were lost to me forever."

She said nothing more, but held her daughter's hand and stroked her hair, as the old, beloved ache was restored.

LXXV

Wyrd-Writere
(OLD ENGLISH)

One Who Writes an Account of Events

he cut healed quickly, and the stitches were removed after a week. Ceres had barely noticed the intervening days go by, so absorbed was she in her new project. Immediately after the stiches came out, she went directly to Phoebe. It was just after six in the evening, but the curtain had not yet been drawn, so the room shed its yellow light on the trees and bushes beyond. Ceres stood by the glass, hoping to catch sight of a one-eyed rook, but there were no birds at all.

"Thank you, anyway," she said. "You won't be forgotten."

She pulled up a chair beside Phoebe, and displayed for her the hard-back notebook she had brought, its first eighty pages now filled with small, neat handwriting. There were few corrections to the text, so naturally had it flowed. As always, Ceres held Phoebe's right hand as she spoke.

"I've written something," said Ceres. "It's a story, and I think it wants to be a book, but it's not finished yet. I don't know how it ends, to be honest. I had no idea of an ending when I started, and I still don't. I thought writers were supposed to know, which made me think I might not be a writer, or not a real one. But you can't have an ending while a story is still unfolding, can you? You have to see where it goes. So let's see where this one goes, you and I, together."

Ceres opened the book, then paused.

"I should say that it's a continuation," she explained, "so it begins a bit oddly, but I think you'll understand why, because you always did like fairy tales."

Ceres took a breath, and commenced reading aloud.

"'Twice upon a time—for that is how some stories should continue—there was a mother whose daughter was stolen from her—'"

And against the palm of her hand, as the pen caresses the page, a finger moved.

Acknowledgments

 had never intended to write a sequel to *The Book of Lost Things*. Whenever anyone suggested I might, I'd reply that the original was a self-contained story and didn't need to be added to. Nevertheless, over the years I've produced tales set in the universe of the book, all of which were included in the tenth-anniversary edition in 2016, for which I gave the original a gentle polish. Then, during the first COVID lockdown of 2020, I worked on a screenplay for a proposed film adaptation. The film didn't come to pass—or hasn't yet—but I enjoyed the experience of returning to the novel, of seeing it in a different light and reimagining it. It made me realize that, despite all my protestations, I had been revisiting the world of *The Book of Lost Things* ever since it was first published back in 2006. I couldn't leave it alone—or it wouldn't leave me alone, whichever you prefer.

I've always loved collecting interesting and obscure words, but *Landmarks* by Robert Macfarlane (Penguin, 2015) and *The Wordhord: Daily Life in Old English* by Hana Videen (Profile, 2021) helped to expand my vocabulary for this book considerably.

As always, there are people to whom I wish to express my gratitude: Sue Fletcher and Emily Bestler, my longtime British and American editors, both of whom shepherded *The Book of Lost Things* to publication, and have now performed the same service for its sequel; the lovely, supportive staff at Atria/Emily Bestler Books, among them Libby McGuire, Dana Trocker, Dana Sloan, Lara Jones, Sarah Wright, Emi Battaglia,

Acknowledgments

Gena Lanzi, David Brown, Dayna Johnson, and many more; everyone at Hachette and Hodder & Stoughton, especially Katie Espiner, Jo Dickinson, Carolyn Mays, Swati Gamble, Rebecca Mundy, Oliver Martin, Alice Morley, Catherine Worsley, Dominic Smith and his sales team; the staff at Hachette Ireland, including Breda Purdue, Jim Binchy, Elaine Egan, Ruth Shern, and Siobhan Tierney; my agent, Darley Anderson, and his team; Laura Sherlock; Ellen Clair Lamb, who worries about a lot of stuff so I don't have to; Cliona O'Neill, whose scientific eye caught many small errors; Jake Nalepa, who helped keep me sane during COVID by forcing me to exercise outdoors for a year or so, come rain or shine, and then threatened to drive me nuts by repeatedly asking if I wouldn't like to reconsider the whole "not writing a sequel to *The Book of Lost Things*" business; Mr.—not Dr.—Robert Drummond, who answered my medical questions about Phoebe's condition and likely care; Dominick Montalto, whose copyediting skills continue to save me from embarrassment; and Jennie, Cameron, and Alistair, who were there for the first book, and Megan, Alannah, and Livvy, who have now joined them for the second.

Finally, to all the booksellers, librarians, and readers who have, over the years, supported and championed *The Book of Lost Things*, as well as my other work: Thank you.